you'll think of me

You'll Think of Me
by Lucia Franco

Copyright © 2013 by Lucia Franco

Edited by Nadine Winningham
Cover Design by Opulent Designs

All rights reserved. No part of this publication may be reproduced, distributed, or transmitted in any form or by any means, including photocopying, recording, or other electronic or mechanical methods, without the prior written permission of the publisher, except in the case of brief quotations embodied in critical reviews and certain other noncommercial uses permitted by copyright law.
This is a work of fiction. Names, characters, businesses, places, events and incidents are either the products of the author's imagination or used in a fictitious manner. Any resemblance to actual persons, living or dead, or actual events is purely coincidental.

All Rights reserved.

more titles by lucia

STANDALONE TITLES

You'll Think of Me

Hold On to Me

Hush, Hush

Say Yes

You're Mine Tonight

OFF BALANCE SERIES

Balance

Execution

Release

Twist

Dismount

To my husband for constantly begging to read my writing even though I wouldn't allow you to.
Nadine Winningham, your support gave me the strength to keep going. You were the fire behind me. Luke is your man.

"We're living in a generation where lying is the new truth, loyalty is a tattoo and love is just a quote. "

—Anonymous

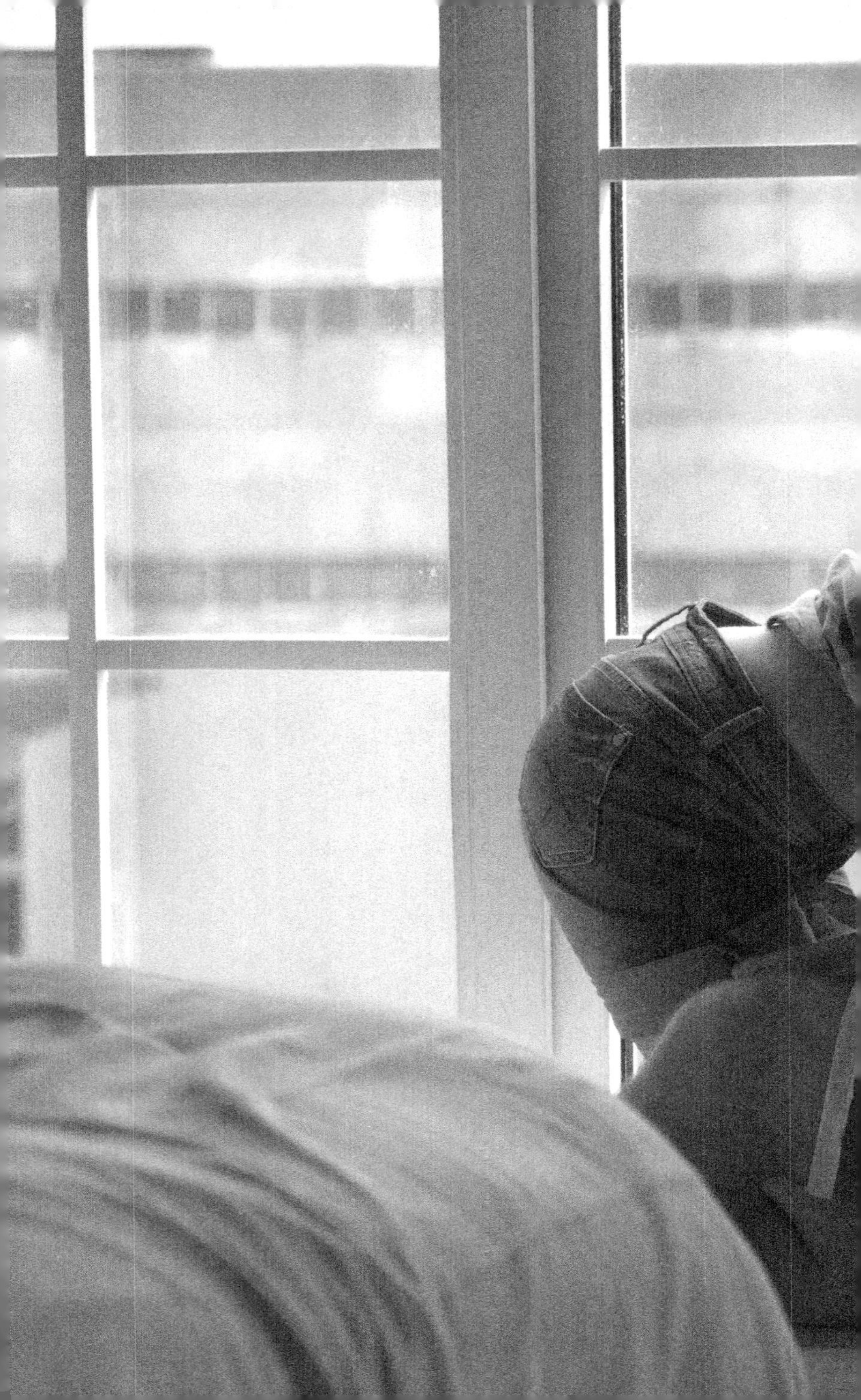

prologue

"You know exactly what I'm saying. Read between the lines, baby. The fact that you knew this weeks ago and never told me has my blood boilin'. Fuckin' boilin'. You led me to think it was settled and we were okay. You lied to my face!" he roared, his green eyes lit with fury. "Excuse me, withheld some major details," he said sarcastically.

Flustered to the core, Ivy shook on the inside. This wasn't what she wanted, but she was so upset and hurt that she couldn't help what flew from her mouth.

"Who are you to tell me I can't leave? That I'm stuck here forever? What's holding me back? Nothing!"

"The one who loves you, that's who! The one who wants to make you his wife one day! Me, that's who! Damn woman, you know how to get under a man's skin like no other. Fuck!"

Olivia cringed. "I never lied to you. So stop insinuating I did."

"But you held back though, didn't you? You left out a few things for the sake of stringin' me along. It's the same damn thing, baby."

"I never *strung* you along. It's not the same thing at all. Not even close."

"If I remember correctly, you said something like, 'It was merely a thought…honestly…nothing more.' Nothing more. Nothing more, Livy? Obviously it was."

"Luke, it's done. I'm sorry, but it's done. Can we stop arguing? I want to spend the little bit of time I have left with you before I have to leave for New York."

Standing from the bed, Olivia wrapped the white sheet around her body and walked over to where Luke was standing.

"You're really doing this? You're really going to leave?"

She nodded.

"Fine. How about we just break it off now? Let's end this —us—right here and save us from the heartache. You go your way, I'll go mine."

Luke saw no reason to keep on going. If she wanted to go to New York, then he would get out of her life now.

Her eyes prickled as tears threatened to fall. Blinking rapidly, she whispered, "No," under her breath. "You can't possibly be serious."

"Dead. Serious. Like a heart attack."

"Luke, there has to be a way we can work through this. Can't we try a long distance relationship?"

"No."

"Why not? Why are you being so irrational?"

"Irr—Too bad, Livy. We're…through." He was fired up, pissed off and needed to stop before he said something he would regret.

"Please, don't end this. Please…" her voice cracked with despair.

Luke bent his head down as she craned her neck to look up at him. A lone tear trickled slowly down her cheek and he wiped it with his thumb, hating to see her cry. Trying to calm his temper, he took a deep breath.

Kissing Olivia's forehead, he whispered, "Goodbye, Care Bear."

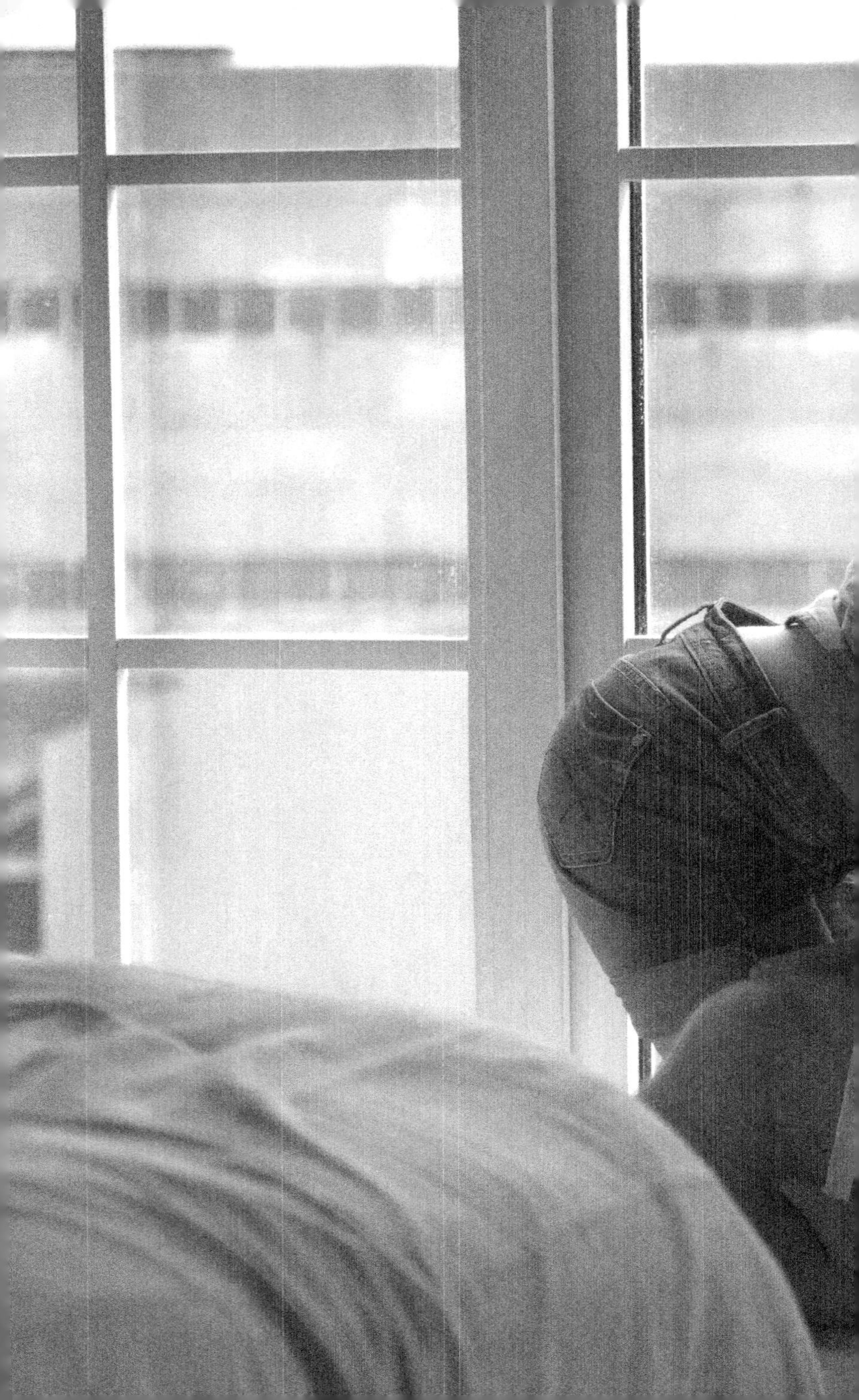

one

present day

Delicate little flurries of snow descended on Olivia in the late night hour while she stood on her small balcony overlooking the city. One by one, the tiny ice crystals landed on her shoulders and hair, around her feet and on her patio furniture. As she drew in a crisp breath of wintery New York air, her lungs tightened and burned. She held it for a moment then exhaled, watching the gray cloud of air flow from her mouth. The low temperatures had her shivering, but she wasn't ready to go inside just yet.

An icy blast of air blew through, causing Olivia's hair to whip across her face. She bit the corner of her chapped lip and winced. After packing for the last few hours, Olivia wanted to take in the tranquility of the night, though it was anything but quiet and calm down below. There was always someone bustling down the streets, racing against time to find the nearest subway station, or hailing a taxi. Manhattan was known as the city that never sleeps, and it held true to its name. Being fortunate enough to live in the city that spanned only three miles wide, Olivia couldn't help but feel as gloomy as the sky looked tonight. It was a bittersweet feeling. Living in New York was some of the most amazing—and difficult—times of her life, but she wouldn't change one day that had passed by. Not one.

The next few months were going to be rough on her once again, but that would be nothing new. If she could live in New York and handle it as long as she had, then she could handle anything.

Olivia was set to relocate in just two weeks, though she wasn't heading back to South Fork, she was moving to Savannah. It had been nine long years—a couple of years more than she had planned to stay—but the time had come. Her heart had been luring her back to the South for quite some time now, and a pull so strong could not be ignored. Savannah was approximately an hour north of South Fork—and the location of her new job. It was a much bigger city than South Fork, which was fine; she'd still be back in Georgia and that's what mattered most to her. Olivia missed home. She missed the comfort of the small town, the easy laid-back lifestyle and surprisingly, the people.

Too many memories were left in South Fork. The past was the past for a reason and there wasn't anything she needed to return to. The only friend she'd stayed in close touch with was Tessa.

Tessa had given her updates shortly after she left, but it didn't last long. Olivia had put a stop to that. It hurt too much. Just a whisper of his name made her chest ache. The first love pain never goes away, right? A yearning, the longing that would always be there, lingered within her heart. She couldn't say it was true for everybody, but it was for her.

No other man she tried to date could erase Luke and how much he meant to her. Even after all these years, Luke could never be forgotten. Lord knows she tried. One afternoon while listening to the radio, it was a total and complete shock to hear his music. Considering there was only one radio station that played country music in New York City, she had no choice but to listen to his voice…his sinfully provocative voice that was still haunting her hundreds of miles away. It had only been a matter of time before his rough southern drawl had been picked up, not to mention his magnetic personality.

A sad smile formed on Olivia's face as she took a sip of her coffee and swallowed the bold flavor. The hot liquid traveled down her throat, warming her. When Luke's music came on it killed her to listen to the whole song. Hearing his raspy voice moved something deep inside, bringing her back to the years they spent together and watching him get deep into writing lyrics. With the knowledge that Luke wrote his own songs, it was only natural for Olivia to try to decipher each word she heard. His life used to be weaved into music, and she wondered if it still was or if it was purely artificial now. Olivia had made a heavy effort to remain in contact with Luke after she left, despite the fact that he claimed he wasn't interested in her anymore, but it didn't last long. She was tough, but she could only handle so much rejection. She had no choice but to move on, but knowing she left him behind never sat right with her.

One night, while feeling exceptionally homesick, Olivia explored job opportunities in Georgia. On a whim, she applied to a few practices looking to hire a neurologist. The next day she woke to an email inquiring about setting up an interview. She felt like it was a sign, as if it was meant to happen. Olivia had vacation days saved and took a few to fly down for an interview.

The other doctor in the office was extremely impressed with her resume and even more pleased with the medical school she attended in New York. Along with the rotations she completed, he felt she would be a great addition. Between taking on a part-time job while in school and doing her rotations, how could anyone not be pleased with her accomplishments? It took dedication and hard work, but Olivia made it happen. It was all she breathed for nine tiring years, leaving her personal life wanting for more. The days were long and the nights were lonely and felt like they would never end. Some days weighed on her like she was climbing a mountain of quicksand, struggling with more than just putting one foot in front of the other. But it paid off.

Oh yes, it paid off. Olivia was headed home and relying solely on herself. It's what she wanted all along: independence. That kind of payoff was what mattered in her eyes. Her parents were saddened that she hadn't chosen to return to South Fork, but they learned to come to terms with it, just like they had when she left.

So there Olivia was, standing on the balcony, sipping the last of her coffee, thinking about how her life panned out. As she thought before, she wouldn't change a thing.

Not a single thing.

Everything happened for a reason.

two

Three months since moving back to Georgia, mental and physical exhaustion had finally set in. Olivia was worn out and tired, ready for the weekend to start. Leaving work after the sun had set and arriving before the break of dawn each morning had caught up with her and taken a toll on her body. It had been going this way since she'd been back, so Friday could not come soon enough.

Jumping up from her chair, Olivia rushed around her desk in an effort to meet her next patient on time. Well, as close to the appointment time as possible, but her white doctor's coat caught on her mahogany desk and stopped Olivia in her tracks. Stepping back, she bent over and unhooked the corner of her coat. In the process, her hair fell in her face and her half-draped stethoscope slid from her neck onto the floor, along with her pens and phone from her pocket.

It had been another crazy and hectic day at the office. Actually, it had been all week. The other doctor in the practice had a family emergency the week before. Olivia didn't have the heart to cancel appointments, so she was working double time by squeezing in her colleague's patients for the past two weeks.

After picking everything up she dropped and placing the stethoscope around her neck, Olivia pushed her hair out of her face. She grabbed her ivory stack of charts and walked out of her office. Making her way down the hall, Olivia knocked on the door to the exam room and entered. After listening to Ms. Nelson berate her about Dr. Thatcher not being there, the small dose of medication and how it wasn't working, she offered to prescribe a different dose to see if it would help. Olivia sighed inwardly. Finally, she was able to move on to her next patient.

Expelling a deep breath, Olivia knocked twice then entered the exam room. The cool air caused a shiver to travel around to the back of her neck. She had been bustling up and down the hallway for a few hours now and was hot, so the air was invigorating against her skin.

As she strode in, Olivia opened the chart for Mr. Nathaniel Alexander and read the notes. He had been dealing with chronic headaches for some time now. Dr. Thatcher had ordered an MRI, since none of the over-the-counter medications were working for him.

"Hello, Mr. Alexander, I'm Dr. King. Dr. Thatcher had an unexpected family emergency so I'll be seeing you today."

"An emergency is always unexpected."

Olivia glanced up toward the low, baritone voice that stopped her from reading the chart.

Well, if that voice wasn't one of the deepest and sexiest southern drawls she'd ever heard. For a split second, if Olivia hadn't seen the name before walking in, she would have assumed it was Luke that voice belonged to. Lazy, deep, and thick, like Tennessee whiskey; and all he said were five words. Olivia's body stirred to life as she replayed the voice in her head. He was one of the youngest patients she'd seen in a while—and by youngest, she meant he wasn't over sixty years of age—and by far the best looking. Amber eyes were framed by heavy lashes and his clean cut, short, dark hair was nearly as black as the ace of spades. He sported a Kelly green shirt and khaki cargo shorts topped off with sneakers. He sat there on the exam table with his hands placed on his thickly muscled thighs.

Then one side of his mouth lifted and he gave an incredibly sexy half-grin. Olivia's lungs tightened up. Sweet Jesus, he was handsome when he smiled.

Clearing her throat, she finally found her voice. "Ah, yes, you're right about that. Excuse me. It's been a long week."

Then the other side of his mouth lifted and pulled into a full on, heart-stopping grin. She needed to get her shit together. *He was a patient for crying out loud!*

"It's all good."

Olivia flipped through the chart, scanned the reports then looked back up.

"Mr. Alexander, what—"

"Nate."

"Nathaniel," she drew his name out. "Are you taking any medication right now?"

"No, Dr. Thatcher said not to until I had the MRI done."

"And you're still not?"

"I stopped taking over-the-counter medication because it wasn't working for me."

"How long have you been dealing with chronic headaches?"

"Around seven months or so."

Olivia paused. "And you're just coming in now? Why did you wait so long?"

"I'm busy and can't take off work much. But I think they're getting worse because it's affecting my vision and hearing. I'm sensitive to a lot now and it interferes with work."

"What do you do for a living?"

"I work in construction."

Well that explained the solid body...

"Alright. I see here the MRI showed acute sinusitis and

polyps within your nasal cavities. I'm not discounting the headaches, because you're definitely suffering from those as well, but it appears the pain is due to allergies. The good thing is there are things we can do to help minimize your symptoms and hopefully remove them completely."

Her patient looked confused.

"I'll explain. Polyps are little pouches in your sinuses that can become swollen and painful. The headaches are most likely from that."

"I think I know what a headache feels like, Doc."

"You would think, right? They're surprisingly similar."

Olivia put the folder down and walked over to the patient. She was going to prove it could be something else.

"Does this hurt?" she asked as she applied pressure to the sides of his nose with her thumbs.

"Yeah. I can feel it in my eyes, too."

"How so?"

"I feel pressure in my eyes when you do that."

"How about here?" she asked as she added more pressure, but this time to his forehead.

"Yeah," he responded in a low murmur.

Olivia had been so focused on explaining everything that she hadn't noticed his eyes fixated on hers. She watched as they slowly traveled down to her lips.

This wasn't good. This wasn't good at all. Olivia stepped back and leaned against the desk.

Clearing her throat she said, "I'm going to give you two types of allergy medication along with something for the headaches. Try to hold off on the pain pills for at least a week until the allergy medication is able to work through any blockage." She crossed her arms in front of her chest. "I'll schedule you to come back in a month for a follow-up with Dr. Thatcher."

"Alright." Standing up, he stepped off the patient table. Olivia silently breathed in as her patient walked toward the door, but he didn't make it to the door. He stopped in front of her.

Nathaniel was tall. He had to be close to 6'1"and built solid and wide as a linebacker. He raised his hand out past her cheek, but dropped it before grabbing a hold of the strand of hair that had fallen from where she tucked it behind her ear.

"Such a beauty," he said softly.

Olivia's heart raced at his forwardness while she stood there digging her fingers into her underarms, unsure of what to do. Mr. Alexander's mouth curved into a smirk and she sucked in her bottom lip between her teeth.

"Don't bite your lip. Thanks, Doc. See you around," he said low, his eyes transfixed on her lips. Then he left.

Holy. Hell.

What just happened?

Wound tight, Olivia felt more alive than she had all week, and by a patient who had her body rousing all in the matter of a quick office visit.

WALKING INTO HER OFFICE EARLY THE NEXT MORNING, OLIVIA noticed the mound of medical files piled up, reminding her that she needed to tackle them. This week had been the longest one of her life, but it was finally Friday.

A vibration coming from her purse startled her. Dropping her purse onto the desk with a thud, she fished for her phone, receipts and makeup spilling everywhere. Sliding her finger across the screen, she saw a text message.

TESSA: I wannnnnna see you. You've been back in Georgia for months now and I haven't seen your face yet! I miss you. I know you're busy, so I'll come to you. Let me know. Xoxox

Olivia smiled, and her heart felt lighter. Placing the phone down, she decided she'd get back to her later. Once settled into her routine for the day with coffee in hand, Olivia got to work. It was still early and none of the staff had arrived yet. She loved the early morning feel of her office; the calm before the craziness. Reaching across her desk, she cranked up the radio volume as *Why* by Jason Aldean came on and she fell into a steady pace of paperwork.

After an hour of sitting in her chair whittling down the paperwork pile, Olivia stood to stretch, and that's when her pleasant morning took an unexpected turn.

"That's country music sensation, Luke Jackson. He's a touring machine! Word on the street is that he's a lady's man. Apparently no one's been able to lock him down until now... A birdie told me he's got a little lady under his wing. So maybe the rumors aren't true after all..."

Olivia's shoulders sagged and her heart fell into the pit of her stomach, a dead weight spiraling down and crashing inside of her. It settled and took root, its darkness spreading itself throughout her body. She felt numb. Regret was like a dirty little creature that just couldn't be quashed. This was why she stopped listening to country music for so long; she didn't want to know any details of Luke's personal life anymore. She had told herself she let it go, so it shouldn't have bothered her, but it killed her inside to hear that. It fucking hurt. Plain and simple. Damn Luke and his music. Shaking her head, Olivia slammed the radio with her hand, not wanting to hear another word, and grabbed her phone.

OLIVIA: *I miss you too! Just crazy busy here. Finally got things together. And yes—We must get together. Hopefully soon!*

TESSA: *How about tonight or this weekend?*

OLIVIA: *Tonight? Possibly! Let's see how my day goes. I'll text you to let you know. Xoxoxo*

Standing up, Olivia shrugged on her white coat and dropped her phone into the pocket. She'd love nothing more than to see Tessa tonight.

The rest of the day flew by like fall leaves twirling in a heavy gust of autumn wind. It was exactly how she felt after running up and down the hallway all afternoon; her head was spinning and her body was going in the opposite direction. Olivia only took part of her lunch break so she could catch up. She let the rest of the staff keep their regular lunch schedules and pulled each patient into the rooms herself. One by one, she saw everyone. It was getting close to the end of the day, and there was just one patient remaining.

Olivia grabbed the last folder and walked down the hallway to the last exam door. She knocked and waited for a response as she glanced at the patient's name.

Jackson.

Her heart skipped a beat then leaped into her throat.

Jackson? Olivia's palms began to sweat and her neck prickled with pins and needles.

"Come in," she heard through the door, but it didn't register in her mind as Olivia frantically searched for an address on the inside of the file.

It was left blank.

Surely... Surely it couldn't be Luke. Jackson was a pretty common name, but she couldn't help thinking immediately of Luke, especially after her morning.

Taking a deep breath and letting it out, Olivia turned the knob and walked into the cold exam room.

three

"Hello?" she said answering the phone with a groggy voice.

"So, any hot doctors?" Lisa asked cheerfully, sounding as if she had been wide awake for hours.

Lisa was her closest friend from New York and Olivia missed her. She had been her one and only real friend there. Lisa was vibrant, outgoing, always with a smile on her face, and not a worry in the world.

What time is it?

Olivia whimpered, throwing one hand over her eyes. She was still in bed and half asleep, but grinned at Lisa's question.

She opened her sleepy eyes and looked up at the white popcorn ceiling through the slow moving fan. It was typical of Lisa to ask that question, always thinking with her eyes and not her head. Lisa continually dated all the wrong guys, coming into her life with serious baggage that no one wanted to touch but her.

"No, Lisa. I'm not looking for anyone 'hot' or otherwise for that matter. Good Lord, girl, doesn't your libido ever stop?"

Lisa huffed on the other end like she was offended, which Olivia knew she really wasn't.

"Umm, no. I'm a normal woman with a healthy sex drive. There is no off button, Liv. I'm not dead! Jesus Christ. I like men, and I like them often." She could just picture Lisa rolling her eyes.

Olivia giggled as she turned onto her side and pulled the comforter over her head. Her hair covered her face and she pushed it aside. "There is no filter with you."

Laughing, Lisa said, "That's true. Seriously, are there any decent guys? And I mean for you, not me. And why won't you look for one anyway? You can't stay single forever you know."

"I don't have time for dating."

Lisa groaned on the other end. "You always say that. You're going to die a born again virgin. I just know it."

Olivia didn't respond—she couldn't. She was too busy laughing at her friend's sense of humor and at how serious Lisa came across.

"When are you going to start dating?" Lisa whined. "I know you're settled in your new little redneck home. Well, your home away from home, so there's no excuse other than your reluctance."

"Something like that... Maybe I'll start, but I'm not on the hunt like you always are. If it happens it happens. If not, that's fine, too. I'm in no rush."

Lisa huffed loudly into the phone. "You're thirty-one! You're not getting any younger, honey."

"Thirty-one is young! Anyway, enough about me. What are you doing up so early on a Saturday?"

Olivia reached above her head, the muscles in her arms stretching as she yawned. Her eyes felt puffy from too much work, but with Tessa coming into town today she needed to get a jump on things. Getting out of bed, she made her way into the kitchen and turned on her coffee pot.

"True, very true, love. I'm just playing with you. I actually just got back from running in Central Park. It's getting cold again and I thought of you as I ran. Then I came home, made a vegetable and fruit smoothie and I'm drinking it while talking to you."

"Getting cold? It has to be close to forty degrees there right now; that's ice cold for me! And you thought of me while running? Why? Is it because I refused to be one of those idiots running in black bike pants, stupid ear muffs, heavy gloves and my eyes watering from the cold wind while the rest of me is covered? All to lose a few pounds in the winter? Thanks, but spare me."

"Exactly! If you could have seen this guy running, Liv. You would've died at what he was wearing. He had his entire face covered except for his Ray-Ban glasses. He wore white clothing and was skin and bones. He looked like something straight out of a movie."

"Ugh. Gross. And believe me, I can imagine it *all*. I'll stick with my hips and the heat and be on my merry way. It's about seventy-five here and sunny today. No depressing gray skies that make you want to slit your wrist with a butter knife."

Lisa groaned in response to the temperature.

"You should come visit me. You might actually like it down south."

"Maybe I'll take you up on that offer one day. I have to check and see if Dan has anything planned first."

"Dan? Are you kidding me? Please tell me you're still not seeing Dan. Lisa, he's married, and a doctor! This isn't good for you or his marriage. This is home wrecker status."

"It's kind of hard to break it off when we work together..."

"You work for him now!" Olivia bit out, muttering a string of curse words.

"It's not what you think..."

"It never is."

"Liv, he said he's miserable with his marriage and wants a divorce but it isn't the right time because his wife just suffered a miscarriage. He has to give her time to heal before he drops the news. He says I'm his morning ray of light when he walks through the office door and he sees me, that I'm what gets him through each day. He thought if I was working in his office it would be a good way for us to be together without getting caught. So far it's working."

"Getting caught? See, that should be an issue," Olivia cried out. "Why couldn't you just wait until he's divorced? And please tell me you didn't fall for his morning ray of light shit."

Silence greeted Olivia. She knew Lisa was in over her head.

"I can't," Lisa whispered sadly. "I think I'm falling for him, Liv. Hard."

"Oh, Lisa…" she dragged out, her heart aching for her friend. "Please think about what you're doing and the lives that are going to be affected over this affair. Think before you act for once. Think with your head first, please? I know most say to follow your heart, but you wear your heart on the outside for the taking. You're not protecting it with any covering. You're bound to get hurt. So please, for once, think with your head."

"I will, Livy. I promise. And don't be so negative. Dan has promised to leave his wife once she's recovered. He loves me and wants a life with me. Would I have held out this long if not?" Lisa finished with a sullen tone.

Lisa had a point, a weak point at that, but she was right in a sense. Olivia couldn't believe her friend was falling for every word 'Dan the Man' was spewing at her. She just prayed it was true this time. Maybe pushing Lisa to visit a little more was what was needed. She hated to see her friend hurt, and flying her down might be the ray of light she needed to see.

"I just don't want to see you get hurt."

"I know you don't," Lisa responded softly. "I don't want to

see myself get hurt either, but sometimes you have to take a leap of faith, you know?"

"Don't I know it…"

"Can I ask you something?"

"Of course. You know you don't even have to ask that question."

"Looking back, do you believe that thinking with your head and not your heart was best for you?"

Olivia's throat tightened. She knew exactly what Lisa was referring to since she had told her every detail about Luke and the damage it had done to her.

"Sometimes you just have to take a chance and see where it takes you."

four

A loud, rapid knocking echoed throughout the house.
Silencing her dog, Tom, Olivia threw the rag she'd been cleaning with into the sink, marched over to the door, unbolted it and swung it open.

And a big grin spread across her face. It was Tessa. They slammed into each other and held on tight with a big hug. No matter how far apart, they had a bond like no one else she knew.

God, she missed her so much.

Tessa and Olivia started speaking at the same time, neither able to make out what the other was saying. They looked at each other, waiting to see who would go first. A pregnant pause, then a fit of laughter followed.

Olivia welcomed Tessa inside her home that was set back off the beaten path with a curvy driveway. It was surrounded by trees with a great deal of land, which was surprising considering she lived in Savannah. She wanted the small town charm but with a city feel. Now she had the best of both worlds.

"I can't believe you're finally here! And I haven't even put my makeup on or showered yet. I must look so messy," Olivia drawled, her accent coming back since moving home.

"I know I was supposed to come later in the day, but I wanted to see you. I waited long enough and wasn't waiting any longer."

"Oh, don't worry one bit!" Olivia yelled out in excitement, batting her hand as if to say it's totally fine with her. "I'm just so happy to see you. You have no idea."

Olivia wanted to jump around like a little girl opening her first Barbie Corvette Power Wheels on Christmas morning. Tessa was her life support, the oxygen she breathed. Countless times over the years Tessa was the one person who kept her going when times were rough.

"Take a seat. I just made coffee."

Tessa looked around, her eyes landing on the round dinner table.

"Well someone had a party last night. Was work so bad? And wine?"

Olivia followed her gaze and stifled a laugh. A box of left over pizza was sitting out with the lid flipped back, a bottle of red wine was uncorked and sitting next to the red Solo cup she had been drinking from.

"Ugh. It has been a long and hard week. The last two days were the roughest. One patient hit on me, I think…"

"No shit," Tessa cut in, looking eager to hear more. Tessa's expression made her think of Lisa and how she would eat this up, too.

Olivia glared at her. "Uh uh. No way am I going out with a patient. I know what you're thinking. Get the thought out of your head right now."

Tessa pretended to pout. "Fine," she said. "You're so boring sometimes."

"HA! He's a patient. That's against code…I think? Though, I swear he was kind of giving off that vibe…"

Shaking her head, she continued, "Anyway, someone else came into my office that I hadn't expected to see."

Tessa's brows furrowed as she tried to think of who it could possibly be in Savannah that Olivia wasn't expecting.

"Let me have my coffee first and then we'll go there. Give me a minute to get changed, too. Come, come. Let's go put your stuff in your room then I'll meet you back here."

Olivia showed Tessa to one of the guest rooms then went to get dressed. She grabbed a pair of white shorts and a yellow tank. She walked into her bathroom, brushed her teeth and tied her hair up, wrapping a hair scarf around it. There. The messy bun look. She applied some makeup, never going anywhere without it. It was a subtle look, not caked on.

Olivia could smell the coffee aroma as it filtered throughout the house. She followed the invisible trail, her feet moving across the soft ivory carpet and into the kitchen where Tessa was waiting for her. She sighed, smiling brightly.

"You look positively happy, Liv," Tessa said quietly.

Olivia fished two mugs out of the cabinet. "I don't think you realize how much I've missed you," she shrugged, "or how happy I am that you came to visit me. I haven't even come to see you yet."

Olivia poured the coffee into the mugs, watching the steam rise from the dark liquid.

"You're just busy getting settled and into the swing of things. I get it. Now tell me who was in your office. I'm dying to know. All you said was that you needed me and had news. What's going on?"

They stood at her countertop filling their coffee with cream and sugar as Tess waited for her to spill. They very rarely kept secrets between each other.

Olivia cocked her head to the side and gave a hesitant half smile. "Okay. But you have to promise not to tell anyone."

Tessa didn't even respond, just gave Olivia a look as if she'd been insulted.

"If I tell you who was there you can't say a word. I'm not kidding, Tessa. I can get in serious trouble for this, not to mention a huge monetary fine."

"Do you really think I would do something to jeopardize your career, Olivia?"

"Of course I don't think you would. I trust you. I've just never spoken about patients to anyone before, so I'm just edgy telling you. I can't reveal why they were there, or give you any information, only tell you who it was."

Silence.

"Well say it already!" Tessa exclaimed.

Olivia took a sip of her coffee and let it travel down the back of her throat. Feeling better with at least a little coffee in her, she spoke up.

"Luke's parents."

Tessa gasped loudly, her hand flying to her mouth. "Luke. As in your ex, Luke?" Tessa was speechless, her eyes as big as her mouth.

"What other Luke would I be talking about? Of course that Luke."

"No way."

"Yes way. Imagine my shock when I walked into the room and saw them. We just stood there looking at each other with uncomfortable silence hanging in the air."

"What did you do?"

Olivia shrugged her shoulders. "I greeted them and made small talk, of course, before we got into the reason for their visit."

"Was Luke there? Did they bring him up?"

Nodding her head, Olivia pursed her lips together. She gripped her mug and said, "He wasn't there, but they did bring him up without me having to ask. They just gave up the information, as if I wanted to know. He's doing well it seems...

Out on tour somewhere and busy. Loves the music and playing for the crowds. I didn't want to ask about him, though..."

Olivia felt a stitch of sadness creep through her. She looked down into her half-full cup and felt her heart sink to the bottom of it.

"Do you ever talk to him? You know, to catch up?"

Tessa's question was laced with a hint of pity. Olivia didn't want pity. She'd made a choice and had to live with it, regardless of whether she wanted to or not.

"No. Never," Olivia responded softly. "There's nothing to talk about. He didn't want to hear from me once I left. I called a few times and emailed, but he never answered. It's been years, Tessa. Years."

"I had no idea you reached out to him. Why didn't you tell me?"

Olivia shrugged again. "There was nothing to tell. He didn't want to talk to me, no matter how hard I tried. That's it. What else is there to tell?" She took a sip of her coffee.

"Wow," Tessa breathed out, running her hand through her blonde hair. "What a couple of last days it's been for you. No wonder you got drunk on wine... Wine? Since when do you drink wine?"

Olivia chuckled. "Occasionally I'll have it. I figured since we were most likely going out tonight that I'd have the good stuff then."

"So what will you do about Luke's parents?"

"I'm going to act like they're any other patient I treat. What can I do? I'm their doctor and they need care. It's what I do. Nothing more, nothing less. Although, they said something that left me feeling puzzled. They said not to tell anyone of their visit, which I normally wouldn't, except you obviously, but that's different. I doubt they ever thought they'd see me, which is why I agreed to their request, but I thought it was strange. It's not like I could reveal information or anything. I'm guessing since South Fork is so small that people talk?"

"Possibly. Everyone loves to talk shit back home. You know that," Tessa stated the obvious.

"Very true. Or else... Maybe their sons don't know about their visit? That's my guess."

They stood quietly, looking at each other for a moment as invisible bubbles of speculation floated in the air around them.

"That's another possibility. Or it could be that Luke's in the limelight and they don't want it getting out? That's what I assumed, but I wasn't going to ask. If they bring it up again when they come back I may. I'm not sure."

"They're coming back?" Tessa asked with surprise.

She knew Tessa wanted more, but that was all she could give. She was already going against the code of ethics.

Changing the subject, Tessa asked, "So, what's on deck for tonight?"

five

past | nine years earlier

Luke took one last pull on his cigarette and flicked it into the grass. Blowing out the dry smoke, he removed the food from the grill. He began grilling soon after he arrived at the lake with his closest friends. Now that the burgers and hot dogs were finished and the chicken needed slow cooking, Luke needed his girl in his arms.

This particular spot near the lake was a part of his youth, where memories were laid but never forgotten. The trees were at a height where they arched slightly over the winding lake, creating a shadow over the water. When the wind blew, he could hear the rustling of the trees that caused the most incredibly cool breeze to brush against his hot summer skin. To most, it looked like nothing but a desolate spot that was home to a bare lake and trees. On Friday nights around a fire, with the sun setting and some music playing, the spot was heaven on earth to him and his friends.

Standing barefoot with her back to him and staring at the lake, Olivia was in her black and white striped bikini, which showed way too much skin in his opinion. Her sexy tanned legs were firmly locked in place while her arms were wrapped around her waist. Livy's dark wavy locks were swept up in a messy tie where a few strands managed to fall around her slender neck. Livy looked so small and lost standing there by herself. Luke wanted nothing more than to hold onto her and never let go.

In a lazy stroll, Luke made his way over to Livy. The high noon temperatures heated the dirt and scorched his feet as he stood behind her, placing his hands onto her sun kissed shoulders. He leaned down and quietly sang behind her ear...

"...why you makin' me fall in love with you, no complications, just easy and smooth love like the summer breeze that drifts through the leaves, baby lean into my kiss, every man needs his own whiskey girl like this..."

"What's going on in that pretty head of yours?" Luke asked, wrapping his arms around Olivia's slender waist and squeezing her to him. He rested his chin on the curve of her shoulder where his stubble lightly grazed the side of her soft face.

Sighing, Olivia paused before she answered. "Nothing, really. Just thinking what a great day it's been." Olivia threaded her small fingers through Luke's large ones, caressing the back of his warm hands with her thumbs.

"You sure, baby? You look like you have a lot on your mind." Gently pressing a kiss to the side of Livy's neck, Luke breathed in her creamy coconut scent as he grazed her with the tip of his nose. She always smelled of coconuts to him. It was mouthwatering delicious in a sense that made him want to run his tongue along her neck until he met her luscious lips and devour them. Not to mention, the taste of sweet tea he knew was lingering on her lips. The combination made him want to consume her every time she was near.

Olivia's body trembled from the small contact. Luke

always managed to ignite a fire inside of her each time he touched her. They'd been together for the past four years, and even before there was always electricity between them.

"Just looking at the beautiful lake, watching your brothers play around, thinking how today was so wonderful. One of the best days of my life. Wondering about where everyone will go now that we've all graduated college."

Luke paused before he replied. "I can always tell when something is stewing in those pretty brown eyes of yours."

Chuckling together, Livy relaxed her head against Luke's chest as they slowly rocked side to side. The sun was stronger this time of year and he could feel the heat beating down on his bare shoulders. It didn't bother him, though. Luke was born and raised in the South, so the exceptionally high temperatures were nothing new to him.

"Yo, Luke! The food done yet? I'm starvin'!" Chase yelled from a distance.

Shaking his head, he turned and hollered back, "Y'all can get your own food!" He'd be damned if he was going to let his girl out of his arms.

As Olivia continued with her unwavering gaze, Luke brushed the wayward strands of hair back and kissed her neck tenderly. He grasped her a little tighter, but wasn't going to let the sense that Olivia was holding back worry him. He knew his girl would open up when she was ready. Absolutely nothing would take this away from him.

In a moment as simple as this, Luke fell in love with Livy a little more.

LEANING AGAINST A GIANT OAK TREE IN HIS NOW DRY SWIM trunks, Luke's arms were crossed firmly in front of his bare chest. He was unmistakably irritated to the point where a tick started in his clenched jaw. Luke didn't want to take his anger out on Livy, so grinding his teeth down was a better choice.

They'd just spent an incredible day by the lake with their friends, swimming and grilling like old times. Luke even played his guitar, sang songs, some along with the radio and others off the top of his head. The singing was mainly for Olivia's pleasure. He loved to watch her face transition through a dozen different emotions while he crooned. Her beautiful brown eyes would light up before trying to conceal them as if she wasn't affected by it, but he knew her all too well. Her eyes would focus solely on the guitar while his fingers caressed the bronze cords and when Luke would add, '*whiskey girl*' to a song, he'd lay it on thick, causing his drawl to come out in a raspy and husky sound that grabbed her attention. Livy's heated eyes would drift up to meet his and they'd lock in place as he sang. A deep tint of pink would color her cheeks and help shape the seductive, yet coy smile that would grace her face.

Whiskey girl had become a nickname he used for her and her alone.

All of their friends had left the lake now and he was having a heated discussion—more like an argument—with Olivia. Luke was trying in vain to keep his emotions at bay, but she took him completely by surprise, and truth be told, it wasn't sitting well with him. He couldn't say he was completely blindsided by it, he felt earlier that she was holding something back. Even then, he wasn't expecting this kind of news.

Tension mounted between them as Luke asked, "What do you mean you want to leave Georgia? So you're telling me you're better off somewhere else? This right here baby," he hitched up his thumb and pointed to the woods behind him, "is the real deal. This is where your heart is, where your friends and family are. It's your home. You're not going to get much better than this."

Luke rubbed his chest as tightness gripped him just thinking about Olivia leaving, an unfamiliar feeling creeping inside. His jagged voice came out in a broken whisper, "It's also where...I am. Take it or leave it. What's it going to be?"

Sitting under a tree on an old gray wool blanket gave her very little reprieve from the sweltering sun. It was late afternoon, but the sun hadn't stopped shining. Olivia glanced up at Luke with her big, round chocolate eyes. She could swear she heard his voice crackle during the last statement he made. It was as if he was saying *take me or leave me*. Goodness, it hurt to hear that since she had no intention of leaving him to begin with. She loved Luke and couldn't imagine not having him near, but hearing him utter such painful words felt like an ultimatum to her. She didn't fancy the idea of being forced to choose between her dreams and her heart.

"*Take it or leave it?* What's that supposed to mean, Luke? Like it's all or nothing with you?" Olivia spat out.

Shaking her head, she pulled her knees to her chest and wound her arms around them. She felt sick to her stomach as she replayed the words in her head. His toned arms and chest were rigid as he stood ignoring her question. His messy sandy blond hair dried unevenly from swimming in the lake and the strands curled just at the tips and framed the sides of his face. A pair of black board shorts hung low on his waist, showing off the slight 'V' that dipped into his suit. It wasn't pronounced, but the thin strip of light hair driving up from beneath caught her attention. Luke wasn't overly defined or full of ridiculous bulging muscles, but he was toned to the right amount of perfection for her. He was exceptionally striking as he stood there, an air of peril surrounded him.

Olivia loved Luke deeply and always would, but she wasn't destined to live in a small town forever. She wanted more than the life she was dealt, so why couldn't he understand her need to at least give it a shot outside of South Fork? Olivia wasn't leaving Luke; she just wanted to see what else was out there.

A current of air glided off the lake, rustling the trees and causing the sun to filter past the rich green leaves and caress her heated skin. Deep down, Olivia had a notion that the thoughts running through her mind would tear them apart. She worried that the decision she was about to make would change so much between them. Olivia knew what she wanted: city lights, four seasons and the hustle and bustle of busy streets. Most of all, she wanted a secure life where she wouldn't have to rely on anyone ever again. It was the one goal and dream she was reaching for, but the thought of not having Luke by her side? Unfathomable.

Olivia picked at her nails as she tried to contemplate an answer that would be the "right one." Answering his question with trepidation, she said softly, "I...I want more. I want to see what other places have to offer. I want to experience life outside of this small town, Luke. And...you should want that too, for both of us. Isn't there anything you want?"

"I know what I want. I'm lookin' at her. And there's no other place I want to be but here with her," Luke refuted in a barely audible tone, his eyes piercing hers.

Pushing off the tree, Luke could feel how tightly coiled his muscles were as he stretched his arms out. The grass was hot as it crunched underneath his feet. Angry wasn't even the word to describe what he was feeling at this very moment. Agitated? Fuming? He wasn't sure and it didn't matter. He was just plain old fucking pissed.

Luke reached into his pocket and pulled out a cigarette. He tilted his head to the side, cupping the tip of the cigarette with his palm as he flicked his lighter. Taking a deep drag, he tried to comprehend exactly what she was implying. Had Luke heard her correctly when she said she wanted to leave? That she wanted to see if there was more out there for her? What else did she need? And where was all this coming from? It blindsided him.

Luke shook his head in denial and increased the distance between them. What the hell was he then? Had the past four years meant absolutely nothing to her? His mind was running a mile a minute, unable to process it all so quickly. Possibly because he didn't want to.

Of course Luke wanted Olivia to do what made her happy. He'd bend over backwards to see her smile, but without him? He'd just assumed they'd stay in Georgia together. The thought of her leaving began to eat him up. Was he being selfish wanting Olivia to stay with him? Probably. Did he give a shit that he was about to be a prick? Nope. Not at all.

Luke turned back toward Olivia with new found determination. Pinching the cigarette between his thumb and forefinger, he gritted his teeth as he spoke, anger laced in his voice. "Fine. Leave. If that's what you want, then go. I hope you find what you're looking for, but know this—I won't be waiting for you when you come back, 'cause baby, you'll be back. This place is in your bones. Mark my words."

Standing up with a blaze of fire in her eyes, Olivia's hair blew in her face as she stomped over to Luke. She was just a few steps away and seething in exasperation, her hands forming small fists at her sides. Irritation rolled down her damp skin in rippling waves that managed to heat her to the core. Leave? Luke just told her to leave?

"Luke! You're being stubborn! We're young, fresh out of college and have our whole lives ahead of us. How do you know you're supposed to stay here? How do you know there isn't more waiting for you somewhere else?" Olivia yelled, throwing her arms around as she spoke. "Is this enough for you? To be confined to this little town with nothing but grass as far as the eye can see? Is that what you want?"

Luke stood still. He had to. The woman was making his blood boil, and not the way she usually did either. He had a feeling he knew where this conversation was headed but didn't want to accept it just yet.

With sheer purpose in his eyes, Luke took one last pull

and flicked his cigarette into the grass. Blowing the final drag of smoke out, he crossed the short distance, eyeing her as if he'd just spotted his prey.

Reaching behind and grabbing the back of her head, Luke fisted a clump of her hair in his hand. He hooked an arm around her waist as he pulled her flush against his heated body. Olivia's back arched and the smooth skin of her stomach connected with his as he heard her breath catch while he held her tightly.

God, how he loved her. Loved her for some time now. *Damn.* Maybe even longer than the four years they had been dating, but now it felt as if she was leaving. He could feel it and was prepared to do anything to get her to change her mind. Call him selfish, but he didn't want to see her go and was willing to use what he could to make her stay.

Leaning down close enough to almost touch her face, Luke searched her eyes for answers as he whispered, "You're enough for me, baby. You. I want what you want and I thought it was here. But now I'm seeing that we might not want the same things." Shaking his aching head, he asked, "What changed, Livy?"

Olivia softened in his hold. He loved that he had this effect on her, that all it took was his touch for her to liquefy in his arms. The air seemed thick as it flowed between them, making it almost unbearable to breathe. He'd like to believe it was the humidity, but they'd always had such chemistry that Luke would be fooling himself thinking otherwise. The softness of her body against his was doing things to his brain. Even mad as he was in the moment, his body was alive and wanting Olivia.

Staring deeply into Olivia's dark brown eyes, he brushed his lips gently across hers. Never losing eye contact, he said breathlessly, "Did you hear me, baby? You. I said you're enough for me. Am I not enough for you?" Then he pressed his mouth down onto Olivia's soft, lush lips. He wanted—no needed—to show her how much she meant to him.

Slowly, Luke slid his tongue along the seam of her mouth causing her sweet lips to part slightly. A sigh escaped her and Luke used that as an opening. He tenderly pulled her bottom lip into his mouth and nibbled on it.

"I need you. Don't leave, Livy."

Olivia tasted heavenly against his mouth as he began caressing her bottom lip with his tongue. The faint taste of sweat tea lingered on her lips and it fueled him even more. Taking charge of the moment, Luke slid his tongue forcefully into Olivia's mouth. The split second he touched her tongue, he put everything into the kiss, crushing her to him.

Pulling her tighter so she couldn't move, he kissed her hard. He kissed her for all the days he'd known her. He kissed her to show her what she meant to him. He kissed her as if his life depended on it. And he kissed her like it was the last chance he was ever going to get. He devoured her lips with such intensity that he was hurting inside from it. It was as if he was overpowered with this need to convince her to change her mind. With a kiss. And he would damn well do anything to get her to stay.

Olivia couldn't even think straight. Luke's kisses always made her dizzy with need, turning her soft and pliable at his mercy. She could feel his body hardening against hers and she loved it; she loved her softness against his hardness. Within seconds, Luke's sinful lips triggered a response from her body. The warm and languid silkiness of his tongue was instant ecstasy. He had serious skills when it came to using his mouth. It may have been a hot summer day, but the only heat she felt was coming from Luke.

As if in perfect harmony, Luke's tongue danced erotically inside her. He touched the roof of her mouth as her hands glided up his arms and over his broad shoulders. Moaning into his mouth, her fingers threaded his sandy hair and she pulled him to her.

Needing to come up for air, Olivia broke the kiss to breathe. Her lips felt swollen and puffy as they both gasped heavily into each other's mouths, seeing the raw passion and need in the depths of his eyes. In that moment, Luke's gaze said more than words could ever express.

Of course you're enough for me, always have been... she thought to herself.

How could she ever leave him?

Olivia stood on her toes and pressed her lips to Luke's cheek, hugging him closely and taking in his heady scent. The sun beat hard onto the open land, but Olivia couldn't tell if the heat was coming from the sun or how agitated Luke was at the moment. Pulling back, she noticed creases around his eyes. That old saying '*the eyes are the windows to the soul*' reverberated through her mind. If that were true, Olivia had all she needed. The truth in his eyes held so much emotion, and it nearly killed her to see it.

In that instant, Olivia made the decision to tell him what he wanted to hear.

"You know... Let's not talk about it anymore. It was just a thought, nothing more. Honestly."

What she failed to mention was that she had already applied to medical schools outside of Georgia. Dropping that kind of news wasn't going to be easy after Luke's reaction today. She was apprehensive about the whole situation and it set her stomach rolling with anxiety. The last thing on earth she wanted to do was lose Luke.

six

Sliding the key into the lock, Olivia opened up the door to the place she called home. It was far from a home these days, but merely a place to sleep. The warmth and love seeped away long ago and loneliness took its place. It wasn't always that way, it just changed as she got older when she learned to be a little less naïve.

For as long as she could remember, Jane and Dave, her adoptive parents, had taken care of her. They had treated her like their own daughter and showed her unconditional love. For whatever reason, her biological parents had given her up after she'd been born and it was something she had learned to live with. Olivia felt she was better off. If they didn't want her, she didn't care to ever meet them.

But as the years passed, something changed in the home and she found herself becoming detached. The care and love she was shown early on began to dwindle away some time towards high school when her father's drunken insensitivity progressed. Small arguments began to creep up more often than she cared to remember, leaving her on edge with anxiety. It went from being a couple of times a month to a few times a week. There was no way to escape the yelling as much as she tried. Olivia would lock herself in her bedroom, push her earplugs in, switch the lights off then crawl between her cold sheets. She'd turn up the newly added music that she knew would be waiting for her on her iPod to help drown out the roaring of voices from down the hall. Luke, her one savior who knew every little thing about her life and accepted her regardless, would upload new music often to surprise Olivia. It was her one clutch, her one grip on normalcy she had left. And she owed it all to Luke. But when that wouldn't work, because there were times when she couldn't stand to be home anymore, she'd run off to his house as her last resort where he'd welcome her with warm, open arms. He'd hold her tight and sing her to sleep.

So much was shifting in her adolescent world when she needed a mother to confide in most. Jane had become distant, unhappiness plaguing her once lively eyes as the years passed by. Resentment filled Olivia for making her feel so unwanted. Music had become an infallible source through it all and her tie to Luke. It filled her with warmth when she was feeling hollow and empty inside, and very alone. They had formed a bond through lyrics that could not be broken.

In return for her defiance, Olivia later learned she came with a paycheck. It nearly broke her on the inside. The first time Olivia heard her father spew the words that she came with a price, she cried silent tears in the shower for days on end. Could it be that no one wanted her?

Any time she rebelled after, her father would dutifully remind her they were paid to take care of her. Jane came to Dave's defense on more than one occasion, pleading with Olivia to ignore him, that it was the alcohol talking, but Olivia couldn't. The damage had already been done the first time she saw the resentment in his eyes as he spoke with clarity one night. With Dave's little reminders, she learned to rely on herself, and by the time her senior year came around, Olivia wanted to hightail it out as fast as she could.

Olivia worked hard in college so she could get out of South Fork. She never lost focus and graduated from Georgia Southern University with a Bachelors of Science in Chemistry. Attending medical school outside of Georgia was something she secretly wanted. New York offered some of the top rated medical schools in the country, along with a rich cultural diversity that she longed to experience. Olivia needed to do this for herself more than anything to prove that she could make it.

Looking around the living room as she walked through the front door, everything was the same as it always was growing up. She spotted her father planted in the tattered blue recliner with his feet propped up watching television. His stomach hung out just a bit from his faded red shirt while his greasy hair was in disarray. The drawn and worn out look of his skin matched his eyes, like he was tired of life and everything around him. It always made Olivia sad to look at her father that way.

"Hey, Dad."

"Hey, sweet pea." His eyes perked up at the sight of her, a smile splayed across his bloated face. "How was your day? Have a good time?"

When he wasn't drinking, Dave was the concerned and caring father who she remembered as a young child. Only when he drank would he become verbally abusive and cruel. He knew which words would cut her down when he used them against her. Overhearing her parent's argue through the walls, Jane had once told her that he drank so much he didn't remember his actions the next day. But Olivia could never forget.

"It was pretty good. We barbequed at the lake and listened to music. It was really nice seeing everyone together."

"That's good. I'm glad you got to see your friends again. You look a little sunburned, though. I hope you put on some sunblock."

"Yeah, it was a scorcher out there today," she said and she smiled. "And of course I wore sunblock, Dad. Is Mom around? I need to talk to her."

"I think she's in the kitchen making supper. Not sure. She's around here somewhere, though."

Olivia nodded her head. "Thanks."

Considering she truly felt he regretted her existence, she was completely bewildered by his gentleness at times. Olivia had come to the conclusion that Dave was the explanation behind Jane pulling away over time. It wasn't Olivia's place to ask, but with the arguments and vile words, it only seemed natural for Jane to retreat. How could she not? It was why Olivia had herself. If what Dave said about her being a paycheck was true, then she was forced to think the worst about him. But Olivia didn't want to come to that conclusion, she'd seen happiness in his eyes once and knew it still lingered somewhere below.

Once it all set in, Olivia didn't hold a tight grudge against her mother anymore. She'd come to terms with it all and accepted it for what it was.

Heading into the kitchen that smelled of garlic and sauce, Olivia found Jane over the stove cooking dinner.

"Hey, Mom."

Jane's brown hair was sprinkled with grey. She turned to Olivia with a genuine smile and asked, "Hey, honey, how was your day?"

"Good. It was good...until the end," she mumbled the last of her response. "I hadn't realized how much I missed everyone. It was like old times like when we were back in high school."

Concern crossed her mother's face. "Up until the end?"

"I brought up the possibility of moving outside of Georgia to Luke. Let's just say it didn't go over well with him."

"I'm sorry to hear that, honey. I imagine he didn't like

hearing that you've already applied to a few medical schools then."

Avoiding eye connect with her mom, Olivia said, "I...ah...didn't tell him yet."

"Liv."

"I know, but I don't want to talk about it, okay? I don't know what I'm going to do. All I know is that I came to talk to you about student loans and what I need to apply for them. I'm stressing about it all and wanted to see if you would help me look on the computer so I can start gathering the right papers. That's all I want to do right now. If everything goes as planned, then I'll decide what to do about me and Luke. Aside from that, I really don't want to talk about him. If it's going to be a problem then we just won't do it."

With a sigh, Jane responded, "Alright. Whatever you need help with I'll help. I just hope Luke will be able to come to an understanding with your decision."

She hoped he did, too.

"So do you think we can start after dinner?"

"Of course."

"Thanks. And I'm sorry for snapping at you. I just have a lot on my mind at the moment. I'm really stressing about everything."

"I understand," she replied softly, using the same tone she would with her father. All her mother could manage to give was a half-smile with her response. Everything was said in that small action.

As Olivia made her way up the creaking stairs to her old bedroom, she looked at the wall of framed photos. Her mother insisted on hanging each school year up. Some were the most embarrassing photos she'd ever taken with puffy, high hair and sprayed bangs, and others that captured an innocent and sweet face to go along.

A strange sadness flowed through her. Reaching out, she ran a finger down one of the wooden frames as she stared at the photo. Just like with any family, they all had their good times and bad, but why was it so easy to remember the bad times rather than the good?

Despite Dave and his drinking, she had a soft spot for him and his willingness to adopt her in the end. He was the only father she'd ever known and appreciated all that they had done, regardless. As she stared at the photos, Olivia felt guilt slither up her body and settle in her heart for her way of thinking.

Opening the door, Olivia glanced around her bedroom. The bed was near the window with the same purple lilac comforter she had throughout high school. Next to the window were her matching desk and bookshelf. Olivia smiled at all the pictures pinned to the old corkboard that hung above her desk. It was a recollection of the past, moments she never wanted to forget that brought back tender memories. Each picture told a different story; some of her and friends during birthday parties and high school football games, but most were of her and Luke. Happiness washed over her as she looked at them, a warm sentiment filled her chest.

Luke.

Olivia sighed inwardly. She didn't know what to do. Uncertainty seeped through her body, disposing of the joy she felt just moments ago. She didn't want to leave Luke, but also couldn't stay trapped in her small town. Deep inside, Olivia knew what she wanted. She knew she should have told Luke about applying to medical school but didn't want to upset him any further, so she had decided to leave that part out. She needed to see how the application process went before she broached the subject of leaving again and go from there.

Walking into her bathroom, Olivia turned the knob of the shower and waited for the water to heat up.

A beep sounded from her phone.

TESSA: *Listen. I've been thinking. How about we plan a night at Smokejacks? The girls and guys…dancing…maybe a drink and possibly getting Luke to sing on stage?*

Olivia shook her head, chuckling. Tessa was the reserved one between the two, except when she drank. Then she was loud and bubbly, which made for fun stories the next day. A thrill ran up her spine just thinking of how much fun they would have.

OLIVIA: *That sounds great. I'm sure the guys would easily agree to going to Smokejacks. The lake was pretty amazing, and I'd love for us all to get together as much as we can before real life takes over.*

TESSA: *Sweet! I'll take care of the guys, you just work on getting Luke to sing. I'll text you later once I have it all figured out.*

OLIVIA: *Got it.*

Luke.

Olivia sighed at the thought of him again. She hoped taking a hot shower would alleviate some of the tension in her neck and wash away her worries. The sun had worn her out, and Olivia would love nothing more than to crawl between her sheets and go to sleep.

Nothing worth having came easy for Olivia. And her bridge to cross had a few planks missing. She'd either have to jump, praying she'd make it over in one piece, or find an unmarked and fresh path that would lead her to a better ending.

Hopefully.

seven

Olivia had been staring at her computer screen for the last five minutes reading the same sentences over and over. She had just opened her email that contained letters from a few of the medical schools she applied to. A distressing and bittersweet feeling formed in the pit of her stomach.

Being accepted to this particular school in New York was a pretty big deal for Olivia. It was one of the best medical schools in New York City and she knew she'd be going against many applicants for a chair. It would be an incredible learning experience in a career she was passionate about. Olivia knew the training would come with long hours that would no doubt wear her down. That wasn't a concern for her, though. Working hard was second skin to Olivia, and it was an opportunity she didn't want to pass up.

A muffled buzzing broke Olivia from her thoughts. She looked over to her bed where her phone was vibrating.

"Hello."

"Hey, Care Bear, what'cha' doin'?"

Olivia smiled at Luke's endearment for her. "Umm…" clearing her throat, she answered. "Nothing…just on my computer checking emails and such. What's up?" She tried to hold her voice steady as she replied. She felt awful for withholding the truth from him.

"You busy? I want to come pick you up and take you somewhere. Just me and you."

Before she could respond, Olivia heard the faint sound of a truck door slamming and an engine revving in the background. "You sound like you're already in the truck."

Luke laughed. "I am. I was hoping you'd say you weren't doing anything. Wishful thinking—and praying—on my part."

"I'm not really dressed and my hair is a mess. I was getting ready to read a book in bed, actually."

"Oh yeah?" Luke's voice grew deeper. "What are you wearing? Actually, scratch that. Change of plans. Stay just how you are. I'll be there soon, and I'm coming through your window. Be prepared."

Sitting up, Olivia laughed at Luke's quick change of plans. "Be prepared for what exactly? And you can't fit through my window. You're too big!"

"Now why would I tell you and ruin all the fun, Livy? All you have to do is just lie there and read your *romance* book while I have my way with you. Don't ask questions, just let me do."

A belly laugh erupted from her when Luke put emphasis on the romance part. He loved to make fun of her romance novels throughout the years, even once saying that if she could read her definition of romance then he could watch his definition of romance whenever he wanted, as if that was even close to the same thing.

"Very funny, Luke. While it may be extremely tempting,"—it was totally tempting to her—"my parents are home, so it's not going to happen. I'll get dressed and head downstairs. Where are we going so I know what to wear?"

"Ahh, that's right. You like to make too much noise and they'll hear you."

"Luke!"

Luke barked out a laugh. "It's a surprise. Dress comfortably."

"Alright, but I'm warning you, I'm not doing my hair or makeup or anything. I'm a hot mess."

"Baby," Luke said in a low, husky voice, "you don't *need* makeup or any spray to fix your hair. You're beautiful the way you are. In fact, I wish you didn't wear any of that stuff to begin with. See you soon, Livy."

Luke hung up and she sat there for a moment processing what he said. He was gentle and affectionate and he may be a smooth talker, but Olivia knew it was honest words coming from Luke. She'd known him too long for it to be otherwise. He was a genuine, good guy.

Getting up, Olivia went to her dresser and pulled out a pair of heather grey lounge pants. Pulling her hair out of its bun, she put on her pants and tied the waistband. Then she walked over to her closet and found her royal blue, three-quarter sleeve Henley and slipped it over a white tank top. Grabbing her black kicks, she slid them on her feet.

Once dressed, Olivia grabbed her phone and purse then went downstairs. She spotted her father who was getting ready to crack open a beer while in his usual chair.

"You goin' out?" he asked.

"Yes, Luke is coming to get me."

He nodded his head. "Alright, be careful. You have your keys?"

Holding up her keys in her right hand, she jangled them. "I do." Olivia looked toward the windows when she heard Luke's truck roar up the dirt driveway. She leaned down and kissed the only father she'd ever known on the cheek. "I'll see you later, Dad."

"Bye, sweet pea. Have fun." Olivia smiled sadly into his gray eyes.

Olivia opened the front door and noticed Luke was

already out of his truck. Pulling Olivia into a hug, he kissed her cheek then reached behind her to open the door to the passenger side of his truck. As Luke helped her in, his earthy scent filled her nose and she had to fight back a hum that had started to work its way up from her throat. He wasn't wearing anything special, yet it was effortless for him to smell so delectable.

Sitting back with an arm draped across the steering wheel, Luke was enjoying the low music on the radio as he drove. The windows were rolled down and Livy's hair was billowing in the wind as she was looking out of the window with her knee propped up against the door. The sweet scent of Georgia countryside mixed with the dry reddish-brown dirt permeated the air. Luke loved it. This was home, his life. He couldn't imagine living anywhere else. He knew Livy was dying for answers, but he wasn't saying anything as he sat there with a smirk on his face under his baseball cap. Tonight was about them.

Turning the wheel, Luke veered to the left as he made his way across a grassy field and parked his truck between two widespread trees about a mile out. Tonight couldn't have been a better night as the sky was illuminated with streams of reds, pinks, yellows and light purples as the sun set on the horizon. There was nothing ahead of them for miles but grass and the stunning sunset.

He turned the ignition so the truck wasn't running, just the battery to keep the music playing softly. Hopping out, Luke made his way around to Livy's side. She tracked his every move, still waiting for him to say something.

"So...are you going to tell me what's up? Why we're in the middle of nowhere?"

"Babe, we live in a small town in the south. We're always in the middle of nowhere."

Olivia didn't even bother responding to his sarcastic answer. He did have a point.

Luke dropped a quick kiss to her cheek and took her to the back of his truck. He dropped the tailgate and climbed in. Grabbing the stack of blankets he brought, Luke began to unroll each one, layering them on top of one another to create a cushion against the hardness of the truck bed.

Once he finished, he looked to Olivia who was watching him curiously. "You done?" she asked.

"Yeah, I think so. Now climb on up here and come sit with me."

A smile graced Olivia's face as she placed her hand into Luke's to help her climb into the bed of the truck. Sitting and leaning back, he turned to his right and reached into a cooler that held ice and beer. Pulling out two cold ones, he cracked one open and handed it to Livy, then did the same for himself.

Bringing the ice cold beer to her lips, Olivia could feel Luke's eyes on her as she took a long sip of the cool, crisp liquid. The first sip was always the best. Turning sideways with the beer still tipped to her lips, she took another sip while she waited for him to say something, anything.

"What?" she said, not really asking him anything. "I like it."

Luke just shook his head as he grinned at her. Taking a swig himself, Luke settled back into the pillows and opened his arm out to Livy. She curled into his side, letting out a sigh of contentment as she rested her head on his chest and draped a leg over his. There wasn't a soul around for miles, nothing but the stillness of the evening and the country music playing softly in the background to keep them company.

Olivia realized why Luke hadn't said a word about where they were going—it wasn't needed. He was showing it to her, how easy and tranquil it was for them even in the middle of nowhere. That it didn't matter where they were or what they were doing, as long as they were doing it together.

How could she ever think of leaving the warmth of Luke's arms now?

. . .

A FEW BEERS IN AND OLIVIA WAS COZYING UP AGAINST LUKE when Billy Currington's *Must Be Doin' Somethin' Right* came on the radio. A lazy smile graced her face as she looked up and said, "I love this song." A soft hum started in the back of her throat.

"Hang on, baby."

Hidden behind the cooler, Luke pulled out a stuffed animal. A *Care Bear*. Olivia's heart melted at the sight of its plush little purple body. Luke had called her *Care Bear* for as long as she could remember. He once told her she was like a little bear that kept people warm and comforted when they were in need. The purple bear was small, and around its neck was a dark blue pouch. Luke held the bear in his hand for a moment before he gave it to her.

"For you."

"What is it?"

"Well, open it and see."

Olivia ran her fingers across the blue pouch before she pulled the drawstring apart. Cupping her hand below it, she tipped the bag and the contents fell out.

Inhaling a breath, she gasped. Olivia looked at the piece of jewelry lying in her palm. Nestled in her hand was a diamond heart necklace. It was absolutely stunning. She picked up the heart and a dainty gold chain dropped from it.

Olivia was speechless. She was caught off guard and wasn't sure what to think of it. He'd surprised her with gifts in the past, but nothing this extravagant.

Looking into his green eyes, they held more emotion than words could ever express at that moment. He loved her. She knew he did. It was almost unnerving for Olivia to see the intensity of love held in his eyes for her. Knowing Luke, he wasn't going to say much about his gesture. If anything, he'd belt out one of his songs instead.

"Luke..." she said breathlessly.

Luke shrugged his shoulders.

"It's...too much... Why? You didn't—"

"I know I didn't have to," he said, cutting her off. "But it reminded me of you when I saw it. I wanted you to have it."

Olivia rolled the necklace around in her palm, the diamonds sparkling with each twist as she thought about his last comment.

Looking at Luke, his backwards ball cap had his curls flaring out along the sides. Leaning in, Olivia inhaled his intoxicating scent that licked across his skin. She kissed the curve of his neck, her lips pressing against his warm skin. He smelled so good her body started to slowly ignite.

Whispering heavily she said, "Thank you. I love it," and continued to softly dust kisses all around Luke's neck, onto his cheek and over to his mouth. He didn't move a muscle, just sat motionless. Olivia gave one last kiss to his lips, pressing hard but letting her tongue just faintly touch his lips teasingly.

Olivia pulled back and watched the muscles in Luke's jaw work as he fought to keep it together. He just kept staring into her eyes with his unblinking gaze. The steady friction between them bubbled into sensual anticipation and all she could think of was being closer to him.

"Just curious, but what made you think of me when you saw this?" Olivia asked as she sat back and licked her lips, tasting Luke on them.

A smile cracked across Luke's handsome face as he picked up the necklace and held it in his hand, admiring it.

"Hmm...I couldn't tear my eyes from it. I was going to walk away, I really tried, but the diamonds caught the light and flickered brilliantly. It's perfect and beautiful just the way it is. It made me think of you. The center is empty, but when it's around your neck it's full, because you've filled it. It's my heart that you've captured and if you're going to hold on to it,

I want you to wear it around your neck...so it's next to your heart."

"Goodness, Luke," was all she could muster up. Talk about aiming straight for the heart.

Both became silent as they stared into each other's eyes. His southern drawl was heavy with each word he spoke, pulling her in deeper and locking her to him in what would be forever. Hearing him express the words she knew came from his heart was both reassuring and painful at the same time.

Painful because she still hadn't told him about medical school.

Not wanting to go there, Olivia pushed the thought out of her mind and put her focus back on the necklace and Luke. It hurt too much to think of anything else.

Luke's heartfelt gesture hit her like a ton of bricks slamming into her chest. Her emotions were climbing and she was unable to form a sentence. Olivia did the only thing she felt was needed in that moment. She reached over and pulled Luke's face to hers, kissing him with as much strength as she possibly could.

She wanted to show him how much his words and thoughtfulness meant to her. She pressed her mouth hard to Luke's, pouring herself into him. Gripping the sides of his neck, her lips tingled as she kissed Luke's lips, tasting the coolness of the beer as her tongue slipped inside. When their tongues collided, they both groaned and consumed one another, as if they were kissing each other for the first time. Olivia felt herself growing wet just from his kiss and she wanted more.

Overcome with desire and emotion, she sat up higher and threw her leg over Luke's lap, straddling him but never breaking contact with his mouth.

"Hang on, baby," he mumbled against her lush lips, "let

me put the necklace around your neck." When she didn't listen, he reached up and yanked at her hair.

"I said hang on, Livy."

Livy's back arched as he held onto her ponytail, breaking the kiss. He traced open mouthed kisses down her neck to her collarbone, running his tongue along the narrow bone. He felt Olivia shudder in pleasure. Reaching behind her, his fingers met and clasped the necklace closed.

"There ya go."

Luke nearly growled when he gripped her hips and tugged her tighter to him. His palms skated down the curve of her ass as he held her to him. Her sigh turned into a moan. She pulled off his hat and ran her fingers through his hair, never letting up. Her actions had his body heating and his cock hard. She rolled her hips into him and Luke almost lost it.

Luke's playful tongue had Olivia pulling on his shirt and trying to remove it as she began to slowly grind against him, creating a steady friction against his zipper. Reaching behind his head, he pulled off his shirt and threw it to the side. Luke gripped her ass tighter and thrust his body back, unable to control himself. His cock was in pain from being trapped inside and wanted nothing more than to sink into her.

She was breathing heavy as he nipped and sucked on the curve of her slender neck. Olivia moaned Luke's name as he ran his tongue below her ear, leaving a wet trail. A soft breeze passed over them and it caused her to shiver against him.

Luke was past aroused. He was fighting the urge to roll them over and make love to her in the bed of his truck, his cock taking on a heartbeat of its own.

Fuck it.

Holding onto her, Luke rolled over Livy until he was on top of her, her legs spreading to accommodate his body. Olivia wrapped her legs around his waist, pressing her heels into him, causing him to push into her sex harder. She moaned and arched her back. His erection was straining to be released. Oh how he would love nothing more than to slam right into her. Livy groaned loudly as she reached down to the waistband of his pants, her fingers sliding over his length, fumbling to unzip his pants and get what she so desperately needed.

"Uh uh…" Luke mumbled, shaking his head slightly. "Shhhh."

Luke grabbed her hand to stop. Taking both wrists, he placed them above her head and held them down with one of his hands. He could tell she was about to speak, but he spoke before she could.

"Let me take care of you. It's about you tonight."

Olivia's body relaxed beneath him, her eyes glazed over. He could smell the sweet coconut on her skin as he kissed the top of her breasts that had risen up from her tank top. She smelled delicious. She closed her eyes feeling her nipples hardened as he skimmed over them, rubbing in circles and then pinching them. Leaning down, he ran his tongue along the tops of her breasts slowly as he created a steady push of back and forth with his hips against hers.

"Luke… Oh, God…" she panted heavily. Olivia tried to pull her hands away, but they were still locked in place.

"I…need you. Please, Luke," she said, biting down on her bottom lip.

With his free hand, Luke gently held her chin, forcing her to open her mouth and release her bottom lip. He knew she was close to climaxing.

"Don't hold back by bitin' on that lip of yours, baby. No one is around for miles. It's just you and me," Luke said, continuing with his exquisite torture.

Nearly crying out loud, she said his name one last time. "Luke, please… I want you in me now."

His throaty laugh wasn't helping. He leaned next to her ear, his breath hot as he said, "Just let go. Let me feel you come against me pushing into you like this. You're so hot and worked up right now that I'd love to slide right into you and feel you gripping me, me pounding into you. Come on, baby...imagine me inside of you right now, sliding in," he rocked against her, "and sliding out" and then he pulled his hips away. "The tension building as I work my cock in you the way you like. Your heart racing, blood heating and beggin' for more."

Luke looked at Olivia's face in the throes of passion. Her head was thrown back, eyes squeezed shut and mouth was open making the most erotic sounds he'd ever heard. He squeezed her thighs, feeling her pleasure as his own.

"Slow...and deep, baby." Luke's voice crackled with arousal. This wasn't easy on him. "I know how you like it. Just picture it." She must've done as he said, because Olivia yelled out loudly.

He leaned down to kiss her aggressively one last time. His hand moved over her nipples, then down her flat stomach where he lifted her shirt and splayed his hand on her goosebump covered belly. Lazily, he dragged his hand in light circles creating a steady friction, teasing her before he made his way further down. He felt Olivia trying to pull her trapped hands out from under his. Luke knew he was torturing her and didn't care. He loved it and got off on it, knowing without a doubt she'd be even wetter from it.

"Luke! Please let go of my hands so I can touch you."

Chuckling, he said, "Nope."

Luke untied the drawstring of her pants and slid his hand slowly over her panties, pushing against her mound with the heel of his hand and feeling how wet she was. Olivia moaned, her body undulating at the spot he touched. He took his time as he slowly rubbed her covered clit. Olivia tried to squeeze her legs shut but his large *turned-the-hell-on* body was in the way and it couldn't be done. Luke was ready to burst at this point. He wanted her so fucking bad, but he didn't want to give in.

Luke moved his hand up to the lace front of her panties, pulled them down and slid a finger in. She bucked, silently asking for more. He pushed harder and rubbed her clit with his finger, using her wetness to bring her higher. Once he moved a little deeper, Luke was able to feel how drenched she was and he growled. God, how he wanted to fuck Olivia right now and would almost give anything to do so, but he wouldn't. It wasn't about him tonight. It was about her.

Luke rubbed her clit with his thumb and slid in and out of her with two fingers, wishing to the heavens it was his dick. His cock strained against his jeans even more when he felt her walls tighten and pulse around his fingers.

"It's right there, baby. I can feel it," he whispered on her lips, biting the bottom one.

"I'm so close…"

"Just let go."

He curved his fingers up and thumbed her clit hard. Olivia yelled into his mouth as she orgasmed immediately. His fingers didn't let up until every last part of her orgasm was pulled from her. Her back arched and her legs were rubbing and squeezing his hips as she purred. Luke knew another orgasm was on the horizon and pulled his fingers out but continued to stroke her wet and swollen folds, not entering her. Up and down he slid, rotating around her clit and down to her entrance just hovering to tease her.

"Luke," she panted, her chest rising rapidly. "Please, I need you in me."

"Believe me, baby, I want to be in you more than you know," he said huskily.

Luke chuckled and then plunged two fingers into her again, ending his torture on her. He curved them and her hips bucked. Olivia bit down on her bottom lip as he pressed down one last time on her sensitive clit, vibrating his thumb back and forth. Luke felt her tighten once more, her thighs quivering as she released again. She moaned his name loudly and thrust her hips against his fingers as she felt her body explode.

This is what he loved to feel... Him giving her pleasure and watching her blow up from his touch. Even through the darkness outside, he could see her flushed cheeks and look of bliss curving her lush lips. Luke leaned down and grinned against her lips. Damn if that wasn't the hottest thing he'd ever witnessed.

eight

Olivia's body stirred against Luke's. She gently nudged him as little sounds traveled from her chest and escaped her parted lips. He watched her hand rise on his chest as she snuggled closer. Their legs were a tangled mess, but he couldn't bring himself to move.

Wrapped in warmth, Olivia knew Luke was awake from the gentle caressing on her lower back. It was a feathery touch that caused her to shiver in his arms. His fingertips were thick and rough, fingers that she loved to watch play the guitar with expertise.

Taking a deep breath, she sighed and stretched her neck up to Luke's face.

"Hey, handsome," Livy said. Her voice was groggy and thick.

Luke nodded, the tips of his mouth lifting into a smile in return. "Care Bear."

Livy's sleepy smile widened.

"Sleep well?"

"Actually, yes. I don't think I moved all night." The scent of early morning dew filled the air as she laid there.

"Been up a while?"

"Not long. Just watching you sleep."

"How are your parents?" Olivia asked quietly. "It's been a while since I've seen them."

"Same old, nothing really new with them. My brothers keep them on their toes. Mama wasn't feeling well yesterday when she got up... Something about a sore throat. Truthfully, I think she's doing too much. She needs to take a break, but I know she won't. Always wanting to do everything. She probably has a sore throat from yelling at the boys all the time."

Popping her head off Luke's chest, she asked, "Want me to come over and take a look at her? Maybe I can help."

He squeezed Livy to him, loving how genuinely concerned she was.

"Awe, Care Bear, you're always wanting to take care of everyone. I'm sure she's fine, but if she complains anymore then you can come and check her out. If I know Mama, she won't utter a word of pain, though. Tough little thing that she is." A rolling sound of laughter rumbled from Luke's chest as he said, "In a way you're like my mother when it comes to caring for people. Maybe that's why I like you."

She playfully slapped his chest. Luke couldn't help but laugh at her.

Their time at Georgia Southern University is where the nickname 'Care Bear' came into play more. He knew Olivia aspired to work in the medical field and assumed she'd become a nurse. She'd mention it here and there, but then just say she had time to decide. Her one focus was school and maintaining her grades and the rest would fall into play, she'd say. Olivia had drive, and Luke admired her for it.

"Fine…but maybe I should come over just to say hi to them. We've been back for a few weeks now and I haven't stopped by…"

Luke smiled at Livy's tenacity. "If you want to, that's fine by me. Don't think I don't know why you're coming by, though."

Grinning from ear to ear, Olivia replied, "Can we go now?"

Groaning, Luke rolled over onto Olivia and kissed her forehead. "Alright, baby. We can go now."

WALKING THROUGH THE DOOR OF LUKE'S HOME, OLIVIA WAS greeted by Luke's brothers having a Nerf gun war. Orange and blue mesh pellets were flying everywhere and sticking to random places throughout the living room. By the smiles that danced across their faces and the giggles that came from deep in their bellies, they couldn't have been happier kids.

"Hey, knuckleheads, a lady just walked into the room. Greet her the right way," Luke exclaimed grabbing their attention. The boys stopped in the middle of their war to look at him.

Luke's expression spoke volumes and the boys obeyed. Luke had always treated women with utmost respect. It was one of the reasons why she fell for him.

"Hi, Olivia," the boys said in unison.

"Hey, boys."

"Hey, Livy." Luke's father, Clark, appeared from the left. He walked right over to Olivia and kissed her cheek then nodded to Luke.

Stepping over toys strewn across the carpet, Luke asked his father, "Where's Ma? She feeling any better?"

"You know your mother. She's got a head like a rock, so stubborn that she won't sit still. She's in the kitchen cooking breakfast."

Luke shook his head in disbelief at his father's reply. Typical of his mother. He knew she had a steel will and did whatever she damn well pleased. Not like his father could stop her. Even while sick, his mother was still catering to everyone's needs. He knew she enjoyed it, but also needed to take a break once in a while.

"Mornin', Mama."

Turning around, Luke could see how sick she truly was just by one glance at her face. No amount of makeup could hide the dark circles or tint of yellow in her eyes. Luke shook his head as he looked at her.

"Goddammit, Mama," he muttered lowly to himself, not allowing her to hear.

"Go sit down and let me take over." Luke stalked around the island and grabbed the spatula out of her hand. He raised his hand and pointed to where Olivia was.

Diane raised her hand and gently patted his stubbly face, her thumb wrapping softy around his jaw. A weak smile tugged at her face and her heavy eyes creased at the ends, showing nothing but pure parental love for him.

"Such a caring young man you are. I raised you right. Let's hope the rest of your brothers follow in your footsteps."

His mother's hand felt warm against his face. Reaching for it, he squeezed and felt the heat pour out of it. Luke pressed his big palm against her forehead; she was burning up. Upset at how sick she was, he accidentally pressed against her a little too hard and she stumbled back. Luke quickly reached around and grabbed his mother by the waist, catching her before she fell. She felt so small and fragile in his arms, not like the tough woman she always appeared to be.

"Hey, Diane, let me help you to the island so we can sit," Olivia said.

"Mama, let Olivia look at you. She might be able to help."

"Oh, honey, I'm fine. Just tired. I'll lie down after I'm finished cookin' breakfast."

Luke squeezed the spatula tightly. He huffed loudly and tilted his head up in irritation. Between Olivia and his mother, he wasn't sure who pushed his buttons more. Steaming with frustration, Luke closed his eyes, trying not to snap at his sick mother. His father would have his ass if he disrespected her.

"Mama, go sit down," he spoke sharply.

Sighing, his mother agreed. "Fine, fine. You have such a temper. You get that from your father you know."

And just like that, his mother was able to calm the tension in the kitchen with her playful charm. When something didn't go her way, she blamed his father, but in a good-hearted way.

As Olivia helped Diane to her chair, Luke turned around and finished cooking the breakfast she had started on the stove top. As he poured more homemade pancake batter into the skillet, he overheard Olivia ask where the thermometer was.

"Well, your fever is awfully high. It's nearly a hundred and three degrees. Luke said your throat was bothering you?"

He could hear his mother grunt before she replied. "Yes... Honestly? It feels like it's on fire."

Luke gripped the metal spatula so tight it was cutting into his hand. He hated to see his mother feel so bad. She was the glue that held the family together. His anger slid through his fingers as he flipped a pancake and slapped it down hard, the batter spilling out of the sides.

"Can you open your mouth so I can see? And tilt your head up so I can shine the flashlight in your mouth. Oh, Diane. Your throat is bright red and extremely swollen. It must hurt to swallow. I suggest you get to your doctor as soon as you're able."

"I've had sore throats, but this one is the worst. I just assumed it would pass in a few days," he heard his mother say.

Luke spun around. "She'll go today," he said, "whether she wants to or not. I'm sure Dad will agree."

"Agree with what?" his father asked walking into the kitchen.

"That Mama needs to go to the doctor today."

"I've been tryin' to get her there. The stubborn woman won't listen to me!"

His mother slumped forward, either in acceptance or exhaustion, he wasn't sure which. She appeared so worn out and it wasn't boding well with him.

"Go lie down and I'll bring you breakfast in bed, Ma."

Diane stood up and said to Olivia in a hushed tone, but not low enough for Luke to keep from hearing her, "You got yourself a good and caring man there. Don't lose him. He's just like his daddy. There isn't a thing he wouldn't do for the woman he loves and I'm not just saying that because he's my son, either."

Diane smiled faintly at Livy and walked down the hall to her room as his father followed.

Olivia met Luke's gaze. They looked at each other quietly, not speaking a word verbally, but understanding one another. Olivia grasped the necklace Luke had given her the night before and knew what Luke's mother spoke was the truth. It's not like she needed to hear it from Diane. She knew a man like Luke was rare to find.

nine

present day

Cowboys was a bar downtown that had a laid back kind of atmosphere with a live band with a dance floor only on the weekends. Olivia knew that Tessa enjoyed music as much as she did and Olivia wanted to show Tessa how similar Savannah was to South Park. It was relaxing and inviting, which was exactly what she needed tonight.

Music blared through the speakers as they waited for the bartender to pour a shot of Southern Joe.

"Here ya go, ladies. Enjoy," the bartender drawled.

"Let's make a toast! To friendship, life and hot as hell bartenders!" Tessa yelled. They raised their shot glasses, tapped them together then brought them to their lips.

Tilting the glass, Olivia tossed the liquid to the back of her throat. She felt it burn as it slithered down, warming her belly and making her shudder at the same time. This stuff could put hair on her chest—not that it was something she wanted. It was just strong as hell, and just how she liked it.

Olivia looked at Tessa, who was taking sips.

"Jesus H. Christ, Tessa! It's not sweet tea!" Olivia bellowed. "Don't sip it. Shoot it!"

Tessa contemplated Olivia's order before she took the shot the right way. That was two shots down the hatch. She knew Tessa wasn't one for shots, but did them occasionally. She was more of a beer drinking kind of girl.

"Let's dance!" Tessa shouted over the music.

Once on the dance floor, the alcohol began to stream through her blood as they danced. Thirty minutes later and Olivia was hot and sweaty. She retreated back to the bar for another drink while Tessa was still going at it. As she made her way through the crowd, Olivia felt the hairs on the back of her neck stand. She stopped to look around and rubbed her clammy neck before she turned back and ordered a Savannah Tea. Olivia would take her sweet tea any way she could get it—and if it had whiskey in it, even better.

After downing the last of her drink, Olivia felt it hit her as she walked through a maze of people onto the dance floor. She let the music course through her body, feeling good and letting go while she danced with her arms above her head and her hips swaying to the beat. She felt each word and each beat as it droned through her body. For a brief moment, Olivia was sucked back to an instance similar to this with Luke. Olivia would let her body take control of the music when Luke sang. His voice, pure euphoric sin coated in sex and whiskey. What more could she ask for?

Olivia's hips swayed seductively as another song started up. Her head angled toward the ceiling, enjoying the ambiance and live band. It had been quite some time since she let her hair down.

Without warning, she felt a body pressed up against her back. Warm hands grasped her wide hips, pulling her to him. Going with the flow, she moved with him, feeling his large jean clad body behind hers. Olivia turned her head to look back, but when she moved her head to the left, the man brought his finger to her chin and slowly pushed her head to look straight ahead, mumbling *no* under his breath.

Olivia leaned back as another song echoed through the speakers. She felt his hands skim down her abdomen, adding a twinge of pressure to her belly, making it flex on its own. His rough fingers grazed across her heated skin where her shirt had risen. Her stomach clenched as she fought back the vibration that threatened to escape her from the feeling of his fingers against her skin. Olivia relaxed into him, feeling every inch of his solid chest as her back started to heat up, wishing she could see who the mysterious stranger was behind her.

As they began to slow down, his fingers moved into the waistband of her shorts. He didn't push them in far, just into the top of the waistband. He rubbed from side to side and she immediately felt her sex heat. He was slowly tantalizing her with his rough fingers that her breath caught in her throat. The man brought his face down to the curve of her neck, his hot breath prickling her skin like jagged teeth. She pushed her hips into his as he rubbed his cheek along hers. Goosebumps broke out over her skin.

Olivia's head lolled to the side, her brown wavy hair falling along the man's arm. The heat of the bodies on the dance floor and alcohol took hold, playing with her, tickling her senses and making her want sex, want him and want him now. Olivia wasn't one for one night stands, but she was ready to throw her inhibitions out the window for just one night... just to let go.

Feeling his scruffy facial hair graze her neck, his fingers danced along the lace band of her panties. The air swirled in a cloud of dark forbidden passion that spoke of hot, steaming sex. The bar was humid and the grinding they were doing wasn't helping her. She was hot and turning into an inferno while his hands and body manipulated hers.

As if he sensed her legs were about to give out, he lifted her closer to him, then twisted her hips around and brought her right back to where she apparently belonged—front to front and up against his dick.

Olivia came face to face with a rock hard chest covered in a navy blue shirt. His hands never left her waist as he shoved his leg between her bare ones and pushed against her wet sex, slowly beginning a dirty dance with her. She moaned in the back of her throat, her eyes closing on their own accord. He palmed her ass with one large hand while he placed his other hand at the back of her head, holding her closer to him. The man had skill. He had her boxed in with his arms and body. Olivia wasn't sure if he knew the power he held over her in that instant, but it was hot as hell.

Before she had a chance to see whose arms she was wrapped in, the scent of spicy sandalwood assaulted her senses. Olivia licked her lips and cracked her eyes open to get a peek at who she had such sexual chemistry with. She looked up to a square jaw covered in stubble. His lips, firm and full that deserved to be sucked on frequently. She locked onto a pair of brown eyes that looked vaguely familiar, flecks of gold swimming in them. They tempted her, lured her in. They were framed by the fullest set of black lashes she'd ever seen on a man. And then he lifted one side of his mouth into a curve and grinned at her, giving her one of the sexiest half-smiles she'd ever seen.

And that's when it hit her.

Shock. Ice cold shock and recognition raced through her body.

Olivia froze. Her mouth dropped open at the same time her arms fell away. She could not believe she was staring back at the eyes of her patient from this past week. He stood there, holding her tight, with a smug look on his handsome face. She placed her hands flat against Nathaniel's chest to push him away, but he didn't budge. He just held her tighter with his stupid smile that seemed to grow at her agitation.

"Move," Olivia ordered. She wasn't playing games. This was her patient for fuck's sake.

"Nope." He barely moved his lips.

Olivia huffed loudly, her nostrils flaring in frustration. She pushed hard and was finally able to move him back.

She quickly turned around to walk away, well tried at least. Nathaniel reached out and grabbed her wrist, spinning her back to him gracefully like a practiced dance move. Olivia fell into his chest with a thump.

"Stop, Mr. Alexander. This can't be happening between us. You're my patient," Olivia said between her teeth.

He pondered for a second then said in a deep voice, "First, it's Nate. I've told you this already. And second, technically I'm Dr. Thatcher's patient. I just saw you since he was out of town, right? And how lucky was I?" He finished, cocking his head to the side with a grin. She smelled the beer on his breath and could see the wicked gleam that stirred in his eyes.

"Doesn't matter. You were still in my office."

The band played a new song and Nate took it as an invitation. He slid his arm around her lower back and pulled her closer, picking up where they left off. Olivia tried to move but when she did, her body rubbed up against his and she groaned. He felt so good. Too good. It wasn't helping that Nate's muscled thigh was wedged between hers. Nate pushed harder into her, causing Olivia to give a throaty moan loud enough for him to notice this time.

"Stop," she whimpered breathlessly.

Nate dropped his head to the curve of her neck. "No. I don't think you want me to stop," he drawled lazily.

"You have to. You're my patient."

"Then I'll get another doctor."

Nate was relentless. He was using his calloused hands to rub along the sides of her waist. She was crossing the line here, she knew it, but goddammit he felt so good that she didn't want him to stop.

"No, Dr. Thatcher is the best."

But her body wasn't listening to her brain. She stood on her toes and reached up, wrapping her arms around his neck. Nate moved in and pressed open mouthed kisses up her neck and nibbled along her jaw, his tongue dancing along her neck. Olivia leaned her head to the side to grant Nathaniel more access when she should have pushed him away. There was something so alluring about him that she couldn't bring herself to do so. So when she moved her head, he moved toward her mouth.

Nate hovered for a moment, his breath hot and heavy against her. She looked up through heavy lids and peered into his eyes. Olivia had a feeling he was waiting for an answer, an invitation to proceed. Her lips parted, a breath escaping them as her tongue slid out to wet her lips. Nathaniel's eyes traveled to her mouth and she could feel his chest moving up and down as he breathed. His eyes darkened as he tried to make a choice. Olivia hadn't moved an inch from his grasp. She only held him tighter and that seemed to make the decision for him.

His tongue slipped out and skated across her lips, closing the space between them. Lightly at first to test the waters, then grazing and nipping back and forth to see how much she'd allow. Unable to conceal the tingling sensation traveling up her spine, she let out a husky sigh. This wasn't what she had expected from him. She expected rough, raw and dirty. Her body was simmering, hot with desire. Parting her lips, Nate's tongue to dip in, touching the roof of her mouth and enticing her further. Olivia tried to ignore the fire building, but couldn't. His moves were seductive and her body responded to them.

He deepened their kiss, crushing her to him. His strong arms held her closer while thick strokes of his tongue delved in and out at the same time his hips moved against hers. His short facial hairs scraping near her mouth only heightened the intensity of the kiss. She relaxed into him fully, losing herself to his skillful mouth. She hadn't been kissed like that in ages, and it felt good.

Nate and Olivia were panting for air once they broke apart, both of their lips swollen and eyes glossy.

Between the lines they just skipped across and the feeling of desire streaming inside of her, Olivia knew she was screwed, blued and tattooed.

ten

Tap, Tap, Tap

Olivia opened the door to the next exam room and her mouth nearly dropped.

"Why are you here? I made sure you were scheduled with Dr. Thatcher…" Olivia said, flipping the chart papers frantically to double check her notes.

"No hi or hello? Or how am I doing?" He questioned with a smirk that made her heart skip a beat. Nate raked his eyes over her, starting from her head and making his way down over her voluptuous hips. Her body awakened from his intense gaze and she cursed herself for feeling it.

Olivia needed to tread carefully. Very carefully.

"Fine," he retorted. "I was scheduled with him, but I called saying the medication wasn't working and needed to come back in. When the receptionist made the appointment, I asked if I could see you instead since we hit it off so well," he winked. "She said it was no problem at all. So here I am."

A cocky smile graced his face. This had to be a dream, and maybe not entirely a good one. Sighing, she pushed a strand of hair from her face.

"Well, that was a mistake, Mr. Alexan—"
"Nate."

Olivia stared pointedly at him and took a breath, trying to keep her irritation in check.

"Mr.—"

"I said, Nate," he reminded her in a deep, authoritative voice. He popped off the exam table and took a step toward her. The room suddenly felt very small as she backed up and hit the closed door.

"Nate, please sit down and we'll discuss why you're here," Olivia said as calmly, trying to hide the nervousness in her. She'd never been in a situation like this before. Just from the two times she had been in Nate's presence, he hadn't taken the word 'no' very well. Nate's presence was strong, and she had found herself bending and agreeing both times.

It's in the eyes, she thought. It had to be. Those sexy damn eyes were draped by his silky kohl lashes. They were a striking yellowish-brown color that reminded her of a lion, slowly calculating when to pounce and mark his claim.

"Nate, please sit back down and we'll discuss why you're here, and two weeks early at that," Olivia requested again, but this time it came out in a throaty whisper. She threw a hand up in the air in an effort to stop him. He had taken three steps and was standing directly in front of her now. She craned her neck to look up at him and her brows angled toward each other, pleading her request.

"No," he defied. "You know, I've been thinking of you since I last saw you. You took off that night before I had a chance to get your number."

"I had a friend in town visiting. We'd been out for hours and wanted to go home."

A fine mixture of insult and challenge clouded Nate's

eyes. "Feisty little thing aren't you," he drawled quietly. "I'd like to see you again. I want to take you out to dinner."

Huffing loudly, Olivia shook her head and blinked her eyes, shutting them longer than usual. How many times had she said no?

"That's not a good idea. I'm sorry but it's just not going to happen."

"Oh, I think it's a great idea, actually," he countered, leaning over her. There was something very appealing about Nate that she found hard to resist.

"See," he drew closer. "I think it's a perfect idea. We do drinks and dinner, or whatever you'd like. I'm pretty laid back. I just want to see you."

Olivia was rendered speechless. She couldn't find her voice with him standing so close to her. *Think. Think. Think.*

"Nate," she said softly, but he placed his index finger on her lips to quiet her.

"Shhh, just say yes."

Olivia shook her head. Her heart was racing a mile a minute and she could feel little beads of sweat forming on the back of her neck. Between the closeness of Nate, his cologne that was pouring off of him and his alluring eyes, Olivia was a wreck. Not to mention that someone could walk in at any given moment and see the predicament she was in.

Nate glided his finger back and forth over her bottom lip, never losing eye contact. His finger was warm to the touch. Inch by inch, he drew closer until she could smell his cinnamon breath. *Figures*, she thought. He's hot as sin and tastes like the devil. He angled his head slightly to the right and inhaled, breathing her in as his eyes drifted shut. Olivia released a heavy breath and a moment later he opened his eyes.

Shit. She knew what those eyes said.

Enunciating each word, he demanded, "What. Do. You. Say? Hmm?"

Panic started to set in, pushing out any thrill she felt earlier. In her haste to get him to back off, she agreed.

"Okay," she breathed against his finger that was still pressed on her lips.

A wicked grin slowly crept across Nate's face, and all she could think of was the proverbial cat eating the canary. Speckles of triumph danced in his eyes. Before Olivia could react, Nate leaned in quickly and snagged a kiss. He grabbed her nape, crushing her lips to his then pulled away.

"Are you fucking crazy?!"

"I'm sorry, but I had to," Nate spoke up before she could even blink.

Flustered, Olivia tried to regain her composure. "You need to leave now. I have patients that actually need me."

"I need you."

"No you don't. What could you possibly need from me?"

Nate deadpanned. "Liv."

"What?" she snapped.

"I need your number to call you for our date," he stated in an obvious tone.

Olivia bit her tongue and took out her prescription pad. Tearing a sheet in half, she wrote her phone number on the back and handed it to him.

A shit-eating grin tipped the sides of his mouth as if he'd just won the battle and war. "Thanks, Doc. Now don't try and ignore my calls, or else I'll have to come back here." He winked at her then stepped back.

Olivia sighed loudly. She threw the pad on the exam table and crossed her arms, frustrated that she let her guard down. Her eyes were sharp as knives as they locked with his and didn't move. She was fuming and he needed to see it.

Olivia hadn't wavered for a man like this in some time, and certainly never for a patient. It had been so long, no one affected her like this. Sweet Jesus, she barely knew the man but Olivia was physically attracted to Nate, there was no question about it. One dinner and that was it. She couldn't allow any more than that.

"So I take it nothing is new with your migraines and the medication is working just fine then?"

"Yup. Working great, like a charm. I'll be calling you later, darlin'." He smiled and left the room, saluting her with a two-finger goodbye.

eleven

Later that evening, a rainstorm had Olivia stuck in her car outside of her house. What started as a sun shower, ultimately turned into a torrential downpour to the point that she could barely see anything in front of her.

As Olivia looked out her car window, she watched as the reddish-brown dirt formed giant terracotta colored puddles around her walkway from what seemed to equate to cannon-ball sized raindrops.

Realizing the rain wasn't going to let up anytime soon, Olivia removed her heels. She slipped her purse over her shoulder and gathered her charts and take-out dinner. She could smell the aroma of barbecued ribs slathered in homemade sauce wafting from the carryout bag. It made her mouth water and stomach growl.

Opening up her car door, Olivia got out and slammed it shut with her hip. The rain soaked her immediately. Thunder boomed across the humid sky making her pump her legs faster. As she made it onto the large wraparound porch, Olivia heard the phone ringing from inside the house while she slid the key into the door to unlock it.

"Hang on, buddy, give me one second," Olivia said to her dog.

"Hang on, hang on, hang on, I'm coming don't hang up," she mumbled, dropping her stuff onto the kitchen table with a clunk while reaching for the phone.

"Hello," she answered breathlessly not bothering to check the caller ID.

"Hey, honey."

"Hi, Mom."

Olivia turned and leaned against the sink, watching heavy droplets of water slide down her dark hair and drip onto her chest.

"How's work been going for you? Finally settled in the office?"

"Actually, it's great. I want to talk more but can I call you back in a few? I just walked in."

"Sure thing, sweetie. Call when you can, but not too late because your father likes to go to bed early you know."

"Right... I'll get back to you soon. Bye, Mom." Olivia hung up before her mom could respond. She was chilled to the bone and needed to get the wet clothes off fast. Before she could reach her bedroom, the phone rang again.

"Did you forget to tell me something? I'm still soaking wet and my clothes are clinging to me Is everything okay?" She was breathless from sprinting back to the phone.

"Well, are you now. Tell me, why are you so wet?"

Olivia stopped walking, wondering who the mysterious caller with the deep voice was.

"I'm sorry, but who is this?"

"Who do you want me to be?"

Not in the mood for games, Olivia got right to the point.

"Listen, I think you have the wrong number. I'm hanging up—"

"Hang on, It's...Nate."

Oh.

"Oh... Hi... I didn't recognize your voice. How are you?" She was completely caught off guard and hadn't expected him to call so soon.

"Well, well, darlin'. You finally greeted me the right way. I'm doing just fine but I take it you're not?"

"I just ran into the house and its pouring outside."

"That it is... So what are you doing?"

Sighing inwardly, she said, "As you heard, my clothes are soaking wet and I need to get changed so I need to hang up."

"Can't do two things at once? Or are you trying to get rid of me? Just change with me on the phone. I'll wait."

Nate had to be the most exasperating man alive!

"You know, I hardly even know you and I find you to be very demanding, pushy and quite frustrating all at the same time. Anyone ever tell you that?" Olivia flicked the light on in her room, walked to her dresser and rummaged through her drawers.

"Yeah, and those are just my good traits." A deep rumble of laughter flowed through the line that made her warm up a little. She kind of liked the sound of his laugh.

"Oh, great... I can only imagine," Olivia said as a small, half-smile formed on her face. "I need to put the phone down. Hang on."

"Go on, princess. I can wait as long as you need me to. I've got time."

My God. Olivia rolled her eyes. The guy was seriously laying it on thick.

"Is this how you talk to all the women in your life?"

"Nope. Just the ones I want."

Olivia shook her head. This guy was unbelievable. Arrogant, cocky and stubborn, and yet there she was talking to him. She put the phone down and peeled the sopping wet clothes off. She then quickly pulled on some lounge pants and a shirt, tied up her frizzy, wet waves in a messy ballet bun and picked up the phone.

"Alright, I'm done," she said, breathing into the phone.

"If you have such a hard time taking your clothes off, you could've just asked for me to stop by and help. I work with my hands, you know."

Olivia couldn't stop the smile that involuntarily spread across her face. Nate was enjoying this conversation a little too much, but in an odd way, so was she.

"Will you just stop with all your smooth one liners already? You got me on the phone. What more do you want?"

She bristled with agitation and her stomach rumbled as hunger set in. She was starting to get moody and wanted to eat. It had been a long day at the office and she was ready to cut back and relax.

"Alright, alright. I wanted to call to set up our date, obviously. What? Didn't think I'd call so soon?"

"Honestly, no. Men don't usually call so soon. Or ever," she said as she opened the crinkled bag of steaming ribs. Thankfully they were still hot. She inhaled. *Delicious.*

"Really?" Nate said. He almost sounded surprised. "How could they not call you? You're beautiful."

Olivia paused. She hadn't been called beautiful in... Well, she couldn't remember. She knew she was pretty, but having lived in New York City around so many women who looked like they were fresh off the runway, it felt hard to compete. It wasn't in her nature for her hair to be perfectly styled, her makeup caked on, or eat an orange a day to be a size zero, or size six for that matter. She had an hour glass figure; wide, full hips and an ass. She was considered hefty by New York City standards. Skinny girls could go starve themselves on lettuce while she ate her ribs and sweet rolls for all she cared.

"Is that all you see when you look at me? My looks? I guess so since we've hardly had an actual conversation."

"No. I noticed your eyes the moment I met you," he

refuted in a serious tone. "They're full of passion, and not the passion that I'm sure you're thinking *I'm* thinking of, either," he said with a good natured laugh. "Passion, as in you care about your job, your patients. Like you truly love what you do. It's a rare thing. So many people work because of the money aspect, but it didn't feel like that with you. I also saw a hint of something else in your eyes... I'm not sure what, but I intend to find out. Your eyes have a lot to say. They make me want to know more about you."

The honesty in Nate's voice rendered her momentarily speechless. He managed to peel back a layer of the thick skin she grew while living in New York with just a matter of a few words.

"Hello?"

Clearing her throat, Olivia answered, "Yes?"

"Thought I lost you there for a minute."

"No...I just wasn't expecting that, is all," Olivia replied truthfully then took a bite of her bread. She kind of felt bad for giving him a hard time now. Maybe she needed to ease off him a little and not jump down his throat so fast.

"So you free on Friday night? I told you I'd like to get to know you better."

There was an underlying magnetism to Nate she would bet women hardly fought. He was uncharted waters for her, ones she wanted to take a dive into. Olivia couldn't figure him out, yet she was intrigued by Nate's relentless nature. Her head was having a tug of war contest with her body, contradicting each other every chance they could. She couldn't quite grasp it all.

"Yes, Friday is good with me. I'm warning you now, I like to eat. I'm no salad girl. That's for the birds."

"Well, don't you know the way to a man's heart?" Nate busted out the first real laugh she'd heard from him yet. It was a full-bodied laugh that went right through her, almost relaxing her tense muscles and her mood. She couldn't stop the smile that lit up her face. Dare she say she actually looked forward to the end of the week?

"Where are we going so I know how to dress?"

"Baby, you can wear whatever you want. But you better have on some high heels."

twelve

Each day quickly turned from dawn to dusk and before she could blink, her Friday night date with Nate was set to start in just an hour.

Olivia's stomach was doing flips as she turned off the shower and stepped out. She was wound tight as a coil, but actually looked forward to going out with Nate. It had been months since she'd been on a date and she couldn't remember a time she had been this anxious.

She did not know Nate very well, though she could tell he was the kind to always have his way. She was sure of that. None of the men in New York had such a demanding personality as Nate did.

Drying off, Olivia decided a glass of wine would help calm her nerves or she'd be a ball of stress the whole night. She padded across the plush carpet until she reached the kitchen where she grabbed the white wine from the fridge and poured herself a glass. Taking a sip while walking back down the hallway and into her bedroom, Olivia went straight into her closet and pulled out a black pair of heels. They were special ones she'd spent a small fortune on when she lived in

New York, and because of that she hardly wore them. She treasured them. Sexy high heels, but surprisingly comfortable.

Olivia pulled out a little black dress from her closet, one that she was dying to wear again. The dress clung to her body's every curve, making her feel extremely sexy. She placed her wine glass down on the dresser and moved on to fixing her hair. Olivia defused her waves to tame them and then applied her makeup; just some black liquid liner, light pink blush, and lots of mascara coating her lashes. Finally, she slipped on her dress and she was done.

Closing her eyes, Olivia grimaced. She couldn't believe she was doing this. It was going to be a one-time deal. In fact, she planned to tell Nathaniel she agreed with him; he needed to find a new doctor. That would be for the best.

She took the last sip of her wine and opened up her jewelry box. She pushed the accessories around looking for something simple, then stopped.

Lying underneath a pile of jewelry was the heart shaped necklace Luke had given her all those years ago. A slow ache crept through her bones just looking at the diamonds as she remembered when he'd given it to her, under the stars, that one summer night. Even though she and Luke hadn't parted ways on the best of terms, she couldn't stand to part with either the necklace or the Care Bear he had given her. It was a time in her life she never wanted to forget, not that she ever could. She loved the necklace and wore it long after she left Georgia, but eventually took it off when she finally accepted that Luke wanted nothing more to do with her. She hated that day and cried while doing so; hated removing a heart that was no longer hers to hold. She ached inside, even though she was forced to accept it. Removing it was like ripping out her own heart with her bare hands.

And now she was treating his mother. It was probably just a matter of time before she would come face to face with him again. That thought alone made her more nervous than anything.

Pushing away her trip down memory lane, Olivia pulled out a pair of long turquoise and silver earrings, found a matching silver necklace with an anchor charm and a few silver bangles. She liked the way the jewelry downplayed the outfit so she wasn't too dressed up.

The doorbell chimed and Olivia felt a set of weights drop into her gut. Tom's bark echoed loudly throughout the house as she made her way down the hall and to the door.

"Hang on!"

Olivia reached down and grabbed Tom's collar to hold him back as she opened the door.

"Hey," Olivia said softly as she wrestled with Tom. "Come on in."

She moved out of the way as Nate walked in while Tom jumped in her grip. Tom was a huge, harmless dog. But his wild wiggling over Nate caused Olivia to put her free hand over the top of the dress, hoping nothing would fall out.

"Back down, boy," she ordered. "Why are you going so crazy?"

"Hey buddy, what are you doing to your little lady here?" Nate squatted in an effort to calm her dog.

"There you go. You like that, buddy, don't you?" Nate said in a tone like he was speaking to a child. Olivia's dog wagged his tail rapidly while Nate scratched the top of his head.

"I'm sorry about that," Olivia said apologetically.

Nate's lips cracked into a lopsided grin. "It's fine. I love dogs and I'm used to it."

Olivia stood up and Nate followed. "You have dogs?"

"I have two little beasts," he said laughing.

She smiled and waved her hand to follow. "Well good, you can tell me about them," she said as she made her way into the living room. "Just give me a sec to grab my purse and shoes and we'll be out..." Olivia trailed off. She looked over her shoulder when she realized Nate hadn't moved an inch to follow her. She frowned, wondering why the sudden change.

"Are you okay?" she asked tentatively.

Nate's heated eyes raked over her length. They traveled down her body slowly. She felt self-conscious and worried she picked the wrong outfit. *If he would've just told her...*

Sweeping away a lock of hair that had caught on her lip, Olivia pressed a hand to her unsettled stomach. Her mouth ran dry as he sauntered over to her, his steady gaze never leaving hers as he stopped directly before her. She swallowed hard and looked up at him, her heart kicking up a notch.

"Everything's fine, just fine, darlin'," he answered in a deep, guttural tone. He brought his hand to her face, his thumb caressing her cheek.

Olivia could feel her cheeks burn and her heart rate spiking. Why was it that the lightest touches from this man could draw such a response from her? Make her heart speed up and feel so anxious?

"Uh uh. What did I tell you about that?" he said, lazily shaking his head. Moving his thumb to her mouth, he pulled out her crushed lip from between her teeth. She didn't even realize she'd bitten down on it. As the roughness of his thumb moved over her wet lips, she found it strangely tempting.

Nate's chin moved down to look deep into her eyes. "I didn't get a chance to greet you properly," he said in a jagged voice, dropping his hand to his side.

"Hi, Olivia," his eyes traveled her face, "You look absolutely gorgeous in that dress."

He stepped in and wrapped his arm around her back to embrace her lightly. With his other hand, he swept the hair away from her face then leaned down and gently kissed her cheek, lingering a little longer. Her pulse was sky rocketing as she found Nate's overpowering presence very exciting.

"Hey...Nate," she whispered. "You look handsome yourself," she got out.

Nate chuckled. "So you're saying you find me attractive? That I look good?" And just like that, the intimate nature of the moment was broken and she chuckled.

Olivia just shook her head as she pulled back and went to grab her stuff from her room. Picking up her clutch and shoes, she turned the lights off and made her way to the living room. She found Nate staring into her unfinished backyard.

"Ah, you're looking at my messy yard. I'm going to have it worked on eventually. It needs some serious TLC."

Bending over, Olivia slipped on her high heels as she held on to the arm of her sofa for balance. She looked at Nate and found him starring at her shoes. Step by step, Olivia walked as seductively as she could to where Nate was standing.

"Approve?"

"Very much so." His voice sounded strangled. "Let's go," he said turning toward the door.

"You don't want to hear about my yard?" she asked innocently.

"Not tonight. Maybe another night. Let's head out. Now."

thirteen

"So, can you tell me where we're headed now?"

"It's a place outside Savannah. Low key."

Olivia wondered if he picked this place because of the whole doctor/patient issue. Truthfully, she didn't want to think about the little predicament she was in and was going to try and ignore it for the rest of the night.

Once they were on the street they drove for about twenty miles. There was a feeling that touched her skin she couldn't quite place. It wasn't strange or awkward like most first dates were, but then again most first dates weren't like this where they'd already had a close encounter…or two.

As they drove, they made small talk for the majority of the time and Olivia was finally able to get a good look at Nate. His dark distressed jeans molded to his legs. The black button down collared dress shirt was rolled to his elbows, a silver watch at his wrist and his hair styled away from his face. Nate was damn good looking.

As they pulled up to a large, dimly lit brick building on the outskirts of Savannah, "Have you been here before?"

"No."

"Well, this is where we're having dinner tonight. And that

right there," he said pointing to the place to the right, "is called Rum Bar. It's a bar that overlooks the Savannah River. It's a real chill, laid back kind of style. It's covered in beach sand and lounge chairs with music that plays all night. It's like being on the beach. They serve these rum buckets that are filled with all different kinds of rum that everyone seems to love. A little too fruity for my taste, though," he chuckled.

Nate pressed a palm to the small of her back. His touch was warm but commanding, sending sparks from his fingertips throughout her body.

They were led to a semi-dark booth that was boxed in with double doors made of wood. She had never seen anything like it before. Between the ambiance and the privacy of the booths, it was an interesting, but perfect place for them. When the waiter came to get their drink orders, Nate nodded in her direction.

"I'll have a 7&7, please," she requested.

"A Corona for me, thanks."

Nate looked at her with a sinful smirk tipping the sides of his lips. "A whiskey girl. I like."

Whiskey girl...

Don't go there. Don't go there...

Blinking away the melancholy she momentarily felt, Olivia spoke up, "Ah, yeah. Normally I like it straight but thought against it tonight."

"You're not going to scare me off, Olivia, if that's what you're worried about. I told you I want to get to know you," he replied, looking into her eyes to make his point.

"Why?"

"Why what?"

"Why do you want to get to know me so badly? You keep saying that. I'm sorry... I'm not trying to come off as a bitch. I'm just curious why you're pushing so hard."

Clearing his throat, his voice rocked through her. "When I see something I want, I go after it. And before you get all pissed off, relax. I know you're not a possession to be kept. I just...wanted to get to know more about you. Not to sound cheesy, but I feel like there's chemistry between us, something worth pursuing. I'm not going to lie to you, I think you're beautiful, so there's that. Can't explain it. Haven't you ever had a pull toward someone that you can't explain?"

Olivia's guilty conscience weighed on her for not being completely truthful with Nate. Her stomach tightened and chest started to ache with the need to tell him it couldn't go past this date. He appeared to sincerely mean what he said about getting to know her.

Maybe in another life time, she thought as she sighed inwardly.

When the waiter brought out their drinks, Nate suggested a toast was in order. She raised her glass and said, "To persistent men and tonight."

A full, heart stopping grin stretched across Nate's handsome face, his white, slightly crooked teeth showing. Her stomach folded over like waves crashing down. If she wasn't careful she could get easily sucked in by his charm.

She brought the glass to her lips and sipped. The dry, carbonated liquid combined with the whiskey moved onto her tongue, burning as it traveled down her throat. Mmmm, she loved this drink. It soothed her stomach and settled her nerves. Nate made her jittery, but a strong drink was just what she needed to relax.

The more familiar Olivia became with Nate over dinner, the more she found herself warming up to him. The conversation was easy and smooth and quite enjoyable. She learned Nate's parents had been divorced since he was a kid. His mother had never remarried, but his father had. Despite the separation early on in his family, Nate never dwelled on it and she liked that about him. She despised when people used past experiences as a justification for the course of their life. Each person has a decision, a path they choose to take. No one can choose it for them.

It turned out his father was the owner of the construction company where he worked. Nate's father planned for him to run the company one day and Nate was actually looking forward to it. It reminded her of what he noticed in the office the other day, about how she had passion in her eyes when it came to her career. She did. It was her life.

Nate-1, Olivia-0, she thought.

An innocent smile curved Olivia's lips as she realized she was keeping score, something she never did before.

"What's so funny?"

Olivia shook her head. "It's nothing."

"Liar. Your face lit up. You're thinking of something. I want to know what made you smile so I can do it again. Your face glows when you smile."

Olivia's smile faltered for a moment. Should she give him another point for his honesty? Or was he just laying it on thick? He was difficult to read and made it harder for her to keep her wall up when he made comments that appeared genuine. Olivia felt herself wavering.

Don't let it happen...

Olivia licked her lips and thought about how to answer his question.

"When you were talking about your job and how you're looking forward to taking over the business one day, I saw the enthusiasm and passion that you said you saw in me. You love what you do. It's hard, physical labor that I'm sure wears your body out more than other days. Some days probably even back breaking work, but you love it. It's obvious."

"That's what made you smile?" He didn't seem to believe her.

"Well, it was the afterthought that made me smile as well.

I like that you love your work... So I said to myself 'Nate-1, Livy-0'."

She took a sip of her drink and waited for his response.

Nate crossed his arms and leaned back. "Ahhh, so this is a competition to you, *Livy*? And I'm winning so far? How does that make you feel," he posed. A grin formed on his face. He was definitely enjoying this.

Olivia puckered her lips and thought for a moment. She didn't want to admit she liked it, that would only lead him on and make his ego grow even bigger.

"Not a competition per se...but just watching how fast you move, Mr. Alexander. How easy it is for you to 'woo me'. I have to be careful. I'm sure you've broken hearts in the past."

A shadow cast over Nate's eyes for a split second, the golden yellow specks abruptly disappearing and leaving a dull, sullen brown. Curiosity weighed on her shoulders. She wanted to know what caused that reaction, but decided against asking since she wasn't planning on staying around. Guilt ate at Olivia again. She was withholding, not being completely honest. And the last time that happened, things didn't turn out so well.

Olivia needed to brush off the sympathy she was unexpectedly dealing with. She couldn't afford to allow herself to fall again.

"So, tell me...Why did you pick this place?"

Nate slanted his head to the side and answered her question. "I knew you were worried about the whole doctor/patient thing so I picked a place where no one would know us. I wanted you to be comfortable with me so you'd want to go out again. Call it selfish, but it's the truth."

She took a sip of her drink and nodded. "I'm comfortable right now and enjoying the night more than I expected. Way more," Olivia answered honestly.

"Didn't think you'd have a good time with me?" Nate

jokingly clutched his chest as if to say he was hurt over her comment.

"It's just been awhile is all. I can't help but be on the fence about how this night came to be. This is very out of character for me."

"Nate-2, Livy-0?" he questioned.

"Slow it down, Casanova, don't get too cocky."

Lifting a brow he said, "Hey, can't blame a man for tryin'."

"Guess not."

"Want to get out of here?" he asked.

Outside, Olivia noticed Rum Bar was livelier than when they arrived and didn't seem to be dying down anytime soon. Nate must have noticed her stare because he asked, "You want to go there sometime?"

"I do," she answered, then realized she answered too quickly.

"Then we'll go."

Shit.

"Nate," she groaned with a sigh. "There can't be anymore dates between us. I'm sorry, but this is the one and only date. I had a great time tonight, but this is it."

"How about you let me decide that," he said in all seriousness.

"No. We can't. As much as I enjoyed myself tonight, this is it. No more. Don't you see the lines we're crossing?"

Olivia's forehead wrinkled with concern. How was it that he didn't have a drop of worry? Was he only thinking about himself?

"I do see that," he said moving in closely, "but I don't give a fuck about any imaginary lines, Olivia. I want you, and I'm pretty sure you want me too. So what's the problem here? And don't give me that patient/doctor shit. I told you I would switch doctors. What's *your* problem? You can't deny the chemistry between us. It's there. It's pulling at us both and you know it. I can read your eyes and see it. It's been there since the day we met. Don't deny it."

Olivia glanced around the parking lot. Deep down she wasn't sure if she was ready to put herself on the line again, but by the deep undertone he used, she knew Nate was fuming.

"I don't have a problem with us. What I do have a problem with is you finding a new doctor. Dr. Thatcher is the best."

"I understand," he answered staring down at her, "but you diagnosed my problem and it seems like an easy one to fix at that. So I could switch doctors with no issue. Nate-3-, Livy, still 0. Go ahead. Give me another reason, Liv, and that will put me at 4 points and you 0, because you know I'll win that one too." He formed his fingers into a '0' as he said it with a know-it-all-defensive-fucking-try-me attitude.

Shit. She was all out of reasons, not that she had many to begin with. She *was* holding back. Her one gripe was the fact that she was his doctor and he just blew that argument out of the water.

Olivia didn't want to get hurt and feared she would. It was a gut feeling she didn't want to ignore. She was afraid to be around Nate. He managed to knock down some of her walls, expose her layers so early on and she wasn't used to it. No one other than Luke had done that to her. She knew she'd fall hard for him, but not until she was ready to on her terms. When the time came she would let go and love again.

"Stop," he ordered.

"Stop what?"

"Stop thinking so hard," he demanded with a drawl. "I can see it spinning in your pretty brown eyes." He was just an inch away from her now and breathing down on her.

"I see what you're doing, finding ways to say no," he whispered. "You're so easy to read, Liv. I know you already in this little amount of time. I paid attention to you, your body. Your incredibly sexy body that I want so, so fucking bad..." Nate trailed off, growling under his breath as he slid an arm around her lower back and pulled her up against him.

"Stop looking for an out," Nate insisted.

"Nathaniel," she whispered. "I can't."

"Says who? You? You're the one fighting me on it right now, Liv. Don't tell me you don't feel it between us. Just let go and give us a damn try."

She did feel it. That's what scared her the most.

"Okay," she said breathlessly.

"Okay?"

"Okay, I'll back down; stop looking for an out, as you say."

A slow, but incredibly sexy grin stretched across his face. Nate's eyes lit up like he'd just won the Heisman Trophy.

What the hell had she agreed to?

"Thank. Fuck," he said and then leaned down for a kiss.

Olivia gripped Nate's shoulders. He pressed his hips into hers, surging against her hard as his other hand held the side of her neck. A small groan vibrated on her lips as Nate pushed her beside his truck and kissed her with purpose.

Olivia's body trembled at the touch of Nate's mouth. She'd never been kissed like this back in New York. She'd almost forgotten what it felt like. Nate sparked something inside of her that had long been buried.

Nate's tongue slid along her lips, as if asking for permission to enter. She obliged and opened willingly, allowing him to take control. This wasn't the first time he had taken over. The control thing with Nate was something she wasn't normally used to, but her body responded like a firecracker from the raw sexual urges in the kiss. Desire streamed through her at warped speed and she needed to take control of herself before things went too far.

Breaking for air, Nate rested his forehead against hers.

"Had I known that you were going to cave so soon, I

would've pushed harder earlier just so I could get that kiss from you."

"You knew I was fighting?" she said breathlessly. Her lips tingled.

Nate laughed, his hand sliding up and down her back. "You bet I did. It was written all over your face. I knew you were going to be stubborn about us the moment I met you, but I told you I wasn't giving up."

Olivia didn't know what she was getting herself into, but this time she was doing what she wanted, what her heart was telling her to do, not her head. Maybe meeting Nathaniel at this stage in her life was right. Maybe it was how her life was supposed to go.

Olivia wasn't sure of anything other than this moment. She knew what she wanted, and that was to take a chance with Nate.

fourteen

past

"Another round, comin' up!"

Finishing off the shots, Olivia and Tessa slammed their glasses down simultaneously on the shellacked wooden counter top. Bringing the back of her hand to her mouth, she swallowed the Fireball Whiskey that tasted like Big Red gum. Her eyes closed shut as they watered for a second. She was definitely a whiskey kind of girl, but taking it straight always drew this reaction from the cinnamon flavored burn.

The bar was packed and rowdy. The easygoing style set the mood. Tessa's plans of having everyone hang out at the live bar panned out, except the part where Luke was expected to sing. Tessa had made it Olivia's job to convince Luke of that, but she still hadn't brought it up to him. He probably wouldn't mind. When he was on stage, he'd pull his baseball hat down low, close his eyes and lose himself to his music and lyrics, as if it was just him and his guitar alone. His mouth and fingers danced at their own tempo, syncing together in sweet harmony, the same way they would graze her skin.

Luke had one of the sexiest voices she'd ever heard. It was

a sexy southern drawl like sweet molasses; dark and thick. Top it off with him fingering the guitar strings and she was done for. People walking by would stop to look and see where the voice was coming from. She liked the attention he received, except when the girls would flock to him. That didn't exactly bode well with her, but then again would any girlfriend like that? Most likely not. That husky voice and full bodied male was hers. All hers.

Olivia had been trying to get Luke to sing more often over the years. In fact, everyone did. He penned his own lyrics that were full of emotion that flowed from his heart. Not that Luke would ever admit it, but she *knew* him. Plus, he had that good ol' southern charm. Really, he was the perfect package.

A large hand slapped the counter, bringing her back to the present. She looked over and saw Luke grinning down next to her.

"Hey, whiskey girl," he said huskily in her ear.

Bringing his other arm around, Luke caged her in. He leaned down and rubbed his nose tenderly against her neck, pushing the hair to the side, causing her to shudder. Olivia leaned against his chest and he nearly growled as her scent drifted up to him. *Damn.* She smelled delicious tonight. Just like coconuts again. It had to be some new stuff she was using lately. He had to admit, he loved the smell on her. It was incredibly sexy and fucking hot as hell. He'd love nothing more than to take her out to his truck and have her climb on top of him. He'd wrap his lips around her taut nipple, tugging on it as he flicked it with his tongue while he manipulated the other as she rode his cock. It was hot, dirty and she loved it as much as he did.

Olivia held onto the chair as Luke spun the barstool around. Her wavy hair lifted in the air as the chair rotated toward him, gently trailing across his chest. The sweet coconut scent drifted up into his nose. He took a deep breath and inhaled the invigorating aroma again. Luke's eyes dilated and rolled shut. Between the scent and the images playing in his head like a movie, he had to force himself not to throw her over his shoulder and head out to his truck.

Livy stopped spinning the chair and widened her legs, allowing him to get closer. He was close enough that he could smell the whiskey on her breath now. She smelled like she had been sunning at the beach with a drink all day.

"You always smell like coconuts to me, Livy..." he groaned.

"Coconuts?" Olivia giggled. Naturally his thoughts wandered to a skimpy bikini she'd probably be wearing with ties on the side. Every time she wore it he had the sudden urge to untie the sides with his teeth. His mouth began to water and all Luke wanted to do in that moment was devour her.

Luke decided that whatever she was wearing he was going to buy stock in that shit and make her soak in it. His dick was rapidly growing hard at the thoughts running through his head.

Peering up through her heavy lashes, Olivia gave Luke a closed lip grin that spread across her face. Her tongue swept out to slowly lick along her lips. He watched a blush bloomed across her cheeks as Luke's eyes trailed down to her tongue. Livy knew damn well she was teasing him.

"Luke," she breathed, trying to whisper his name behind a not so innocent smile. Why did his name have to sound so damn sexy coming from her mouth? She rose up to sit taller, tilting her head and giving him a doe-eyed look. Olivia squeezed him with her knees—little minx that she was. He tried to conceal the guttural sound in his chest as he pushed his hips into her.

With his right hand, Luke cupped the side of her thigh. He slid his hand higher and inched down her silky smooth leg, stopping just above the hem of her jean shorts. Thank goodness she was wearing tight shorts that hugged her thighs and ass, and not those flared out cutoffs he loved. Otherwise she'd be showing everything at this angle and he couldn't have that. Livy was *his* girl.

"Baby." Luke growled with a lopsided devilish grin. *Two can play at this game.*

Livy bit down hard on the inside of her lip. She reached out, taking hold of Luke's wrist.

Breathlessly she whispered, "Stop."

"Awe, baby girl. You think you're so slick, don't you?" he said close to her face in a hushed, lazy tone.

Olivia giggled.

"Teasing me in a bar with people around and thinking that I would just sit back and take it? Well it's not going to work."

Luke gripped her thigh tighter, rubbing his thumb in circles, making her squirm.

"You think I won't take you out to my truck and have you flat on your back in seconds? Hmmm? Or how about I make you get right up on me and ride my cock as I take you reverse cowgirl style? I bet you wouldn't be saying 'stop' then, now would you?"

Olivia's breath hitched in her throat. Aroused by Luke's dirty mouth, Olivia was seriously contemplating taking Luke up on his offer.

"I think I would be the one taking you…"

His eyes darkened. "You'd like that, wouldn't you, baby?" He playfully breathed into her. "It's alright. You don't have to admit it, but I can see your nipples harden through your shirt." Luke chuckled as Olivia's cheeks deepened in color.

Pressing her hand to the solid wall of his chest in an effort to push him back, Olivia could feel the heat pulsating off him. "Settle down, big boy," she said and then puckered her lips together.

Luke dove in for a quick kiss, wrapping his lips around her mouth and pulling. Before she could respond, the kiss was already over. The tips of Luke's mouth curved upward like the devil himself was planning something.

She slapped his chest and tried to push him away. "You're mean."

Luke didn't budge. His eyes focused as he bent down near the back of her nape to the place he needed to taste her. He could smell the whiskey coming off her as she released a breath of hot air. Livy automatically gave him access, tilting her head to the side. He flattened his tongue against her flesh, pressed his lips down and suckled.

Olivia grabbed the back of his arm, squeezing as hard as she could. Her skin was on fire as he teased and taunted her with his mouth, her panties wet. If Luke wanted to carry out his plan in his truck, no way in hell would Olivia object to it.

"Don't tease me if you can't handle it, whiskey girl," Luke breathed hotly behind her ear. His sinfully hot voice was a low and husky drawl. Damn man was sex on a stick!

"Hey, get a damn room you two!" Ash, one of their friends, yelled.

Luke's head snapped up and this time Olivia was able to playfully push him away. Not that she really wanted to. All of their friends were looking at them and it made Olivia's ears get hot when she realized she and Luke had created a scene. She was so caught up in the moment with Luke that she wasn't even aware of everyone around.

"So you gonna sing or what, Luke?"

Luke's brows furrowed at Tessa's question.

"Sing?"

Looking at Olivia, Tessa's mouth dropped open in astonishment. "You didn't ask him?"

"Ahh, sorry. I didn't get a chance to," Olivia said, lifting her shoulders in an apology.

Tessa cried out, propping her hand on her hip. "Ugh, Liv!"

"Luke," Olivia said in a sugary sweet voice, "will you get

up and sing for us tonight? Please?" Olivia asked batting her lashes.

All the guys groaned in unison at her request; it was the last thing they wanted.

"How are we ever going to get some ass if you're always stealing our thunder?" Chase said.

"For real, bro. I ain't ever gonna get laid with you always serenadin' the ladies. Cock blocking and shit. You got a girl for fuck's sake," Ash complained.

"And you never will have a lady with that kind of mouth," Tessa swiftly said. "Who's gonna want that," Tessa said, waving her hand up and down the length of Ash's body, "when we can have this?" She turned and finished in the same gesture she used to refer to Ash, but this time Luke. Ash's face didn't move a muscle while Tessa stood there, proud of her little dig at him.

Olivia hugged Luke's side and smiled up at him. "Please? For me?"

Luke looked down. "If you want it, you gotta beg me to sing," he finished with a wolfish grin.

Olivia pulled his head to hers. Leaning so her mouth was aligned with his ear, she said slowly, "I'm not going to beg now, but how about I beg for something else later? Or maybe we can play out that scene in your truck tonight?"

Luke's eyes grew dark with intent, his lids closing halfway. Clenching his teeth, he gritted through them, "Little hell cat. I'm getting you for this," and smacked her ass.

Olivia jumped at the slap and smiled. Luke released her, and Tessa cheered loudly knowing they would get what they came for.

"Let's get one more round of shots first," Ash said. "I'm definitely gonna need another drink now. I ain't gettin' cock blocked again."

"You kiss your mama with that mouth? Seriously Ash-*hole*," Tessa yelled toward Ash. "Do you really think you're ever going to find a woman, a respectable woman at that, spewing that kind of garbage?"

Ash threw back his shot, his Adam's apple bobbing as he swallowed. Ash and Tessa had gone toe to toe since high school, constantly pushing each other's buttons.

"It's *Ash*, sugar tits. And I ain't looking to take anyone home to mama tonight. I had you once though, didn't I? I bet I could have you again if I wanted."

Olivia's mouth dropped open, nearly hitting the floor. What…? When…? Ash and Tessa? How…?

As Ash leaned on the bar nursing his beer, a cocky gleam resonated in his eyes. He was clearly taking pleasure in the bickering with Tessa. Ash was waiting for Tessa to act so he could verbally pounce on her again. It was evident.

"Should I tell them how much you liked it? How you called out my name and begged for more?" His head bobbled side to side with the widest, sneakiest grin she had ever seen.

"Ha! You wish Ash-*hole*! I did no such thing," Tessa bellowed loudly, jamming her index finger into his chest. Ash grabbed her finger and held it.

"It's Ashmore to my mama and Ash to my friends. Get it right, sugar," he replied in a deep drawl, not even hearing the 'r' at the end of sugar. Ash had one of the strongest southern accents she'd ever heard. Olivia had to admit, it was pretty damn sexy.

"Whatever." Tessa yanked her finger away and wiped it on her shorts as if his touch was disgusting.

Ash pierced Tessa with his eyes and laughed. "What? You don't like my touch all of a sudden? Since when? Cause that's not how you were acting last week on the back of my bike."

Daggers were getting ready to fly from Tessa's eyes as her nostrils flared. He was making public their apparent secret relationship. Tessa's reaction just confirmed Olivia's suspicion and before it went any further, Olivia jumped in and changed the scene.

"Hey, where's that round of drinks? I could always use another shot of whiskey." Olivia moved to Tessa and nudged her covertly from behind. She hoped that no one saw her movement and prayed that Tessa got the hint to tone it down a notch.

The round of shots came and they all threw them back. Letting the liquor coat the back of his throat, Luke smacked Livy with a kiss again and then sauntered toward the stage and gave them the performance they wanted.

fifteen

Giggling with a playful smile, Olivia pushed against Luke's bare chest to move him off of her. He didn't budge one bit, not that she expected him to. Luke just laughed at her effort. There wasn't a chance in hell that she would be able to lift his big frame anyway. The guy was solid as a rock. And truth be told, she was quite content with him lying across her body.

Luke was propped up on both his elbows looking down at Olivia's face on her bed. She had her hands drifting softly back and forth on his shoulders while she lay naked beneath the sheet. The sheet was only a thin barrier that did nothing to hide her responsive body. He was singing one of his impromptu songs again. Luke had always sung them to Olivia for as long as she could remember. Even though they were cheesy at times, some of them really struck a chord with her.

"let's make a memory we'll never forget…me and you baby on a bench… taking my hand and saying yes…"

But the song he sang was different this time and the lyrics felt oddly real. There was a look in Luke's eyes that said so much more, as if he truly meant each word. Like he was giving her an opening into his heart and asking her to read between the lines to know what he felt. Was there a difference in the way she received them this time? She was coming to realize that Luke spoke through his music more so than in words.

Luke stared down at Olivia's sleepy, lovable face. She was pinned beneath him with her brown hair splayed out on the white down pillow. Her espresso colored eyes beckoned him with each glance. He wanted to fall into those eyes each time she looked at him.

Olivia ran her fingers gently through Luke's hair. It brought a sense of peace over her, something she loved to do and did often. Luke didn't seem to mind when she did it. Her eyes were locked on his mouth as he continued singing, watching his lips as his heavy drawl came out more and more.

"...I bet she don't know the feeling that she gives me... I bet she don't know how much I want to love her forever... nothing but sweet and easy love for as long as she'll let me. And maybe we can even get a dog down the line..."

Jokingly, she slapped his shoulder and turned her head into the pillow.

"Luke! Stop. You're makin' me blush with your silly song."

But he continued on. Olivia could feel the vibrations from Luke's chest with each word. It was a deep rumble against her own chest that caused her body to slowly awaken, igniting once more. Watching Luke's lips move and then take breaths between words to lick his lips did something else to her. She wanted to reach up and lick his lips for him. It was damn hot and knowing it was just for her was enough to send her body into overdrive. Squeezing Olivia tighter between his arms, Luke continued...

"...I just wanna love her body with my mouth...lay her out and feel her beneath me...caress her skin with a whispering touch...when a moment like this is all it takes to know she's mine..."

Olivia couldn't control the groan that escaped her lips. "Luke..."

"Ah, baby," he said thickly, nuzzling the side of her cheek, "I'm just singing random words. Relax."

Relax? As if that was possible in Luke's arms.

After they left the bar the night before, Luke made damn sure he and Livy acted out that scene in his truck. They worked out that whole scene he taunted her with. He knew she wasn't expecting it, but it ended up being one of the hottest things they'd ever done. As Olivia rode him, bringing them higher and higher together, Luke had her wrists clutched behind her in a tight hold, immobilizing her. He watched as her hips glided up and down painfully slow over his hard cock. And when she had his entire length firmly rooted inside of her and close to reaching that high she desired, Luke grabbed a hold of her hair and pulled her head back as his hands pushed on her back, not allowing her to lean back. Olivia's back arched and she moaned so loud it took everything inside of Luke not to bust in that moment. With the truck parked in the middle of nowhere and the windows rolled down, the breeze cooled their damp skin as they came together, Livy more than once.

"Are those goosebumps? Is my baby cold? Here," he said lifting himself and the sheet from her body, "get under the comforter with me."

He slid his body right between her legs while covering them with the comforter. Leaning down, he breathed heavily against her jaw and then over the hollow of her neck where her necklace laid. His jaw raked against her as he continued a low humming in her ear. He worked his fingers through her scalp, kneading them as her body warmed from his touch. He began a slow rock against her sex knowing his touch would set her on fire.

"Let me fall...into...you," he breathed against her lips.

His hoarse voice had her thighs quivering and her body wanting more. Olivia's hips rolled up as he positioned himself at her entrance, nudging her opening but not pushing in. Instead, he teasingly ran the head of his cock up and down her wet slit, licking along her neck until he couldn't take it anymore and had to have her.

Reaching into the bedside drawer, Luke quickly grabbed a condom and covered himself. *"Let me fall...into...you..."* he repeated before sliding into her warm receptive body at a dangerously slow pace, taking her mouth at the same time.

Groaning in unison from the connection between them, Luke started a steady rhythm. He withdrew slowly and then surged back in, hitting as deep as he could go, causing Olivia to throw her head back. She pressed her breasts against Luke's chest, her nipples rubbing his bare skin as she squeezed her inner legs. Olivia knew he was struggling to keep it in check just as much as she was. The feeling of him penetrating her slowly then quickly built up a sizzling sensation from the tips of her toes to the top of her head.

Once he was settled in as deep as he could reach, Luke held there for a second or two then pulled out and then rushed back in. Their eyes locked and her body felt like it was ready to burst into flames. All the while, Luke continued to sing. She didn't know if he was making it up or singing a song he already knew. It didn't matter at that point, she could hardly think straight when her body felt like an inferno. On the verge of climaxing, but needing to finish with Luke at the same time, Olivia could hardly take it anymore and took control. She reached up and kissed Luke deeply, plunging her tongue into his mouth as she met his strokes with her hips. She sucked on his tongue and clenched her sex at the same time, moaning as they came undone together in a blissfully high climax.

Luke held still inside of Olivia while he caught his breath. His cock twitched from the orgasm he just had while he floated high as the clouds. Man, it just got better and better for them. It was an unexpected moment that happened to play out quite well. He hadn't planned to have another go around, but he wasn't complaining.

Looking down at Livy, her face was beautiful in the afterglow. Her chest rose slowly as she took deep breaths. Dark, thick eyelashes lay closed together forming half circles and her cheeks were flushed with the slightest blush of pink. Her lush lips were parted and swollen from kissing. For Luke, Olivia was the most beautiful woman he'd ever laid eyes on. He loved her so much at times it hurt just looking at her.

Leaning down, he whispered against her mouth, *"my girl,"* kissed her softly before withdrawing. He rolled to the side and headed toward the bathroom.

Olivia was unable to move. She was completely and thoroughly depleted of any energy after their second tumble in the sheets. She decided the most she was capable of doing was turning her head to watch as Luke's muscled legs took him into the bathroom. His backside was a work of art, sculpted to just the right balance of muscle and definition. A faint tan line sat low along his waist from the days they spent by the lake, and in her eyes, he was perfect.

Olivia heard the shower turn on while she lay there. She pushed the hair from around her face and then toyed with her necklace, tracing the heart shape with her finger. She thought back to last night when she missed a phone call at the bar right before Luke had snuck up and teased her. There were so many reasons why she could not have answered it.

A muffled ringtone distracted Olivia from her thoughts. She leaned over the bed and grabbed her purse, pulling her phone from it. Her long hair fell around her shoulders as she brought the comforter up to cover her body as she looked at the number on the screen.

Shit.

Shit.

Shit.

Her heart beat rapidly against her ribs. She couldn't ignore the call this time and knew she had to pick it up. Panic started to set in knowing Luke was in the shower and could be out any minute. She hadn't planned to be around Luke when she took the call, but now she had no choice.

Olivia chewed the inside of her lip and silenced the ringer. She needed to get her emotions under control before she picked up.

Taking a deep breath, she answered.

"Hello?"

"Hi, Olivia King?"

Olivia rolled over to the other side of her bed, her back to the bathroom. She needed to make this call as quick as she could and keep her voice down.

"This is Olivia King."

"Hello, Olivia. My name is Mark and I'm the assistant to Dean Richard here at Columbia University. I hope I'm not bothering you and that you have a few minutes to speak. I tried to call last night but got your recording."

A few minutes…

She perked up. "Yes, I'm available right now. I didn't see your call and heard the message earlier this morning. I apologize about that," Olivia lied.

Clearing his throat, he said, "No worries. I wanted to congratulate you on being accepted to Columbia University. Every year we review thousands of applicants and only a fraction are accepted. That being said, we grant scholarships to students for a number of reasons. Your MCAT scores along with your undergraduate transcripts were quite impressive and we would like to extend an offer to you. What really moved us was a call from one of your professors from Georgia Southern, who happens to be a colleague of the dean. He spoke very highly of you and insisted he be included as one of your recommendations. He emailed a letter to the dean to have it on record."

Olivia's mouth hung wide open while she stared at the wall, incapable of forming a sentence or even thinking straight. She was speechless. She couldn't afford to pass up an offer like this. It was the chance of a lifetime and she'd be stupid not to take it. It's what she wanted…right?

Perplexed, Olivia asked, "Which professor of mine was it? I'd like to thank him."

"I'm sorry, but he actually asked if we could keep it anonymous. Only that you were one of the most ambitious students he had and saw a great deal of potential in you."

Olivia was stunned into silence. If her heart was beating hard before, well, it was nothing compared to how fast it was racing now. This is what she wanted, what she worked so hard for, and she wasn't even sure how to feel about it. Too many emotions were running through her veins to comprehend what she had just been offered.

"Wow. That was very generous of him to do. I'm a bit shocked right now."

Mark chuckled. "You should receive the scholarship papers in the mail in the next few days. Please review them and send them back as they are time sensitive."

Closing her eyes, she rolled onto her back. "Alright, I will. Thank you for calling. I wasn't expecting this one bit. I don't think it's even hit me yet," she said softly, rubbing her forehead with her hand.

Mark gave a heartfelt laugh. "That's understandable. I'm glad to hear that you're coming on board. It's a great opportunity, one that shouldn't be passed up, truthfully. We think you would excel with us, especially after your professor's glowing letter. Have a great afternoon, Olivia, and welcome to Columbia."

"Thank you, Mark. You have a great afternoon as well," she responded, pulling the phone away and blindly pressing the end call button.

"Who was that?"

HOLYSWEETJESUSMOTHEROFALLGODS!

Luke scared the shit out of her. He stood holding the towel wrapped around his waist with one hand. Water dripped from his wet hair onto his shoulders and trickled down his body, past his six-pack abs and into the towel. When had the shower turned off? She hadn't heard it, but she had been so caught up with the conversation to become aware of anything else around her. How long had he'd been standing there?

"Who, Olivia?" Luke bit out in a low tone. "What did you just accept?" he asked confused.

Olivia laid there looking up at Luke. She had to choose her answer carefully. Biting her lip, she contemplated her response, knowing there was no good way to really go about it.

"It was a school."

"A school? For what?"

Olivia closed her eyes briefly before opening them and slowly answered Luke. "It was a medical school I was accepted to in New York City."

"What...what are you talking about?"

Luke couldn't believe his ears. Shock hit him with a force so strong he could barely form a sentence. Was she serious?

"You heard me, Luke. I said, New York."

Unbelievable. He was furious, fucking pissed off. When had she applied to medical school without mentioning it to him? And of all places, New York? Accepting an offer to medical school meant one thing... Olivia was leaving.

"Are you going?"

When Olivia didn't answer his question, Luke shook his head, water dripping from the ends of his hair. Unbelievable. Un-fucking-believable. He couldn't even look at her right now. She'd straight out lied. Not only had she lied, but she kept a huge secret from him. Looking around the floor of Olivia's bedroom, he eyed his balled up pants from where he dropped them the night before.

"You lied."

"I did not, Luke." she countered.

Dropping the towel, he skipped his boxers and reached for his jeans. He slipped them on but didn't bother to button them.

"Oh, no? That day you said moving was a mere thought, that's it. That it was nothing more. Obviously it was. And it's not just a move. It's medical school in New York! That's called a lie, Olivia."

"No it's not, Luke."

"Fine. You omitted a few details," he said sarcastically using air quotes.

Luke couldn't deal with this unexpected news. He was seething with anger and needed to get the hell out of her house before he said something he'd regret. She lied. Flat-out fucking lied to him. And if she said she didn't lie again, he couldn't be held responsible for his words.

This moment would change everything for them. Luke couldn't even stomach looking at Livy so the only thing for him to do was to ignore her.

"Luke," Olivia breathed, gripping the sheet to her chest, "please, talk to me."

Stopping dead in his tracks, questions popped into Luke's head that baffled him.

"When the hell did you have time to take that test for med school? And without me knowing? When did you submit your application? And where was I when you did all of this?

Because If I remember correctly, we were always together at GSU."

"The MCAT? I studied at the library or in my room when we weren't together, any chance I could. I always had my nose in a book, so you didn't notice it."

Luke huffed in disbelief. "I can't believe you. I can't believe you hid something like this from me. Olivia, did you really think you wouldn't have my support?" he asked, hurt that she thought she couldn't tell him. "You know what? I'm done. Done with this, and done with you."

Olivia's heart cried out knowing Luke was upset. This wasn't the way she wanted it to happen. The plan had been to ease into it. Hurting Luke was the last thing she ever wanted to do.

"Luke, Columbia is a top rated school. I can't afford to pass it up. Plus, it's in one of the biggest, most vibrant cities to live in. There isn't a dull moment there like there is here. I want to attend this school, and you should want it for me. Not to mention, they're offering me a scholarship."

"I don't see why you can't go to a medical school like that here or even in Tennessee so you'll be close. Why do you need to go hundreds of miles away? What happens after the four years of medical school?"

"It's not the same and you know it. You're not seeing it from my point of view. You know I've wanted to get out of Georgia for some time now. That's no surprise to you."

"What happens after four years, Livy?"

"Luke, you know how hard I've worked for this!"

"Olivia, what happens after four years? Stop trying to dodge the question."

She treaded carefully. "Medical school is longer than four years, Luke. But I guess I would either stay there or come home once it's complete. It's up to me."

Dumbfounded, he stated with a bite, "So that's what it comes down to? Only what you want and not a fuck about what I want? I can give you everything. Just give me a chance, Livy."

"Oh, come on, Luke! It's not like that, not even close. I don't doubt that you could give me everything and more. I know you can, but I need this for *me*. I need to do this to prove I can make it on my own. It's not about you or money or anything else. It's about me planning out my future and my career. I need to provide for myself so I never have to rely on someone to take care of me again. I worked my ass off at Georgia Southern, you know this."

"You're being completely selfish and not seeing it through my eyes. What happens to us? Do I suddenly mean shit to you because all I heard was 'I, I, I, I,' in that sentence. Your decisions are going to hurt people. Can't *you* see that? Why can't you rely on me and let me take care of you? You're not even giving me a chance." Luke's temper rose as he fought with Olivia to change her mind. He felt like a bolt of lightning struck his chest over this mind-blowing news.

"I'm not that woman who's going to end up barefoot and pregnant in the kitchen two years down the road in some hick town. Not that there's anything wrong with it, it's just not me. Never has been. I want a career. I want to continue school, and the way you're behaving right now is unbelievable."

"I understand that you want to go to school, Livy, but why didn't you tell me? I can't believe you didn't tell me. And in New York? Why can't you stay closer to me?"

Olivia shrugged sadly. "I was scared to. I think because I worried about your reaction? I had a feeling you wouldn't want me to go so far…"

The more upset Olivia became with Luke, the more her bones began to rattle. Tears of frustration were making their way up and forcing themselves to sit on her eyelids, but she wouldn't allow them to fall. She worked hard and she shouldn't be made to feel ashamed for wanting it. How could he not understand how much this meant to her knowing so much about her past struggles?

"I guess I am selfish then...because I plan to accept their offer once I receive it. I want this really bad, Luke."

"Yes? Yes... You said yes? Without even thinking about us or discussing it with me?"

"There was never anything to really discuss with you," she stated pointedly.

"Bullshit," Luke mumbled under his breath. He spotted his shirt and fisted it. Fuck this. And fuck her. He needed to get out fast and find something to punch and then a few beers to ice his hands.

"This is fucking bullshit. What have I been this whole time to you? These past four years in college and before that? A piece of meat to fuck whenever you want?"

Olivia flinched, her heart shattering. Her voice dropped as she said, "You know that's not true, Luke. You know how much you mean to me, more than anyone."

"Yeah? Because it sure as hell doesn't sound like it if you thought there was nothing to discuss with me."

"I thought I'd have your support in this, that you'd be happy for me knowing how much I hate it here and the family I had growing up. I assumed we'd continue our relationship, but it'd be a long distance one."

"Well, Olivia, you assumed wrong. If you thought you'd have my support in this, why the fuck didn't you tell me from the beginning? You're not making any sense." Luke never called her by her full name. "You know what, if you hate everything here in this bum town, then go on up and become a city person."

"What are you saying?"

"You know exactly what I'm saying. Read between the lines, baby. The fact that you knew this weeks ago and never told me has my blood boilin'. Fuckin' boilin'. You led me to think it was settled and we were okay. You lied to my face!" he roared, his green eyes lit with fury. "Excuse me, withheld some major details," he said sarcastically.

Flustered to the core, Livy shook on the inside. This wasn't what she wanted, but she was so upset and hurt that she couldn't help what flew from her mouth.

"Who are you to tell me I can't leave? That I'm stuck here forever? What's holding me back? Nothing!"

"The one who loves you, that's who! The one who wants to make you his wife one day! Me, that's who! Damn woman, you know how to get under a man's skin like no other. Fuck!"

Olivia cringed. "I never lied to you. So stop insinuating I did."

"But you held back though, didn't you? You left out a few things for the sake of stringin' me along. It's the same damn thing, baby."

"I never *strung* you along. It's not the same thing at all. Not even close."

"If I remember correctly, you said something like, 'It was merely a thought...honestly...nothing more.' Nothing more. Nothing more, Livy? Obviously it was."

"Luke, it's done. I'm sorry, but it's done. Can we stop arguing? I want to spend the little bit of time I have left with you before I have to leave for New York." Standing from the bed, Olivia wrapped the white sheet around her body and walked over to where Luke was standing.

"You're really doing this? You're really going to leave?"

She nodded.

"Fine. How about we just break it off now? Let's end this —us—right here and save us from the heartache. You go your way, I'll go mine."

Luke saw no reason to keep on going. If she wanted to go to New York, then he would get out of her life now.

Her eyes prickled as tears threatened to fall. Blinking rapidly, she whispered, "No," under her breath. "You can't possibly be serious."

"Dead. Serious. Like a heart attack."

"Luke, there has to be a way we can work through this. Can't we try a long distance relationship?"

"No."

"Why not? Why are you being so irrational?"

"Irr—Too bad, Livy. We're...through." He was fired up, pissed off and needed to stop before he said something he would regret.

"Please, don't end this. Please..." her voice cracked with despair.

Luke bent his head down as she craned her neck to look up at him. A lone tear trickled slowly down her cheek and he wiped it with his thumb, hating to see her cry. Trying to calm his temper, he took a deep breath.

Kissing Olivia's forehead softy, he whispered, "Goodbye, Care Bear."

sixteen

present

It was about time she went home to visit with her parents.

A million emotions were running through Olivia during her drive. South Fork was a place filled with memories, both happy and sad. She hadn't come home much over the years, it hurt too much.

"Mom?" she yelled walking through the front door.

Olivia's mother rounded the corner. She wiped her hands on her jeans then pulled Olivia into her arms. "Olivia!"

"Hey, Mom."

Hugging Olivia tightly, Jane said, "I've missed you so much. I can't believe you're finally back in Georgia."

"I know. It's kind of surreal, but I'm happy to be back. I feel bad for not coming here sooner, though," she said apologetically.

"Oh, honey. I know you were busy but that you'd come when you could. A move like that takes time for the dust to settle. How about you go get situated and come back down so we can catch up over supper?"

Olivia nodded and grabbed a hold of her bag. The wheels from her suitcase rolled up each carpeted step with a thump.

Plopping her luggage on her bed, Olivia sat down and scanned her phone.

NATE: *Hope you made it there safely. Now hurry back.*
OLIVIA: *I did. <3*
NATE: *Good. Don't forget about me while you're there.*
OLIVIA: *HA! As if I could. You're either harassing me or trying to seduce me any chance you get.*
NATE: *You like it. Say it.*
OLIVIA: *No.*
NATE: *Liv...Don't make me cancel our date I had planned. I know you've wanted to go to this specific place...*
OLIVIA: *LOL! You wouldn't dare.*
NATE: *Liv.*
OLIVIA: *Nathaniel?*

Olivia knew Nate was purposely baiting her.

NATE: *Say it first.*
OLIVIA: *Nope. Talk soon.*

The relationship between them had been going better than she'd expected. Yet, Olivia still found herself holding back. She still kept her heart on reserve. It was automatic.

For the past month, Nate and Olivia settled into a natural and easy relationship—minus the sex. They had gotten to know one another on a more personal level. Between the texts and calls, they saw each other as much as possible and spent many nights at each other's home. Olivia wasn't ready for the next phase just yet, and thankfully Nate wasn't pushing her. Sure, she wanted him and sometimes wanted to give into him desperately, especially when she woke up wrapped snuggly in his strong arms. Nate could hardly take his eyes or hands off her when they were together. He seemed to adore her, like she was the center of his whole world. It wasn't in her nature to open up so easily on an emotional level, but she was beginning to expose pieces of herself to Nate. But Olivia knew once sex started, heavy emotions would be involved, and she wasn't sure she was completely ready.

Olivia blew out a weary breath and ran a hand through her hair, pulling on it in frustration. Truthfully, the question wasn't whether she was ready for it or not. It was if she could handle *all* of Nate, plus her emotions. She had a sinking suspicion that he was going to consume more than just her body. She didn't want to jinx something that hadn't started, but when it came down to it, Olivia wasn't sure she could handle another heartbreak. It was why she barricaded her heart long ago and closed off her emotions.

She never wanted to feel heartache again.

THE NEXT MORNING, AFTER BRUNCH WITH HER MOTHER AND catching up, Olivia realized she needed to see Diane Jackson sooner rather than later. A few questions popped into her head in the middle of the night so she called ahead this morning to let them know she was in town and would be stopping by. She'd be lying to say she wasn't nervous. Stepping into Luke's childhood home after all this time wasn't going to be easy. Olivia wasn't sure if Luke would be there and if he was, she wasn't sure what to say to him. *Hi? Hello? How are you? How have you been?* It had been nine years since she'd seen him; they were virtual strangers now.

Driving down the dirt road with the windows down and music playing, Olivia was hit with the memorable aroma of fresh cut grass, red dirt and humidity in the air. It was an earthy mixture that was home to her. She smiled widely and cranked up the radio, but just as she did, one of Luke's songs began to play. Figures. The longing in his voice, the pull in the lyrics, the hint of smokiness, sent a shiver through her body and her smile faltered.

...she's the one with the lips I miss...but never want to see again, the tears I never want to taste again...who left a bruise under my ribs from the pounding it took...baby, I'm gonna keep on lovin' you with the words you want to hear...that feeling, been there so many times it's like a second home to me...you deserve the heartache, that aching pit of regret while I keep on lovin' you...

His voice was the same as she remembered—raspy, but sexy as hell.

She could just imagine his green eyes penetrating her resolve as his fingers strummed the guitar... The swipe of his tongue across his lips to wet them right before he sang...

Would it always be like this? Would there ever come a time when she'd be able to listen to one of his songs without feeling anything at all?

Nostalgia came back full force as she pulled into the driveway. The Jackson house looked exactly the same. Olivia took a deep breath and exhaled. It was a home she spent many hours in growing up before they turned into a couple. As kids, they always ran around barefoot through the woods trying to catch fireflies in the dead heat of summer nights. The summers, when their only responsibilities were to brush their teeth before bed, were long gone.

Making her way up the steps, she rang the bell and waited. Seconds later the door flew open by a young man who was wearing nothing but denim shorts slung low on his hips. His hair was disheveled but he had the same prominent jaw, just as she remembered Luke having.

This had to be one of his brothers, she realized.

His eyes narrowed and his head angled, sizing her up. "Olivia," she said before he could guess.

He paused, and then eyes, a shade darker than his

brother's, lit up in surprise. A wide smile stretched across his face as he looked her up and down again.

"Hey, Livy, how you doing! It's John," he said excitedly.

"It's good to see you, John," she said. "I can't believe how much you've grown."

John chuckled. A crooked grin twisted the corner of his mouth. "I'm not a kid anymore, if that's what you mean," he laughed. "Honey, it's been like ten years or something."

Honey? *Honey?* Olivia nearly balked at honey.

Trouble. This one is definitely going to be trouble.

Clearing her throat, Olivia said, "Yes…almost ten years. Are your parents home? I was in town and wanted to stop by. It's been a while since I've seen them."

"Not here to see Luke?"

Open curiosity was laced in John's question. Her heart practically skipped a beat at John's question.

"Ah, no."

"Oh, well, that's a good thing because he's not here anyway. When was the last time you saw him?"

Olivia breathed in a sigh of relief and thanked her lucky stars. Just as she was about to answer John, Luke's dad pulled the door completely open. The strained lines on his forehead seemed more visible than when she last saw him.

"Hey, Livy," he said gruffly and pulled her into a bear hug. "Good to see you again."

Out of the corner of her eye, Olivia saw John's brows scrunch at his father's last statement. Evidently he had no idea they'd been to Savannah.

"You too… Thought I'd stop by and say hi."

"Sure, come on into the kitchen and let me fix you a drink."

Turning to his son, he said, "Go on upstairs and take a shower. You have community service to do today." The deep groan from John was one of annoyance. His eyes squeezed shut and his head rolled back, the veins in his neck jutting out. He clearly wasn't looking forward to this community service.

"Go on," Clark ordered. "Or else they'll tack on more time. Next time don't screw up and mind your manners so you won't have to do this."

John stomped his way up the stairs, leaving them alone.

"Come on in, dear. Tell us what's going on."

seventeen

"Well hello, Dr. King," Mrs. Jackson winked and went in for a hug.

"Please, Diane," she said. "just call me Olivia. I've known you for too long."

She patted Olivia's hand and nodded. "So, what brings you here, honey?" Diane walked around and sat down on a barstool across from Olivia.

"Is it alright to talk freely here? I wasn't sure if anyone in the family knew you'd been to see me." It almost came out in a whisper.

"No, we haven't told anyone yet. We didn't want to worry any of the boys. With Luke on tour, the twins always busy with sports, and John who can't seem to stay out of trouble, we didn't want to worry any of them. We figured once the results were in, then we would decide what to do. But you can go ahead and speak."

"Well for starters, why did you wait so long to do the blood work? I almost called you to see if you had done it but then your results finally showed up."

Her lips formed a thin line. "I was feeling fine after I saw you. I thought it was in my head so I figured I didn't need it. Just thought I pushed myself too hard like I normally do."

"She's hardheaded, that's why," Clark chimed in. Diane's hand flew back and playfully swatted her husband's stomach.

"I am not," she replied. Clark looked at Olivia with eyes that said 'yeah right' and a smile curved Olivia's mouth.

"Care to tell me what happened?"

"Well," she started, "I became extremely tired again, more so than usual. Before, like I said, I thought I had pushed myself, but this time I hadn't done anything out of the norm. I watched myself closely. My joints were aching again, and the numbness and tingly sensations were all over my body this time.

"Plus, my vision is off. Sometimes I wear my contacts too long, and thought I needed to change them, so I did. It's strange… It comes and goes. Everything kind of just flares up I guess," she finished using her hands as if to show a mini explosion. "I knew it was something more, and that I couldn't ignore it anymore."

"You didn't tell me about your eyes, Di."

"I didn't want to worry you anymore."

"Honey, I'm your husband," Clark said with sad eyes, his graying brows pinched together. "I want to know what's going on with you at all times. I know you like to take it all on like Superwoman, but I'm here to help. Let me know when you need me for anything, please."

Diane nodded in agreement. A fragile smile shifted her face as their eyes met. "Okay," softly rolled off her lips.

"Okay… What about fever? Headaches? Dizziness? Inflammation? Any of those?"

"Well, yes, but I didn't think that was anything to complain about. Who doesn't get headaches? I have all boys. I'm bound to get a headache here and there." She took a sip of her sweet tea.

"I need to hear everything, Diane. Even if you think it's nothing, it could be something that could change the game plan for me. Trust me," Olivia said as she placed her hand over Diane's.

Diane nodded. "Then yes to all of those."

"Alright, so blood work is a good thing, but also confusing. Your results show that you may possibly have an autoimmune disease, but autoimmune disease can be many different illnesses—which are treatable. It's really difficult to tell without further testing, to be honest, and I don't want to diagnose without doing so.

"It's one of the reasons I came out here to see you. I didn't want you to have to make another trip to Savannah just for this information and since I was visiting my parents I figured I'd stop by. I'm going to order you a series of tests to be done and once they're completed I'll look over the results and we can go from there."

"What kinds of illnesses are associated with autoimmune disease?" Diane sat quietly, her face turning pale as her husband posed the question.

"Well, there are a number of them. Some mimic others, which is why multiple tests should be done. They'll help in ruling the other issues out. It just takes a little time. I'll give you the information for facilities in Savannah that do these tests. Once the appointment is set, you go. Don't back out because you're suddenly feeling better, Diane. This could take weeks, so be prepared to wait. I may order one test after another just to be sure. But don't worry, we'll figure it out together."

"Thank you, Livy." It was barely audible, but Olivia heard it and felt awful. That was one of the reasons why she never planned to treat family or anyone she considered family. Not that she had much family, but throw relatives and friends in the mix and it was an emotional career.

Olivia got up from her barstool. It was time for her to go. Being in this house and speaking with Luke's parents about a possible lifelong disease was really weighing on her. She thought of Diane as her second mother.

"I'm going to head out. If you have any questions, I'll give you my personal cell phone number and you can contact me anytime. I don't normally hand out my phone number, but these circumstances are a little different and I trust you with it." Olivia jotted her number down on the back of her business card and left it on the table for them.

"Thank you," Clark said. "We really appreciate you coming out here."

"Oh, it's really no problem."

"Umm, Olivia? Did...you ah...want to know how Luke is doing?"

Uncertainty was written all over that question and hit Olivia hard. Of course she wanted to know about Luke. She always wanted to know, but she wouldn't dare ask. If she did ask, then she wouldn't feel like she wasn't staying true to Nate. But if his mother did...well, she would listen.

Olivia pushed her hair behind her ear and answered. "Yes, I would like to know, actually. I just didn't think it was appropriate to bring it up at a time like this." Her heart beat rapidly as she waited for her to respond.

"Oh, nonsense!" She shooed her hand forward with a large smile, her eyes lighting up. "He's on tour at the moment so we hardly get to see him, but he's building a large fan base," she said enthusiastically. "He performs as much as he can, working to the bone it seems. It's hard to believe my baby boy is playing on stage. He's coming home soon. I can't wait to see him!"

A large grin crossed Olivia's face. She was genuinely happy for Luke. She once told him long ago that he belonged on stage, that it was where he was born to be.

"Well, if you need anything call my cell," Olivia said again over her shoulder then walked out the door.

"We will. Thank you again, Livy."

And in that instant as she left their house, all Olivia could do was pray that everything would be fine.

eighteen

"Come in, Shelly," Olivia said, not even bothering to raise her head up from the previous patient's chart. She knew it was Shelly. The woman still insisted on giving two knocks and waiting for permission to enter. Some days it annoyed her to no end and Olivia just wished the nurse would walk in without hesitation.

Shelly poked her head around the door and said, "You have a call."

"Who is it?"

"He wouldn't say…only that he insisted you speak with him. He swears he knows you very well and would talk to him when I told him you were busy."

Must be Nate. She'd have to call him back when she got the first opportunity. She was too swamped at the moment.

"Take a message for me. I'm very busy right now, Shell."

Shelly paused. "The thing is he's very insistent. When I told him you were busy and I would take a message, he told me to call you 'Care Bear,' whatever that means. He wouldn't say—"

Olivia snapped her head up, her eyes popping out and her stomach in her throat. She was suddenly frozen in her chair.

The only thing moving was the rapid pounding of her heart against her ribs. Only one person knew that name.

"I got it. Thanks, Shelly," she responded with a fake smile. "You can leave now."

Shelly smiled wearily, closing the door behind her. Taking a deep breath—or five—Olivia tried to calm her nerves before she picked up the tangled corded black phone.

"Dr. Olivia King."

"Olivia..." a deep voice echoed over the line.

Chills flitted over her body. It reminded her of his lyrical flames of poetry that used to flicker against her skin. All it took was four syllables and she knew who it was even without the endearment he used with Shelly.

Olivia couldn't believe she was hearing Luke's voice. It had been more than nine very long years since she'd heard a peep from him. Not that she expected to. He ignored every email and every phone call, disregarding all her efforts to stay in contact.

Trying to play it cool, Olivia responded after clearing her throat. "Yes, this is Olivia. What can I do for you?"

"Olivia, it's...Luke. How...How are you? It's been quite a while."

"Hi...Luke. I'm well," Olivia answered, trying to keep it cool. "How are you? I heard you're on tour right now. It seems your singing career has taken off."

Olivia silently cursed, using every word she could think of. She squeezed her eyes shut for being such an idiot. He wasn't calling to talk to her, obviously.

"Ahh, yeah," he said then let out a low chuckle. "The tour's over so I'll be headin' home," Luke answered. "Listen, I wanted to talk to you if you have a minute."

"I do. What's up?"

"Good... Thanks... I heard my parents came to see you. I had no idea that you're a doctor now. That's amazing. Good for you."

Olivia flinched at his openly honest statement. Had she not left for medical school? While there was no way of him knowing what she had done for the past nine years, why was it that she knew what he had done with his life?

"I am... I'm a neurologist now, obviously. And thank you."

"Livy—"

Cutting him off, Olivia said in a hurried professional voice, "What can I do for you, Luke?"

There was a slight clearing of his throat before he answered. "After what I've been told, I'm concerned about my mother's condition getting out. Well, any condition she may have. I know we didn't leave off on the best terms, but I'm asking you, please, to not say anything to anyone."

"Luke, I'm a doctor and there are laws I *must* follow," she said. "I would never say anything to anyone about your mother's condition or anyone else's condition for that matter. I take my medical oath very seriously. I would never violate it, not for anyone. No one will know anything about your mother or any treatment that she may or may not need. My staff is trustworthy."

Olivia waited for Luke to respond. She loved what she did, every draining minute of it, and she wouldn't jeopardize it for anything, or anyone.

"That's a relief to hear. Thanks, Livy. I honestly didn't think you'd say anything, just needed to hear it from you to be sure. I can't help but have my doubts. I know my family is worried about what the town would say, which is why I understand they came up to Savannah. That town loves to talk shit, plus with people always wanting info... We don't need that on top of everything else."

It was as if he was expecting her to say the opposite. Olivia pursed her lips together and glanced around her office. Luke's tone hit a low and deep spot inside her. His voice sounded like gravel rubbing against smooth asphalt.

"Nothing to worry about, Luke. Like I said, I take my job

very seriously. Though, I'm a little offended you would think I'd talk to people."

"Right... Well, I apologize. I tend to have a hard time trusting people in my line of business. Just know I appreciate what you're doing."

"Well, you're welcome, Luke."

"When I was told my parents went to see you, I wasn't told much else." Luke paused for a moment. His voice started to crackle at the beginning of the last sentence. "Is... everything going to be okay?"

"Ah, Luke, I just told you that I couldn't reveal any information about any patient, including your mother's. What makes you think I'm going to disclose anything to you?"

Luke chuckled. "Well, I thought since it's Mama that you would, considering our past."

"Water under the bridge, Luke. That doesn't even factor in. You thought wrong if you expected me to utter a word to you."

"Olivia, I'm not asking for a lot here. Just let me know if she's going to be okay, please. I can't think straight while out on the road knowing that she was at a neurologist's office. I'm thinking the worst here. My mind is running a race with itself over all the possibilities. I haven't been able to sleep since I heard the news." The faint sound of a lighter sparked in the background.

People heard the word 'neurologist' and thought the worst. She'd seen it over the years during her training and working in the field. Her heart was aching knowing how difficult it must be on him, especially being so far away.

"I'm sorry, Luke. I can't say anything." She hated having to do this with him, knowing he was suffering.

"Dammit, Livy. Clearly, I'm not going to say a damn word. It's my mother. Just give me something, anything."

"I...can't. Luke...ugh..."

"*Care Bear*...please..."

Just hearing Luke's voice crack across the phone made her reminisce about the past. Taking a deep breath, Olivia closed her eyes and counted to ten. She knew she shouldn't, yet Olivia couldn't stop the words he wanted to hear from flowing from her mouth.

Quietly she whispered into the phone, "Don't worry. I'm just waiting on some tests results to come in, but she should be okay. It's nothing we aren't capable of treating."

A snide, snickering laugh coming from Luke made her skin crawl, like hundreds of red ants coating her body. Shit. She knew immediately that she screwed up. Irritated with the situation, she squeezed her eyes shut, shaking her head. What had she done?

"Was that all it took? A few lines of begging and pleading for you to give me info, Livy? Was it that easy for you to break your oath?"

"Luke, I... I was." Olivia was stammering now.

"Ah, ah, ah. You were what? Breaking your doctor's oath? Seriously, Livy. This is my family you're caring for, not to mention, there are fans following me trying to get any little piece of information about me. How the hell am I supposed to trust you with my mother's life if you give it up to me so easily?"

"You're playing dirty. That's not fair. And don't ever mock me again."

"All is fair in love and war."

"Love and— What love? What war? Are you kidding me right now? You're at odds with me for what? Over something that happened years ago that you apparently can't seem to get past? Don't act like a child, Luke. I'm not going to play games with you."

Not only was her blood boiling because she'd been tricked and fell for it, but because Luke was bringing up the past and using it against her.

"I told you because I didn't want you to worry. I'd never

do that for anyone else. I actually have a heart and feelings, unlike you." After pausing for a brief moment, Olivia decided it was time to finish this conversation. Just before slamming the phone down she said, "And Luke? Don't call me 'Care Bear' *ever* again."

Closing her eyes, Olivia couldn't believe what had just transpired. She rubbed her throbbing temples and contemplated whether or not to just take the rest of the day off. It had crossed her mind at one point that once she began treating Luke's mom she would probably encounter Luke. She just hadn't expected it to be this soon.

Standing up, Olivia smoothed down her white lab coat and made her way around the desk. She still had half a day left and she was determined to finish it out. Luckily for her, it was Thursday, which meant drinks with Shelly after work. At least she had something to look forward to.

Sweet baby Jesus, Olivia thought at the blaring alarm clock. It sounded like a freight train coming straight through the bedroom. Turning her head under her pillow, her eyes felt like sandpaper as she peered to the right to read the clock.

4:30 a.m.

How stupid was she to stay out late with Shelly?

Livy…Care Bear…

Not wanting to go there, Olivia raised her arm and slammed it down on the snooze button. The black alarm clock tilted on its side and fell flat with a clang. Just a few more minutes…

Rushing through the back door of the office building and into her office, Olivia threw her purse onto her chair. After snoozing through her alarm, she over slept and woke in a panic.

Pulling her thick waves into a messy bun, a knock sounded at the door. *Jesus Christ*. Why couldn't Shelly just follow directions and walk in?

"Yes, Shelly!"

Shelly hesitantly opened the door, alarmed by Olivia's tone. "Umm…you have a call."

"Who is it?"

"It sounds like the guy from yesterday…the Care Bear guy. He won't tell me his name."

"Thanks, Shell. I'll take it from here. I, ah, didn't mean to snap at you." Shelly gave a timid smile and left her office.

Picking up the phone, Olivia felt like death inside. She had a hangover like never before and her stomach was in knots. She was never drinking tequila again. Her eyes burned. All she wanted to do was go home, close the blinds and crawl into her soft down bed and go to sleep. Too bad that wasn't happening any time soon.

"This is Dr. King. What can I do for you?" Olivia said in her sweetest, sugary voice possible.

"Livy—"

"What, Luke? I don't have time for your games today." Not bothering to hide her feelings of disgust.

"Damn…you sound sick. Are you okay?"

She knew she sounded worn out. Olivia had been working herself to the bone, and last night didn't help.

"I went out last night and had a couple drinks." Why was she telling him that?

"Ah…whiskey girl. Not drinking whiskey anymore I take it? Because your voice never sounded like this." Luke laughed lightly.

"Don't call me that. I wanted something a bit stronger last night, not that it's any of your business. I had more than usual but then again I don't get out much." Seriously, why was she telling him this? And why did he have to bring up the past yet again?

"Right... Anyway, I'm calling because I wanted to apologize for tricking you yesterday. It was wrong of me. I was worried and upset and took it out on you."

"Right. I'm an easy target."

"Well, for what it's worth, I'm sorry."

"It's fine. This is an unusual situation, and I need to remember that. Listen, Luke," Olivia said rubbing her eye with the heel of her hand and collapsing into her chair with a huff. "I've never released information about a patient to anyone before. Nothing. You have to trust me and take my word on this," she said tiredly. "It's someone's life I have in my hands and I take it as seriously as I take my own. You're just...different. I guess maybe because I didn't want you to stress while out on the road? Oh, I don't know. Just know that I would never hurt your name or your mother's. I swear to you."

Luke was silent. At one point she thought he'd hung up.

Finally, Luke asked, "Listen, do you want to maybe catch up and do lunch sometime when I get back?"

Olivia gulped. "I'm not sure. I'd have to check my schedule."

"Alright. I'll take it. And Olivia? Thanks. I really do appreciate what you're doing. I know what I did was sneaky, the way I went about it and all. I'm sorry. I just freaked out."

Clearing his throat, he said, "I had no idea you left New York."

Could he make her morning any worse?

"Yeah, I'm back in Georgia, but I live in Savannah now. Listen, Luke, I need to go. I have patients waiting."

nineteen

Luke's eyes zoomed in to make sure he wasn't hallucinating.

And he wasn't.

He also couldn't believe *that* was his whiskey girl, either.

Luke watched Olivia from his parked truck on the side of the commercial street as she shoved the heavy glass door open, emerging from her office building. With the puffy, light purple circles under her eyes, Olivia looked beyond exhausted and worn out as he stared through his windshield at a face he hadn't seen in many years.

After his flight landed in Georgia last night, guilt left him restless all night. It wasn't normal for Luke to be conniving, so he needed to apologize for acting like an ass. He did a little research and within three minutes found out where Livy worked, jumped in his truck and hightailed it north. Judging by the looks of her, Luke partially blamed himself for the tiredness in her eyes, or at least blamed himself for adding to whatever was going on in her life. But as his heated gaze traveled down her body, he noticed how much Olivia had changed over the years.

Holy. Hot. Damn.

Olivia had always been beautiful to him, but over the years she'd changed into a stunningly, gorgeous woman. Just a glance and his body roared to life.

Granted, Luke hadn't seen Livy in ages, but Lord have mercy. The white collared shirt was plastered to her chest and the buttons down the center looked about ready to pop. The outline of her bra held much fuller breasts as his gawking gaze traveled south. He'd never seen a woman look so curvy in all his life that left him hard and wanting so bad so quickly. She looked mouthwatering in the tight navy blue skirt that hugged her new curves—and he meant hugged her wider hips to her thighs and down to her knees. From the looks of it, Olivia had softened around her hips over the years. And it looked fucking amazing on her. Sexy as hell. The skirt was glued to her like a glove. Man, he'd love to see what was underneath it too, in an honest way of a hungry male who saw a beautiful woman that made his jaw drop. Luke's imagination was running wild. He pictured his hands slowly skimming up the inside of her thighs, squeezing every few inches as he went, making her sigh and purr in pleasure from his touch as he eased his way closer to her.

Olivia's long brown hair billowed around her face in the breeze, and Luke noticed the worn out look once again. It was a look she often wore while back in college when studying for exams. His chest seized at the memories of them studying together on his bed all those years ago, remembering how it would turn into more than just studying. Now he couldn't help but wonder if his behavior yesterday had given her the drained look she wore in her eyes.

Luke had to admit he was edgy walking up to Olivia. Adrenaline combined with anxiety pumped through his veins and his body didn't know how to react. He was jittery and had a love/hate relationship with this kind of high. Luke wanted to walk right up to her, but he'd be fooling himself if he said he wasn't nervous as shit. It had been a long time since they'd seen each other and he wasn't sure how she'd react to his presence.

When Luke planned to return home after tour, he never expected to see Olivia, let alone talk to her. He thought he'd just go back, kick it with Chase and visit his family. But with the news of his mother and the way he treated Livy on the phone, Luke's plans changed the moment he walked on the plane.

Seeing Livy so close, literally just steps away after no contact after so many years, was a lot to take in. He didn't think he'd be so nervous about walking up to a woman, but then again Livy wasn't just any woman. Memories of them from the past surged through his brain and he instantly felt like an ass for being so condescending to her.

Pulling out a cigarette, he lit it and took a hard drag before he strolled up to Olivia. He watched the tip turn into a blaze of crimson gleaming in the shadow of his palm. He exhaled, the dry smoke rolling casually from his lips. Once in front of Olivia, blocking her path, he waited for her to look up from rummaging through her purse.

"Hey, Livy."

Olivia's head snapped up and she stiffened. Luke was standing larger than life in front of her. The sound of the noisy street faded into the distance as she stared. The only thing Olivia could hear was the pounding in her chest as her body went on high alert. Luke wore a ball cap, just like he used to with his dirty blond hair flaring from the sides, and gold aviator sunglasses shielding his eyes. She couldn't help but look him up and down, more so in shock than anything else. His skin tight white tee was paired with dark jeans and finished off with tan combat boots. It seemed not much changed with his attire.

"It's Luke."

That voice... That smoky voice sent a tremble throughout her body that she wasn't prepared for. It was deeper than she remembered and made the beat of her heart speed up even more. Closing her mouth, and her eyes because of the embarrassment she felt for gaping at him, she cleared her throat and finally she responded.

"I know."

Luke grinned broadly at her. "So you remember me."

Not finding his humor funny in the least bit, Olivia quickly grew irritated. Standing taller, she answered him.

"Of course I remember you," she deadpanned. "As if I could forget. You're on the damn radio all the time. What are you doing here?"

"Just wanted to make sure you knew it was me. It has been a long time and all."

Looking into Livy's eyes, Luke shifted from one boot to the other. He took another pull from his cigarette that was pinched between his thumb and forefinger. Blowing the smoke out to the side, he said, "I wanted to come and apologize in person for what I did yesterday."

"I didn't think you were already in Georgia."

"I flew home last night, actually. I have some time off and wanted to come home."

Luke had a few days off and drove up to Savannah to see her? The thought tickled her even when it shouldn't.

"Oh…well, there was no need to make an apology in person since you already did earlier on the phone. Or did you forget? Savannah is a small hike from South Fork. You just wasted a good part of your afternoon coming up here. Thanks, I guess, but I need to get going."

Luke reached out to stop Olivia, but pulled back quickly before he touched her. She looked down at his hand and then up to Luke with a question in her eyes.

"Did you need something, Luke? I already told you I'll keep everything strictly private. No one in my office will know who you or your parents are."

"Can I make it up to you?"

"There's nothing to make up. I'm on lunch right now and have a lot to do. I need to go."

"So...where are you headed?"

Olivia's nostrils flared. She was growing more and more agitated by the minute. She didn't remember him being this persistent, or was it something he acquired? Luke may have been pissed with her for leaving, but she was just as angry for him shutting her out completely.

"I just told you, Luke. I'm on my lunch. I'm headed to get the fattiest, greasiest burger I can find with fries. Happy that you know my plans now? Anyway, it was nice seeing you, but seriously, I need to get going," she answered brusquely.

Olivia placed the strap of her purse on her shoulder and walked around him on the sidewalk.

"Livy— Wait."

Olivia spun fast and looked back at Luke, but as soon as she did she regretted it.

Fuck. My. Life, she cursed under her breath.

A hangover.

Luke.

And the suns strongest rays burning a hole into her eyes.

"Shit," she muttered, placing her sunglasses on her face. Not only was she seeing bright silver circles, she could feel moisture trickling down the hollow of her breasts from the high humidity.

"What, Luke? You and I have nothing to talk about. I'm treating your mother, not you. What part of that don't you understand? Or is it the fact that you probably have people kissing your ass on a daily basis and aren't familiar with anyone telling you 'no' so you're being an asshole and won't leave me alone now?" Olivia snapped. She couldn't help the attitude.

"Want to get lunch together? Maybe catch up?" Luke gave Olivia a lopsided, cautious smile.

Olivia's mouth gaped open, completely dumbfounded by his question. Was he joking?

"Are you out of your ever loving mind? Catch up? Catch up on what exactly? The past nine years? We're completely different people now, Luke. There's nothing to catch up on. It would take entirely too long to even begin that voyage down memory lane, and quite frankly, I'd rather leave the past in the past."

There. That wiped the smug smile right off his handsome face. She needed to be done with this conversation ASAP.

Luke couldn't believe his eyes—or ears. He had to fight the grin that tugged at his mouth. Olivia had just chewed him out and he took it all, not giving it back to her. Hell, he was caught off guard by her spicy mouth that he couldn't stop himself from asking her to lunch. Seeing her eyes flare the way they just did made him want more. Luke had forgotten that Olivia hardly ever took his shit, and it was one thing he loved about being with her. He'd watched her face heat and her eyes flicker as she became exasperated while he toyed with her. It fueled him now just like before.

"Bitter about the past, are we? I don't think you have any right for the bitterness, to be honest. And all I did was ask if you wanted to get lunch together, not go for drinks."

"Bit—," Olivia had to bite her tongue. She was dangerously close to going off at this point and had every right, just as he did.

"No, Luke, I'm not bitter about the past. I'm hungry and hungover and want to be left alone. All I want is a damn burger with a lot of ketchup and to be on my merry way," she said emphatically. "We have nothing to discuss. We're not friends anymore. Friends talk, they keep in touch over the years. We didn't. I'm treating your mother and that's as far as it goes. How many times do I have to repeat myself?"

With that, Olivia turned around and crossed the street. She couldn't believe the nerve of him asking to catch up.

Catch up on what, exactly? He was being friendly simply because of his devious little plot and the fact that he brought up their past to get what he wanted? She didn't give a shit how rude she just was. She hoped she got through to him. He may be a country rock singer now, but he was still small town Luke to her and she wasn't caving in to him or his charm. It also wasn't helping that while he stood inches from her she could feel the heat bouncing off his unyielding body. Luke had grown into one hell of a man, and she couldn't stop her body from reacting to him. Even though she told herself she was long over him, her emotions were saying otherwise.

Walking a few blocks normally didn't bother Olivia, but today it did. Her high heels and pounding headache combined with the heat was something she was in no mood to deal with.

But neither was running into Luke.

Olivia opened the door to the burger place and was hit with a big draft of cool air that felt so good against her scorching skin. She grabbed the lunch order that she had called in earlier and began eating. She pulled her phone out of her purse when she heard something smack her table and looked up.

Was he serious? For the second time today, Olivia was momentarily rendered speechless.

"You have got to be kidding me," she muttered shaking her head. A sexy smirk panned Luke's face. He was too handsome for his own good with a smile like that.

"What? I drove a while to get here. I'm hungry too. And since I don't know the area I followed you here."

"It's a strip mall full of places to eat. You just had to pick this one?" She shoved a fry into her mouth then cut her burger in half.

Luke watched as Livy licked her plump lips. Who knew eating could be so sexy? He couldn't resist not following her here. Not only was he hungry, but watching her parade down the street in that skirt she wore like a second skin had his mouth watering.

"Listen, I just wanted to talk. I feel bad still and can see you had a rough night. I can only assume it was my doing that caused it."

"You assumed right, Einstein."

Luke nodded then reached over to grab the other half of Livy's burger and took a bite. "Wow. This is good!" he exclaimed between his full lips. He hoped he could lighten the mood if he changed the subject.

Olivia's eyes narrowed. She knew what he was doing and to be quite honest, she was so drained that she didn't feel like fighting anymore.

She shrugged. "It's my favorite hangover place."

Luke cocked a grin and said, "A favorite hangover place? I can see why."

Olivia angled her tray toward Luke to share her fries. "Yeah, well Shelly and I like to go out occasionally on Thursday nights. Sometimes I'll hit this place up for lunch the next day."

"Where do you go? And last I remember you didn't get hangovers."

A conversation with Luke was not something Olivia wanted to have for a multitude of reasons. For one, it made her hyperaware of every move he made, every bite he took, and each time his lips wrapped around her straw to sip the drink he snagged from her. Or how his long thick legs would move under the table and brush along her calf. Luke had packed on muscles over the years, his presence was so powerful that it was impossible not to notice everything he said or did. She needed to prove to herself that she wasn't easily affected with him so near, but was doing a piss poor job.

Not to mention, his raspy voice sashayed dangerously across her skin, spiking her pulse while her heartbeat pounded against her ribs.

Olivia shrugged. "Oh, around here. I work a lot so I don't like to wander far since I'm usually up before the sun rises. There's a bunch of places with live bands and cheap drinks," she said smiling at the live music part. "We'll either hit them all up, walking from place to place, or just stick to one. I guess it depends on the mood we're in."

"So you're still into live music?"

"Some things never die," she answered bobbing her head.

Hearing Livy was still into live music surprised Luke. Music is what pulled them together, locked them in from the beginning. For some reason he had figured she'd stop listening to it once she left.

"That's good to hear, Livy."

"Can't help it I guess," she continued, and looked deep into Luke's eyes. "I love live music more than anything, especially from the newbie's trying to make it in the business. That was the one good thing about living in New York. Gavin DeGraw opened a bar in downtown New York where singers can perform all week long. It was my favorite place to go when I needed time away from life. The feeling it gave me, the harmonic emotions would flow right through and crash over me in waves, sucking me under and making me feel each and every word. I loved it. There's nothing better. All it took was a beat, a few hooks and everything fell into place. It's real and it's raw. Songs tell a story that I want to know more about, their sorrows spoken through lyrics that cannot be said in person. It kind of just takes over and I feel free… I just let go and find my center. Yeah…I still love it. Plus whiskey, I still love that, too." She laughed casually, almost as if time had never stopped between them.

Her smile wavered when she noticed Luke's piercing eyes. Burning. Predatorial. Heated. He eyed her like a vulture looming in and gearing up to dive down.

"Luke, what's wrong?"

Luke snapped out of his stare at the sound of Livy's soft

voice. He couldn't believe what she had just spoken. No one, none of the women he knew had ever said that about music before. Most were into the idea of a singer, the fame and glory that followed, but they didn't understand the concept or what occurred behind the strings. But Olivia did. She understood it and obviously still loved it. Always had, he'd just forgotten.

"Nothing," he lied. Luke needed to get out of there immediately. In the last couple of years with women coming in and out of his life, none had ever uttered words even closely resembling those Livy had just said. Truthfully, it moved him so deeply he wasn't used to the feeling. It was an awakening that boiled down to one clear objective. It was the quintessence of music for Luke. And the one person who understood his world he had told to get the fuck out of his life.

Luke adjusted himself in his chair, trying to get comfortable with the growing bulge in his pants. Nothing was hotter than a beautiful woman who loved music and understood it. And Liv did. She understood every aspect of it. Not only did she have beauty and brains, but the love of music as well. She was the perfect package and he had thrown it all away because of his stubbornness.

Too bad they finished years ago. And didn't that just put a damper on his mood.

Clearing his throat, Luke said, "I'm going to head out. I want to see my brothers with the little time I have. It's been awhile, being on tour and all."

"How are you brothers? I saw John the other day. He looks so much like you now. What a heartbreaker he must be."

Luke paused. "You saw John?

Olivia chewed her fry slowly. "Yes… I was at your parents' house. Didn't you know?"

"No. I had no idea."

"Oh... Then how did you find out about your parents?"

"John told me, but I didn't ask many questions. He was pretty vague about it all, just gave me your number and said I needed to call you. I assumed he overheard them talking. He didn't tell me you came by, though."

"Well, I was in the area. I went home to see my parents. It was the first time I was able to since I moved back to Georgia. I figured since I was close that I'd make it easy on them and stop by."

Luke contemplated what she said with a nod. He knew she'd gone home occasionally over the years, so no one would think anything with her stopping by. He was more in shock she'd been by his parents' home and John not telling him.

"Just out of curiosity, Luke, where do you live now? You said you came home for a few days, so do you live at home still?"

He bellowed out a laugh. "No, I don't live at home, Livy. I had a house built near them, though."

A lazy smile slid across Olivia's face and her eyes softened. She remembered how much family meant to Luke.

A snippet of a country song played loudly from her cell phone and Olivia glanced at it. Picking it up, she smiled as she read the name across the screen. *Nate.*

Looking up she said, "It was good to see you Luke. I can't say I'm happy due to the circumstances, but...I'm glad to see and hear you're doing well. Your mom told me. She's very proud of you."

A text message came through and Olivia looked down at it.

"You asked about me?" For some reason that idea excited Luke.

"Well, no. She voluntarily told me."

Luke's shoulders slumped slightly. "Oh."

"Guess I'll see you around."

"Yeah. Later, Care Bear."

It didn't even register with Luke that he had used his nickname for her.

And with that, he walked back to his truck.

The whole drive home, lyrics and notes hit him hard to the point where he couldn't wait to put them on paper the first chance he got. Maybe even cracking open some beers, too. The feeling pulsating through Luke was one he hadn't felt in ages, and he welcomed it with open arms. Back in college, Luke never had a problem writing melodies or songs for fun. They always came to him easily with Livy nearby. The words would fly faster than he could write, page after page. But somewhere along the way, the ease of song writing drifted and he found his words watered down and more difficult to pen.

Had Livy become his muse long ago but never realized it until now? If she was just a stone's throw away, Luke's world would tilt off its axis. Nothing else mattered for him. Everything had always been about Olivia and what he wanted with her, for them.

Music and Livy were a powerful concoction. Always had been in memory, but in the flesh it was exceedingly stimulating. It was a high he craved often, and coincidentally he'd just had his first dose. Luke was only getting started as it slowly crept its way through, invigorating the blood in his veins and transforming his deep thoughts into music once again.

twenty

Nate kept his word and took Olivia out the following weekend.

Pulling up to a bar north of Savannah that was surrounded by palm trees, Olivia was still cautious about being seen with a patient. She didn't want to admit it, but Olivia felt like the forbidden aspect added excitement and fuel…and she liked it. But did that take away from her actual feelings for Nate?

Nate held Olivia's hand as he led her through the crowd and out to empty colorful Adirondack chairs that were scattered around the sandy deck that overlooked the Savannah River. Deck lights were attached all around the wooden railing and reflected onto the tall trees that glowed over the black lake, giving it the image of smooth satin.

As a waitress moved through the crowd towards them, Olivia was getting ready to order her usual whiskey when Nate stopped her.

"You ask to come to Rum Bar and you're ordering a whiskey? Nope. Not happenin', darlin'. You're getting a rum bucket. Here, look at all the different ones they make," he said handing her a menu.

Olivia glanced over the menu with Nate. Holy rum her eyes nearly popped out of her head!

"Wow. All that rum. Six different flavors seem like a lot, but sound good." Nate's incredibly sexy grin met his eyes as his dark hair glistened in the moonlight. Olivia's heart fluttered at the sinful gleam in his eyes. He reached for her hand and laced his rough fingers through hers. Nate's personality might be a little stronger than what she'd been accustomed to, but deep down he was a true southern gentleman.

The waitress returned with their drinks and Olivia looked down into the bucket that was filled to the brim with ice and her peachy pink drink. It was the size of a small sand bucket kids build sand castles with. She took a small sip from her straw as Nate watched. The humidity was thick, but the air coming off the river cooled over her body as Nate leaned in and dropped a kiss to her cheek.

"This stuff is dangerous. It tastes like fruit juice, but it's actually pretty good."

"Better than whiskey?"

Olivia giggled. "Well, I don't know about that, but it comes close." Olivia angled the straw toward Nate, offering him a sip of her drink. He paused to look at her before he covered the straw with his lips and tasted the frothy concoction. It was oddly intimate watching Nate drink from the same place her lips had just been.

She settled into Nate's side and listened to the live band. He stroked her arm softly and kissed the top of her head. Somehow they'd fallen effortlessly into a really good relationship that she had no complaints about. It was almost too good to be true.

"How was visiting your parents?"

Olivia swallowed and answered. "It was better than expected, actually. My mom appears to be happy, so that's a plus. I know she'd like for me to move back to South Fork, but

I can't see myself living there again. I love my life in Savannah now."

Nate's arm tightened around Olivia's shoulder after hearing how happy she was in Savannah.

"I love it here, too. I don't know if I'd like it down there, but if you decided to go back, I guess I'd have to follow you."

Hearing Nate would follow her should have brought happiness to Olivia, but it did the opposite.

Pulling Olivia from her train of sad thoughts was a loud voice booming over the music playing. She couldn't see where the voice was coming from, but noticed a crowd forming around a few guys. Just when Olivia was about to take another sip, she thought she saw a glimpse of a face she recognized, but then it was gone just as fast. She was trying to get a better view as Nate spoke to her but, didn't want to make it obvious.

"Liv?" Nate shook her arm. "Olivia?" This time it came out louder and deeper, grabbing her attention. She looked up at him with questioning eyes.

"Yeah?"

"Did you hear anything I was saying?"

Shrinking back apologetically, she answered honestly. "No...I'm sorry. It's just that I could swear I know that guy over there..." Her eyes glanced to where the scuffle was.

Nate's eyes followed. "You know them? I thought you didn't know anyone here?"

She swallowed a sip of her peach drink. "Well, I don't know anyone here. It's just that one guy looked familiar to me." Just then the crowd broke apart and she caught sight of the face again, and it hit her.

John! Luke's brother! Her eyes popped and Nate noticed.

"I knew it! I haven't seen him in... Well, he's not even old enough to be here."

"Who?" Nate asked confused, but Olivia didn't listen to his question as she stood. If Diane and Clark knew he was here... Olivia shook her head. She knew John was trouble the moment she saw him at Luke's parents' house.

Nate reached out and gripped her arm firmly, pulling her to a stop. Olivia stumbled and Nate caught her side and brought her to him.

"Where are you going, Olivia?"

"That's John, Luke's brother! I want to stop whatever is going on before it gets worse," she stated it as if he knew what she was talking about.

"Luke? As in ex-Luke from your past? Luke, the one who wouldn't go to New York with you? He has a brother? But why would you care what his brother is doing? And how do you know if that's him if you haven't seen him since you left?"

Olivia flinched on the inside. She wasn't sure how to answer his last question. Hopefully she could dodge it.

"Yes. He has a few brothers, actually. I know his parents wouldn't want to come all the way up here. Come with me and let's see what's going on." She pulled on his hand to follow, but he didn't budge.

Olivia waited for Nate's response. He scrubbed a hand over his face, contemplating what to do. She could tell he was deciding if he wanted to be bothered by what was going on.

Nate sighed deeply and said, "Alright. Let's go. But stay close to me."

Olivia stood on her tiptoes and kissed his lips quickly and turned to go. He wrapped his arm around her back and pulled her tight to his side in a guarded, possessive manner. She grinned down at the sandy beach deck floor, finding it somewhat comforting. Typical Nate.

Nate's grip tightened on her hip as they made their way through the growing crowd. The shouting became increasingly louder as a myriad of colorful curse words were being thrown around.

John forcefully shoved another guy across the floor. The other guy was provoking John, saying something about a girl.

She looked over at John's eyes and saw fury in them. The cocky guy across from John placed his arm around some bleached blonde's shoulders with a smug look. The blonde didn't seem thrilled, but went along with it by wrapping her arm around his waist and placing her fingers into his pocket.

Olivia watched the scene play out.

"What the fuck, Alyssa! What the hell are you doin'?" she heard John yell, his eyes filled with rage. Alyssa, the bleached blonde, just shrugged her shoulders again. Clearly she couldn't care less because she didn't answer. She just laid her head on the other guy's chest while smirking, which fueled John's temper even more.

"Man, you're just like all them other hos, ain't you? Go ahead and fuck around with him. He ain't nothin' but a piece of shit white trash anyway. Just like you," John slurred.

Olivia's mouth dropped in shock over John's language. She saw the hurt in Alyssa's eyes for a split second before it disappeared. Alyssa raised her head up and brought her lips to the guy's cheek for a kiss. But just before she could, he turned his head, grabbed Alyssa by the jaw and kissed her hard. John's breathing got faster as he watched the two lock lips in front of everyone. Olivia couldn't believe what she was seeing. The sweet and innocent John she remembered as a child playing in the lake was now reaching out and grabbing a beer from his friend's hand and slamming it back. He threw the bottle to the floor and began stalking toward the two who had finally come up for air.

Shit... She knew where this was going and had to do something to stop him. Now.

Pushing forward, Olivia parted from Nate and made her way through the crowd. She yelled for John, but he didn't hear her over his own yelling. She reached out to grab for his shirt, but he swatted her hand away and kept walking to where the other guy was waiting for John.

"JOHN!" Olivia yelled and grabbed for him again. He

went to push her away but she held on tighter and yelled his name again until he looked at her. "JOHN! It's Livy. Olivia!" she exclaimed, stumbling into him.

Recognition finally formed in John's green eyes—eyes so similar to Luke's she thought. A sneaky lopsided grin slid across John's baby face as he drawled drunkenly, "Well, hey there, Livy. Whatta ya doin' here?" He placed his arm around her and pulled her snugly to him.

"What's going on, John?"

"Livy…ain't nothin' goin' on here, doll, except for my girl fuckin' around with this low life scumbag…"

"I'm not your girl, Johnny," Olivia heard Alyssa yell. He looked up with eyes thinned into slits and snarled.

"It's *John*! You fuckin'…"

"John! How much have you had to drink tonight?"

John shuffled side to side. "Not much, doll. Coupla' beers."

Yeah, right.

"How about I—"

"Go with it," John whispered and she smelled the vile stench of alcohol on his breath.

"Huh? Go with what?"

"This." John planted a wet kiss on her lips.

Fuck. Fuck. Fuck.

Olivia pushed on his chest trying to pull back. After what seemed like minutes, she finally was able to free herself from his drunken kiss.

"John! How dare you! What the hell?"

John didn't hear her. Instead, he looked over her head at Alyssa and she saw the gleeful revenge dancing in his eyes as he did so.

"Alright, let's go, John. We'll take you home." She took his hand and pulled him from the swarm of people surrounding them. Making her way to the entrance, she looked for Nate every few steps she took.

"You gonna stay if you take me home? Luke's home you know. All he's been doin' is talkin' about you since he saw you. I'm sick of hearing it, to be honest."

Olivia's body tensed. Luke was still home and he'd been talking about her? She prayed Nate hadn't heard what John just said…

As if he could hear her thoughts, she felt a searing glare on the side of her face. Olivia looked over her shoulder and found Nate watching her. His eyes became intensely hot, matching the redness that most likely graced her cheeks.

"Let's go."

"So you're stayin' then? Thank fuck," John drawled.

"Staying where," Nate questioned as he approached, eyeing John.

"Nowhere. I'm going to take John home. So if you could, can you please take me home so I can get my car? It's a long drive to where he lives."

Nate stood silently watching Olivia. "I'll drive you both." She could tell there was a lot more on his mind than just annoyance at ending the date early.

"Who's this guy?" John asked, sizing him up and down.

"Nate."

"Her boyfriend," Nate chimed in.

"My boyfriend."

"Well, well, well…"

"Shut up, John. Let's go. I think you've caused enough trouble for one night. Can't imagine your mother would be happy right now if she knew."

John stopped walking to the truck and pulled back. "What's going on with her? Why did you come over? And don't worry about takin' me home. I can get a ride. Go chill with your boy."

Nate stepped in this time. "Who's going to drive you? I bet all your friends are probably as drunk as you."

John stepped up to Nate, looking as if he was ready for a fight. This was utterly ridiculous and needed to end now.

"John, who would be driving?" Olivia put the emphasis on who.

"Me."

"Oh, hell no, you're not!"

"John, you heard Olivia. We'll take you home."

John snickered at Nate's comment. "Olivia?" he said as if it sounded foreign to him. "Nah, I'm good. I'll see you around, *Livy*."

Reaching for John yet again, she demanded his phone from him. If he wasn't riding with her and Nate, then she'd get him a ride. The problem was, she could only think of one person to call to come out and get him at this time of night. Chills broke out over her skin just thinking about calling him. She didn't want to call, but what choice did she have?

Olivia ignored both John and Nate's stares as she swiped her finger along the phone to look for the number. Her heart battered against her ribs, fingers trembling as she scrolled through his numbers to the letter L. Olivia looked up at John as she found his brother's number. His shoulders relaxed and his eyes danced with mischief as he looked back at her.

As her shaky thumb hovered over the number, Olivia took a deep breath then looked at Nate. He was completely closed off and difficult to gauge.

Olivia pressed send and brought the phone to her ear. The pounding in her chest was making her nauseated and jittery as she waited for the other line to connect. She began pacing back and forth, hiding her face as the line picked up.

"Yeah...what's up, John?"

Good God. His rough voice rolled over her heated skin and she felt it down to her belly. She must have woken him for him to sound so hoarse. Olivia could just imagine him rolling over and reaching for his phone, hair all messy around his face and probably shirtless to boot. A thin sheet barely covering him slowly falling around his perfectly cut stomach, sitting extra low on his waist. Her stomach clenched...

"John?"

Olivia's thoughts were interrupted as Luke cleared his throat.

"Luke." It came out as a soft whisper, which was not her intention.

"Livy... Livy? Is that you? Wait. Who is this?"

"Luke, it's Olivia."

"Livy? What's happening? Why are you calling me from John's phone? Everything okay? Where are you? What's going on?" Luke threw a million and one questions at her before she could even answer the first one. She heard a shuffling in the background, most likely from Luke sitting up in his bed. That roughness in his voice disappeared and now he sounded wide awake.

"Relax, everything is fine. I, ah, happened to run into John tonight up here along the Savannah—"

"Savannah! The fuck..."

"River. To make a long story short, he needs a ride home. I told him we'd take him home but he said no. I didn't know who else to call..."

Luke sighed and asked as calmly as possible, "Jesus H. Christ. Is he okay, though?"

"Oh yes, he's fine. He just had too much to drink tonight. I'm not going to replay it all. I'll let him tell you. Are you able to come and get him?"

Olivia rolled her lip between her teeth. It just dawned on her that Nate and Luke would be meeting face to face. Maybe she needed another rum bucket.

"Yeah, just text me where you're at and I'll jump in the truck. And Livy? Thanks for calling me." Olivia heard shuffling in the background and a faint soft voice before Luke clicked the line dead.

. . .

About an hour later, her past was meeting her present.

Olivia had decided that another rum bucket was not the best idea. She could handle a glass of whiskey, but six different flavors of rum in a sand bucket was enough for one night.

Luke walked up to Olivia like he owned the place. His tired eyes were trained on hers and she felt it to her core. He took one last puff of his cigarette and flicked it ahead of him, stepping on it as he continued walking. His eyes were mostly covered by his hat that was pulled low, but she could still feel them on her. Sand fluttered onto his light colored jeans with each step he took. For rolling out of bed, Luke looked damn good. She may not be in love with him anymore, but she sure wasn't dead either.

Nate wrapped his arm possessively around Olivia's back. He leaned into her ear and whispered, "That's Luke? Your ex, Luke? As in Luke, the country singer, Luke Jackson?"

Shoot. Had she not told him that little tidbit? "Um, yes, that's him."

"And you didn't bother to tell me that he's somewhat of a celebrity here in Georgia? Are you *fucking* kidding, Olivia? What else are you holding back from me?" Nate's amber eyes pierced Olivia with dark suspicion, his deep voice cutting through her angrily. When she didn't reply, his eyes rolled closed and he shook his head at her. Nate was pissed off and knew she screwed up royally by not telling him who Luke was.

Luke stopped in front of them. He shoved his hands in his pockets and said hello to Olivia then looked at Nate curiously.

Olivia cleared her throat. "Hey, Luke."

Luke bobbed his head. "Livy."

"This is Nate."

Nate shook Luke's hand and said, "Hey, man."

"Thanks for coming out, Luke. We told him we'd take him home, but he refused."

"Of course, Livy. He's my brother. Stubborn as fuck and always wanting to rebel. Ah, so where is he now?"

Olivia looked over her shoulder. "He's off sitting in one of the chairs, pissed at me for calling you now that the alcohol has worn off. I could give two shits—"

"Pissed off at you? That's fucking rich," Nate heatedly said. "*I* should be the pissed off one here."

She looked at Nate, embarrassed over his outburst and saw his jaw flex. Oh, he was angry alright, but was it aimed at her or John, or both?

Luke crossed his arms against his chest defensively, his head cocking to the side. "Oh yeah? And why's that, huh?"

"Why's that?" Nate barked back. "Because that little punk ass brother of yours put Olivia in harm's way trying to act like hot shit. Olivia could've gotten hurt when he pushed her. He's lucky—"

"Well, in his defense, he didn't realize it was me," Olivia said quietly, cutting Nate off. She bit down on her lip and looked at Luke whose face had changed to concern, his eyes traveling the length of her body. She could feel Nate's glare scorch the side of her face as he continued. "And then he had the nerve, the nerve to fucking kiss her. He kissed *my* girl in front of a crowd of people."

Luke's lips slowly tipped into a devilish smirk, and for the love of God she didn't want to find his grin incredibly sexy, but she did.

"If he wasn't a kid I would've knocked him the hell out—"

"Knock him out? *Knock him out?*"

Jesus Christ. Two grown men acting like children. Maybe she should have had another rum bucket after all.

"Yeah. That's right. It's too bad Olivia was genuinely concerned about his wellbeing that she attempted to break up a fight *he* was about to start. Someone needs to keep that boy in check. No one touches Olivia but *me*. And no one puts their mouth on Olivia but *me* and they sure as hell don't put Olivia in a situation like that!"

"Is that right?" Luke retorted coldly, slowly drawing out each word as if he was ready to test that theory. Nate tightened his arm around Livy, and that only seemed to taunt Luke more. The air thickened around them and crackled with tension.

But Nate wasn't backing down either. "You got that right." The past and present were about to collide in a matter of seconds, and Olivia's one goal at the moment was to stop it from happening.

"Alright," Olivia said calmly as she stepped in the middle of them. "Luke, get your brother. I don't know what your problem is, but just get John and go."

Luke wasn't sure what his problem was, either. He should've been mad at John, and here he was throwing it at Livy and this Nate guy. He turned and walked toward his truck as a loud whistle carried through the air. "John! Let's ride."

"What the hell was that about?" Olivia demanded from Nate, slamming his truck door loudly.

"You tell me, *Livy*."

Livy... Nate was mocking Luke. Nice.

"Tell you what? What the hell did I do? You're acting as if what happened tonight was my fault!"

Nate started the ignition quickly and drove out of the parking lot, the tires spinning and spitting the gravel.

"Slow it down, Nate."

Scoffing, he said, "Well, for starters, it *is your* fault. You should've just left that kid alone and stayed with me, but you didn't. Then he puts his hands on you, *kisses* you and I find out your ex-boyfriend is a celebrity. Real nice, Liv. Real nice. You fuckin' kept out important shit about your past. How could you not tell me who he is? I knew he did a number on you emotionally from what you told me, but for Christ's sake, *him*? You didn't think you needed to let me know? Oh, and let's not forget the part where you saw him recently. Tell me, when did you have time for that little rendezvous? When? Are you seeing him behind my back!" Nate yelled as he punched the steering wheel twice, his fist springing back. "Fuck!"

Olivia cringed as Nate's voice reverberated within the confines of the truck.

"I never mentioned it because I never thought I'd see him again."

"Olivia, he lives in your hometown. Your small hometown! How did you not think you'd ever run into him again? Are you serious or just deluded?"

"Don't be asinine, Nate."

"Don't tell me how to be. I'm allowed to be whatever the fuck I want to be right now. You purposely withheld that part. Now he's back…or you're back… Are you seeing him? I'm not quite sure and don't know if I can even believe anything that comes out of your mouth right now. How do I know he's not back for you?"

"He's not." *That ship sailed long ago…*

"You don't know that. I saw him look at you. It's how *I* look at you. Shit, he'd be stupid not to go after you. He eyed you like a piece of candy. Did you see him when you went home? Is that why you went back? Were your parents just a cover to see him?"

Olivia rolled her eyes. Nate was being completely ludicrous. "You're jumping to conclusions, Nate. Have I ever given you any reason to doubt me?"

He paused. "Not until tonight. I feel like I don't even know you right now."

"Just stop. You sound absolutely ridiculous and taking it all out of context. You don't know what you're talking about, Nate."

"The fuck I don't! You both have history. And I'm not

stupid. He's a famous country singer with girls chasing after him. Why did you see him?"

Olivia brought her leg up and propped it against the door. "I can't tell you, Nate. Please understand that I'm not hiding anything from you, I just can't tell you. You have to trust me on this."

"You actually expect me to trust you right now?"

"Yes, I do. Again, I ask, have I ever given you a reason to doubt me?"

A cold, unspoken feeling drifted through the air when Nate didn't respond. And for once, she was content with the silence between them. It might only be for a matter of minutes, but she didn't have anything left in her to fight. She was hurt over the fact that Nate suddenly lost his trust in her, but she couldn't tell him about Luke's mother.

"Just take me home, please. I'm done with tonight," she said softly, her head resting against the passenger window.

"No, you're coming to my place tonight."

"I really don't want to. I just want to be alone."

"Too bad. Plus, my place is closer."

Olivia sighed heavily. She was only five minutes from where he lived. "Fine. I'll walk home."

"As if I'd let that happen. Either you're at my place or I'm at yours. That was the plan, and we're finishing this wreck of a date."

twenty-one

past

Drunk. Inebriated. Smashed.

That was the state of mind Luke was in. Drunk as fuck but damn it all to hell, he fucking wanted Livy bad. He leaned against the brick wall in Chase's backyard thinking how much this night had taken a nasty turn. Livy was like a tattoo under his skin. He couldn't even begin to describe the anger or confusion he felt inside after what happened earlier. His chest ached and tightened with each breath. Never had Luke thought Livy would leave Georgia. Leave him.

The heated argument they had. She fucking lied to his face four weeks earlier at the lake. This whole time... This whole time she knew she might be leaving and never said anything to him.

What the fuck? He grabbed another beer, popped it open and downed a long swig while pacing back and forth.

But if he was being honest with himself, there was a part of him happy for her. He always wanted her to have everything. He understood why she wanted out, the shitty childhood she had and all. He wanted to grant every wish

Livy had, and he would if she let him, but this one he refused to. He just couldn't. It wasn't as though he didn't trust Livy. Luke just couldn't deal with the idea of her being so far away from him. What kind of relationship was that? He wanted them to grow closer, not apart. And with her hundreds of miles away, that's exactly what would happen.

What hurt the most was that she hid it all from him. The studying, the test, and the excitement when she received her acceptance letter. Everything. How could she?

Trying to ignore the pressure building in his chest and the need to go to her, Luke kept downing cold ones as he watched Livy with her friends by the fire pit. He hoped that coating his blood in alcohol would help ease the pain of the situation. There was a good possibility she was telling Tessa what an asshole he'd been, and he had been one, but she deserved it. Luke wasn't sorry for what he said or did, and sure as hell wasn't apologizing, either.

They were all chilling at Chase's house tonight, but Luke was so worked up that he separated himself from Livy as much as he could stand. By the look in her eyes and how relaxed her body was in the lawn chair, she'd been drinking too. Possibly as much as him after the bone jarring decision he'd made. He wanted her so bad, even if just to hold her, but couldn't.

With the summer stars against the heated black sky, Luke hadn't been able to take his eyes off Olivia. His need for her only grew as her skin glowed between the flickering blue and orange flames of the fire pit.

Pushing off from the wall, he made his way to the kitchen where he grabbed another beer. He listened for the crisp sound as he cracked it open and took a long chug from it, feeling the iciness slide down the back of his throat. Damn it tasted good. How many beers was he on tonight? Eight? Nine? Twelve? He lost count at this point and sure as fuck didn't care.

Hearing the sound of Livy's voice, Luke glanced over his shoulder and through the handprint covered glass door. She looked so perfect sitting by the fire with her hair cascading over her shoulders as she leaned over, laughing at something Tessa must have said. Her thick waves caught his attention and all he could think about was running his fingers through the softness. On any normal night she'd be sitting on his lap while they chatted with their friends. But not tonight, or ever again.

Fuck.

Luke squeezed his eyes shut as the now familiar ache settled in his chest, one he did not welcome.

Looking through the sliding glass door again, Luke watched as Olivia removed her shoes then grabbed her purse from the ground. She was slightly unsteady as she stood, probably due to the whiskey he was pretty positive she drank liberally.

Assuming Livy was coming into the kitchen for another drink, Luke left the area and made his way around the corner to check the score of the game playing on the television. He was trying his damndest to not be next to her. Olivia was like a flame crawling underneath his skin. He wanted her so bad it hurt. And not because of her looks, but because of her heart, the way she cared about people, her soft eyes, because of her strength over her childhood, what she wanted in life. Between the beer and complete confusion over what he was feeling speeding through him like a freight train, Luke was ready to explode. It didn't help that he wanted her six ways to Sunday right now, either.

When Luke told Livy to stay away earlier, he saw the pained look in her eyes and hated himself for making her feel like that. Or not? He wasn't positive, just so perplexed over everything. He was contradicting what he thought just moments before. It made his head spin. One minute he wanted to take her and fuck her until she screamed his name in pleasure, and the next minute he wanted to walk away from ever knowing her.

Luke tensed when he heard the glass door shut. He clutched his cold beer and stood staring at the television. He hoped she was headed into the kitchen and then back out. Otherwise if she had to use any other room in the small house, she'd have to walk past him.

His neck prickled in awareness as he felt the presence of her in the same room. Turning his head, his cock jumped at the sight of her.

Olivia gasped when her eyes connected with Luke's. Desperately trying to not look at him, she quickly glanced down as she placed one foot in front of the other and walked.

Just as Livy tried to pass him, Luke snaked his hand out and grabbed her by the elbow, pulling her close to him. "Come here, girl," came out in a heavily, slurred drawl.

Yup, she'd been pounding them back too. Good. He could smell it on her breath when she fell into his chest.

Luke stared into Livy's brown eyes. It was obvious she was hurting and he felt like an ass. Her normally deep brown eyes were puffy and red rimmed. Even through his drunken haze, it was evident she'd been crying and he hated it was because of him. Luke loved Olivia. He didn't like seeing her in pain, but he was in pain himself.

"Yeah…" Livy breathed, straightening herself. Luke still had a firm grip on her arm. She stared at his plump lips—lips that could turn from sensual to rough in a second. She wanted so bad to reach up and nibble on the bottom one and suck it into her mouth, but couldn't. Not after how he broke things off between them. Finally, Olivia regained her composure.

"Luke…what do you want?"

Lifting one corner of his mouth into a smirk, Luke let out a small grunt then said, "You."

"Let go of me. You told me to leave you alone. So I am."

Luke tightened his hold on Livy's arm when she tried to yank it away.

"Baby...*my* Livy. Don't play stupid. I want you and you want me. It's okay... You don't have to say it. I just watched you stare at my mouth with hungry eyes. It made me so hard just watchin' you. Damn, what you do to me..." Luke said in a voice as rough as sand paper. He leaned down to inhale her scent and shifted his hips into her. Olivia couldn't move. She was rooted firmly in place knowing what Luke said was the truth.

Stifling a groan, Luke's eyes closed. He tugged on her hand and slid it down to his bulging erection.

"Luke...I thought you said we were done," she breathed as her hand cupped him.

Chuckling, Luke said, "Done with you? Ah, Livy, I'll never be done with you. Can't imagine how that could ever be."

Luke pressed his lips just above Olivia's collarbone, his tongue sneaking out. He opened his mouth and scrapped his teeth across her neck. Olivia drew in a breath as he slowly licked and bit his way up her neck to just below her ear. He tugged her skin into his mouth, sucking deep. He let go with a pop then pulled her earlobe into his mouth.

Olivia let out a strangled breath, a tingly warm hum drizzling down her spine. Damn traitorous body. She was worked up by Luke's words and by his touch. Olivia turned her head into Luke's cheek as he came up, slowly scraping his stubble against her face.

Swiftly, she tried to pull away and continue to the bathroom.

Luke placed his beer on the nearby mantle, grabbed Livy's arm and yanked her around. No way was she getting away from him. He gripped her chin and pulled her to him. He peered down and whispered, "You. Are. Mine." And then he smashed his lips to hers hard.

Luke's fingers dug into her head as he held her close and

pressed harder onto her mouth as he kissed her roughly. She was pushing and shoving against him, yet little did she realize she was rubbing her body along his, igniting him more.

A dangerous concoction of anger, painful arousal, and fury rip roared through his body. Not over Livy fighting him, but because of their future and what they would never have now. He hated that she was leaving him. Luke leaned into her, forcing her to take a step back as she fisted the front of his shirt. They both may be drunk, but he didn't give a fuck. He needed her.

Livy tried not to kiss him back, but it was futile. His lips were always her biggest weakness. She wanted him exactly as he claimed she did.

Coming to her senses somewhat, Livy broke contact and pushed as hard as she could against the solid wall of his chest, shoving him toward the opposite wall. She tried to move out of Luke's reach, but she was unsteady and tripped. He caught her by the waist and quickly pushed her back into the wall. Within seconds, he had her leg up and hooked around his hip as he pushed into her with a smug grin.

Luke's feral eyes were locked on her swollen lips. He pushed down the little strapless dress she was wearing and growled in the back of his throat before he licked his lips and wrapped them around one of her nipples and pulled it into his mouth.

Olivia drew in a breath and moaned Luke's name as he flicked his tongue across her tight nipple and gave it small bites. He was pure temptation. She tried to resist, but her body didn't want to fight. She felt her resolve weakening and her sex growing wet for him. Would it always be like this? The chemistry between them had always been off the charts.

"Oh, God, Luke. We can't...please stop." She quietly moaned and pressed his head into her breast, contradicting her words.

Luke lapped at her rosy, taut nipple like a lollipop then

kissed his way up her chest to look at her. He grinned and kissed her again.

Judging by her tight grip around his neck, she was enjoying it just as much as he was. Luke knew all he had to do was slide her panties to the side and he could sink right into her. She'd take all of him, welcoming him into her heat. He pinched her hardened nipple and said, "You gonna tell me you don't want me now?" Then he shoved against her, biting her lip and rubbing his erection on her clit.

Olivia's heavy lidded eyes were glossy as she looked at Luke, her body a blaze of heat. Her skin was damp as she tried to catch her breath. He was playing with her emotions and she didn't like it. It wasn't fair.

"Fuck. You. Asshole."

"Nah, baby, fuck you," he responded, grinning seductively at her. He pushed on her sex at the words 'fuck you'. Luke went back in for more.

"We can't, Luke. Just stop. Please…"

"We are."

"No."

"Just give in, Livy. I know you want me. I bet if I slip my fingers inside you right now I'll find you wet and wanting. You're not getting away from me tonight. You'll always be mine, Livy. Always."

"No… What… What if someone walks by? We're in the hallway where anyone can see us."

"I got you," he said as he lifted her other leg up and wrapped it around his waist. Olivia placed her arms around his neck and held on. He couldn't wait to have her in his arms again. He nearly sprinted into the bathroom and shut the door with a kick of his foot. Turning, he slammed Livy against the closed door, holding her there with one arm. Her legs tightened around his waist as he quickly undid his jeans with his other hand. He slid them and his boxers down, and then ripped her panties away.

Within seconds, Luke rubbed the tip of his hard cock against her soft folds, sliding up and down then thrusting into her as far as he could go. She took him to the hilt. They both groaned loudly as Livy's tight sex hugged his cock, gripping him hard and adjusting to the tightness.

"Fuck..." Livy grunted, her head falling back against the door.

"Oh, baby...I plan to." Luke groaned. "Damn, you feel so good. Never...felt this good before, baby...different. Can't stop..." He pulled out his cock and pushed back in, a wet suctioning sounded from it. His cock throbbed to the point of pain inside of Livy's welcoming heat. It was incredible being inside of her, he could never get enough. Like he was home.

Livy was thinking the same thing when it dawned on her...

"Luke!" she shrieked in his ear. He stopped abruptly, but didn't pull out. "You're not wearing protection!"

Luke said nothing. He paused for a moment, then his eyes grew heavy as he penetrated her sex again, slowly sliding in and out with his bare cock. He grabbed the back of her thighs hard, digging his fingers into her skin as her clit began to pulse at the touch of each thrust, her heart battering against her chest. It was almost too much to take and she was ready to burst at any minute. Her swollen lips hugged his dick, the tension building higher and didn't want to stop.

"Luke, I'm not on birth control...you don't have a condom."

How she managed to get that out she had no idea. She clutched his arms as her breath heightened. She couldn't stop him. Olivia was too into the feeling of his cock pulsating inside her. She knew this wasn't the brightest of ideas but she couldn't ask him to stop at the same time. She could only muster one thing.

"More. I need more, Luke."

Luke picked up the pace as he pounded into her. Using

the door to help hold her up, Luke moved his hips in circles against her. His legs were aching from holding them both in the same position, but no way was he stopping. Livy's breathing was heavy and erratic and he could smell the whiskey rolling off her lips.

"More. Give me more. I'm so close, Luke."

"We finish together, got it?"

She nodded her head frantically.

Bending down, Luke took her nipple into his mouth once more and bit down. Thrusting in three more times with long and hard strokes he said, "Now."

Livy exploded, milking his cock dry with her inner walls as she convulsed rapidly around him. She yelled out his name, pulling on his hair.

But Luke didn't let up. He kept going and going, prolonging their mutual orgasm. It was like an intense cluster of stars falling into one another and then exploding into more. Luke continued slamming into her, digging his fingers into the backs of her thighs as he hit as deep as he could. Olivia's legs squeezed his hips from the powerful orgasm that racked her body.

Needing to muffle her moans, Luke slanted his mouth over hers and kissed her deeply. He pushed as if he was trying to climb inside of her…and maybe he was.

When he finally let go, he whispered against her mouth, "I…love you, Livy. My…Livy."

At the sound of Luke's affection, she squeezed him with the walls of her sex and held him to her as tight as she could.

twenty-two

Lying back on her bed, Olivia threw her arm over her eyes. A single tear dripped from the crease of her eye that she fought so hard to hold in. She placed her hand on her hollow chest and fingered the heart necklace Luke had given her.

"Hmm...I couldn't tear my eyes from it. I was going to walk away, I really tried, but the diamonds caught the light and flickered brilliantly. It's perfect and beautiful just the way it is. It made me think of you. The center is empty, but when it's around your neck it's full, because you've filled it. It's my heart that you've captured and if you're going to hold on to it, I want you to wear it around your neck…so it's next to your heart."

A month had passed since the ugly fight and the night of drunken sex with Luke. Those days had been the longest days of her life. No sleeping, and if she did, she'd wake up shortly after. Too much was on her mind to fall into a peaceful slumber. Her mind raced back and forth at night, running with different paths she could take. In the end, each street led to the same destination: a future without Luke.

After that night at the backyard bonfire, Luke wouldn't answer her calls. He completely ignored any conversation she tried to start with him. He closed himself off from her completely, except when she asked about his mother.

Finally, one night at Ash's house Olivia was able to corner him. The fact that he'd been drinking heavily might have worked in her favor. They say the truth comes out when drunk and Luke said a lot that night.

Finding the courage she needed, Olivia spotted Luke standing off to the side and walked over to him. She gazed up and into his eyes, eyes that were now empty and raw. Lately, she'd heard from friends that he was hitting the bottle harder. Truthfully, whiskey was her best friend at the moment so she knew what it felt like. Despair. Emptiness. Loss.

Her heart pounded as she took a chance and made a move. She stepped closer and slipped her small hand under his shirt. She needed to feel her skin on his. She needed his heat, his warmth, his love. Putting her lips to his mouth, she kissed him.

Only for Luke to grab her wrist and stop her immediately.

"What do you think you're doing, Livy?" he asked in a languid drawl.

Stunned, Olivia's mouth dropped open and her eyes bloomed. The white rings of her eyes were stark against the rich brown that Luke almost lost himself in them.

"You think you can just come on over to me and act as if it's okay now? Well, it's not. Don't think you can have me and then leave. You want me again? Fine. You can have me whenever you want. I told you this, but you gotta stay in Georgia with me. I'm not goin' to be your booty call 'cause you're drunk. So don't even try and tempt me with that sexy little body or that mouth. Not goin' to happen." Luke eyed her entire body with a heated gaze.

Olivia's breath caught in her throat. The jolt of pain from his words stabbed her chest and she could hardly breathe. Luke still had her hand in his grip. He began rubbing the center of her palm in soft circles. Bringing it to his mouth, he kissed her fingers.

Luke's tone completely switched, his eyes softening as he continued speaking to her, "Stay with me, Livy. Don't leave, please. I need you...

want you. I'm asking you not to do this. Don't tear us apart." Luke pleaded with heartbreakingly sad eyes and voice to match. Just for a moment, Luke unmasked his emotions for her to see the depth of pain he was in, how raw he was inside. It hit her full force. She was going through the same emotions. Olivia wanted so badly to stay, but couldn't. She needed to do this for herself...that's what she kept saying over and over again in her head.

Softly she replied, her voice cracking with her heart, "I...can't."

Luke straightened his back and stood to his full height, dropping her hand. "Then it's done. Get outta my face. I want you...fuck, probably always will want you, but I can't do this," he sneered quietly, only for her to hear. "I can't be with you without you being next to me in the flesh. I want to be able to reach out and touch you when I want. I want to hold you next to me at night, not have you hundreds of miles away. I want to kiss you when I want. Be able to pick you up and go for a drive. It's not the same and you know it. None of that could happen with you so far away. So go. Leave. This is our goodbye. I hope you think of me every damn day and regret leaving. You won't ever find what we have with anyone else. What we have is real and it only happens once in a lifetime. Remember that. I'm not afraid to say it. You're it for me, Livy, but obviously I'm not it for you. So I hope you dream of us, that you wake thinking of me and wishing you could go back but knowing you never can. This is all on you, baby. Have a nice life. I'm out."

Tears filled her eyes as he used his hand to wave her away, dismissing her, but it was his words that cut the deepest.

The heartache and the suffering Olivia dealt with over the past couple of weeks ripped her apart. It was a slow torture of deep, invisible slices that were rubbed down with salt whenever she thought about Luke. Each memory tore through her, exposing her heart and slicing her body open on a daily basis that she worried would never heal at the seams properly. And if they did? Well then they'd never look the same. From the outside there would never be a single solitary scratch, but inside she'd bear the marks of a broken heart because of a decision she made. She should have told him from the beginning. It was like a rusty knife slowly slicing inch by inch through her heart and down into her stomach. Olivia was a mess and she only had herself to blame. She couldn't think straight and couldn't sleep. Even eating had become a problem. She had completely lost her appetite, her stomach rebelling against almost anything she tried to eat.

Letting out a heart-wrenching sigh, Olivia sat up and ran her fingers through her tangled hair, or at least tried to. She hadn't brushed it in days and quite frankly she didn't see a reason to. She no longer had Luke, and she had hardly left the house lately unless it was absolutely necessary.

One more day was what she kept mouthing as she made her way into the bathroom. Tomorrow she would say goodbye to Georgia and hello to New York. It's what she wanted, right?

Olivia looked in the bathroom mirror and didn't recognize the person staring back. Her dark eyes stared back looking hollow and lifeless. There were blue-black circles under them showing her lack of sleep and stress. She looked like death, and truthfully, it was an apt description for how she felt. Olivia's usual full-bodied wavy hair was lank and lifeless, a perfect definition of a rat's nest. She needed to get her ass into gear but how could she when she felt like her whole life had been sucked from her?

Stripping off her clothes, Olivia peered down at her body and saw the change that had taken place since that painful night. Her stomach was starting to become concave from the lack of interest in food. Interestingly, it was how her heart felt too. She could start to see her hip bones beginning to make an appearance and her legs were thinner as well. Olivia turned the shower on and waited for the water to heat up. In her entire life, the shower was the one place she allowed herself to cry. She detested when anyone would see her shed tears because then questions would be asked, and she hated discussing her feelings.

After finishing in the shower, Olivia towel dried her hair and walked to her closet. She slipped on a hunter green dress that normally clung to her body but now hung loosely.

Picking up the phone, Olivia dialed Luke's number again. This was the last time she was calling him. She knew he was upset and didn't want to speak with her, but was he really not going to say goodbye to her? Would he just let her leave like that?

Pick up, pick up, pick up, Olivia chanted quietly. But when his voicemail chimed, she knew that was the end of the road. She didn't want to leave a message but she couldn't help herself.

"Luke..." her voiced cracked, "I just wanted to say goodbye. I wish things didn't have to end the way they did. But know that you'll always have a place in my heart. I never meant to hurt you or lie. I swear. Take care. I'll miss you so much."

Another tear rolled down her cheek sliding into her mouth. Tasting the salty wetness, she deflated even more.

The roaring sound of an engine echoed outside her bedroom window. Olivia looked out her window and was astonished to see Luke's truck driving up toward her house. She was mentally exhausted and had to be delusional at this point because it couldn't possibly be him, right? Any minute she was ready to watch the truck reverse out.

But it didn't.

Olivia watched as Luke's truck slowly rolled to a stop just a few feet back on the red dirt driveway of her home. She couldn't believe her eyes and waited to see his next move. He sat in his truck for a moment before opening his door and stepping out. His head was angled downward while he walked around to the front of his truck. He leaned against it and crossed his legs in front of him, shoving his hands into his pockets.

Finally, in what felt like centuries, Luke glanced up toward Olivia's window and silently acknowledged her with a nod.

He was here to see her go.

Her heart dropped into the pit of her stomach.

Turning away from the window, Olivia ran out of her room. She sprinted down the hallway and flew down the stairs. She was going so fast that she tripped over her feet on the last few steps and hit the floor. Taking a deep breath, she regained self-control. Right before opening the front door, she glanced into the mirror hanging next to it. "At least I took a shower," she said to the emotional mess staring back at her.

Opening the door, the humidity hit Olivia in the face immediately. Luke's name was a whisper on her lips. She could already feel her eyes beginning to water while her chin gave a small quiver. She ground her jaw in an effort to stop her emotions from taking hold of her.

Suck it up, don't cry.

She shut the door behind her, making her way down the driveway to Luke. The entrance to her home and the surrounding land was covered in large bushy trees throughout and gave a decent amount of shade from the heat, not that she would even feel it. She had been pretty much oblivious to everything around her the last couple of weeks. The normally bright blue sky was swathed in miserably gray clouds of melancholy, mimicking her mood. The air was moist and dewy with a chill. A storm was about to rain down on them, she could feel it in the air.

Olivia's heart pounded like a jack hammer going off inside her chest. A burning sensation danced its way up her spine, around her neck and outward. Her ears began to heat, and the back of her neck was clammy and tense. She felt so unprepared for this meet with Luke, but truthfully, there was no amount of preparation for a moment like this. Olivia didn't know what to say and was completely at a loss on how to act. Luke had been her best friend, confidant, her shoulder to lean on, her everything for years. He gave her security when she felt lost. Even before they started dating he had always been there, she just hadn't yet opened her eyes to notice him early enough. Now she felt so distant, like she was a stranger to him. She hated it. Hated the circumstances because she knew what was coming and how it was ending.

Olivia stopped just steps from Luke. She wanted nothing more than to reach out and grab him. Her heart ached for his touch.

Luke hadn't moved a muscle or even shuffled a step from his position. He stood stone cold and waited for her to go to him, like saying this is as far as I'm going, as much as I'm willing to give. Time stood still.

Lifting his head and tilting it to the side, Luke's jaw was locked and his lips in a firm, grim line. There was no mistaking his eyes now. Even with the hat pulled low, his green eyes blazed as they shot through her.

"Hey," she said softly.

"Yeah," Luke responded briskly. "Got your message, ah messages. I wasn't going to stop by... Not sure how I ended up here." Luke shrugged, his eyes still trained on her.

Olivia didn't know what to say. Were there any right words now? Probably not at this point.

He cleared his throat. "So you're leaving today, huh?" he said uncomfortably, moving his head in small bobs before finishing the question. He couldn't even look at her.

"Um, I'm leaving tomorrow, actually."

Unable to stop herself, Olivia stepped forward to close the distance between them, but before she could take another step, Luke's hand shot from his pocket flying up to stop her. Her breath caught in her throat and her stomach tightened. All she wanted to do was wrap her arms around Luke but he clearly wanted nothing from her.

Just kill me now.

"Don't. Can't be held responsible for my actions if you

come closer..." he muttered. "Have you been eating? You're looking way too damn thin," he stated, eyeing her up and down. She was withering down to almost nothing. Luke noticed the heart necklace lying around her neck and instantly felt like an ass for giving it to her. He had opened himself up to her that night, probably more than he ever had and now she was leaving.

"How about getting rest? You got black circles under your eyes too, Care…"

Don't hold back, she pleaded internally. *Care Bear*. He was going to call her Care Bear but stopped. Her chest ached and she could hardly catch her breath. Shit, this was killing her.

Self-consciously, she tucked a strand of hair behind her ear and wrapped her arms around her waist. She hadn't been able to eat or to sleep. Depression had taken over rapidly and she lost her appetite.

Looking at the ground for a moment to collect her thoughts, she ignored his questions. In a delicately soft tone she said, "Heard you've been around the bars lately, drunk as all hell and stumbling out. I heard you were playing your guitar for some girls…even singing to them. Is... Is it true?"

Just uttering those words had her eyes watering. She was nearly destroyed when she heard the latest news about Luke and didn't want to believe it could be true. But when it happened night after night and from multiple witnesses? Yeah, talk about dying a slow death. Had he moved on so quickly?

The tips of Luke's lips curled just a fraction.

"Doesn't matter what I do now, does it? You know how small towns are, word travels fast and shit gets turned around and taken out of context. But that's another reason why you gotta leave, right? Why you need to up and go?" Luke pointedly accused her.

Olivia shuffled from one foot to the other. "Luke, it's not like that…"

"I didn't come here to argue with you, Livy. Just came to say goodbye and good luck. I hope it's everything you want and that you'll have a good life."

"Come with me."

"I'm not leaving my family to be a city boy and play in the snow, honey," he said in a sharp drawl. "That's not me, it'll never be me. I know what I want and who I am, and that's to be here." He finished jabbing his thumb at his chest. Luke pushed off the truck. "So yeah. Hope it's what you want."

"What I want is you, you know this. Why can't we try a long distance relationship? I don't understand. Why are you so adamant against trying to work through this? People do it everywhere!"

"You must not want me bad enough for you to leave," he snapped angrily. "You must not want us. I would never think of leaving without talking about it with you first. Guess in the end I wanted you more than you wanted me."

Nearly compressed of all air, she could not believe Luke's words. The ache in her chest tightened. "You know that's not true. Why do I have to choose? That isn't fair, Luke." Olivia's voice was rising with each sentence. "I would never make you choose!"

"Oh, but you are, baby girl, you are," he countered with a sly sneer. "You're making me pick between my family and you. Now is that fair, eh?"

Upset and beside herself with a heavy heart, Olivia was enraged. Her heart battered against her ribs, the skin of her fingers tightening as she fisted her hands, every nerve ending in her body standing on edge. It didn't have to come to this. Luke was testing her self-control, but with every right. Even if he felt a minuscule amount of sorrow for what she was going through, surely he wouldn't act so cynical? Right?

She couldn't take it anymore. Olivia was dealing with such a hefty amount of emotional grief that she propelled herself forward, shoving Luke as hard as she could in the chest.

Momentarily stunned, he fell into the front of his truck while she pushed and shoved and beat on his chest with her hands repeatedly. The truck dug into his back as tears of agony, pent up misery from the last month, started to run freely from the corners of her eyes as she called him every name in the book she could think of. Olivia kept pushing and shoving Luke with all her might, taking her frustration and pain out on him. His body was her punching bag and he allowed it as she fought angrily over her decision to leave, his refusal to go with her and that they couldn't come to a compromise. She wanted to fall to the ground and cry her eyes out knowing this was the end. That after this day it was over for them. Silently she prayed he'd do something, anything, to make it okay for what she was doing, but he didn't. Luke was letting her take her aggression out on him instead of batting her hands away. Fragments of her name were being called out, yelling for her to calm down, but it didn't register. She wasn't letting up just yet and he knew it.

Hot tears streamed down her cheeks and her nose turned a pinkish-red from crying. Olivia's dry lips pulled tight as her heart came through her eyes in waves, but she didn't care. Her hair flew around and stuck to her tear soaked face as she cried and beat against Luke. She reared back to slap Luke across the face, but Olivia's foot slipped on the dirt and Luke reached for her instantly, pulling her small frame into his torso.

"Stop. Get your hands off me." Olivia resisted as he gripped her body. She was aligned with his chest and refused to pick her head up.

"Livy. Relax—" he said as he gripped her arms tighter.

"Screw you! It doesn't have to be like this! It doesn't have to be like this! You're not even giving us a chance," she sputtered between angry tears, her head lulling back, crying her heart out.

Luke hated to see her in pain, but he was in pain himself. Reaching down, he grabbed her chin in his hand while the other one tightened on her arm. In a moment of weakness, Luke pressed his mouth to hers and kissed her hard. He needed to feel her. How could he be with her but not kiss her when he wanted to? It would never work. Olivia tried to push away, but Luke held tight, not letting her go.

Luke had her locked in now.

Within seconds Olivia caved and allowed Luke to take over her mouth. As soon as their tongues collided, they groaned into each other's mouths. She grabbed for the top of Luke's shirt, fisting it in her hands and pulling him to her with all her might. It had been weeks of no touching and no kissing. How was she supposed to survive in New York without his touch?

Luke loosened his hold just enough to slide his hands up and wrap them around the sides of her neck, locking her in as he kissed her with every ounce he could muster. His thumbs grazed her jaw as he lapped at her lips, putting everything into the kiss, knowing this was the end for them. That after today, Olivia King would no longer be his to hold, his to kiss, his to sing to when she was dealing with too much and needed to be calmed down. He wouldn't be the one she confided in who could relax her with the touch of his hand or a melody.

Olivia moaned in response when he suckled her tongue, throwing her arms around his neck and holding him in a death grip. She thrust her hips into his groin; the hardness she felt couldn't go unnoticed. Luke was just as aroused as she, yet he was denying them, even though his body screamed otherwise. She began slowly grinding against his pelvis and it was his turn to groan into her mouth as they continued to nearly bruise each other's lips. Luke slid his hands into her hair and roughly worked her scalp as they fought for each other with their mouths. And in a way they were. They were fighting for one another, but both just being stubborn.

Olivia slid her hand down his rapidly panting chest, past his stomach and over his pants to the outline of his shaft. She stroked him through his jeans from base to tip, squeezing at the tip each time. A growl erupted from his throat and he thrust his hips into her hand then fisted her hair. Olivia stood on her tiptoes, lifted her leg up and draped it around the back of Luke's leg trying to bring her sex into line with his, needing to get as close to him as she could. Sweet pains of desperation sliced up her belly and straight into her hammering heart. She wanted Luke so bad she could hardly stand it. And if this was the last time they were going to be together, then so be it.

Luke reached down and pulled her other leg higher, lifting her off the ground as he spun her around to place her on the hood of his truck.

A deep roar of thunder ripped across the clouded gray sky in the background, but did not register in Olivia's mind. She was too preoccupied with Luke's body so close to hers and his sinfully wicked mouth that it was all she could think about. They were together in this moment and that's all that mattered. Nothing else.

Olivia felt as if she was in the eye of a hurricane. The past couple of weeks had hacked through and roughed her up pretty badly. And now the hurricane was at a standstill, the eye, that intense serenity and eerie calm that she knew would pick back up eventually and tear through once more, damaging her irrevocably, leaving behind a slow and raw ache. And just like with a hurricane, she would rebuild in time, but the inside would never, ever, be the same, no matter how hard she'd pound those nails in to secure the seams back together.

In that moment, Olivia despised herself for the decision she had made. She wished she had never applied to medical school so far away or even contemplated leaving Georgia. How was she going to get by without Luke?

Salty tears slid down her cheek and into their joined mouths as Luke made love to her with his tongue. "Luke," she said, sucking in air between gasps.

"Shhh, Livy."

"Please," she breathed. "Make love to me."

"Stay with me. What we have is good."

Olivia fractured inside. She let out a huge gush of air that might be mistaken for pleasure, but was most definitely not. It was the sound of sweet suffering and pure agony. She squeezed her eyes shut and felt her mouth form a frown.

"Please," she pleaded sadly. She needed to feel him.

Olivia needed Luke. Not just for the sex, but for the closeness she had always felt between them, that special connection, that feeling only two people who are meant to connect feel. She sucked in her bottom lip and rolled it between her teeth.

Pulling back, Luke's gaze bore into hers. "Stay with me and I'll make love to you every day for the rest of our lives. Don't leave like this, Livy."

Olivia was breaking. Her legs loosened their hold on him. She didn't want to let go, but she had to. She pushed at his chest to move him off of her, feeling the rejection from deep inside as another round of thunder rumbled across the darkening sky.

"Please."

"Uh uh... Can't. We're outside, Livy, for fuck's sake."

He was refusing her, making her feel even worse. Like shit. Her legs skated down and behind his thighs. She was weak. Luke's mouth never moved from her neck as she attempted to create space between them. She pushed him away when what she really wanted to do was pull him closer and never let go. But she wasn't getting very far with Luke's tongue and body touching hers. She was past the point of quivering in arousal.

Luke stopped kissing her neck, raised his head and looked deep into her eyes. He slapped his hand down on the hood of his truck hard, jarring Olivia and making her jump. The banging sound of his hand slapping the hood nearly scared the life out of her. This wasn't a side she'd ever seen before from him. There was no mistaking the raw passion and fervor in his crazed green eyes. Olivia was motionless, stunned. Just as he made his move, the clouds parted and the skies opened up above them.

"Hold on," he grunted. "Put your arms around my neck." She did without hesitation. He lifted her by the underside of her thighs and carried her around his truck. The rain was coming down so hard that puddles were forming in the dirt driveway quickly. Climbing into his truck, he laid Olivia onto the seat. Luke slammed the door and looked at her. Heart and emotions slipped from her bloodshot eyes as she exposed how she truly felt inside.

"Get up," he ordered.

Luke sat back against the leather seat and reached for her. She went willingly to him as he grabbed a hold of her slimming hips, lifting her to straddle his waist. He lifted her dress out of the way and grabbed a hold of her ass. His legs widened as she sat down on him, feeling for that right spot. She went to reach up to put her hands on him but Luke stopped her. Olivia looked into his fiery eyes and felt her throat climb into her mouth. He was stopping her, again.

Grabbing both wrists, Luke placed them behind her back and immobilized her. He pressed on her lower back with their hands clamped together, shoving her sex into his cock. Olivia's eyes fluttered shut and she felt her body loosening up. She hated how he was purposely provoking her. She was at war with her body, didn't want to take it, but couldn't refuse it.

Luke leaned forward and ran his tongue along the mounds of her breasts, lingering over her collarbone and then up her neck. Olivia whimpered and rocked into him. Turning her head, she found his mouth and nudged at his lips with hers only for him to rear back. He wouldn't even let her kiss him. She struggled to release her hands from Luke's tight grip, but he wouldn't budge. Olivia was on the edge of release with the way Luke was manhandling her. He'd never been this hard on her before, but by god, she loved it. The flame that had been ignited by Luke's erotic kissing began to burn deep between her legs. Luke was her fire, but would eventually ruin her too.

Olivia gently pushed into his face with hers, forcing his head back into the headrest. He wasn't expecting it and she was able to wiggle one arm free and quickly reached for his cock. Luke's jaw was wired tight as she stroked up and down through his jeans again. He released her other arm and Olivia started to work his button. She rose up and pulled his neck into her mouth at the same time, flattening her tongue against his skin and licked, something that he loved for her to do. It was like his kryptonite and she was using it to her advantage.

Olivia managed to unbutton and slide the zipper down. He grabbed her hips in a bruising grip, freezing her in motion and she panicked thinking he'd stopped her once again.

"Livy," he moaned lazily.

"Yeah."

Luke didn't respond, just moaned her name again. She knew he wasn't going to ask for it, his pride kept him from doing so. He was hurt. She knew Luke like the back of her hand, so she took matters into her own.

"Lift up and help me," she said.

Olivia rose up on her knees and went for his waistband. His hands met hers and they pulled down his jeans and boxers. His erection sprung free but then became sandwiched between them when she sat back down on his lap. She grabbed Luke's face and kissed him, feeling the heat coming from his dick as it twitched against the thin layering of her wet panties. He lifted the hem of her dress again and slid his hands up her smooth thighs to the crease of her hip, rolling his hip toward her. His fingers ran along the seam of her panties, a low moan rumbling through Olivia's body. With one hard tug, Luke ripped her panties in two then slipped his fingers into her wet sex. Olivia was on fire, panting into him. The truck's air was stuffy, thick with tension as desire swirled much like Olivia's blood while it continued to rain outside. Luke stroked Livy's wet folds with two fingers back and forth, closing her eyes from the pleasure of his fingers on her and rocking into his hand.

"Look at me," he grounded out. Livy's head snapped up and her brown eyes met his wild, untamed ones.

"Stay with me. This is the last time I'm askin' you," he said then as he slid a finger along the seams of her wetness as his eyes bore into hers. Slowly building pressure on her clit, Luke rubbed in circles as she rotated her hips on his fingers.

At his pleading, her chin quivered knowing the one answer he wanted she couldn't give.

"Hold still."

A finger teasingly hovered over her entrance before he pushed inside fast and stopped once it was as far as it could reach. A smoky sigh escaped Olivia's lips. Luke slowly pulled his finger out and rubbed her clit in circles to the point where it was just enough to stimulate her but not enough to push her over the edge. He was tormenting her purposely.

Two can play at this game.

Olivia reached down and rubbed her hand along her sex, coating her palm with herself. The feral look in his eyes spoke volumes. His chest rose quickly, revved up and ready to take control in a matter of seconds. Grasping his length, she stroked Luke with her wetness from tip to base. She repeated the motion, her hand hitting a trail of hairs on his mound. Olivia wrapped her hand around the swollen head of his shaft and squeezed, stroking up and down so she could slide right on him.

Luke groaned loudly, not hiding his own gratification.

"Fuck, Livy. What are you doing to me?" Luke groaned somewhere between gratification and despair. She pushed up and onto her knees and bent forward, pressing her breasts into his chest.

But she wouldn't slide down onto him.

No.

It was a power struggle of wills. She wanted him to want it every bit as much as she did.

Olivia hovered above him as he looked at her, expecting her to make the next move. Leisurely, she grazed the tip of his plump crown with her warm silky smooth folds. Their eyes never left each other. She sucked in her bottom lip and rolled it between her teeth as they waited in unspoken tension. Knowing Luke was wild with desire only made her decision to wait that much better. She needed him to take her, not the other way around.

Finally, in what felt like an eternity, he grabbed her hips and aligned her entrance up with his cock. He squeezed her pelvic bones in a painfully tight grip and then shoved her down over his raging hard cock, taking her all the way. They both yelled out so loud that she was thankful for the pounding rain bouncing off the hood of his truck that masked the sound of them. Without delay, Olivia immediately started a steady rhythm. She slid up and down, so wet and slippery that it caused a delicious fiery friction. It was sexy and it was electric. She grounded down on his dick, her clit pressing down on his mound each time. Her breath heightened with each pressing second and it sent chills down her spine. Olivia's stomach clenched and she could feel the walls of her sex tighten around his cock, soaking up every inch of him. Luke yelled something inaudible as he palmed her breasts and pinched her nipple through her dress while his other hand slid over her rear, dancing dangerously low. The tips of his fingers grazed the wetness produced by them as one and he nearly lost it.

Luke placed both hands on her hips and started a fast but steady dance of heady sex.

The games were over.

"Yes... More."

He didn't stop. Luke just kept driving himself into her, pounding into her sex, a slippery suction that pushed her even closer over the edge.

"Don't stop," she panted.

"Not even if I wanted to could I stop fuckin' you," he drawled.

Shit. She was close. So. Fucking. Close. "Close...so close."

Luke groaned, "Come with me."

So weak. Olivia was so weak that she was actually happy Luke had taken control. Her heated body was like hot molten lava as he fucked her roughly, but she loved every minute of it. Her skin was on fire, moist with perspiration. She started to pulse and squeeze around him in an attempt to find release.

"I don't want...to come yet. I want...it...to last."

Luke clutched her neck, his arm wrapping around her waist and shoving her down on his enlarged cock as he thrust desperately inside of her. She was trapped, unable to move as his cock plunged into her with short, hard stokes. It was the best of both worlds for her. He was as deep as he could go and hitting her clit.

"Ahh..." she moaned.

Olivia's plump lips coated him once more as she felt herself beginning to spasm.

"Now. Come with me now," he said through clenched teeth.

Olivia reached for the back of his head, seized his damp neck and bit down on Luke's lips as they came together in a blissful, mind blowing orgasm. It rippled across her skin, pouring through her in sweet rapture. Her nails dug into his shoulder as Luke ate at her mouth with a vengeance, moaning and sighing in between breaths. The kiss only heightened the orgasm that hadn't yet died down as they rode each other's ecstasy.

They were as close as they could possibly ever be in that moment.

twenty-three

present

"I'm sorry," Nate murmured from behind. He wrapped his arms around Olivia's waist and leaned into her. "I was a dick last night."

She could feel the rise and fall of his breathing against her back.

"You got that right."

After a restless night, she finally decided to get up and cook them breakfast. Olivia was still upset from what had happened at the bar between Nate and Luke.

"I'm a bit of a hothead who's dating a smart and beautiful woman. Liv, I get jealous when some guy kisses you. What guy wouldn't get upset? Then your ex shows up? And yeah, I nearly lost it. You have no idea how hard it was to rein it in. I wanted to kick his ass. I wanted to beat him within an inch of his life, but I didn't." Olivia tensed. "I didn't because of who he was to you. Now had it been anyone else…" Nate wrapped his arms around Olivia and held her tightly from behind.

"But, Nate, when have I ever given you a reason not to trust me?" she asked softly. Olivia was still upset.

"You haven't and I'm sorry, Olivia. I admit I was wrong to jump to conclusions. I just…"

"Just what," she said as she turned off the water.

Olivia felt Nate take a deep breath and then said the last thing she was expecting to hear.

"That I'm falling hard for you. The kind of falling where the words 'I love you' usually follow soon after, Liv."

Olivia was stunned. Unable to think…move…speak.

"Nate."

"You don't have to say anything," his baritone voice washed over her skin. "In fact, I didn't realize it until last night. Lying in bed next to you, with you curled up away from me, I felt like shit over our argument. I wanted nothing more than to reach out and hold you, but I knew you didn't want it so I backed off. Last night was supposed to be us ending the night with you in my arms, like usual. Waking up next to you is something I love doing more than you can imagine. I didn't like going to bed with you mad at me, and last night it killed me, Liv. I've fallen harder than I realized." Nate brushed away her hair from her nape and tenderly kissed her, his stubble scraping her neck.

"I'm sorry for the way I acted." Nate inhaled deeply and wound his arms tightly around her, pulling her back to his chest. She tried to turn around but couldn't.

"Loosen up for me, Nate."

"No. I can't even look at you right now. I'm embarrassed of how I acted."

"Nate, I swear I'm not going behind your back with Luke, but you have to trust me on this one and the reason I can't tell you why I saw him."

"I know you're not. You haven't given me a reason to doubt you. I do trust you. I was just completely blindsided by Luke showing up, his brother kissing you and hearing you saw him. But if you're asking me to trust you on this one, I will. I have no choice not to trust you.

"I want you, Liv. I have from the moment you came into the exam room looking overwhelmed. Something about you draws me in, but it's more than being gorgeous, though." Nate's deep voice sent shivers throughout her body. "You're different and I'd be stupid to let you get away from me. It's why I pushed so hard for you, why I didn't give up. And you know what? I don't think you want me to stop. I think you want me to push to see where this can go, but you're still holding back. I can feel it and I can see it in your face. You're still questioning 'us'. Let go. Fuck the rules and live. Live with me. Feel the moment with me."

Goodness, why did he have to go there? Why did Nate have to go and lay it on the line like that? Olivia had been so good at keeping the walls to her emotions solid and only lowering them to breathe. What he just said was so honest. Real. She was on the verge of tears, her chest contracting as she desperately fought to hold them in. Every minute with him, he pushed past the barriers she had erected over time.

Looking into the sink full of soap suds, a nervous tick in her knee caused her to bounce. Olivia wanted to give in, she did, but she was so scared of getting hurt again. Was the possible heartbreak worth what they had right now?

"Olivia," Nate whispered near the nape of her neck. His voice was rough and his breathing hitched. He moved his hand from the counter and placed it on her hip, asking for more. The heat from his hand flamed her skin as it glided along her belly, bringing her closer to him.

"Please," he pleaded and pressed his hips into her.

Squeezing her eyes shut from the sting of tears, she relaxed into Nate, answering his question with her softened body. Olivia could feel the heat pouring off of him as she burned for Nate. She turned her head to the left, moved it against his chest and inhaled his heady scent as it drifted over her, overwhelming her senses. His other hand grazed her jaw, his rough fingers helping guide her head up to his.

As she followed the movement of his hand, Olivia opened her eyes. Nate was so close she could see the black hairs along his square jaw. His eyes. His eyes always got to her. They were shooting to the center of her body, full of crazed passion and intensity. Her eyes fastened on lips she wanted to taste as Nate's hand circled her stomach, his fingers creating a steady ache below while they stood there waiting for time to fast forward.

Nate had asked, and she'd given a partial answer. Now was time to deliver.

Standing on her toes, Olivia closed the distance with her mouth. She pressed her lips to his. It was an odd angle, but she made it work. Nate hadn't moved his mouth at the touch of her lips, but his hand continued running in circles across her stomach, increasing the friction between them. She pushed harder with her mouth and he responded only just a bit.

When Nate didn't respond like she thought he would, Olivia second guessed herself and pulled her mouth back to get a good look at him, but he pressed on her stomach with the heel of his palm in an effort to bring her back. She knew what he was doing. The press of his hand was saying she needed to make the effort now.

Nate was dropping his guard and letting her see what he truly felt. It was written all over his brazen body, his face a cast of smooth sensuality. Olivia realized he was putting it on her, that it was for her to decide on the next step. It was a daring decision, one she still was nervous to take. She knew Nate was waiting for her to say yes, that she wanted to screw it all and be with him. Olivia knew what she needed to do. What's life without taking a chance, right?

The next move in the game was hers to take.

Turning around was her answer, because Nate said, "Nate-4, Olivia-0." Then he smirked and she shoved her mouth onto his.

Nate's calloused hands slid down her backside and over her hips, his fingers leaving a trail of heat she felt down to her core. Growling, Nate thrust his hips into hers, his hard erection strained against her belly. His hands traveled down to the back of her thighs and he squeezed.

"Hold on, darlin'," he ordered against her mouth and picked her up, placing her on the edge of the counter. He moved between her legs so that their sex aligned perfectly. Olivia sighed, wrapping her legs around Nate's waist and locking her ankles in a tight hold.

Olivia's body was on fire and trembling with need. Nate's hands didn't stop moving over her, working her into a frenzy of desire. Their tongues moved, biting and nipping, sucking and stroking until they were panting and struggling to breathe.

"Nate," she whimpered.

"What do you want? Tell me," he replied in between kisses.

"Please, Nate… Please…" she trailed off, silently wishing he could read her mind. Nate broke the kiss and grabbed her face between his hands. He looked straight into her eyes and said with a firm, deep drawl, "What do you want, Liv? You have to say it, baby."

Olivia's breathing became more and more labored. What did she want? Did she even know?

As if he knew, Nate pushed forward and grinded against her hips. Olivia's head drifted back from the pure erotic delight she felt. He swiftly moved his hand from her jaw to bring her upright.

"Say it," he demanded.

Licking her lips, "You. I want you. Happy? You *know* I want you."

A shit eating grin stretched over Nate's handsome face and his eyes lit up with hunger. The need was there before, but it was as if a cloak unveiled his desire at her words. He was so incredibly sexy that her breath caught in her throat. Nate smashed his face down and kissed her deeply, consuming every inch of her mouth. He slid his hands under her ass, cupping her rounds to him as he thrust against her again.

"We need my bed. I'm going to make love to you for the first time, and it sure as hell won't be against a wall or on a sink," Nate said, breaking the contact to mutter against her lips. "I want to do it right."

"Okay," she breathed into him.

Olivia squeezed him with her legs while his rough fingers danced along the bottom of her ass. She felt herself grow wet even more from his touch and her belly flipped.

Shoving the door open, Nate brought Olivia into his dark room. She held onto him as he laid her gently onto the bed. The light from the hallway glowed into the room, casting a shadow across Nate's scruffy face. Goodness. The emotion rolling through his eyes was so much for Olivia to handle.

Nate pulled back and stopped. His hands splayed across her stomach, sliding up and down her bare skin.

"What are you doing?" she asked breathlessly.

Shaking his head, he said, "Just looking at you. You're so beautiful. Your lips are swollen from my mouth on them. I can't wait to feel you... I just need to look first..."

Olivia puckered her lips together suddenly feeling self-conscious. She pulled her arms up to her chest and tried to close her legs.

"Don't. I want to see your beauty. Take your shirt off for me," he ordered.

Olivia contemplated for a moment then slid her feet down his jean covered hips to rest on the bed. She sat up to remove her shirt but left her lacey bra on as she looked to Nate waiting for her next order.

Locking eyes with Nate, he slowly skimmed his hands over her hips and to her heavy breasts where he palmed them. Where her eyes were slightly glossy from her emotions running rapid, Nate's were burning with need. A dark, deep passion built inside that looked like it was ready to let loose at any given moment.

Nate kneaded her breasts, sliding his thumbs over her lacy covered nipples. Her breath hitched as he began to massage circles. Olivia's eyes rolled shut and her legs quivered with desire.

"Open your eyes, Olivia. I want to see them," he demanded.

Nate kissed her neck slowly, her head falling to the side to allow him access. She worked her hands into his hair and pressed into him with an arch of her back, her breasts pushing higher. Nate's tongue scraped along her skin and lapped over her nipple, lingering as he wetted the spot as much as he could through the cloth.

Olivia sighed loudly in pleasure, her sex thrumming in pain as she leaned back onto the plush bed. Nate loomed over her as her legs opened wide, permitting him to lean down and press his body to rest onto hers. She rotated her hips into his and he reciprocated, feeling the delicious straining of his hardness. The rigid muscles on his back stood out against her fingers as she gripped his backside. Stopping to admire his taut chest, a smile danced across Olivia's face.

"Like what you see?"

"I do," she said huskily. "Very, very much."

Slowly, but attentively, he slid the straps down her shoulders then removed her bra, freeing her heavy breasts. Her nipples puckered from the cool air for a split second until they relaxed. She watched as his mouth lifted up into a heart stopping grin. Leaning down, he wrapped his tongue around her nipple and tugged hard with his lips, his tongue swirling around the hardened flesh. Olivia groaned from the sensations speeding through her body as he showed her other nipple the same treatment.

"Please…" she whimpered.

"What, honey? What do you want?" he groaned, pushing his dick into her again. Olivia's hips rose at the feel of him and said low, "You. I want you. Now."

"Liv…"

"Nathaniel…I *want* you, please," she begged, not even realizing she hadn't abbreviated his name.

At the sound of her request, Nate yanked as hard as he could until her denim shorts and panties were pulled off. He threw them over his shoulder, hitting the carpet with a soft thud then removed his pants.

"Yes…" he managed through a guttural moan and stroked her wet slit with a brush of his fingers. He manipulated her sex, massaging it and adding slight pressure, causing her back to arch off the bed. Olivia was ready to combust at the touch of his skilled fingers.

"Nate…" she groaned. "Just stop playing with me and take me already," she begged.

A deep rumble of laughter escaped Nate. "Gladly."

"I can't hold out much longer," she sighed, rolling her hips. Nate removed his jeans and boxers just in time as Olivia reached to stroke cock. Her hand worked him good. He sheathed himself quickly then positioned himself at her entrance.

"Please, Nate. If you don't get in me soon, I'm going to come before it even gets started."

He laughed, finally pushing into her. "Not gonna happen on my watch. Don't worry, honey. I'll take care of you the right way."

Fisting the sheets in her hands, a slight burning sensation tore through her. It had been some time since she had sex. Nate pulled out then surged back in, hitting deep and holding there. He leaned down, crushing her and kissed her hard.

Nate pulled out and then rushed back in. He developed a steady rhythm that was climbing on the inside. Olivia grabbed hold of his bare back and held on tight as their hips met. Their mouths parted and they panted into each other.

"God, you are a stunning woman," he stated. "Your body beneath mine as I glide in and out... What you're making me feel right now, Liv. Your heat wrapped around my dick. Fuck," he groaned and captured her mouth once again with his.

"I want to hear you, Liv. Let me hear you."

"More..."

"More what?" he asked prominently, pumping into her.

"More, Nate, please..."

"Come on baby, let me hear you... Tell me how you want me," he demanded.

Olivia knew she couldn't last much longer when Nate rotated his hips and then thrust in again. Finally she yelled, "Stop teasing me and make me come." She breathed out heavily as she ran her nails down his back, scoring his damp skin. She was sure he'd have marks tomorrow.

That did it.

Nate drove into her hard and fast one last time. Olivia convulsed around Nate, milking him for all that she could as he came too. Their bodies pulsed, joined together, moisture coating their skin making them stick together as they reached a high like never before.

With her heart pumping fast against her chest, Olivia couldn't stop the sadness that slithered through her bones for some unknown reason despite the bliss she momentarily felt.

twenty-four

Two weeks later, the results were back from Diane's tests. She had Multiple Sclerosis.

God. Seeing the diagnosis in writing hit Olivia harder than she expected. She had known from experience that Diane had some sort of autoimmune disease, but it still wasn't going to be an easy task delivering this news. Normally she was able to detach herself from the emotions of the situation, but this time it was a totally different ball game. Such sadness in the simplest form sat at the tips of her fingers.

Olivia rounded her desk and walked down the hall to where Diane and Clark were waiting in the exam room. She had personally made the call and told Diane the lab and test results had come in. Clark had gotten on the phone at that point, asking if they could come that very afternoon. Olivia didn't have the heart to make them wait so she agreed.

Olivia knocked twice and entered the room to three grim faces, Diane, Clark, and surprisingly Luke. She knew he was going to have a difficult time accepting his mother's diagnosis, even though MS was manageable. Luke stood in the corner of the room with his arms crossed, removing himself from the situation as much as he could. His usual hat was nowhere in sight. Instead, his wavy hair was pushed back behind his ears, thicker and fuller than she remembered.

Sighing inwardly, she took a deep breath before she began.

"So all the results are finally in. I'm going to be frank with you, it's not good news," Olivia said as she watched Clark grasp his wife's hand.

Clark answered for Diane. "And what's the diagnosis?"

Olivia bit down on her lip. "The findings of all the test results regarding your symptoms show that you have Multiple Sclerosis." Before Olivia could finish, she heard a loud gasp erupt from Diane. "But, I am hoping we have caught it early enough for oral medications to help slow down and reduce the severity of the MS symptoms and shorten the attacks."

Silence.

"How could this have happened?" Luke asked bleakly, the color draining from his face.

"Multiple Sclerosis is a very difficult autoimmune disease to diagnose, which is why there is so much testing and lab work. There isn't a specific medical trigger in a person's life that it develops from. This is the kind of illness that lies dormant until it makes its presence known."

Looking at Diane, Olivia had compassion for the woman. "I know that this is a lot for you to process right now, but know that we have plenty of options to tackle this head on."

A raw ache in her gut slowly made its way up her body and she fought the emotion that she knew would show through her eyes. She sat down on the doctor's stool and took Diane's hand in hers.

"Clark, Diane…if you want a second opinion, I will understand. I can send my test results to any doctor of your choosing. Or if you don't want me to treat you due to the history I have with your family, I also understand. As doctors, we try to detach as much as we can emotionally, but to be honest I'm not so sure we all could do that." Olivia glanced up at Luke who hadn't moved a muscle.

With a bleak look, he said, "You'll be my mother's doctor. There's no need to go anywhere else."

"Luke, I think it's up to your mother and father to make that decision. Not you."

Clark shifted around to his son and said, "She's right, son. We'll figure it all out, together. Don't worry one bit."

Luke's jaw shifted and her eyes darkened. "Like I said, not for you to decide."

Olivia was shocked at Luke's outburst. Looking back to Diane, she stated, "Diane, you're the patient in this. I want you to be comfortable with who your doctor is."

Luke paced back and forth like a caged tiger. Why couldn't she just agree to treat his mother? He knew second opinions were always mentioned as options, but he was going to make damn sure Livy was his mom's doctor. No doubt his trust in people had pummeled through the floor over the years, especially because of the line of work he was in, but for some unknown reason he felt a drop of trust in her even when he shouldn't.

It had to be Livy or no one else. He'd talk to his parents to make it happen.

Olivia shook her head at Luke. She turned back to his parents and said, "Why don't I give you some paperwork about the different treatment plan options and then you can go home and decide what you'd like to do. I just want the best for you." Olivia smiled softly as they nodded.

"Livy."

"Luke, I need to speak to you in the hallway, now," she demanded. "Excuse us," she said then smiled at his parents.

Olivia left the room and walked down the hall to the last exam room, Luke following her.

Throwing the file onto the table nearby, she spun to yell at Luke, but before she could say a word he grabbed her by her face and kissed her hard. Shock reverberated throughout her body at the touch of Luke's lips on hers. The feel of his lips, the closeness of his body, and his scent wrapping around her as his tongue sought entrance into her mouth. He was aggressive with his mouth, his hold on her tight as her body tingled all over for him.

Forcing her to step back, Luke trapped her against the table. He was wild with need, wanting desperately kiss her. He wasn't allowing her to get away as pure animalistic need coursed through his veins. Luke traced over her sweet lips and pulled the bottom one into his mouth. Olivia gasped and Luke used that as his opening to dive in. Their tongues collided, touching for the first time in nearly a decade. It was savage, it was pure, and it was raw. It was all consuming.

Finally.

But then they turned it down a notch and began gently lapping at each other slowly. As if they were trying to memorize each other with the touch of their tongues. Her heart ached. Breaking away, they breathed heavily into each other's face looking completely surprised and unsure of what to do next.

"Luke," she whispered. What did he just do?

"I'm sorry, Livy. I had to," he whispered back, looking into her wide eyes. "I needed to. Don't be mad, please. I'd do it again if you let me."

The last thing Luke expected to do was kiss her. He expected to go toe to toe with her, but watching her in the exam room do her thing moved him. And when she ordered him out of her office? He nearly lost it. Luke knew he had to have her. He knew he shouldn't, but he didn't care. Never had he felt such an overpowering urge to kiss anyone like he had Olivia. So he did. He'd lay his lips down to hers again in a heartbeat if she allowed it.

Olivia's mouth was dry and her thoughts were a jumbled mess. She didn't know what to do, what to think, what to say.

All she knew was that Luke had just kissed her. Kissed her after nine years because he needed to.

He. Needed. To.

Bringing her hand up to her mouth, her fingers danced across her swollen lips. She was so confused. This wasn't what she anticipated when she walked in here. Shaking her head, she said, "Luke."

"Treat my mother, Livy. Please, if she'll allow it. Please?"

Olivia held her hand up to stop him. "It's not your call to make, Luke," she said quietly. A tick started working in Luke's jaw. It wasn't his decision to make and he knew it too.

"*If,* a big *if,* Luke. If she says yes, then I will. But I don't want to see you pressure her about it."

Sighing, he agreed. Luke agreeing so easily was another thing Olivia hadn't expected. Her brows angled up as she looked at him, still confused with what had just transpired. The tone between them changed and she could feel an invisible pull between them, a longing that clearly had never died.

Clearing her throat, Olivia said, "We need to get back to your parents."

Luke walked back to the exam room while Olivia went to her office to retrieve all the information she had promised Diane. Once Olivia took a seat, Diane's soft voice broke the silence. "I think you're right. I'll go home and sleep on it all and then make my decision in the morning."

Olivia handed all the paperwork to Clark and Diane. After an hour of explaining and repeating to Clark that there was no cure for MS, she tried to clarify that it could be slowed down with long-term medication. It killed Olivia to see Clark so distraught over his wife's condition, fighting to keep it in, but knowing deep down there was only so much that could be done. Olivia felt hopeless, completely and utterly hopeless. Not once in her medical career had she felt like this. Then again, she never cared for a patient so close to her before.

The whole time, Luke sat stoically off to the side, not saying a word after Olivia had put him in his place. She felt terrible, but none of these decisions were his call to make. His green eyes were trained on her, it unnerved her with him so close and watching her. Olivia fought hard to focus, but once she did, she tuned him out and did her job.

But now Olivia was drained. She was worn out and mentally exhausted from this afternoon's visit. She felt as though an imaginary set of weights were slowly pulling her down and shackling her to the floor, especially now with Luke on her mind even more.

Jason Aldean's *Night Train* played softly from within her lab coat. "Excuse me a moment while I get this."

Stepping out into the cold and quiet hallway, she answered her phone.

"Hello?"

"Hey, darlin'."

"Nate," she said, instantly feeling guilty, "I'm still at work with some patients. Everything okay? Can I call you back?"

"Well, that's why I'm calling. I called your house but you weren't there. Listen, babe, I'm going to have to cancel tonight. I need to head up to my mom's house. She needs help and I don't think I will be back in time for our date. I'm sorry, but she needs me right now."

"Is everything alright with her?"

"Oh yeah, she's alright. Just needs help fixing some things around the house. She's alone and has no one else, you know, so I run whenever she calls. Can I have a rain-check for tonight?"

"A rain-check?" She was intrigued. "And when do you plan to use it?"

"Whenever I damn well please. That's when."

Olivia giggled. "Is that so? Well I kind of like that idea. Go. Take care of your mom."

"Liv, I really am sorry about tonight."

The disappointment in his voice was loud and clear. "It's alright."

"Are you sure? I can try and make it back in time."

"No, no. It's okay. After I leave here, I'll call Shelly and see what she's up to. Maybe she'll want to head over to Castaways Pub with me."

"You alright, Liv? You sound like something's up."

Was something up...

"Yeah...I'm fine. Just a little worn out is all. See you tomorrow, then?"

"Sure thing, baby. I'll make it up to you."

Olivia sucked her lip in anticipation. "Bye," she whispered.

Sighing, Olivia walked back into the room to find Luke pacing back and forth. Not even wanting to go there, she looked at his parents and decided to close it down for the evening. She'd done all she could. Now they just needed time to digest it all.

twenty-five

Carrying a few shot glasses, Luke walked over to where Olivia was sitting.

The distressed jeans were dropped low on his hips, the lip of his boxers peeking out and begging for her attention. Could the black crew neck shirt get any tighter on his arms? Even after all these years, Luke still made her heart speed up.

Luke's eyes were apologetic as he handed her a glass of amber liquid. Olivia decided after the appointment with his parents today that there could never be a relationship, friendship, or whatever, now. How could there be?

"Take it, Livy," Luke drawled, his eyes locked on hers.

Olivia glared at Luke.

"Livy," Luke said between clenched teeth. "Take the damn whiskey. Consider it a peace offering."

Not uttering a single word, Olivia grabbed the shot and threw it back, her eyes never leaving Luke's gaze as she did. She let the burn of the spicy liquor soothe her. Olivia commended herself for not clenching her eyes shut as it moved down her throat and warmed her belly.

"Thank you."

"Don't thank me, Luke. I wasn't taking it as a peace

offering. I just wanted it. You can go now."

Man, she was really pissed at him. Guess she wasn't impressed with his kiss. He'd have to try harder next time.

"Well then, would you consider this one a peace offering?" Luke inquired as he gave her the second glass.

"No. What are you doing here, Luke?"

Luke shook his head at Livy's stubbornness. Instead, he took the shot and threw it back. How she drank this stuff straight he didn't know. After a few beers it wasn't that bad, but it wasn't his choice of poison. It tasted like gasoline.

Placing his hands on his hips, he waited for her to say something, anything, but Livy never did. Her brown eyes peered from under her heavy lashes as if she was trying to burn a hole through his head. Luke turned and walked back to the bar to order a few more shots. He'd get her to open up soon enough, even if he had to coerce her with whiskey.

Holding up two fingers, Luke shouted over the music to the bartender. *"Yeah, can I get two more rounds!"*

Grabbing the four shot glasses, Luke positioned them between his fingers and went back to Livy. He placed the drinks on the table then took one of the chairs and flipped it around to straddle it. Leaning over the back of the chair, he slid one shot to Livy, keeping one for himself. He watched as she eyed the glass, knowing his whiskey girl couldn't say no. As if he didn't know her. *Please.* She fought with herself, biting that lip of hers then reached for a glass. As she reached for it, so did Luke. *That's my girl.*

Their eyes locked and they drank at the same time.

"Why are you here alone tonight?"

"How'd you know...?" Luke smiled as soon as Olivia spoke. He knew the Fireball would work. He cocked his head to the side, lifted his eyebrow and waited for her to respond.

Luke could be so exasperating at times. After two shots and a 7&7, Olivia didn't have it in her to fight anymore. She tried to ignore Luke, but could only do so much with him sitting just inches from her. She felt her resolve breaking down, herself loosening.

"Nate," she emphasized his name, "had to back out to help his mother. *I* needed to get out for a bit, so here I am. Why are *you* here, hmm? Not like it's that close to you."

"Heard you on the phone. Knew you'd be here, so here I am."

Olivia's eyes narrowed to slits. There had to be more than just that. "You were listening to my conversation?"

"Not exactly." Luke shrugged nonchalantly. "The exam room door wasn't shut all the way and your voice carried."

"So you followed me here? What are you? A stalker now?"

Luke gave Livy a droll stare. "Like I need to stalk you, Livy."

"Oh, that's right. You're a famous country singer now. *Excuse me.*" Her voice heightened as she placed a hand across her chest, her southern accent coming out. "I'm sure you have women flocking to you in droves. In fact, the night I had to call you to come pick your drunk ass brother up, I'm pretty sure I heard a woman in the background. Why don't you go back to your flavor of the week and leave me be?" Olivia grabbed the last shot and tipped it back. When she'd heard the sound of a woman in the background that night, her heart churned with bitterness.

Well, this just got interesting. A slow and methodical smile curved his lips. If she only knew how fabricated those tabloids were. "Is that jealously I hear, *Care Bear*?"

Her jaw set tight, teeth clenching. Olivia was pretty sure she'd ask him before not to call her that again.

"What do you want, Luke? There's not really anything left to say. We've said it all. We can't be…friends or whatever this awkwardness is between us." Venom dripped from her words. The whiskey was not only loosening her up, but heating her blood.

Taking the last of the shots, Luke didn't want to fight with

Livy. He wanted to explain his actions but knew he would get nowhere trying tonight. Instead, he decided to try a totally different route.

Luke held his hand out while looking at her.

"What?"

"Come dance with me."

Scoffing at his request, Olivia glanced around the bar before she replied. "No. I don't think, *actually I know*, it's not a good idea."

"Stop using that big brain of yours for a minute and dance with me. Old friends hanging out. Nothing more."

Old friends...*old lovers*, she thought.

"I really don't think so, Luke."

Absolutely nothing good could come from being that close to Luke. Nothing.

"Don't you ever just cut back and relax?"

Olivia shrugged and leaned back into the booth. "Not really. Never had much time to relax."

"Well you do now and you have no excuse. Take my damn hand and dance with me woman. Let's go," he demanded thickly, his southern drawl coming out heavier from the liquor.

Reluctantly, she placed her hand in Luke's inviting palm. His hand was solid and firm as he closed it around her small hand. This wasn't a good idea and she knew it, but she didn't stop herself either.

Sliding out of the booth, Olivia made her way over to the semi-crowded dance floor with Luke. He turned and grabbed the belt loops of her jean shorts and hauled her to him, brushing into his body. She could smell his old, yet familiar scent as she came face to face with his chest. Taking a deep breath, she inhaled. Goodness, he smelled just like she remembered: woodsy, sun-kissed skin.

Reaching up, she rested her arms on Luke's shoulders as he spread out his hands on the small of her back and drew her in closer. The hot touch of his fingers against her back shot sparks throughout her entire body. Her heart pounded against her ribs. Olivia needed to get herself under control.

Trying not to make eye contact but not wanting to stare at his chest either, Olivia looked up at the ceiling. The bar radiated warmth and comfort with its southern charm, the dim lights setting the relaxed mood as they began to sway. Vintage looking crystal chandeliers sparkled all around, reflecting the wood tones. From tawny pink to espresso, the earthy colors shined all around the room making it look like the crystals were in fact those colors.

"Why are you really here, Luke?"

He shrugged. "After hearing about my mother, it was a lot to take in. Once I took my parents home, I watched as my dad took her to their room. I knew he was putting on a brave face for her. When he didn't come back out of the room, I went home. But once I was there, I couldn't take the silence in the house any longer and I needed to leave. I didn't want to be alone. So here I am."

"But why not call one of your friends?"

He shrugged. "You were my friend once."

All around them the air suffused with tension. Her heart ached at the sound of Luke's confession. They had been more than friends. She knew it was a lot for him to deal with.

"Well, I'm glad you're here then. I mean, I was surprised when you walked in and it confused me to see you, but I understand why you're here now."

"I didn't want to be around anyone else but you tonight, Livy. You were the first person who popped in my head when I ran out of my house. I wanted you."

Chris Cagle's *Miss Me Baby* streamed through the speakers as they rocked from side to side. Listening to the lyrics, the chorus hit her chest like a ton of bricks. Tightening his arms around her waist, Luke began crooning near her ear along with the song, breaking down her resolve. The deep, raspy southern drawl melted her on the inside, making her body flare to life.

Continuing to sing only for her, Luke placed emphasis on certain words and pulled her tighter to him, almost as if he was afraid to let her go. His stubble would graze her face each time he got too close to her ear. The cracking in his voice was not something he could stop. He was aching inside, not just with her in his arms, but also because he was stressing big time over his mother and he needed someone to comfort him. He needed his Care Bear.

Olivia could feel the heat radiating from his body, the muscles tense in his arms. There was nothing better than listening to Luke sing. Even when he wasn't singing, just watching his fingers caress the bronze cords when he played acoustic guitar was enough for her. Aside from the undeniable chemistry, music was what pulled Olivia and Luke together and locked them in. They would lose themselves in the moment, the sound of the strings being thumbed. At times he'd stop to tune his guitar if a string was off, and it was like he was tightening her to him even more. Music had always been everything for Luke early on, but now she couldn't help wondering if he was like that with other women after she'd left.

In that moment, deep down Olivia regretted ever leaving South Fork. The regret was like shards of glass roughing up the scar tissue every time his songs came on the radio. It sat heavy in her stomach, fermenting with each thought. She tried to keep space between them as they slow-danced, but as the whiskey took root in her belly she felt herself moving closer to Luke. Something was different tonight with Luke, she couldn't quite place it, but she could feel it in his hold. He needed her, and she wanted to be there for him.

Luke watched Olivia closely. He could feel how tightly coiled her body was enveloped in his arms. It was written all over her face. She was like an open book to him when it came to her emotions, so easy to read yet she still tried to conceal them.

"Livy," Luke said. Olivia gazed up at him with wide eyes full of question.

"Don't think," he demanded. "Just feel. Just feel the music and let it run through you. Feel it up in here," Luke drawled as he placed the back of his knuckles to the side of her face and began a tantalizing downward spiral. "And let it flow slowly through you here," he finished grazing over her heart.

His voice was a steady deep hum of intense desire as he ran the back of his hand down her neck and over her chest, then around the curve of her breast exceedingly slow. His thumb swept out and grazed the fullness of her breast, lingering while he stared into her eyes and then moved down to her waist. Olivia's body alighted with hunger as she struggled not to tremble from his touch. It wasn't right, yet she couldn't control her body's reaction. She shouldn't be craving his touch, yet she burned for it badly.

Not breaking their stare, he lifted the back of her shirt and began gliding his hand back and forth just above her shorts.

"Let it take you away and live in the moment with me," he tugged her closer to him, tightening his arms around her.

Gently and effortlessly, like honey sliding down hot butter, Luke touched her so softly that her lips parted and her body ignited. A flush crawled up her chest and into her cheeks as she forced her eyes not to shut at the stroke of his knuckles caressing her.

Luke knew he needed to stop touching Livy, but fuck, he just couldn't. His dick was struggling to keep calm with her so close, aware of every inch of her lush body pressed against his. Having Livy back in his arms was something he never thought would happen, and to be quite honest, he was going to take advantage of the moment. Screw everything else.

His touch must have affected her because he noticed a

tremor work itself across her body. Goosebumps were plainly visible on her arms even in the hot and stifling bar. Her eye lids were heavy as she replied, "With you. Live in the moment with you? Hmm...that's not so easy."

"Yes. With me. Two old friends, remember?" Luke reaffirmed once again.

He pulled Olivia to him so they were now hip to hip, pressing his aching lower half into her. He leaned his head down to the curve of her neck and rested it there.

"I've missed you, Livy," Luke whispered thickly against her neck. And he did. He could swear he heard a purr escape her lips as she let out a gasp. Olivia's breasts smashed against him when she tightened her hold around his neck knowing she felt what he admitted. Hell, he did miss her. She turned her head to the side and laid it on his chest, causing her long hair to dance across his arm. At this point he could hardly think straight. He was going to have blue balls for sure.

Maybe Livy was right. Maybe this dance wasn't such a good idea.

Against her better judgment, Olivia rested her head on Luke's chest and allowed her eyes to roll shut. Their faces were so close they were breathing in each other in. She could hear his heartbeat as they moved to the music and everything else faded away. She couldn't respond to what he just said. The truth was she missed him too.

Arousal was streaming through her whiskey coated veins and all Olivia could do was hold on. Her heart fell into sync with his. Tightening her arms around Luke's neck, she ran her fingers gently through his hair. Why did it have to be the smallest, most insignificant moments when it came to Luke Jackson that would turn her body up and her world upside down? She was soft and pliant, wanting Luke now more so than ever. It was wrong of her to think like that, she knew it, but there was an aching place in her heart for Luke that just never healed. Sometimes all it took was one song for the memories to come surging back as if they happened yesterday, when in reality they happened nine years ago.

Once the song ended, she was going to flee from Luke's arms and lock this moment away so she'd never forget. Until then, Olivia was going to bathe in it, because once it was over, it could never be allowed again.

As Luke was living in the moment, he felt the hook of a new song come to him. He whispered roughly near her ear...

"...baby, if you're missin' me turn up the radio...my songs tell a story...is it too late, too far gone to fix what we had...lean into my mouth and taste the truth on my lips...it's been so long, have you forgotten..."

One of Luke's hands was still drifting lazily on her lower back and over her hip while the other one was higher up, holding her securely. He didn't want to let go of her, and his body demanded that he not. Luke pressed harder against her back, pushing her into his cock. Her deep groan caused the slightest vibration in his chest. "

...remind me again what your lips taste like, what your body feels like under mine, I want the touch of your fingers on my skin as we give in to each other...let me be your shot of whiskey, heating your body with mine...turn up the radio if you're missin' me baby...

As Luke finished the last line, he placed a finger underneath Livy's jaw and tilted her chin up so her soft eyes met his. Her lips parted and a breath rolled off her lips. God, she was beautiful. So soft and luscious. He could feel the heat of her breath roll out heavily against his face. He wanted so badly to lean down into that mouth of hers and kiss her hard.

Too close...too much. If anyone had told her months ago that she'd be back home and dancing with Luke she would have laughed.

Now he was taunting her with his wicked mouth and

seductive words, knowing full well what they did to her. Her head was spinning, her breathing erratic, and a multitude of sensations whooshed through her body as she was being sucked back in to Luke. She was hypnotized by the pull he always had on her. Her eyes fastened on Luke's plump lips as he continued to sing.".

..with just a kiss, that's all we need for you to fall into me, whiskey girl, and not ever leave..."

Fuck. Olivia needed to leave. Like now. He was stripping away each hardened layer with a stroke of his hand, but in this case with his voice. His music always did this to her. It was like a drug to her. All she had to do was look into Luke's eyes and the rest would fade away.

Just like it used to.

"Livy," he groaned.

Olivia looked into Luke's green eyes that were focused solely on hers. He was telling her to unwind, to let go, but how the hell could she when he was running his hand down the sides of her body and singing to her? Between the soft caress of Luke's touch, to the rubbing of his leg between hers, Olivia felt herself dissolving. His touch was like a firefly flitting across her skin, leaving a trail of heat that made her hot and bothered. For him.

> *"...hold onto the memories.... Its heartache that never goes away ...fall into me, and feel the good times beat against your skin, whiskey girl..."*

"She licked her dry lips and watched Luke's eyes trail her tongue. She hadn't meant to get his attention that way, but she began to like it.

"Olivia..." Luke pleaded as he ran his hands up and down the sides of her waist. Olivia's eyes locked on Luke's mouth and she felt her body surrendering to him. Her heart raced and she wanted to give in to him.

Luke began closing the distance between them and she hadn't yet moved.

Time stood still as their mouths touched ever so gently, barely there, but *all* there. He grazed her plump, sugary lips with his, sliding back and forth, creating volcanic like heat around them. Earlier in the day, he put a lot into that unexpected kiss, but now he wanted Olivia to want it like he did.

Hell, Luke wanted Livy the moment he saw her again. He wanted to wrap her in his arms and hold her to him and never let go. He didn't care how long it had been. She was still his Livy, he knew it. She was the beat to his melody and the only one who made him feel alive.

Luke couldn't hold back any longer. She was too tempting, so soft and warm. His tongue peeked from between his lips and when it touched her top lip, his cock jumped. Damn, he wanted her. Fuck the boyfriend, Luke wanted Livy like old times. Realizing she hadn't withdrawn from him, Luke put more into the feel of the kiss and pushed into her mouth.

Thank fuck she responded. Olivia leaned into him.

And he took her for all he could.

She moaned.

Into his mouth. Hell, it was hot as fuck. And then she kissed him back harder sealing the kiss.

Their tongues collided in a fury of desire, reawakening the emotions and passion that had been dormant for so long. He tasted so good that she moaned into his mouth. Luke devoured her mouth with a ferocity she'd never known, and she was allowing him. Stupidly, stupidly allowing him in again on so many levels she didn't want to process. Olivia needed to break the contact but fought with herself to let go. She knew if she did, it was going to be the last time she would ever feel this way. The last time he would hold her close with his hands on her.

Groaning in both pleasure and regret, Olivia reluctantly pulled back and broke the kiss. She licked her lips and opened her eyes to peer at Luke. Silently they said so much to each other without having to say anything. Desire. Regret. Longing. Nothing about it felt good. Just reading his emotions made her chest ache with regret. Whether it was from her leaving him behind or because she was with Nate, she wasn't sure. And how screwed up was that?

Scrubbing his face with his hand, Luke stepped back and mumbled, "Livy, I—"

"Shhh…"

Olivia softly pressed a finger to Luke's swollen lips, silencing him mid-sentence. She didn't want to hear his apology. Instead, she rose on her toes and placed her hands on his shoulders. She could feel the warmth radiating from his palms when he gripped her hips tightly to steady her balance. The heat of his hands seared Olivia's flesh, his fingers dug into her while a flood of feelings rushed through her body.

Olivia hovered closely in front of Luke, her eyes trained on his parted lips as she leaned in closely, her heart picking up speed. Olivia met Luke's rousing gaze for a moment before she licked her lips and closed the distance, giving him the softest kiss imaginable. A valediction kiss.

It was still there for him.

Walking off the dance floor, Olivia strode through a mixture of smoke, the husky scent of humidity, and the faint scent of aftershave.

The familiar aroma stopped Olivia dead in her tracks.

That scent…she knew of no other who wore it except for one person. Olivia glanced around the darkly lit bar but she was unable to get a glimpse of anyone through the mass of people. As quickly as her legs would take her, Olivia hightailed it toward the door and went home. Alone.

twenty-six

A loud, consistent banging woke Olivia from her drunken slumber.

Moving the mop of hair from her eyes, she looked over at her clock but it only blinked. The power must have gone out in the middle of the night. She grabbed her cell phone to check the time but noticed a text.

Tapping the message icon, she read the text.

LUKE: Listen to the music, it tells a story…

Her heart skipped a beat. And another. And goosebumps broke out on her skin.

She knew the full meaning of those words.

Her heart. His music. How the truth was secretly woven in the lyrics all along. This whole time she thought Luke had moved on, but he hadn't.

Now that she knew the truth, her whole world changed again. Knowing what she did now, she knew the choice she had to make.

Olivia rubbed her eyes and made her way to the front door. When she looked through the peep hole, no one was there. The banging picked up again and she turned toward the back of her house. Oh, that's right. She scheduled to have Edison's Construction come and redo her yard, and like an idiot, she agreed to a timetable that started at the crack of dawn on a Saturday.

Gazing out the window, she spotted the three men who were working on the deck and yard. Landon, Lorenzo and Lukas were dressed in old ripped jeans with no shirts. She wished Tessa was there to witness the hunky trio. Considering it was nearly eight-five degrees this early, she could understand the minimal amount of clothing. Not that she was complaining or anything.

Nate... Shit. What was she going to do? Obviously she needed to come clean about the night before, but was terrified about doing so. She scratched her itchy palms, nervous and unsure about the whole situation. Another loud noise was coming from outside, this time it was definitely from the front door.

Looking through the peep hole once again, Olivia froze.

Nate. Taking a deep breath, she answered the door.

"Hey," she said sweetly.

Nate's jaw was clenched. "Hi."

"Come on in."

Nate strode in with his arms crossed against his chest.

"What are you doing here? I mean, I thought you were at your mom's house."

"Weren't expecting me, were you?" His voice, so cold and hard, was completely unlike Nate.

"Well, not this early, but I'm happy to see you," Olivia said, reaching forward to wrap her arms around him, only for him to give her a stiff hug in return. She felt like she was hugging a stranger.

"Okay...well, I'm just making coffee. Would you like some?"

"Yeah. Sure." Tension radiated from Nate, and she had no idea what was going on with him.

Walking into the kitchen, Olivia grabbed the milk, coffee mugs and sugar. Nate showing up unexpectedly was a sign that she shouldn't wait to open up and confess.

"So, how's your mom doing?"

"Alright, I guess."

"You guess? What did you need to do over there?"

Taking a sip of his coffee, he replied, "A little this, a little that."

"Could you be any vaguer?" she muttered under her breath.

"What?"

"I didn't say anything," she stated.

Standing up, Nate made his way past the breakfast nook to where Olivia stood in the kitchen.

He eyed her up and down before countering sternly. "What did you say? I didn't quite hear you."

"I… I didn't say anything…"

"Right," Nate slowly drawled out as he glared at her.

"Nate, what's wrong? What's going on with you?"

A will to breathe kind of need swirled in those brown eyes of his, but also something else she hadn't seen before. As if he was holding back on the strand. Nate wasn't his usual playful self today and it confused her.

"Is everything okay with your mom? You're acting strange."

"Strange? Strange maybe because I need you more than ever and I feel like you're not here."

"Not here? Where else would I be? I'm standing right in front of you."

Shrugging, he said with curiosity, "I don't know. Where else would you be, Olivia?"

"Nate, I can't read minds. Please, what is it you want?"

"Want?" Nate's eyes heated her skin as he eyed her up and

down. He pressed up close, backing her against the counter. "I want you. Right here, right now. Just like this in your lacy white underwear and overstretched shirt. I want you with your makeup smeared, puffy eyes and hair a wild, tangled mess. I want you to want me like I do you. I want nothing between us. I want honesty and I want all of you. Can you give that to me? Can you give all of it to me?"

Olivia's mouth popped open.

Nate grabbed the back of Olivia's head and hauled her into a surprising kiss. He pressed on her lips, flattening them to him then pushing her mouth open with a tilt of his head, thrusting his tongue in. It was almost brutal, possessive. Normally she liked this side of him. Nate's kisses usually triggered a small heat inside of her. Now they did nothing. Not even a spark.

"I... I don't know if I can," she whispered honestly against his lips.

Nate recoiled as if he'd been slapped in the face. "How do you not know, Liv?"

She shrugged remorsefully. Olivia knew the answer.

"Where do I stand with you?"

"Where... Where do you stand?"

"Is there anyone else?"

That caused Olivia's eyes to widen.

"No?" he countered. "God, I hope there's not, I really do. Otherwise, what am I fighting for?" he said and kissed her again. The little simmer she once felt with Nate was gone.

Her fire only burned strongly for one person... Always had for him.

"Please, Nate. I don't know if..." she breathed against his mouth with regret. Olivia pulled away. It was now or never and she knew it.

Nate hauled Olivia up by the backs of her thighs and carried her out of the kitchen. He sat down with her on his lap when they reached the couch.

"It's you, Liv."

Confused, she asked, "What?"

"You asked me what I want. I want you. I want all of you. But most of all, I want your heart."

Olivia cracked inside at his honesty. He wanted a heart she didn't have to give him.

"What makes you think you don't have it?" she asked curiously into his amber eyes.

"I don't know... I'm not used to feeling like this. Wanting a woman as much as I want you." Nate laughed. "I'm just not used to letting anyone this close to me. I guess I'm just second-guessing everything I do and say. It's pretty much all new for me."

Sadly, Olivia wasn't truly in love with Nate. Cared for him deeply? Yes. Lusted after him? For sure. But did she love Nate? No. She had given her heart to one man long ago.

"What do you want?" he asked patiently.

What did Olivia want? A month ago, she would've said Nate, but now that she knew where Luke stood, her answer to Nate's question had changed. To know that there was a chance to reconcile her past with Luke, there was no way for Olivia not to want that. Their history was just too steep to ever forget. And truthfully she didn't want to. Luke singing to her, the truth in his words, they were all too much to forget. They were too deep and too real to ignore.

The bridge between Olivia's eyes started to throb. She squeezed the skin between her eyes and blew out a long breath. The sound of Olivia's phone chimed. She looked down and saw a text from Luke.

Of course.

Nate nudged his head against Olivia's shoulder and looked down at the screen with her.

Luke: time fades...but the music never stops

"Luke?" Nate stated, dumbfounded.

"Yes…"

"Luke texted you? You gave him your number? Since when?" he asked incredulously. "What aren't you telling me, Olivia?"

Olivia looked into Nate's eyes, feeling guilty about so much more now. "I'm sorry, but I can't tell you, Nate…"

"What do you mean you can't tell me? Why can't you tell me?" he asked with agitation.

Olivia sighed and removed herself from Nate's embrace. She took a few steps and turned to look down at him. Pressing the heels of her hands into her eyes, she said, "I'm Luke's mother's doctor."

She instantly hated herself for telling Nate that. "I gave him and his parents my phone number in case they needed anything."

"His *mother* is your patient. Not Luke," Nate clarified. "He doesn't need it Olivia. Since when do you give your personal cell out?"

"This is a little different, Nate. I know them personally," she said, drawing out personally. "I grew up in a small town with Luke. Nearly lived in his house. I can't *not* be there for him."

Brooding, Nate stared at Olivia before he asked, "How long?"

"How long what? Has he been texting me? I don't know… Since the beginning?"

Nate's eyes were a blend of hurt and simmering rage. "Why didn't you tell me?" he demanded in a low, deep tone.

"Why would I need to tell you? I'm treating his mother."

"You know why," Nate refuted as he stood. "You have a past with him, Olivia. A long one. It's like you hid it on purpose. Did you really think I would be okay with this?"

"It's my job, Nate. And it wouldn't matter if you're okay with it or not."

Nate cocked his head to the side, took two steps and leaned into Olivia's face. "Really?" he questioned her quietly.

"Yes, really. I'm trying to alleviate stress for him while he's out on tour so he doesn't have to worry or come home."

"Worry? Come home? That's not your job, Olivia," he snapped. "How many times have you seen him?"

Feeling her heart kick up a notch, Olivia ground her jaw back and forth, debating what to tell him.

Nate closed his eyes. "Why would you not tell me, Olivia?"

"I didn't think it would matter."

"You're kidding, right?" he deadpanned.

Olivia shook her head. "I'm just answering his questions about his mom. Why is it such a big deal to you?"

"What else, Olivia? What else are you not telling me? How about we just air it all out now so we don't have to go through this again? Because I'm not so sure I would want to."

As Nate waited for her to respond, Olivia tried to take deep, slow breaths as inconspicuously as she could. Nate locked eyes with her. He was a smart man and knew something else was coming.

Her phone chimed again and she groaned. *Damn Luke.* They both stood still.

"Something else you need to say to me, Olivia?"

Rolling her bottom lip between her teeth, she bit down so hard she tasted blood. Olivia said nothing as anxiety pulsed through her chest from Nate's hardened gaze. The last thing she wanted to do was answer him.

"How often do you see him?"

Her shoulders tugged upward. "Whenever he's in town."

"Don't play dumb with me. I know you know how often."

Olivia wanted to lie, but wouldn't. She needed to get it all out. If what Luke said was true about his music, then deep down she knew what she needed to do.

"He's been to an appointment here and there... We saw him at Rum Bar."

"Plus all the text messages. Which I'm going to say wouldn't be just about medical updates, would they?"

She didn't respond.

"What else?"

Olivia gulped, took a deep breath and looked into Nate's scowling gaze. She tried to start off slowly. "He..." she said, trying to ease her way into it, but that was laughable. There was no way to ease anything when it came down to it. "He came to the bar last night. He showed up unexpectedly."

Nate said nothing while he waited. Olivia chewed her lip as nausea took root in her stomach.

Nate scoffed. "This must be good."

"I was feeling lonely and had a lot on my mind."

"Get to the point."

"I'd had a drink. Then Luke bought me a few..." she trailed off.

"So you're drunk now. With Luke. Keep going."

"We ended up dancing together... We danced to a few songs..." Olivia took a deep breath, placed her hand on her neck and said, "Luke and I kissed."

Olivia's eyes revealed her sorrow. The guilt was like a snake slithering inside of her, wrapping its way around her chest and squeezing.

Nate snickered. "And the night just gets better and better."

"Nate—"

"Let me guess. It didn't mean anything, right?" he mocked while he began to walk through her house.

Olivia couldn't answer the question because it *did* mean something to her. "Let me explain," her voice cracked with despair.

Just then, her phone rang.

Fuck her life.

"Answer it." Nate walked over to her. Reluctantly, she did as Nate demanded.

"Hello?"

"Hey, Care Bear."

Nate's eyes flared, the gold flecks turning dark. Nate mouthed 'Care Bear' silently and glared at her.

Clearing her throat, she responded. "Hey, Luke, what's going on?"

"Just... wanted to see what you're doing."

Olivia gripped the phone tighter. A dark and uncertain air current circulated around her and Nate. "Working on it. Listen, I need to get going. Talk to you soon."

"Later, Livy."

"He calls, too," he said in utter disbelief. "Is there anything else?"

"No, that's it."

Determined steps took Nate to the front door. Before he could grab the doorknob, Olivia whispered, "Where are you going?"

Glancing over his shoulder, Nate looked deep into Olivia's eyes. "I need to leave before I'm forced to regret something else."

That stung.

"We all make mistakes, Nate. It was just a kiss."

Nate dropped his hand from the knob and faced her. "Are you seriously going to tell me you didn't kiss him back and that it was only once?"

Olivia began to stutter. "I... I didn't."

"Here's something for you, *baby*. When we spoke, I heard how much you needed me, so I raced back and went to the bar since you weren't at your house. Imagine my surprise seeing you in Luke's arms with his hands all over your body. You have no idea what it took for me not to go and rip you from his arms and beat the ever loving shit out of him. It's bad enough his brother kissed you; he's a young kid and was drunk, but not Luke. Luke is a grown ass man and knew what the fuck he was doing. I watched him kiss you, Olivia. I *watched* you kiss him one last time before walking off the dance floor. So don't even give me shit that it was one time and meant nothing. I saw it!" Nate's voiced boomed around the room, slamming into her like a freight train. Jesus.

"You saw?" Then Olivia remembered the faint smell of aftershave that reminded her of Nate...

"Damn straight," Nate bellowed while walking towards her. "It destroyed me to see you in his arms, Olivia. I hated you. Then I see you now, like this, with your stretched out shirt and your wild hair, and all I can think is how much I want you. That maybe I could let it go and forget it all happened, that I was taking the higher road and willing to be second best for you. But being here in front of you and seeing in your eyes that I'm not where I should be in your heart, I can't."

"But you almost made love to me, did you not?" she stated confusedly.

Nate shook his head sadly. "When it comes to you, Liv, I...just don't know."

"Please..." Olivia's jaw quivered. She didn't know what she was even asking for. Maybe forgiveness?

"You're asking a lot right now, baby. You know that, right?"

Olivia squeezed her eyes shut. "I do," she whispered.

"And I just can't give it to you."

Olivia placed her hand on his forearm, but he pulled it away as if she'd burned him. "I'm so sorry," she whispered.

"Did you ever really want me?" he asked softly, changing his tone. His eyes were so sad it pained Olivia to look at them.

"Nate," Olivia said, her voice cracking. "I'm so sorry. More than you'll ever know. I never meant to hurt you."

"Funny thing is, I think you do you mean that."

"Please..." Olivia pleaded for him to believe her. "There

is no excuse for my actions, I know that. You need to know that you were the first person I truly cared about since Luke. That's the truth. You were never second best, Nate. Don't ever think that. I fucked up, I know that."

"Were."

Olivia looked puzzled.

"You said 'were.' Everything you just said was past tense. Tell me, Liv, when did it change?" he asked in a broken whisper.

Bringing his hand up, Nate cupped her cheeks. "This is where the road ends for us, Liv. You go your way and I'll go mine. It's as good as it can ever be, but it's not enough," he said as he pushed a lock of hair behind her ear and cupped her face, his thumb grazing her jaw.

Tightness suffocated Olivia's chest as she replayed Nate's words in her mind. They weren't cruel or harsh, but spoken with a sad clarity that racked her soul.

"I think I've been fooling myself all along. When I watched Luke look at you that night at Rum Bar, I knew. I just didn't want to accept it."

Olivia heard nothing except for the pounding against her ribs. Everything was a blur around them, fading as his words struck the center of her.

With an ache in his voice, he continued. "You love me on some level, but it's just not the same kind of love. I *hate* knowing you share a connection with another guy just as strong, if not more. And before you say you don't, take it from an outsider's point of view, you do. Would it be fair to string us both along when we both know in the end it's not what you truly want?"

Nate placed his arms around Olivia's shoulders and pulled her close. Her eyes were rimmed with tears, tattered from admitting the truth, but from hurting Nate most of all. She wrapped her arms around his back, her small hands fisting his shirt and held on. She licked her dry lips and bit down hard, trying to ease the now agonizing pain that lacerated her heart. She never meant to hurt him.

"It's alright, Liv. I understand it all too well. Just...let me down easy."

Olivia's emotions swelled painfully inside of her. Her legs were weak and her heart heaved as she fought the tears that streamed down her cheeks. She did love him on some level, but he was right. It wasn't enough. It would never be enough.

Placing his forehead against hers, he whispered, "It's okay...Liv. I'm disappointed and pissed off at myself for thinking I could be enough this whole time when all along I never was. I fought hard for you in the beginning, but if I can't have all of you, then I don't want any of you. This is a two way street, honey. I hate to admit it, but Luke is one lucky guy."

"You say that like I'm going to run into his arms."

"Maybe not right now, but you will."

Nate opened the front door and walked out, Olivia silently followed him wrenched with sadness Olivia said, "Look, Nate—"

"Don't, Olivia. This is the end of the road for us. Just know that I loved you and could've loved you more than any other woman if you had let me, but you couldn't. And it's okay, baby. I'm not mad. I'm just hurt. It's written in your eyes, Liv, you belong to someone else. I want to be able to love my woman fully and completely without holding back. You're worth fighting for, don't misunderstand me, but not when I'm dealing with a heart I never had to begin with. That guy is going to be one lucky man. Just wish it could've been me."

Hot tears threatened to spill down Olivia's cold cheeks listening to Nate's straightforward words. They were painful to hear and struck a chord deep inside her heart, even if they weren't meant to, and she knew they weren't full of malice. That's not who Nate was, but that's exactly how the truth was. It showed an ugly and depressing side of things people chose to ignore and only listened to when forced. People didn't like the truth if wasn't in their favor.

Finding her voice, Olivia tried to speak, but it came out in a whisper. "Alright, Nate. You win." She could hardly meet his eyes.

Nate let out a sad chuckle over the irony of Olivia's last statement.

"No. You win. Nate-0, Liv for the win," he finished.

A loud sob erupted Olivia's throat as she broke down and cried harder. The truth hurt. Big time. Reaching over, Nate pulled her into his arms.

"Just wait," he murmured into her hair. "Let me hold you one last time, a few more minutes."

And so she did. It was the least she could give him.

Later that night was painfully quiet for Olivia, a certain calmness settled in the air as she lay alone in her bed.

The hurt ran deep.

twenty-seven

"So he left? Just like that?" Lisa asked on the phone.

"Yeah, but can you blame him? I probably would have too if I'd been in his place."

"I guess so. And you haven't heard from him since?"

"Nope. Not one word, Lisa." Olivia took a deep breath, relaxed into the couch cushion. "I fucked up. I don't know why I would expect a call."

"You totally fucked up. Considering your past, and how much you hid from him, I'd be surprised if he ever spoke to you again."

Leave it to Lisa to give it to her the only way she could: blunt honesty.

Olivia had given Lisa a replay of everything, from the episode at Rum Bar to the break-up.

When Olivia hadn't heard from Nate, she caved and called. But after four days, she stopped.

"What about Luke? Have you told him to stop with the messaging?"

"No. I can't, Lisa. I mean, I probably should, but *I just can't*. How would you feel if you were hundreds of miles away and couldn't do anything to help your mother?"

Sarcastically, Lisa said, "My mother's dead! So I really can't see your view point or his."

"Lisa!" She chuckled at Lisa's warped sense of humor. "Come on. Be serious for once in your life and give me your honest opinion."

Lisa groaned into her answer. "I guess I see where you're coming from..."

Pulling the blanket up to cover her legs, Olivia whispered, "What am I supposed to do, Lisa?"

"You get over Nate."

"Thanks," she retorted dryly. "You know, this is your fault. You're the one who pushed me to date Nate. I blame you for it all," Olivia said playfully.

"Hey, sometimes you have to take a chance, right? Liv, let me ask you a question, but you have to answer it honestly."

Olivia straightened. "Alright..."

"After all you've told me about what's been going on, do you think it's possible you still love Luke?"

"Jesus..." Talk about getting to the root of the issue.

"Hear me out. I'm being real right now." Lisa laughed. "I know, sounds comical coming from me and all, so don't laugh. In all seriousness, everything would make sense if you do, Liv."

"I never hid the messages, Lisa. Just didn't think I needed to tell him. It wasn't as though I was doing anything wrong."

"You know what I mean, Olivia. Don't beat around the bush trying to ignore the question, and don't even try to lie to me. You totally kept those messages from him. Just think about it for a minute."

Olivia thought about Lisa's question before she responded. Would she be lying if she said her body didn't respond to being in Luke's arms? *Yes.* Would she be lying if she said the connection with him was completely gone after all these years? *For sure.* Oh, who was she kidding?

Maybe her feelings had never left, but they weren't the same people. But was what he sang really true?

Clearing her throat, she gave Lisa her honest answer.

"Truth is," she said softly, "I think I'll always love him. I can't help it. It's just…always there, but it doesn't mean I can't love someone else. We can love more than one person, right?"

"You're asking the wrong person that question, honey."

Oddly enough, Olivia felt like a weight had been lifted from her chest. She breathed in a sigh of relief.

twenty-eight

Olivia's phone was ringing and it took her a few moments to rummage through her purse to locate it.

Thankfully, Diane had informed her that Luke was back in the studio recording a new album, so she didn't have to face him, but they continued to text. Though, Olivia only gave him so much information about his mom. It was up to Diane to tell Luke the rest.

Olivia silenced the ringing.

This time a text message came in.

LUKE: *Pick up the damn phone Olivia.*
OLIVIA: *No. I'm working. What do you need?*
LUKE: *I need you to pick up your phone. I have a question.*
OLIVIA: *I'm right here. What's your question?*
LUKE: *I'm miles away and need to hear that my mom is okay. I spoke with her today and she didn't sound right. Just answer your phone.*

Shoot. Olivia didn't want to answer, but if there was something truly wrong with Diane then she needed to pick up.

OLIVIA: *Ok.*

Not even thirty seconds went by before it rang again.
"Luke."
"Olivia," Luke growled. "I know you're probably pissed…"

"You know I am! You knew about Nate and yet you put your stage face on and played me. You sang to me, sang about our past, *fucking kissed me*, and for what?"

"…but my mother's life is on the line here. Put your silly, childish feelings aside and answer your phone. Do your job!" Luke shouted.

"Screw you, Luke! I am doing my job. I have been doing my job my whole life. I've done everything I'm supposed to, to keep this completely platonic between us and less stressful on your mother. I look at Diane as more than a patient, so it's not easy separating feelings from work."

Luke sighed loudly into the phone. "Olivia, if I call, answer your phone. I'm hundreds of miles away. I can't think straight, can't physically see her. I'm worried about my mother and you won't answer your phone. Can you think of someone else for once in your life? I'm calling for one reason and one reason only. My mother. Not you."

"Don't be an asshole, Luke. Those years don't interfere with my job, trust me. I'm doing this as a *favor* to you. I'm treating Diane, not you. I don't have to give you shit. I pick up calls when they're from a patient in need, which you're not. That was a low blow taking a hit at my profession like that."

"Tough shit! My brothers are too young to know anything and John is fucking around as usual which isn't helping. Dad doesn't tell me anything and I know my mother is lying to me to protect me when all the while I can *hear* it in her voice. Will someone cut me a fuckin' break and tell me the truth? I just want to know how she is doing. After her phone call this morning, I'm ready to say fuck my next album, fuck my agent and hop on the next plane to come home."

"Luke, I know it's not about us...or me." She softened, feeling sorry for him. "I know that. It's just that I care about your parents and I'm trying to keep it as professional as I can. I'm going out on a limb giving you information that I shouldn't be." Olivia paused and then sighed. She didn't want to fight with him. "Tell me what happened and I'll see what I can do."

"She sounded like she was in pain, more like agony, this morning when I called. It was around 11:00 a.m. and she was in bed. In bed, Olivia. She's *never* in bed at that time. She said she just had a headache."

"It's not all that uncommon. She probably did have a headache. Luke, you have to remember that she's going to live with some form of pain for the rest of her life. There's no cure, all I can do is help lessen her symptoms."

"So it was a headache then?"

"If that's what she told you. But I'll call just to check."

Luke was silent.

"Luke?" Olivia said softly. Her heart was reaching out to him beyond the arguing.

Clearing his throat, he replied. "Yeah, ah, thanks, Livy. This is harder than I thought," Luke choked out. "I know she'll be fine, I have faith she will, but I also know she's trying to be strong. I think she's been hiding it for longer than she let on. Just wish I could be there instead of miles away."

Trying to ease his pain a little, Olivia took it down a notch. "It's not all an act, Luke. Your mother is a strong woman. Your father is there for her so try not to worry as much. Remember, he bends over backwards for her. The medication will take time depending on her body, but I'll call if you want."

Luke chuckled. "Yeah, you do that. And Livy?"

"Yes?"

"Thank you for everything. I wouldn't have been able to deal with this had it been anyone else. I mean it. I want apologize, and let you know I'm so grateful for what you're doing. I'll try to keep it to texting, just got worried when I heard her voice."

"It's alright. You know I'm here when you need me." Olivia knew she was stepping out of bounds with their agreed setup by saying more, but she couldn't help herself. "So...how is everything else with you?"

Luke let out a gruff sigh. "Honestly? It's been difficult. Real difficult, Livy. I'm taking my frustration out on people who don't deserve it. I'm the one starting the arguments...my manager, agent, friends, crew, everyone. I need to relax, but for some reason I just can't. I have a lot on my mind other than my mom. Pile it all up together and my head is throbbing all the time."

"Sounds like you're the one who has a headache."

Luke laughed. "I think you need a vacation."

"The same could be said for you."

Silence drifted through the phone line. An unspoken longing touched them intimately, pulling them together. It was there. They both could feel it and sense it.

Olivia smiled sadly to herself. "I haven't been on vacation in..." she paused to think. "Actually, I don't think I've ever gone on vacation."

How pathetic was that? That she never took time out for herself?

"How is that possible?" Luke questioned with surprise.

"I don't know...just haven't had time. It's a vicious cycle I brought on myself, I guess." Just thinking of having no time to breathe was exhausting in itself.

"Anyway," she said breaking the silence. "If you feel like you're falling again, just pick up your phone and send me a message. I'm always here."

"Thanks... Listen, I'm sorry about that night at the bar. I

know it was wrong of me, but I don't regret it. I know... I shouldn't have even gone, but when I overheard you on the phone that you'd be alone, and I was alone at home, I knew I couldn't stay away. Then having you in my arms like old times... Yeah. I guess I couldn't resist."

He's sorry for that night...he couldn't resist. Could not resist. Why did it suddenly feel like Luke threw a curve ball at her?

Luke sighed into the phone. The grudge she erected over the years was crumbling at her feet.

"I don't know what came over me, Livy. I bet Nate is pissed about it all, let alone that you're treating my family. I know I sure as hell wouldn't."

When she didn't respond, Luke edged into the question slowly and asked, "You haven't told him, have you?"

"No," she answered quietly. She didn't want Luke to know she and Nate were no longer together yet.

"Can I ask why not?"

"I haven't worked up the courage?"

Incredulously, Luke asked, "You? Not able to work up the courage? That's not the Livy I remember."

Olivia's back went ramrod straight. "I guess I'm not the same Livy I was."

"I find that hard to believe. I bet she's still there under that starched white lab coat waiting to be free again."

"I just... I'm scared."

"If you're worried about losing him, don't. Judging by the brief moment I met him, if he's the kind of man I'm assuming he is, he'll want to beat the shit out of me. Can't blame the guy. But if he walks away, he'll only come to regret it down the line. Trust me."

He'll regret leaving... There was no way for her not to wonder if Luke was speaking from personal experience.

"Thanks, Luke." She smiled sadly.

"Hope he makes the right choice."

A small smile tugged at Olivia's mouth.
"Bye, Luke."
"Later, Care Bear."

twenty-nine

Pulling up to Smokejacks, Olivia took a deep breath before getting out of the car.

Tessa's call to let her know about a little reunion couldn't have come at a better time. The reunion was something her friends did once a year, but Olivia had never be able to attend for many reasons.

Making her way inside, she noticed it looked just as it had years ago. A sense of nostalgia washed over her. Memories resurfacing from old times, she glanced at the now empty stage. It was dark and bare.

Olivia took a seat at the bar and ordered a drink. Just as she finished, Ash, Chase, and Bradley filed in one after another and made their way to the bar.

…and then Luke?

Jesus. Lord. What. The. Hell?

Olivia's heart sped up as Luke walked in like he owned the place in a lazy glide with a grin plastered on his face. She couldn't pull her stare away, he was spellbinding. His long strides were accompanied by his infectious smile as he made his way over to the bar. He was straight up sexy. Olivia couldn't deny how much he still got to her.

Olivia left her barstool and walked over to Tessa, who had just walked in and nudged her with her elbow.

"I thought you said he wasn't coming," Olivia said, eyes as wide as saucers.

"I swear I didn't know, Liv. I promise. I was told he was out of town. Don't let it bother you and have a good time. I think you need this more than anyone right now."

Tessa gave a heartfelt squeeze to Olivia's hand. The guys were doing the quick "what's up bro" half hug with each other while getting their respective orders and leaning against the bar.

"Looking good, Livy," Ash said flirtatiously, dropping a peck to her cheek.

She giggled. Still as playful as she remembered. "Thanks, Ash."

"Hey, Chase. It's good to see you again."

"Likewise, Olivia."

Bradley lifted Olivia off the floor into a bear hug. He crushed her in a tight embrace that felt like all the air had squeezed out of from her lungs. She grunted, "Hey, Bradley."

"Hey, girl. Long time no see. Glad to hear you're back."

"I'm glad to be back, actually," she breathed out.

"Alright, put her down, B. She's gettin' blue in the face."

Olivia tensed as Bradley lowered her to the floor. She looked over his shoulder and spotted the voice that had always tipped her world.

Luke could feel Olivia's presence the moment he walked into the bar. His eyes zigzagged across the low lit room in an effort to locate her. And when he did, his gaze zeroed in on her curvaceous body as he felt his own roar to life. His eyes blazed full of want as they traveled the length of her body, his cock jumping at the sight of how sexy she looked in jeans that hugged her body like a glove. Man, she got him going every damn time he saw her.

Luke needed a drink. Fast.

He knew she was going to be there, but most likely with her stupid boyfriend. Where was he anyway? Luke glanced around looking for Nate but didn't spot him. Nate probably wanted nothing more than to knock his sorry ass out for layin' lips to his girl...Nate's girl...what the fuck ever.

"Hey, Care Bear. How you doing?" He looked around. "Where's that boyfriend of yours?"

Olivia chewed her lip nervously. "Ah, he couldn't make it tonight."

Luke smirked on the inside. There was no way he was holding back from hugging Livy knowing Nate wasn't around.

"That's too bad," Luke lied. He leaned down and enveloped Livy in a tight embrace, dropping his head into the curve of her neck and inhaling her soft hair. Just the way he remembered. Coconuts. *Hell yeah.* He inhaled again, squeezing Livy to him and feeling her breasts against his chest. Luke's blood warmed from the feel of Livy in his arms, he loved the softness of her body. His fingers grazed the sides of her breasts as he held her close.

She whispered thickly, "I didn't know you were going to be here."

"I usually try to, but I don't always get the chance. Luckily I was able to get away for a few days."

"Well, I'm sure your parents and brothers were happy to see you since you hardly get to come home."

Luke pulled back and his hands slid to her hips, holding her in place as he eyed her.

"Your mom misses you and worries about you." Olivia shrugged nonchalantly.

"You spoke to her recently?"

"Do you mean do I talk to her outside of being her doctor? Then yes, sometimes I do. Just a quick hi to see how she's doing."

Luke huffed and scrubbed a hand over his face. His chest softened at the sound of Livy's genuine concern for his family.

"Don't know why she worries. I'm fine. She needs to worry about herself and my brothers, not me. I'm not a kid anymore."

A sweet, half smile graced Olivia's lips before she said, "I don't think a mother ever stops worrying about her kids, Luke. It's only natural. I'm sure one day you'll be going through the same thing with your kids, regardless of their ages."

Inadvertently, Luke gripped Livy tighter. He needed to keep his thoughts locked in, but he was already having a hard time. Here she was talking about him having kids one day. Luke thought about it for a moment but couldn't fathom having his own children with anyone else other than Livy. She was working her way under his skin again. He imagined her with a swollen belly carrying his child...her face glowing as they found out the sex of the baby...

The awkward silence was broken when Chase yelled for shots.

Saved by whiskey. Thank you, Mr. Jack Daniels!

As Chase handed the shots out, the old friends held them in the air. "A toast to old memories, new memories and friends."

"Can't get any cheesier than that, Ash," Tessa laughingly said.

Ash slammed back his shot. "Screw you."

"Nah, I'm good."

"So long as Luke doesn't cockblock like he used to...we're all good," Ash laughed.

"Or could it be because no one wanted your lame ass?" Tessa yelled then turned to Luke and batted her eyes up at him. "Hey, Luke, sing for us?"

Ash turned around and eyed Tessa up and down like she was a piece of meat. She scoffed and turned towards him. "You pig."

"That's not what you said last time."

"Get over yourself, Ash-*hole*."

"I'd rather be over you."

Tessa's jaw locked. "Not going to happen." She turned to Luke and said sweetly, "Luke? What do you say?"

Luke mumbled something under his breath. He wasn't really up to singing for anyone right now. As much as he loved it, he was on a break and just wanted to cut back and hang with his friends, but Tessa was giving him her puppy dog eyes and pouty lip routine, begging him to sing like old times. Old times…when Livy was his girl.

Chase, being a wiseass said in a high-pitched, girly voice, "Yeah, Luke! Sing for us!" He clutched his beer to his chest and tried to bat his eyelashes like Tessa did.

"Man, shut up. I ain't singing."

"But Luke! You have to! Just like old times!" Tessa whined.

"Yeah, Luke!" Chase mocked.

Luke looked at Livy as he said, "Times have changed, Tessa. Not going to happen."

With that, Tessa stomped back to the bar to order another drink. "Want me to sing to you, baby?" Ash asked Tessa in a smoky voice, mimicking Luke's. Olivia chuckled at his attempt.

Disgust appeared all over Tessa's face. "God, no. Now go away." Ash reached out for Tessa but she pulled away quickly before he could touch her.

"Alright. I got you," he nodded, arrogantly accepting her answer.

Olivia noticed Tessa in the corner of her eye trying to fight the grin that curved the corners of her mouth. Tessa was enjoying it much more than she showed.

Two hours later, Tessa had finally coerced Luke to sing on stage.

But that's not what bothered Olivia, or the slew of young college girls yelling his name and singing along to his songs.

"You doing okay, Livy?" Tessa asked.

Olivia nodded her head automatically. What bothered her was *what* Luke had just sung on stage.

...everyone needs a whiskey girl...

Four times. Luke said it four times, and every time he did, a drunken howl from the women up front would sound right after. At first she thought he slipped, but when he did it again, she knew he hadn't.

It was almost laughable that Luke crooned in the background as she sipped on her whiskey. But then, during a small intermission, he sent her a text.

LUKE: *Listen to my lyrics, they tell a story...*

Chills broke out over her skin, her phone almost slipped from her fingers. Why would he send her something like that? Her chest tightened and her body had gone completely numb. He was deliberately testing her patience and it just wasn't fair. Olivia did everything that he asked of her and this is how he repays her? By singing *"whiskey girl"* in front of everyone? Granted, no one knew, but that wasn't the point.

When Luke finally strolled up to the stage after much nagging from Tessa, Olivia sat at the bar for another drink so she wouldn't have to watch him. Luke knew it was a childish move to taunt her. He would purposely lock eyes with her and stare. How the hell could he not?

After a little while, Olivia slipped away to the ladies room in the middle of a song. She needed a break from listening to Luke on stage. Even furious with him, warmth surged through her body at the sight of him. Her heart was laden with memories as she watched Luke grab a lonely guitar and play with expertise. He held and caressed it intimately. Olivia tried to mask her emotions to those around her, but it wasn't easy. As much as she told herself she was over Luke, she couldn't help but still love him. Watching him on stage again, it was all too much for her to handle. His voice would drop low as if he fell into another dimension, luring her into his black hole. And when that happened, nothing mattered anymore but him. Time stopped and she felt what he felt, the beat of the drums, that one hook in the song that meant more than any other, the clenching of her stomach as he held a note. The rush of performing. As if his voice took them to another place together from a single strum of his finger on the strings. Her love of watching Luke sing still hadn't died. It never would.

Reaching the semi-dark area outside the restrooms, Olivia waited her turn in line. She closed her eyes, leaned her head back and took a deep breath. Cheers and chants echoed from the crowd, signaling the song was over.

"Thank you, thank you."

His voice…sounded so hoarse. *God.*

"I'm gonna take a little break for now. Maybe I'll be back."

The cheering only grew louder.

Luke made his way off stage with determination. He had watched Livy from the stage, watched as she avoided looking at him and stared down at the glass in her hand. Why couldn't she see what he was trying to say? He managed to catch a glimpse of the look she used to have. It was a look full of want and need that he had fulfilled in the past.

Pushing his way past people on the dance floor, Luke knew the bar like the back of his hand. He'd come here often after she left, sit in a booth and slam back beers as he put his feelings on paper to cover his emotions. It was how he coped with the loss. Yeah. He wrote those kinds of songs because of a broken heart. Fucking sap that he was.

Luke found Livy in seconds. She was leaning against a

dirty wall in the hallway waiting in line. Her head was dropped back against the bland gray wall, looking so tired and worn out. Luke marched right up, grabbed her arm and pulled her behind him, dragging her toward the door labeled "Emergency Exit", not even stopping for Livy to gather her footing.

"Luke, what the hell? Let go!"

Discombobulated from the shock of Luke dragging her outside, Olivia tried to yank her arm back, but had no such luck. "Luke! Stop!"

Luke kicked out the door and swung Olivia outside and pushed her up against the brick wall in the dirty alleyway. "Why'd you do it, Olivia?"

Perplexed, she bit out through clenched teeth, "Huh? Do *what* exactly, Luke?"

"Why'd you turn your back on me once I got up on stage?"

"Are you kidding me? You manhandle the shit out of me, drag me outside, slam me into a wall and that's all you say? What the hell is wrong with you!"

Luke retreated a few steps back as shock flitted across his face. His eyes traveled every inch of her body looking for any marks. Hurting her physically was the last thing on earth he'd ever want to do.

"Dear God," he whispered, "I would never lay a hand to you, Care Bear. Did I hurt you?"

Olivia rubbed her arm. "I'm sure I'm fine, but don't ever do that again."

Luke was not the kind of man to raise a hand to a woman, it wasn't in his bones. He wasn't trying to hurt her... Rubbing a hand across his tightened chest, Luke slowly took a step closer.

"Livy...I would never..." He couldn't even finish the sentence. Luke leaned down and pressed his forehead to

Livy's, holding her face between his palms. It would take nothing for him to lean down and rest his lips against hers.

Unable to look into Livy's eyes, he closed his own before he said, "I could never hurt you. You have to believe me." Her hands fisted his waist, gripping his shirt and holding him. She made the smallest move and leaned into him.

She knew. Olivia knew Luke wasn't capable of hurting her. She was just taken aback by it. Taking a few deep breaths, Olivia relieved Luke of his suffering.

"I know," she whispered. "You scared me."

"I just wanted to talk."

"Talk?" A laugh escaped her lips. "What could you possibly want to talk about?"

Lifting his head, but not dropping his arms, Luke looked into Livy's eyes and spoke as earnestly as he could. "Why did you ignore me when I got up to sing? I had no intention of singing at all, but I looked at you when Tessa was begging me and thought I saw hope in your eyes for a split second. So I caved. Because of you. I sang because of you. But when I got up there, you wouldn't look at me, like you couldn't stand to hear me."

Luke's eyes pleaded for an answer. Olivia had no idea that ignoring him would hurt him so much. She did it to protect herself.

For her. Luke sang for her. Olivia wasn't sure what to even think. "Why would you do that?"

"Because I remember how much you loved it."

"Luke," she shook her head. "That was long ago."

"Did you?"

"Did I what?"

"Did you like what you heard? I sang it for you."

"It doesn't matter what I like anymore."

"It does to me."

"Why, Luke? Why? Why does it matter whether or not I like it?"

Luke shrugged. Why couldn't she just answer his question? "It just does."

"Well, that's a stupid answer."

"Why can't you just answer me?"

"I could ask you the same thing. Never mind. I need to get back inside."

"Is it as good as when we were together, Livy?" His voice was hoarse. He knew he shouldn't ask, but he also needed to know how she truly felt.

Olivia glanced up into his eyes. Her heart raced as she tried to find the right words.

Luke saw the look in her eyes that revealed her answer. "Nothing could be as good as when we were together," he whispered, answering for her. Luke couldn't resist tasting her. He leaned down and kissed her hard, savoring her mouth. She responded immediately and took all of him in a heart stopping kiss.

Breaking the kiss, Luke asked between pants, "Tell me. Does he make you happy?"

Olivia felt her jaw quivering. She thought about her answer carefully before she spoke.

"At one point Nate made me happy more than I thought possible."

Luke cringed on the inside at her confession. He wasn't expecting *that*.

She let out a sad smile, her eyes soft with repentance. "I once loved a guy long ago so much it hurt. I never thought I'd feel that way again."

Pulling away, Olivia turned to leave, but Luke kept a hold of her hand. "I write them for you." His voice cracked along her skin like sparklers.

"Write what?"

"My music. The songs I sing. All I have to do is think of you when I'm stuck and it just flows from the tips of my fingers." Luke chuckled dejectedly. "It's almost like you're my muse. All of my songs have parts of you in them. You just have to listen closely."

She couldn't handle it any longer. Luke was making her chest hurt and her head ache. He wanted her, he didn't. Which was it?

"I don't know what happened, Livy. I drank a few beers and was all good, but once I began to play my music...you paid no attention to it... I'm sorry. Lame excuse, but I was sucked back into the past and couldn't control myself. I wanted to go back and feel it all again with you, even if it was just for one night."

Olivia smiled sadly. Squeezing his hand she said, "I have to go. I have a long drive ahead of me." As she went to open the door, she glanced over her shoulder and saw Luke standing with such a heartbreaking look that she found herself saying, "I listen to all of your music, even if it hurts to."

thirty

Luke was too stressed out with everything going on in his life. His mom, Livy, work, touring… It was all becoming so exhausting mentally and he needed a damn break. Livy took up most of his thoughts, those of the present and past. Watching her in her doctor's office being able to do what she loved really got to him. He knew what she wanted at a young age, and she went after it. But the truth was, he couldn't help but "what if" himself to death over the choices he made.

So he flew home the moment his tour ended. He hopped on the next flight out, only after sitting with his manager for over three hours discussing the next phase of his life, and then he bolted. He hadn't even stopped to see his parents, didn't mention he was coming home, just went straight to his house and threw himself into his empty bed and passed out. He needed some serious down time. But before he crashed, he shot Livy a text.

LUKE: *I'm home…was thinking we could get lunch while I'm here.*
OLIVIA: *Sure. I'd like that.*

A few days later, Luke was finally rested with a clear mind.

> LUKE: *How about I come pick you up?*
> OLIVIA: *Umm… Where are we going*
> LUKE: *Wait, is this going to be a problem with Nate?*
> OLIVIA: *No.*
> LUKE: *Good. We're going out to lunch, remember?*

Shoot. Olivia wasn't even thinking and had completely forgotten about Luke asking her to lunch. She wasn't in the best frame of mind and her emotions were all over the place. Her only plan for Saturday was to plant flowers all day on her newly finished deck.

> OLIVIA: *I'm working on my deck and around my house all day…Sorry. Maybe tomorrow?*

Luke laughed. Livy wasn't getting off that easy.

> LUKE: *That's fine. We'll just take a ride and get a late lunch instead. Be sure to wear jeans*
> OLIVIA: *Okay.*

Olivia put the phone down and got back to planting. *Would it be okay with Nate…*if he only knew. Olivia shook her head. Taking a ride with Luke meant what? Where were they going? Where would they get lunch? What would they talk about? Luckily she was able to push that back until tomorrow.

Two hours later, sweat trickled down the swell of her breasts and her hair sticking to the back of her neck. With her fingers covered in dirt and all over her clothes, Olivia stood up and wiped her forehead then grabbed a water bottle. It was a scorcher outside, and she could feel how hot her cheeks were. She pressed the ice cold bottle to both cheeks before she opened it and drank it all.

Her dogs barking brought her gaze to the sound that echoed down the street. She patted Tom's head and peeked through the trees.

Her mouth dropped. Luke? *On a motorcycle?* What was he doing here?

The roar of the pipes grew louder as she watched the bike draw closer.

Olivia shook her head. Of course it had to be Luke.

One more crank of the gas, and Luke rode onto Livy's driveway and flicked off his bike. He couldn't stop grinning at her expression. She obviously wasn't expecting him, or for him to ride up on a bike.

Holding the handle bars steady, Luke tilted his bike to the side and dropped the kickstand. Gently, he eased his bike down and stood, swinging his leg off. Removing his jacket and then his helmet, Luke shook his head, allowing his hair to breathe after being trapped under the helmet for nearly an hour. Livy still hadn't moved from her place, her mouth hanging open.

Luke smiled. "Hey, Care Bear."

"What are you doing here?"

"Taking you out for lunch."

Her brows furrowed. "That's tomorrow."

He glanced at his watch. "Well, it's already three p.m. and when you said you were working on your deck all day, I knew you wouldn't be leaving so I came by today instead. I figured I could help with your planting then we could catch a bite to eat."

"I'm not getting on that bike."

Luke's grin stretched bigger. "Yes, you are."

"No way in hell. When you said take a little ride, I thought you meant in your truck! Not on a death trap!"

"Livy, as if I'd let anything happen to you. And we are

taking a ride, a ride on my bike. You need to let go and let the wind hit your back and not give a damn for once in a while. I just got my license to ride, so you're safe. Let's go."

Her mouth dropped with her shoulders, fear clouded her senses. "You just got your license? When?" she whispered thickly.

Long strides took Luke toward Olivia. He shrugged. "I think...two weeks ago?"

"Two weeks! There is no *way* I am getting on there with you now," she retorted, taking a few steps backwards. "You shouldn't even be riding alone yet, either. That's too soon!"

"Livy," he warned. "Let's go."

"Luke, I'm a doctor! I know what risks I face riding those things. No! Plus, you're not experienced enough to ride."

"Baby, I know how to ride," Luke smirked.

Olivia couldn't stop the smile that tugged at her face at his innuendo. He was picking up speed and closing the distance between them. No way was she riding a motorcycle with an inexperienced driver.

Turning, she took off running barefoot through her yard. She rounded the corner of her house and looked over her shoulder to see Luke trailing her.

"Luke!" she yelled. "Stop! I'm not getting on your bike!" She was giggling at being chased and then started running in zigzags to create distance between them.

"Like hell you're not. I'm taking you for a ride. You need it more than anyone," he said catching up to her. Luke wrapped a strong arm around her stomach and hauled her against him.

Olivia yelled somewhere between a scream and a giggle at being captured. She wiggled out of his hold quickly, giggling the whole time. She took three steps before he captured her again and tumbled them to the ground.

Out of breath, Olivia tried to roll and escape him, but he pinned her down with his body on the grass. She squirmed and twisted under him, legs scissoring the sides of his waist as her hips lifted, trying to push him off.

Luke stared at her laughing face and he realized how much he missed seeing her glowing smile. Her eyes lit up and they sucked him in.

"You're not goin' anywhere except to change and get on my bike."

"Luke, I am not riding that thing," she breathed.

"Baby, yes you are." He smiled at her. "You'll love it. I know it. It's what you need. Trust me."

Her smile faltered at his endearment.

"What's wrong?" he asked, his brows furrowing. If she really didn't want to ride, he wasn't going to push it anymore.

"You called me 'baby'." Luke's eyes softened with his body. He looked at her dirt smeared face and realized that calling her baby struck a chord. Looking at her lips, he wanted so bad to lean down and kiss her. Instead, he took a hand and moved her hair from her face, dragging his knuckles down the side of her head, causing her eyes to drift shut. She tugged her bottom lip into her mouth and bit down, knowing she was fighting the feelings coursing through her body, just like he was.

"So I did," he said softly. "Does that bother you?"

She shook her head no. In fact, she liked the sound of it on his lips.

"Good. So you ready to go?"

She gripped Luke's shoulders with apprehension and asked, "Did you really just get your license?"

His green eyes lit up and his lips curved at the tips into a heart stopping grin.

"No, I've had it for years, actually. I was just busting your chops." Her eyes rolled and she chuckled. Leaning down, he couldn't resist softly kissing her forehead. She looked so adorable under him on the grass that he had to do it. Her hands that were on his shoulders gripped him harder and she tensed.

Pulling back, he asked, "Are you ready to go?"

"I'm pinned beneath you and full of dirt." He looked down at their bodies and a half-smile tipped his lips. "So you are."

She pushed at his shoulders but got nowhere. "Well, will you move so I can get changed and we can ride?"

So we can ride? Damn. Luke was having a hard time with moving. He was sandwiched comfortably between her warm thighs and didn't want to move. "I kind of like where I am actually," he said as he wiggled his hips, which was a stupid thing to do. It only made his cock hard.

Olivia clenched her stomach as she held in a groan. Why did Luke have to do that? She was completely aware of every inch of his body trapping her to the ground. She squeezed her legs and inadvertently rolled her hips into his, feeling his hardness press against her sex. A small breath rolled off her lips. Luke's eyes darkened and his jaw flexed.

Taking a chance, Olivia ran her fingers through his hair. "I've wanted to do this for a while now," she said softly when he tensed. At his confused look, she answered him. "I wanted to run my fingers through your hair since I saw you again. Remember how I used to do it all the time?"

With both hands, she gently trailed her nails along his scalp, fluffing up his hair and watching it fall through her fingers. For some reason she had always found it relaxing in the past, and felt the need to do it now.

He had forgotten how much he loved when she did that. Her touch was soft, arousing.

Luke's arms tightened around her as his dick strained against his pants. There was no way of hiding his erection and knew Livy could feel it too, yet she wasn't stopping with her hands. She was watching her fingers in his hair, but his gaze was locked on her lips and if she didn't stop, he was going to be kissing her in seconds. The look in her eyes had his body heating all over. So instead, he laid his head down on her chest and listened to her heart beat as she continued with his hair. He hoped he wasn't crushing her, but her touch was so comforting that he didn't want to move.

Olivia wasn't sure what came over her, but she had to run her fingers through his hair. She was lost in the softness when Luke laid his head down. Running her fingers through his hair used to bring calmness to her, and she realized it still did. Maybe that's why she started doing it. Maybe it was because she missed the feel of him on her even when it wasn't sexual, just when they were lying together. He brought her a sense of security.

Taking a deep breath, she wrapped her arms around him, holding him to her as her heart ached for the closeness with him.

That's when it hit her. This is what she had yearned for in the past that no one could deliver. "What are we doin'?" she asked quietly.

"I'm doing whatever you want, baby."

Olivia squeezed her eyes shut. "I'm going for a ride with you."

Once she dressed in jeans and boots, Olivia was standing in front of Luke's bike, watching him buckle his helmet. He undid the smaller helmet that was fastened to the back of the second seat and walked to her.

Biting her lip, she said, "I'm scared, Luke."

Luke dropped his arms. "Olivia, I would never let anything happen to you. I promise. We'll stick to the back roads if that makes you feel better." She nodded.

Placing the helmet on her head, he said, "Lift your chin," then buckled the straps.

Luke looked in her eyes and saw that she trusted him. With a grin he said, "Let's ride."

Swinging a leg over the bike, Luke sat down on the leather

seat and put the weight on his right leg as his left boot flipped the kickstand back. He switched the key and turned on his bike. Twisting his wrist back, Luke listened for the cracking sound of the pipes roaring to life.

He glanced at Olivia who was as pale as a ghost. "Get on." She nodded stiffly and swung a leg over. Looking into his rearview mirror, Luke watched as Livy looked around frantically for something to hold on to.

Looking over his shoulder, Luke said, "Scoot down as close as you can get to me."

Olivia did as Luke asked and her legs were snuggly cupping him. She wasn't sure where to put her hands so she placed them under the seat and grabbed a hold of the metal railing, gripping it for dear life. Maybe this wasn't such a good idea…

Luke chuckled at Olivia's tense body. He dropped his arms and turned around halfway. Holding the bike between his thighs, he grabbed one wrist, then turned the other way and grabbed her other wrist. Pulling her forward, he wrapped her arms around his waist and locked her around him. Glancing over his shoulder one last time, he said, "There. Now hold on tight and don't let go."

Luke revved the engine, the loud pipes roaring as Livy scooted even closer and squeezed him hard. "Lighten up. I need to breathe, Livy," he laughed.

"Oh, sorry," she mumbled.

Slowly, Luke turned his bike around and it rode forward. His boots skated lightly over the gravel until reaching the end of the driveway.

"Which way to the backstreets?" She pointed and told Luke. Nodding, he accelerated and skimmed his feet along the road until he picked up speed then placed them on the foot rest and rode out.

At first Olivia thought she was going to be sick. She tried not to squeeze Luke so hard, but she had never been on a motorcycle before and it frightened her. Once they hit the street, Olivia watched as Luke held the steering bars and rode with confidence, only then starting to relax a little. It was exhilarating and she felt free, but that didn't mean she lightened up on her hold. Olivia found the front pockets of Luke's jacket, slid her hands into them, took a deep breath and relaxed into his back. She turned her head to the side and laid it down watching as the world passed them by while they rode to virtually nowhere.

Luke had always brought her a sense of comfort when they were younger. He knew about her alcoholic father and his outbursts, her adoption and rebellion as a teenager, and he was constantly there to calm her down when she was losing control. He knew the right words to say and if that didn't work, he'd sing to her. He was the one constant in her life she could rely on back then. And now when she was at a time in her life when she felt like her control was slipping, he showed up on his bike.

Olivia knew she was falling for Luke again, not because of his looks or their undeniable connection, but because aside from everything in her life she dealt with, he got her. He understood her. He knew her, and he accepted her past, something she had never shared with anyone. He was her best friend and confidant. Olivia forgot how much she missed his friendship.

Tilting his head to the side he yelled at her, "You good?"

Livy propped her chin on his back with her hair billowing in the wind and answered him. "I'm good."

It was the best she's been since she left Georgia.

thirty-one

A little over an hour later, Luke veered off to the side. After riding for that amount of time he wanted to give Livy a chance to stretch her legs out. He got off the bike, undid his helmet, then hers.

"Here, let me help you off the bike. Stand up on the foot rests. The pipes are hot and you'll burn your leg pretty badly if you hit it."

"Really?"

"Oh yeah, I've don't it a few times. Hurts like a bitch."

Olivia looked down at the shiny silver pipes then back up, listening to them sizzle as they cooled down. She stood on the pegs and reached for him. Luke grabbed her by the waist and lifted her up, bringing her chest parallel to his face. She wrapped her arms around his neck and bent her knees as he carried her away from the bike.

Stopping, Luke slowly lowered Olivia to the ground, but they never left each other's embrace. "Did you like the ride?" he asked, staring into her eyes, her hair a tangled mess.

"I did."

"Would you want to ride with me again sometime?" he grumbled, hoping she'd say yes.

She bit her lip, and nodded.

Luke smiled and kissed her forehead. "Good. Now let's go get something to eat." Luke broke contact and took hold of Olivia's hand. He began walking, but she stopped.

"Oh my god," Olivia yelled out, bending over to look between her legs as Luke laughed. She began walking with bowed legs. "I feel like I went horseback riding! My legs are sore!"

Luke chuckled. "Come on, cowgirl."

The sun was setting around them as Luke and Olivia had a late lunch on one of the wooden picnic benches scattered outside the little diner. "How are your parents doing? I haven't seen them in years."

Olivia averted her eyes. "My mom is good I guess... Dad is the still the same. Nothing has really changed between them."

"So he's still drinking I take it?"

Olivia sighed. "Mom says he's slowed down, but I don't know if I believe her. I want to, but I haven't been home enough to actually witness it."

"You never went home during the holidays while you were in medical school?" he asked in disbelief.

"I did, but only for a few short days. It was hard to find time between school and work. Like I said, I never stayed long enough to have to deal with his verbal attacks. I think Dad tried to hide it from me when I was there, truthfully."

Luke shook his head. "Remember when you used to sneak over to my house at night?"

Her eyes met his with a smile. "What made you think of that?" she asked.

Luke thought for a moment. "I'm not sure." He took a sip of his soda then said, "My mom said she knew you would sneak over at night. She could tell something was going on with you, just wasn't sure, but that she also trusted us so she didn't get involved. Apparently your mother knew it too."

"What! She did?" This was news to her.

"Yeah, she told me after you left, actually. It was surprising to hear."

"Huh. Maybe that's why I never got caught sneaking in or out of my house. I mean, Dad was too drunk to wake up to noise, but I'm sure Mom would have heard."

"Beats me."

"You know..." she said, easing into the next part with a smirk on her face, "the majority of the time I came over was because of what was going on at home, you knew that, but sometimes it was just because I wanted to be near you. So I'd sneak into your room and sleep with you."

"Funny you say that because I could usually tell when something was up at home when you came in. Your body was usually wound tight, scrunched up and shaking, begging me to hold you and to not let go. So I did. I'd wait until you fell asleep and then I would too. But there were a few times when I couldn't figure out what was bothering you, so I left it alone."

Olivia gulped. His memories hit her gut, the reminiscences of him holding her, putting her to sleep, trying to erase her nightmares to create happy memories. "Your home felt safe to me. It was warm and inviting, unlike mine. Your mom always had a smile on her face and your brothers were happy. Being there with you felt right."

"For what it's worth, I'm glad to hear that, Livy." She nodded with a tight smile.

"She trusted us..." Olivia giggled, shaking her head, remembering that more than sleep was going on.

"Yeah, it's a good thing I knew how to keep you quiet back then," Luke said, a wicked grin spreading across his handsome face.

She threw a french fry at his head, which he dodged. "Luke!"

"Ah, back in the day when we were wild and free..."

Luke's eyes traveled playfully to the sky as he thought back to them naked between the sheets at night.

"Luke. Stop. I know what you're thinking about. Just stop."

A sinful gleam resonated in his eyes as another french fry went flying toward his head.

"Down by the lake..."

"Luke!"

"In the back of my truck..."

"That's it. I'm going to kill you!" she yelled, rising from the bench and laughing.

He got up from the bench and stepped back. Teasing her, he continued. "In the woods after the bonfire that one night..."

"Oh my god." Olivia stepped around the table trying to reach him but he moved too fast.

"Your screams went on for miles..."

She almost grabbed his shirt but he moved out of her grasp. "I swear to God, Luke, I will sell all your dirty little secrets to the tabloids if you don't stop. Like how you like to talk dirty!"

He stopped. "You wouldn't dare."

"I would," she laughed, looking to see which way was closer to reach him. "Or how you're actually soft and sweet and like to cuddle. Or how you like to sing impromptu songs in bed. I bet that would take away from your rock image."

"No one would believe you," he deadpanned.

"Yes, they would. I can see it now on the front cover of the tabloids." Using her hands, she said, "Ex-*girlfriend to pen tell all about singer/songwriter Luke Jackson.*"

"Go ahead and try it." He hadn't moved from his spot.

"What makes you think no one would believe me?" she asked, edging closer to Luke.

"Because I never did any of those things with anyone except with you."

"What?" she breathed in, all humor dropping from her face.

Luke walked to where Olivia was firmly rooted in place. "There was no one else, Livy. No one else got what you got. Those were our moments, and ours alone. I wasn't going to recreate them with anyone else."

Olivia's wide eyes held her from looking anywhere else but deep into Luke's. She was lucky she managed a sentence at this point. "But didn't you have a girlfriend? I assumed you would with her," she whispered.

"Well, yeah, of course I had a few here and there, but you assumed wrong because I didn't sing to any of the girls. Ever."

Being on the road didn't allow him to have a girl of his own long-term. And contrary to what people believed, he wasn't the kind of guy who slept with just anyone. Sure, at first it was all fun and games. He tried to lose himself in his music and any woman who didn't resemble Livy. Luke was young and fortunate to be doing what he loved, but in the last few years, he'd grown and shied away from the camera, wanting more privacy. Thank goodness he had considering the state his mother was in now. He kept his personal life on the down low as much as he could. Since then, he had only been with a few women, but none of them came even remotely close to the one standing before him with anguish in her eyes.

"I had no idea. Maybe I won't sell all your secrets after all."

Luke grinned. "I would hate for the world to know what we shared."

Olivia stared into Luke's eyes that held so much honesty. She couldn't believe what he was telling her. That even after everything that had happened, he still held onto them.

"Why?"

"Why, what?"

"Why didn't you sing to any of them? Why didn't you give them what you gave me?"

"Listen to my words," he emphasized, reminding her how his feelings and emotions were weaved in his music. Luke brushed away a tangled lock of hair from her face. "It was only you, only you who got the real me. And I wasn't going to ever share that with anyone, Livy. Even though we had split, it still meant too much to share. It didn't feel right letting someone in on our private moments." Cupping the sides of her face, he finished with, "So I never did."

Olivia's mouth gaped open. "How do I know you're not lying?" Her voiced cracked.

"I promise you I'm not," he said seriously. "Go ahead and share our intimate details and watch how many chicks go after you. I'm telling you the truth, Care Bear. There was no one else but you. Only you got the real me. I learned early in my career to wear a mask, but with you I never needed to. I swear."

Olivia searched Luke's green eyes for the truth...and found it. She saw it, even when she didn't want to accept it; it was right in front of her eyes. She didn't know what to think. He saved their precious moments for them only. It made her jaw quiver with too many emotions knowing he spoke the truth. Olivia could feel tears rising up and settling on her lids. This whole time...she'd been so stupid.

Her breathing accelerated and she did the only sensible thing that she could think of. Olivia grabbed the sides of Luke's face and pulled him to her, smashing her lips to his. She stood on her tiptoes and leaned into him as Luke grabbed her hips in shock, digging his fingers into her. Olivia kissed him with force, with emotion and with heart. As Olivia wrapped her arms around Luke, he kissed her back slowly but then pulled away. Stormy need laced with confusion swirled in his green eyes. They hit her hard, and she wanted to fall into them. She went to reach for his mouth again, but he stopped her.

"As much as I love your lips on mine, what about Nate?"

Olivia gulped and she loosened her arms. She averted her eyes and bit her lip. Quietly she said, "I don't want to talk about him."

Luke wasn't a cheater by any means and new Livy wasn't either, but he had to ask about Nate. As much as he loved the feel of her in his arms, her mouth on his as she kissed him with such intensity, Luke felt bad for the guy. He watched Livy's shoulders sag and felt her regress. He knew something was going on with Nate, he just wasn't sure what. It wasn't his business to ask anyway. Not right now at least while she was staring at his mouth, clearly wanting more of him.

"You sure?"

Olivia nodded. "So would it be okay if I did this?" he asked, brushing his lips across hers.

"Yes. Trust me," she mumbled into his mouth.

"You sure?" he asked before pulling her back to his mouth and taking control.

Olivia nodded her head and then rose up on her toes once more as Luke sucked on her bottom lip. He tightened his arms around her waist, pulling her to him. Luke lapped at her lips, kissing her back with the same passion. He was showing her how much she still meant to him, that after all these years and with what he admitted tonight, the burning need for Olivia King could never be extinguished.

Just like it never had for her.

thirty-two

A month had gone by since riding with Luke on his bike. At this point, Olivia was miserable and angry over her breakup with Nate and falling for Luke again.

Olivia silently berated herself as she sipped her whiskey and continued rearranging her furniture. It had been almost one month since Nate had ended things between them. Usually the whiskey calmed her nerves and made her giddy, but tonight it was doing the complete opposite. It was firing her up the way it burned down the back of her throat and settled in her stomach as she reminisced about the past. She was trying to find justifications for everything. Her emotions were battling with her brain. She just wished it would stop for a little while.

Let me down easy, Liv.

Those words had replayed over and over in her head for weeks.

Another sip.

Just her letting him down, easy.

But it really wasn't easy in the least. She could read Nate's emotions as clear as day as he tried to mask them. Sadness had layered his handsome face like translucent skin. She had never felt worse. A low ringing sound pushed through her thoughts.

Grabbing her phone, Olivia picked it up to see Luke calling.

And life just got sweeter, didn't it?

"What, Luke?" she snapped.

"Whoa. What's wrong, Care Bear?"

"Don't call me that!" Olivia squeezed her eyes shut in frustration. *Care Bear.* She knew exactly where that stupid stuffed animal was sitting.

On her shelf. In her living room. With all her books. Just like it had for many years, and in every office she'd ever had, only this time she moved it to her house. She seemed to create her own misery everywhere she went. Now she felt like gutting the damn thing and watching its white fluff drift aimlessly to the floor. Then she would stomp on it while she laughed maniacally.

"What do you need, Luke?" she seethed into the phone, gripping it hard in her hand.

Olivia heard a lighter strike, a long, deep inhale and then release. "Just needed to call ya," he said, his southern drawl came out stronger.

She shook her head. "For what now?"

"Nothing, really. Maybe to see if you wanted to go for a ride again."

She'd actually love to do that, but she was too worked up at the moment to say yes. "Listen, Luke, I'm in no mood today. I'm hanging up now."

"Livy, what's wrong?"

Olivia fought the urge to snap back. Her emotions were already running wild and she did not want to be questioned by him. Instead, she huffed into the phone.

"Everything going okay with you and Nate? Why are you breathing heavily?"

Olivia stopped in her tracks. "I'm trying to move furniture, and it's... It's none of your damn business!"

"Okay..." Another puff of smoke.

"I'm rearranging my furniture. That's why I'm out of breath!" Olivia couldn't contain herself. Every time she answered Luke, she yelled at him. "And sweet baby Jesus, would you stop smoking those cigarettes? They're going to kill you and ruin that raspy voice of yours everyone loves."

Luke snickered into the phone. The guy literally snickered.

That did it. She clicked the phone off and threw it onto her wood table with a loud clang and watched it slide across and drop to the floor.

She needed music. Music always helped when she was feeling down and sad about things going on in her life. It brought her to a place where she was free from everything and let her forget her troubles from the past. So she cranked up the stereo and thanked Mother Mary she didn't have neighbors to complain about her music.

Thirty-five minutes later, after moving the furniture back to where it originally was, Olivia was breaking into a sweat.

What the hell had she been thinking? Wiping her forehead with the back of her hand, her dog started barking from the loud banging coming from her front door.

Peering to the right, she looked out the side window and stood still.

You have got to be kidding me.

A stupid grin spread across his handsome face, reaching his eyes—green eyes that were shadowed by a hat of course. Unlocking the dead bolt, Olivia opened the door. She stood still staring with her jaw set tight.

"Umm, what are you doing here, Luke? You sure love stopping by my house, don't you?"

Luke looked down at Olivia and continued to grin at her. She was all worked up, her hair a hot mess and clothes all twisted from sweating. *Damn*...a wild mess and she still looked good.

"Come to think of it, I never asked you how you found out where I live in the first place. How did you find my address?"

"My people."

"Your people?"

"Yeah."

"Could you get anymore clichéd?"

"Aren't you going to let me in, *Livy*?"

"Not 'til you tell me why you're here, *Lukey.*"

"Lukey? Come on, baby. Couldn't you come up with a better one than that?" Olivia glared at him and began closing the door in his face.

"Wait... Wait!" Luke stopped the door with his hand.

"Just let me in."

"What for?"

"Because clearly your dickhead boyfriend isn't here to help you with your...rearranging."

Her eyes were suddenly watery as she tried to hold in the tears.

"Olivia, please, let me in."

There was nothing he hated more than seeing her cry. Olivia stepped back and allowed him in. When he heard her voice on the phone earlier, he knew instantly she needed someone. The pain in her words pulled him in, so he hopped in his truck and hightailed it north.

Once she shut the door behind him, Luke followed silently down the hall, not saying a word. Hell, no way could he speak a word right now if he wanted to. His eyes were glued to the two plump rounds moving up and down as her feet patted down the hallway. Luke followed her, the music he could barely hear from the front of the house getting louder, into an open room in a massive disarray of furniture.

She was really moving the furniture herself? Was she out

of her damn mind? He placed his hands on his hips and looked around. It was a good thing he had called her when he did. She'd been on his mind all day and fought with the urges to call her.

"What's next?"

Olivia pointed to the loveseat then the empty spot where she wanted it.

He moved it.

"Next?" Again, Olivia said nothing, just pointed. He knew she was hurting but also knew she wasn't going to open up until she was ready.

Luke watched as the stress started to fade away from her beautiful chocolate eyes as she lifted the small glass of amber liquid, swirled it then brought it to her lips. Using the hem of her shirt, she wiped her face and forehead, exposing her pale belly. The soft and smooth skin rose and fell as she breathed. Luke had to shift his gaze away quickly so his dick wouldn't get any ideas.

After a little while, she turned down the music and looked over at him. "You want something to drink? I have whiskey, water…whiskey… Maybe a beer layin' around somewhere… I don't know…"

"Yeah, I'll take a beer if you have it. Thanks. Where do you want these books?" Luke asked as he began pulling them off the top shelf so he could move the bookcase for her. Olivia looked around. "Here, give them to me." She traded the beer for the books.

After emptying the first three shelves, Luke squatted down to the fourth one, and then stopped.

Nestled in the corner and leaning against a thick medical book was the little purple Care Bear he'd given her many years ago. Luke reached for the bear. Clutching it in his hand, he stood and turned to Olivia.

Olivia's breath hitched at the sight of what Luke was holding. Her heart contracted as he stood there looking dumbfounded between her and the bear. She'd completely forgotten the bear.

"You kept it? After all this time?"

"Of course I did, Luke."

"Why?"

Olivia walked over to Luke and reached for the bear but he swiped his hand away before she could grab it. Blowing her hair from her eyes in frustration, she placed her open palm out. "Hand it here, Luke."

"No. Tell me why you kept it first."

Olivia rolled her eyes.

"Did you just roll your eyes at me?"

"Men are so dense," she mumbled. "Of course I kept it. But your grubby hand is getting it all dirty. Now please, give it back."

"These grubby hands are helping you while your boyfriend is MIA. So answer the question." His eyes were hard and unnerving. "Why did you keep it?"

"Because we grew up together? You were my best friend and you meant something to me, dammit. What? You don't have anything sentimental?" She sighed heavily while answering.

Astonished, he stared at the bear as he asked, "But Olivia, it's been, how many years?"

"What does it matter?"

"It's just a piece of pillow stuffing, Livy. It's nothing."

Olivia felt the tears prickle her eyes. Her jaw burned as she fought to stop it from quivering. She refused to cry over a stuffed animal that obviously meant nothing to Luke. *Just a piece of pillow stuffing?* He obviously wouldn't understand.

"To you maybe." She held out her hand and asked softly, "Can I have it back now? Please?" That bear meant more to her than the medical books on her shelves. It was priceless. And if anything happened to it, she didn't know what she would do.

Luke looked at Livy's puffy, tear rimmed eyes and handed the Care Bear back to her. He hadn't expected her to keep the bear. Then something dawned on him.

"What about the necklace? Did you keep that too?"

Livy brushed a hand down the front of the bear feeling the downy softness. Of course she kept the necklace. A sad smile that didn't quite reach her eyes formed on her face.

"It's because of you, you know. Nate's not here because of you," Olivia whispered, dodging the necklace question.

Luke's head snapped up at Olivia's words. Had the bastard actually left her?

"You're kidding, right? When did he leave?"

Olivia sighed and placed the bear on top of the book pile with great care, as if it was porcelain. She took a deep breath and ran her hand over her knotted hair. Walking into her kitchen, she grabbed another beer for Luke and poured two fingers of whiskey into her glass.

Handing him the beer, she said, "It was over a month ago. The day after the results of your mom's tests came in, he broke it off."

"That long ago? Why haven't you told me?"

She shrugged, shaking her head. "Do you want the truth? All of it from the beginning?"

"Indulge me."

With a heavy heart, Olivia decided to let the words flow that she had kept locked inside for so long.

"Truth is, Luke, I came back here because of you. I didn't want to admit it at first, but there was a pull so strong that kept screaming at me to come back to Georgia. But like the incredibly stubborn woman I am, I kept ignoring it. Even though we had been over for years, and I had no hopes of ever reconciling anything with you, I still had to come back. I don't know why, and I know it doesn't make any sense. I just needed to be here too. It's one of those things you can't explain, just that I knew I had to do it."

Olivia's heart was racing a mile a minute, battering against her ribs. Luke just stared at her, not saying a word.

"After everything I dealt with growing up, I needed to prove to myself that I could survive on my own. That going to school in a new city far away was the right thing. I was devastated after I left, you have no idea. There were times where I was ready to drop med school, pack up and come home. The first year was the most difficult, and a few times I almost caved. Thankfully, the overwhelming amount of school work kept me busy. I told myself that I was happy with my new life, that it was what I wanted. It was what I wanted, just not without you. So I stuck it out and stayed. After I completed everything I went to New York for, I worked for a little while until I couldn't take it anymore. I was...done. I wanted to come home. Now when I look back on it, I can't believe how selfish I was. I was stupid to be so single-minded and not thinking about who I was hurting."

Olivia inched her way to Luke, taking small steps and scrunching up the bottom of her shirt in her clammy hands. She was nervous as hell and starting to tremble, but desperately fought to keep it from showing. She wanted to appear cool, calm, and collected. That she could handle even an admission as simple as this. But this wasn't simple. Not in the least.

"Nearly every day I put on a brave face while dying on the inside trying to be someone I'm not. I was hollow, empty without you. I suffered day in and day out without you for years until I finally let go. Now I'm wondering if I made the right decision to come back to Georgia. I never expected this. You, being around again, near me, surrounding me, taking up my thoughts and what could have been. What I threw away. Everything is so messed up."

Swirling her glass, Olivia watched the smoky liquid spin into a funnel. She took a sip of whiskey then set the glass down on the table. "Nate left me because he saw what I couldn't admit. He saw what you mean to me. *I* didn't even know," she said, placing a hand against her chest, "but he did. It didn't help that I wasn't upfront with him over the phone calls. Or all the texts. With anything that involved you."

Olivia looked at the bear, then to Luke. "You wanted a reason why I kept the bear, Luke? There it is. You're the reason. I thought I had let go, but obviously I never did. I don't know if I'll ever truly let go. How pathetic am I? I'm thirty-one years old and still in love with my first love."

Luke didn't utter a word as she finally broke the dam that was holding back everything she had bottled up inside.

Clutching her hands to her chest and swallowing her anguish, she kept talking. "I missed you so much, Luke. Each and every day I thought about you, what we had, and how stupid I was to walk away from it. I screwed up. I can't take it back, and as crazy as it sounds I wouldn't. But I'm here now pouring my heart out to you."

Olivia didn't know where this courage was coming from. Liquid courage? It didn't matter. It was now or never that she be truthful to herself and to Luke.

"Had I known how things were going to happen between us, I never would've left. But I don't feel bad about leaving, either. And how fucked up is that? I'm so fucked up... My mind is all over the place..."

Luke hadn't moved a muscle or spoken a single word the entire time. She couldn't even gauge his thoughts. He just stood there with his arms crossed in front of his chest with a pained expression. She couldn't interpret what he was thinking. Luke just stood there, his silence was deafening.

Grabbing her drink, she sipped it. "You know what? It doesn't even matter anymore. I'm not even making sense. The past can't be changed and everything is such a joke. It is what it is. No matter what, I'm always going to want more..." She mumbled the last sentence to herself. The whiskey infused her blood, and she let go, opening up to Luke and letting it all out so he knew where she stood. That he could take her or leave her.

Take me or leave me, Luke once said to her. Now she knew the full impact of those words.

Luke didn't know whether to throttle Olivia or throw her to the floor and take her right there, which he was positively sure she'd allow. He definitely didn't see this coming, dumbfounded by her confession.

He took another swig of his beer as he thought back to the day he'd seen her after all these years. She looked as beautiful as the first time he laid eyes on her when they were teens. There had always been an undeniable connection with her. The lure in her eyes, her pouty little lips, it was all damning to him. In that moment, he hated himself for not following her.

Taking a swallow of his beer, he placed the empty bottle on the table and stalked his way over to her.

"Why, Olivia? Why, now?" He growled in the back of his throat. She gave a hesitant shrug.

Slowly, he leaned into Olivia, crowding her space. "What makes you think that I want you after all these years? Because of a few kisses? A few songs I made up?" he asked, cocking his head to the left. "You," he said pointing at her chest, "left me."

Olivia took a couple of steps back. She understood he was still angry about the past and how easily she threw it all away. Luke may have moved on, but she was the one that killed him on the inside. No one had ever compared to Olivia King.

Wired and ready for a fight, resentment filled his green eyes with fire even though his body was hard and ready for her.

"I...I...didn't say..." Olivia felt a twinge of uneasiness settle in her stomach.

"No. No you didn't say I still wanted you, but that's what you're hoping for, isn't it? That I'd drop everything and run back to you now that Nate is gone? Or was it because we shared a kiss?" Luke asked, still wondering where this admission of guilt was heading.

"Luke, I...ahhh..." Olivia stammered. Luke was in her face, invading her personal space. Taking another step back, she placed her hand behind her, feeling blindly around the newly arranged room.

"You 'ahhh' what? Huh..." Luke mimicked with a cocked eyebrow. He was livid and wanted her to feel what he felt.

Boxing her against the wall with his arms, Luke leaned close to her face. He could smell the whiskey on her wet lips and the smell of flakey coconut drifting all around her. It took everything not to press into her soft body.

Close enough to touch his lips to hers, he rubbed his stubborn jaw line across her smooth face as he whispered, "You what...baby?"

Gasping, Olivia lost all train of thought as she replayed what Luke just said in her head. *Baby.* She was lost as she stared into his eyes. One minute he was in her face, the next she saw tenderness.

Moving one arm from the wall, Luke tugged on her hair, forcing her to look directly at him. With his other arm, he snaked around her waist and pulled her tight to him. She was face to face with him now, no place to go.

Without thinking, Olivia brought her arms up and slowly wrapped them around Luke's shoulders. She had no idea what she wanted to say at that point. She couldn't even think straight being in his steely arms, his body pressing into hers. There was no mistaking the hardness of his erection pressing against her stomach letting her know he still wanted her even if he stated otherwise.

Luke's voice was a broken whisper as he stared into her eyes and said, "Livy...Care Bear."

He kissed her softly, slowly running his lips tenderly across hers. Olivia's lips were warm and supple, and damn how he missed the feel of them against his. She responded to his kiss by leaning into him with a soft whimper, but before she could get any further with him, he abruptly broke away.

Confusion etched across her face. Olivia was breathless and waited for him to explain why he stopped.

"You had your chance but lost it. I gave you an option and you ran the other way."

Olivia's mouth dropped with her heart. She tried to pull away only to have Luke pull her tighter to him, squeezing her.

"Luke, let go of me," she squirmed in his arms.

"You think you can just say all those things to me and then finish with 'it is what it is' and kiss me like that? I don't think so. I gave you an option, you ran. That's no one's fault but your own."

Olivia stopped twisting and snapped her crimson eyes to Luke's. "That's what I told you! That I fucked up! I'm sorry! I made a mistake. I apologized ten thousand fucking times already. What more do you want me to say? You could have come with me and refused. So this is on you too."

Placing the palm of his hand on her face, he gingerly caressed her reddened cheek. The regret in her pink-rimmed eyes hit him hard. She looked like a mess with her long hair wrapped up at the top of her head, strands falling wildly around her face. As much as he wanted to make her hurt, he just couldn't bring himself to do it. His resentment was an opened wound, and he was only clawing deeper, causing more pain. But she already felt his pain, and it was time to move on.

"Livy."

"Just shut up and let me go!"

"We can't go back, can we?" he drawled. "It's been so long. You only want me now that Nate is out of the picture," Luke said, pulling the tie out of her hair. "And the worst part is that I'm almost willing to cave," he whispered with his forehead against hers.

Olivia felt like a fool for opening up, embarrassed that she did and wanting to get away from him now. Luke threading his fingers through her hair and massaging her scalp wasn't helping her move her body from his. He was calming her with the touch of his hands and soothing her with his words.

"Don't presume to tell me what I want," Olivia spat out.

"I get it, Livy. I get how you feel because I still want you after all those years even when I shouldn't," he admitted.

"Olivia," Luke muttered. "We're both in a tough situation. We never really had closure, so we're hurting and taking things out on each other. You're hurt over dickhead leaving you. You're also angry at me because I forced you to deal with my mother, forcing you to deal with me. It was wrong of me, but I knew deep in my gut I could count on you to take care of her. Despite my worries and misgivings in the beginning, I knew I had to take a chance with you. Almost like it was meant to be. You and me. Again."

Her eyes traveled along his prominent jaw to his lips as he breathed. "I can't keep up with you, Luke," she mumbled.

Olivia stopped resisting his hold. Arching his hips, he held her nailed to the wall with his body as he placed his hands on the curve of her shoulders. She rested her forehead against his chest and let out choppy breaths trying to calm herself. "Everything's so messed up, Luke," she sniffled. "I don't know what to do, who to talk to anymore. I feel...so lost. I've never felt like this before. Why do I have to mess up everything good in my life? I'm such a fuck up," she sobbed softly, clutching his shirt in her hands.

"Hey," he said softly, "look at me." Olivia shook her head no.

Grabbing the sides of her face, Luke gently turned up her face and forced her gaze to his. "Livy, look at me." Olivia opened her eyes and his chest tightened at the pain and sorrow in them. He wanted more than anything to make her feel better.

"You're not a fuck up. Stubborn? Damn straight. But not a fuck up. Nate will regret leaving you down the line. Trust me on that one, baby." He bored into her eyes, trying to show the truth in his words.

"But you don't trust me."

"Who said I don't?"

"I just…"

"Do I regret not going with you to New York? Damn straight I sure as hell do. Don't think for one minute I don't regret not going with you. But then maybe you wouldn't have become a doctor. And then maybe I wouldn't have sat in those bars and gotten drunk on your memory and written all those cheesy-ass ballads that ended up landing me a record deal. Truthfully, I love my life, and I think you love yours, regardless of everything. Life works in mysterious ways, Livy. Nothing is set in stone, the course is still unwritten. We make our decisions, no one else. We can 'what if' it all we want, but things happen for a reason. If we sit and think about why things happen the way they do, that's just more precious time being wasted. Enough is enough. In the end, we're where we're supposed to be."

Olivia nodded her head, silently agreeing with him. The tears that finally fell from her eyes were caught by the pads of Luke's thumbs as he wiped them away. She licked her lips and blinked her eyes, suddenly feeling exhausted. She needed a break. A break from life. A break from reality. Just a break from everything.

Grinding his teeth together, Luke was fighting with his emotions as he watched her slowly run her tongue along her lips. This was Livy. His Livy. Could she be thinking the same as him? That he wanted to consume her mouth and every inch of her body? He sure hoped so, because he was about to take a chance.

Massaging his hands slowly down her face and neck, he watched Olivia's head loll back while her eyelids grew heavy.

Luke smirked when she released a purr-like moan and felt her body softening under his touch. She may not even know she was doing it, but by God was it hot.

"Let's stop this cat and mouse game we've been playing. Let's move forward and start new. Together. Don't deny us," Luke said huskily.

He took her mouth in his with a breathless kiss, and pressed his body into her. Thrusting his tongue in, Luke sucked the air from her as she gasped and he consumed her. Greedily he took from her as much as she was willing to give. Sucking. Pulling. Biting. Tongue fucking. He didn't care. Luke was okay with it. She wasn't pulling away and that said it all. It was clear, they needed each other. The arousal building inside Luke was becoming painful, but after everything said between them, he wasn't sure if he could push for a little more even though his cock was telling him to try.

"Luke..." she mumbled against his lips.

"Alright. Up you go." He lifted her with ease.

"Where are we going?"

"*You* are going to bed."

"Well, where are you going then?"

"Home."

"Luke, that's a long drive. Stay here. You can stay on my couch."

"Nah. I'm good. I can drive home."

"But you've been drinking."

"Babe. I'm good. Trust me."

"Please, stay here. You'll have me worried all night if you drive home."

Luke debated with himself whether to stay or not. He wanted to. But there was no way he'd be able to keep his hands to himself if he did.

"I'll stay with you for a little while, but then I'm leavin'. I'll be back in the morning to help finish. Hey, why the hell did you do that anyway?"

She shrugged hopelessly. "I wanted to take my mind off things, I guess."

"So you decided to do it with a bottle of whiskey and some heavy ass furniture moving? You could've hurt yourself."

Olivia sighed. "Well, I didn't say it was a smart idea."

"Don't do something like that again. You need something, you call."

"Alright," she replied softly.

Luke lowered her down and then kicked his boots off before he climbed in. He nestled into Livy's backside, draped an arm over her belly and pulled her close to him. It took everything he had in him not to groan out loud from the softness of her body.

"Go to sleep, Care Bear." Talk about pure agony. Livy's lush body was snuggled against his and there was nothing he could do about it.

"Don't leave…"

"I won't."

'Luke' was a whisper on her lips as Olivia fell into a deep slumber.

thirty-three

Running her palm along the cold empty sheet behind her, Olivia's stomach dropped a little at the loss of Luke not snuggled up behind her.

It had been such a long time and she had forgotten what it was like to be wrapped in Luke's arms. And what did it feel like to her? Comfort…security…and home. It was just like the times when she'd sneak out of her house once her father had fallen asleep and run down the street to his. After her father had consumed too many beers to count and took his anger out verbally on Olivia, Luke would hold her tight and take all her fears away.

Olivia's eyes were scratchy and swollen as she opened them. She was physically and mentally exhausted. Her body had been running on empty lately. Yawning, she stretched her arms above her head and turned over to look at the clock. *Eleven o'clock?*

Standing from the bed, she made her way to the kitchen to brew her favorite addiction. Halfway through the living room something caught her eye and she paused.

To her astonishment, her living room, down to the books being placed neatly on her shelves, was completely finished.

Her mouth dropped in shock as she scanned the room slowly, taking it all in.

Luke had finished it for her while she slept.

And sitting in the center of the room on her mahogany coffee table was the tiny little purple stuffed animal. He left it there purposely for her to see.

Olivia walked over to the table where she grasped the bear in her hands and stared down at it. A soft smile tugged at her lips knowing Luke must have done it after she'd fallen asleep in his arms last night where she was dead to the world. Her heart softened at Luke's thoughtfulness and realized that the mean front he put on was just that—a front.

After her coffee, she was going to jump in her car and take a little ride down south to thank him properly.

"Hang on! Be right there!"

Olivia tapped her foot nervously while her stomach twisted in knots as she stared at the blue front door. She wasn't sure why she was all wound up, it wasn't like she hadn't seen Luke recently, but her nerves were on edge and jittery as she waited for the door to open.

The door flew open and Diane's eyes grew wide. She beamed happily and said, "Well, hey there, Olivia. What brings you here? Come into the kitchen and I'll get you some tea."

Olivia smiled nervously. "I'm actually here to see Luke. Is he around?"

Tilting her head to the side with inquisitive eyes, Diane asked, "Luke? Well, he's around. But Olivia, he doesn't live here. He's at his own home." She said it as if Olivia should have known that.

"Oh, that's right... I'd forgotten he told me he built a house. I guess I just assumed he'd be here. Would it be too much if I asked where he lives now? I need to talk to him."

Diane pondered Olivia's question with a glimmer in her eyes. She felt like an idiot coming to South Fork to see Luke. She should've just called to thank him. Now she was standing in front of Diane asking for his address while Diane pursed her lips in thought.

"I'll give it to you, Livy, but you have to make me a promise."

Olivia's eyes furrowed. "Okay…"

Taking hold of Olivia's hand, she nicely requested, "You have to promise me not to hurt him again. He was a wreck after you left. He'd kill me if he knew I was telling you this, but as a mother I feel it's my duty to. And one day when you're a mother you'll understand, too. I watched him for months and the agony he went through without you by his side. I know Luke and he'd never admit that, but a mother knows these things. That's what hurt the most…being a mother and not able to fix the one thing only one other woman could. So please, promise me you won't hurt him again."

Olivia rolled her lip back and forth between her teeth as her jaw trembled. Her heart pumped hard as it cracked down the center, struggling to stay together after hearing Diane ask that she make this promise to her. She never ever meant to hurt Luke to begin with, and she sure didn't want to ever again.

Swallowing the lump in her throat, Olivia took a big breath before she spoke.

"I promise you, it wasn't just Luke who was hurting, Diane. If you only knew…" She shook her head. "But I promise not to hurt him again. All I want to do is thank him for last night."

Diane's pleading gaze morphed at her reply. Her eyes were perplexed with so many questions swirling in them. She touched her dainty fingers to her mouth and pulled back just a bit.

Breaking their silence, John tumbled down the stairs like a bat out of hell. He was in a hurry but managed to say, "Hey, Livy. Good to see you again."

"Where you off to, John?" Diane asked him.

"To see Alyssa."

Diane dabbed her cheek with a finger and slanted it to the side. John leaned over and pecked his mother's cheek before he left.

Alyssa? The one he was yelling at that night at Rum Bar?

Diane glanced back at her and said, "Alright, Livy. I'll give it to you. Just go easy."

thirty-four

As Olivia turned into Luke's home, her eyes widened. The wrought iron gate was wide open for anyone to enter and she wondered why Luke had left it like that.

Driving up the winding driveway, Olivia parked her car and stepped out. She took in the land surrounding his home in awe. She could smell the newly fresh cut grass and the moisture in the air. Luke had done an impressive job just from what she'd seen so far and she could only imagine what the inside looked like. Her knees locked in place just thinking about being inside his home. *Shoot*. What if someone was there? Like another woman?

Olivia groaned. She should have called first, but she wanted to thank him in person and wasn't thinking when she jumped in her car and hightailed it down south.

She took a few deep breaths and began walking up the pebbled driveway to Luke's large front door. Olivia was focused on the gray and white little pebbles beneath her feet when a sound caught her attention.

Standing before her was Luke, barefoot in ripped jeans. His arm was propped against the door as he leaned into it, the muscles flexing to hold up his weight, a cigarette dangling from his fingers. Her gaze traveled the length of him and Olivia ground down on her jaw at the sight of Luke's stance; his body was built to near perfection.

Olivia shyly smiled and then waved.

She waved. Like an idiot.

Luke took one last pull on his cigarette then dropped it into the ashtray outside.

"Can't say I'm not happy to see you, Livy, but what are you doing here?"

"I wanted to talk to you."

Luke's mouth quirked up. "Figured you weren't coming for a swim."

"Can I come in? I mean, if you're available and don't have company or not busy."

Luke took in Olivia's demeanor. He could tell by just glancing at her how nervous she was on the steps to his home. He never expected to see her there.

"You mean, like a female?" He chuckled. "There's no one here but me. Come on in, Livy."

Luke held opened his front door that had to be at least ten feet tall. As she brushed by, her senses became aware of every inch of him and she tried to hide the shudder that rolled through her body.

Damn. As Olivia glided past him, he once again took in that sweet flakey coconut smell that he only associated with her. It assaulted his nostrils in all the right ways, making his body hard for her. He instantly wanted her back in his arms again, and now that there was no barrier between them after what she told him the night before, he wanted to make it happen.

But it wasn't just the familiar smell of Livy that attracted Luke, because that would be disturbing. It was so much more. The fact that she was standing before him in his house after everything that happened, her generous and caring heart, the way she could sit and watch the sunset, her love of music especially, the way her coffee-colored eyes pulled him in…

Luke wanted Livy desperately. He wanted to feel it again with her. All of it. She was like listening to his favorite artist on repeat, he could never get enough. The beat to his music. The pure bliss of waking to her every day. She would always be his Livy, but now she was adult Livy and she made his heart beat faster and his blood roar even stronger than before. Nothing stood in their way now.

When his mother called and informed him that Livy was on her way, he didn't ask questions. Luke hung up, opened the gate to his home that was normally always bolted shut and quickly got dressed, throwing on whatever he could find.

Watching Livy's lush body fall into a deep sleep, sighing and mewing sounds broke free from her parted lips. He'd forgotten what it was like to have her wrapped in his arms and didn't want to leave, but knew he couldn't stay. He wasn't sure where they stood and he wasn't going to make assumptions, but he had hope and was wishing on a prayer that it would go his way.

Luke flew down the interstate in record time, but he hadn't been able to fall asleep once he got home. Olivia was on his mind and no way would counting sheep work for him. He wanted to take a shower after working up a sweat at her home, but he didn't want to wash the smell of her away. He knew just thinking that made him sound like a whipped man, but Luke didn't give a shit. When he had finally succumbed to sleep at the break of dawn, his mother had called what felt like only ten minutes later. He was half dead but perked right up at the mention of Olivia and got his ass in gear.

Olivia turned on her heels slowly, taking in all of Luke's home that was so him. It felt quaint and homey, which she wasn't expecting. A round table sat in the center of the entry way with mail strewn across it. Dark wooden beams crossed the white ceiling diagonally every few feet and there were pictures all over the walls. Rugs covered the wood floor that led into a living room. To her left were stairs to the second floor. She had to admit she was surprised at how nicely decorated the house was.

"Wow, Luke, you have such a nice home." She breathed in.

Luke shuffled on his feet. "Uh, thanks, Livy."

Luke could feel the anxiety dripping from Olivia's skin. He felt bad seeing her body so tense. Wanting to ease her discomfort, he asked, "Want me to give you a tour?" She nodded and her shoulders dropped.

"Well, this is the foyer, obviously." He smirked as his arms opened to showcase the room. "Come." Turning and walking toward the living room, Olivia followed behind a few feet. She listened to him as he showed her each room. Luke was dying to ask what was on her mind, he wanted to know her thoughts, but he'd wait until the time was right.

Making his way to the huge sliding glass windows that captured the most breathtaking view, Luke slid one of the doors open.

When Luke had the blueprints drawn up, he made sure to have a tall set of lengthy windows to display the view ahead of him. He knew once the dust settled the sunset would be the most amazing sight glistening off the lake. And he was right. Luke loved sitting on his porch watching the night fall. It was peaceful and provided much needed downtime after being on the road.

The only thing missing from the page was the one standing next to him staring straight ahead.

Olivia looked over the trees surrounding the lake. It was a picture perfect view with a tree swing to top it off. Luke had a huge piece of land that went as far as her eyes could see. To the right was a small home, which she assumed was a guest house.

"How much land do you own?" Olivia asked.

He shifted on his feet uncomfortably. "I don't know... Give or take twenty acres..."

Olivia's eyes bulged. "That's a lot of land, Luke. How do you keep it up?"

"I hire people."

"Oh yeah," she said, feeling stupid again. It would make sense hiring someone. "Are you home often?"

"Not as much as I'd like to be. Though, it does get pretty lonely out here when I am. Maybe that's why I'm hardly home all that much. If I had something or someone to come back to then that would be a different story," he said, looking deep into her eyes.

Trying to change the subject, she asked, "Do you have any animals?"

"No. I'd like a few dogs, but I don't like the idea of them being alone out here, not that anything would happen. Sure I could hire someone for that too, but I just can't. It wouldn't be right to the dogs. Plus, I don't know if I could trust someone to care for them."

God, how he missed Olivia and in that moment he wanted her back so bad.

Taking a chance, Luke held out an open palm. He wanted to walk onto his deck hand in hand and show Olivia. He wanted to stroll through his woods with her by his side. He wanted to sit on the swing and rock with her, not just now, but at night too. He wanted to show her his little studio he had added onto the house where he made his music. And just like all those years ago, as if in that moment nothing changed, he still wanted everything with her. He wanted to feel it all with her again. It was easy and simple, but that's what they always had together.

Take my hand...

Olivia looked down at Luke's inviting hand. Her breathing became erratic as emotions were bubbling up inside of her, threatening to escape. She tried to hold it in, but Luke noticed the change in her and he took a step closer. Her heart gave a little pitter patter at the nearness of him, the heat coming off his body as she watched him take deep breaths. She wanted desperately to take hold of Luke's hand and never let go, but was scared. She was scared of wanting everything with him again but not having it. Scared of how he made her feel. Scared at what he'd say. Scared of his rejection again. Luke always had such control over her, making her feel so much. Her heart was open and exposed more than it ever had been. Letting Luke completely back in was a chance she wanted to take, but was terrified to do so. She wasted too much time doing what she thought was right and not what she truly wanted deep down.

Most of all, she was scared that she had unintentionally hurt someone else in the process. Nate. She didn't want to run back to Luke like he swore she would, but the pull was too strong, too demanding.

Her vision became blurry as tears welled in her eyes and her jaw trembled. She couldn't take his hand. It felt guilty doing so, yet there was nothing more she wanted in the world.

Jesus. This woman had to be the most stubborn one he'd ever come across in his life. Luke could see the internal battle in her pretty brown eyes. He wasn't asking for her to marry him, not yet at least, just to take a walk. Then something happened. Whatever was running through her mind caused tears to form in her eyes and he knew she was fighting to keep them in. If he knew Olivia like he had, she was probably over thinking everything. If she wasn't going to take that extra step, then he would. Too much time had passed, and he wasn't going to let another day go by without her next to him. They were both stubborn and wanted something more all those years ago, but fate had come full circle and brought them right back to each other. No way was Luke going to allow her to leave again like he had nine years ago. It was the biggest mistake he had ever made.

Luke drew closer. He watched Livy's shoulders lift with each intake of air. Every time she took a deep breath, her breasts threatened to spill over her top.

"Take it," he demanded.

Olivia shook her head. She couldn't tear her troubled eyes from his hand. In a strained voice that killed him to hear, she whispered, "I can't."

"Olivia, look at me."

He stepped closer while she took a step back.

"No."

A lone tear slid down her pink cheek. When Luke saw it, he made the decision for both of them.

"Fuck," he muttered and pulled Olivia to him, feeling the far away connection finally close. He wrapped his arms around her back and held her tight. At first she tried to twist away with her small fists shoved up against his chest, but she quickly gave up and sagged into him. She let the tears flow freely. Her back vibrated from the emotions ripping through her body and he hated it because he understood what she was dealing with all too well. He felt it too. He felt every waking moment of it. The distance between them over the years was unbearable at times. The little sounds she made busted him open and all he could think of doing was making it right for both of them.

"Shhh... It's okay, Livy, I got you."

That only seemed to make her shudder harder so he dropped a kiss to her head.

"Baby, Care Bear, please don't cry. You know I hate seeing you like this," he begged.

"Don't let me go," she whispered between tears. All Luke could do was hold on tighter.

Too many emotions, too many memories, feelings, whatever it was, hit her all at once and she let go. It felt like waterfalls flowing from her entire being, signifying the struggles of the past that she held on to for so long. As humiliated as she felt, it felt even better to let it all out. Like a weight was lifted, the sun came out…and she could breathe again.

Olivia took a deep breath and slid her arms around the sides of Luke's waist and held on. She turned her head to the right and laid her head gently on his chest, looking out at the lake. She sidled up to him and pressed her body against his as he rocked her slowly and exhaled.

"Stay," Luke's voice splintered. "Stay for the night."

What the hell was he doing? Luke didn't want to push too far, but it was now or never. He knew she was dealing with a lot on her plate, and he didn't want her to do it alone.

Olivia froze and Luke felt it. Before she said no, he quickly spoke. "Not in my bed, Livy. Of course you're welcome there," he nervously laughed, "but you can stay in a guest room I have. Just stay with me tonight."

"I can't."

"No one is stopping you."

"I have to work in the morning."

Luke chuckled. "That's your reason why you can't? How about I make a deal with you? I'll set every alarm I have to make sure you're up early, even the coffeepot so it automatically brews you coffee in the morning."

Olivia seriously contemplated it, she shouldn't be, but she was. "I don't think—"

"Don't think. Just do. You're always thinking too much."

She sighed heavily. "We'll see."

thirty-five

It was early evening and the sun was getting ready to set. Luke poked the wood in his fire pit as Livy watched nearby on his couch. He finally managed to calm her down. She hadn't yet agreed to stay the night, but he hoped she would. There was one part of the house she had yet to see that meant more than any other room in his home.

"Want see why I had the house built the way I did?

"Sure," she replied softly.

Reaching out his opened hand, Olivia threw her legs off the couch and put her hand in his to stand. She was exhausted and mentally drained but she wanted to see what sold him on this particular piece of land.

Olivia noticed Luke's gaze and followed. Her small hand was enveloped in his large one. Just looking at it made her heart skip a beat. Slowly, Luke opened his fingers and laced them between hers, wrapping them tightly in hers so she couldn't pull away. He was testing the waters, and she let him.

Giving a light squeeze she said, "Lead the way."

Luke's face lit up as he threw a blanket over his shoulder and made his way toward the sliding door. What he planned next was something he dreamed of often, but never thought it would happen. It was easy and simple and he knew Olivia would appreciate it.

For a few minutes, their bare feet carried them across the dewy grass until they reached the tree with the large swing on it.

"Take a seat."

Livy let go of his hand, and Luke immediately missed the feel of it.

The custom made cushioned swing was built so that his legs and body would not hang off uncomfortably. He rested his arm along the back of the chair and motioned Olivia over.

Olivia curled up to Luke and rested her cheek on his chest. He reached over and took her hand and positioned it over his stomach, holding her to him. Time passed as serenity brought peace.

"I can hear your heart beating," she said quietly.

"Oh yeah? What's it saying?"

Olivia thought for a moment. "That it's beating as fast as mine, like our hearts are in sync almost. You're just as anxious as I am, even though you give off the complete opposite vibe. I would've never thought it'd be racing."

"I'm always nervous around you, Livy. You made my heart beat fast all those years ago, and you still do today. Nothing's changed for me."

Olivia squeezed her eyes shut at his truthfulness. She didn't know what to say other than to tighten her arms around Luke.

"Not that I don't mind the quietness between us or you being here, but why did you come over today?"

She sighed heavily. "I wanted to thank you for moving the rest of my stuff around last night, but also to apologize in person. I said some things I probably shouldn't have and acted like a total ass."

"No need to thank me for anything, Livy. Just glad I

decided to show up when I did. You could've seriously hurt yourself."

"Psshhh... I'm stronger than I look."

"Believe me, I know that more than anyone."

Luke rocked the swing back and forth with a gentle kick of his heel and got a little more comfortable. The sun was finally setting across the horizon, exactly what he wanted Livy to see.

"All the colors... It's so pretty," she said quietly. Olivia had never seen such a picture in all her life. A huge streak of orange hues rippled across the sky that was sandwiched between baby blue tones and faint gray clouds. It was like she was looking at a water color painted canvas. Absolutely beautiful. This was why she had moved back home. Something as simple as this.

"I could watch the sunset until dark and fall asleep out here. It's so peaceful."

"I agree. When I was shown this land, it happened to be around sundown. When I saw it, I knew it was the one. Took me all of ten seconds to decide."

Luke had bought the piece of land and had a home built on it after his first paycheck from the record company. He didn't want to forget where he came from or who he was at the end of the day.

"I can see why. It's stunning. We didn't have sunsets like this back in New York."

Luke took the blanket he carried out and draped it over them when Olivia shivered after a draft of wind blew across her skin.

"I know. I've been there. Nothing like the South and home."

Olivia's head snapped up. "You have? When?" This was news to her.

"I went after I signed my life away for music in the

beginning. I was there for a few weeks opening for some groups."

"Why didn't you call me, message me, text me? Anything?"

He shrugged, unsure of what to say. "I don't know. I wanted to, but it had been some time after you left. About a year or so later. I figured you didn't want to see me since I refused to talk once you left and all."

"Luke..." Olivia shook her head, irritated that he hadn't made an effort to see her after she tried hopelessly to keep in touch with him.

"I didn't say I didn't look for you, only that I didn't call."

Confusion set across Livy's face as Luke opened up to her. "Truth is, I looked you up before I went to New York. The internet and Facebook are a fabulous invention." He smirked. "I knew all along you went for your doctorate. I followed everything you did for years, but eventually I let go. I had to, just like you did."

They both had let go when it was the last thing they wanted to do. Olivia shook her head and went to stand. She needed to walk off what Luke was throwing at her. He looked her up and was even in New York, but wouldn't see her? It was like a weight slamming into her chest and knocking her down.

Luke yanked Livy back to him and pulled her close to his face. No way in hell was she getting away.

He breathed into her, "I saw you, Livy. I saw you come out of school one day with some redheaded girl. You were laughing and smiling as you walked down the street and into a pizza place. You looked happy so I didn't approach you. God, though," he shook his head, "now I wish I had. So stupid..."

Olivia's lips parted in surprise over Luke's admission, and the fact that his lips were just mere inches from hers. He was so close that she could taste him. Her body tingled as he looked deeply into her eyes that promised so much more.

"I guess I wanted you more since you never looked back. You went to New York and that was that."

Olivia's mouth dropped. Talk about a slap to her face.

"Are you kidding me? How dare you say that? You know it's not true, Luke. I wanted you just as much."

"Calling and emailing doesn't mean jack, babe. Sorry, but it doesn't constitute a thing. I waited to see what you would do after your time was up. Your actions said it all."

Shaking her head, she looked directly into his eyes. "Believe what you want, Luke. Just because I left doesn't mean I stopped loving you or wanting you. I stayed in New York because I had nothing to come back to. You acted like I didn't exist."

"If only that was possible. You were on my mind twenty-four seven."

The silence coming from Olivia had Luke wanting so bad to sink into that mouth of hers and kiss her the right way. He wanted to feel her lips on his without any obstacle separating them. He wanted her body against his, naked, for no other reason than to just let go and feel her.

Staring at Luke's lips, Olivia said, "I need to go."

She couldn't handle anymore. So much was spoken, the stream of emotions coursing between them and pulling them together. They both wanted more, but teetered on the rope that bound each one together.

"Don't run, Livy. Stay."

"I'm not running, Luke. I just can't stay."

"I told you I'd make sure you'd be ready in the morning. Plus, there's a part of the house you haven't seen yet."

She shook her head no.

Cupping the side of her face, Luke's green eyes pleaded with her to not leave. She was so close to his face that it wouldn't take but a deep breath to bring her to him and close the distance. He watched Olivi stare at his mouth. He swept a finger under her chin to bring her eye level to him.

"So you gonna kiss me or what?" Luke asked with a sly grin.

"Huh?"

"You gonna kiss me or what, woman? You can't tear your eyes from my mouth."

"I... I don't know... I wasn't planning on it."

"Livy, stop thinking for once in your damn life and just act. What's stopping you now?"

"Nothing, but... But how do I know that you want it, too?" She was starting to stammer like a fool.

Luke chuckled. "You can't feel it?" he pressed her hand to his chest.

With a bashful smile, Olivia realized she did want to kiss him. "Maybe another day, Luke."

"Didn't think you were ready, but I had to ask with the way you were staring at my mouth, like it's candy and all."

She smiled sheepishly, her eyelids growing heavy.

"But that doesn't mean that I don't wanna kiss the hell out of you."

Olivia's eyes widened just in time to see the blur of Luke's hand fly past her face and his mouth smash to hers.

Luke held onto Livy for dear life. She was the rhythm to his life and having her so close was too painful not to dance. Desperate, he couldn't take it anymore and needed to feel her. He refused to allow her to back down, so Luke put everything into that kiss. Plunging his tongue into her mouth, Luke kissed her as deeply as he could. Rolling over her, Luke pushed Olivia down onto the reclining swing as he continued to kiss her with his all. Her leg hitched up and leaned on his hip, her hips rotating into his. His hands found their way into her hair and worked her scalp as his tongue tantalized every inch of her mouth. He must have been doing something right because Livy arched her back and pressed her breasts against him, feeling her hardened nipples strain against his chest. Her legs widened and he settled between them. Luke groaned into her mouth at the feel of her body so tight to his. Dear God, those beautiful breasts of hers were begging for his touch. His cock throbbed in pain just thinking about holding them. His hips thrusts against her sex and she surged in return. Olivia brought her hands up to his head and ran her hands through his hair tugging at his scalp. The sensation of her under him, her soft pliable body, her hips undulating against his, and the sexy purrs that seeped through her lips had Luke rock hard. He wanted nothing more than to sink into her and make love to her for hours.

"Stay," he mumbled against her luscious lips.

"No."

"I'll keep kissing you until you change your mind."

So he kissed her again, and she grinned. "Luke. Please…"

More kisses, but this time he peppered them around her jaw, down her neck, then back to her lips. "Was that a please for more or a please to stop?"

She paused and answered honestly. "I'm not sure?"

A cocky grin spread across Luke's face before he leaned down for another kiss. "So you're saying I have a chance?"

Olivia shrugged. She wasn't sure of anything at the moment except that Luke always had a chance with her.

"Let's just take it slow."

"Okay," she whispered and returned to his lips as he leaned back down, kissing her deeply.

thirty-six

Luke tugged Olivia toward the little house she spotted when they first stepped out of his home. Night had fallen so she could hardly see a thing in front of her as Luke guided the way. The only light was from the full moon and the muted light from his house. Their bare feet crunched the twigs and the grass was cold beneath her feet, but Luke's hand radiated warmth throughout her body.

"Is this where you wanted me to sleep when you said I could take a guest room?"

Luke looked at her like she'd grown three heads and barked out a laugh. "Livy, I'd like you to sleep against me in my bed with my arms around you, but I'm not pushing my luck. I have guest rooms in my house. This is where I make my music."

"Like, where you record it?"

"Yeah…where I go to lay a track, write a song, play my guitar, if I need inspiration or whatever. It's my favorite place to be. I didn't like being away from my family as much as I was in the beginning, so I had a small studio put in."

Luke put the code into the door and turned the knob. Switching the light on with his other hand, he watched Olivia look around his office. At first he watched her eyes, but when he trailed down to her mouth he noticed how raw and pink her lips were from their kisses. His body hardened and he wanted to feel her mouth on him once more. All Luke could think of doing was throwing her onto his couch and making love to her right then and there. God, how he wanted it more than anything.

Hell, he had to have another taste of her again. Luke reached over and grasped Olivia, taking her head into his hands and smashed his lips to hers. Luke kissed her speechless, feeling his tongue spoon hers, pulling her into him. He needed her so badly that he ached all over.

Backing her against the couch, Olivia's legs met the couch cushions. He pressed her down, and laid his weight on top of her. Dear God, how she felt heavenly under him, just how he fantasized many times. His cock was solid, dying to slide right into her and he worried he'd bust before she was ready.

Luke released his hands from her face and worked them over her body. He palmed her breasts and kneaded them as she moaned. He made his way down the sides of her breasts, past her stomach, over her belt buckle and zipper to her sex. As Luke cupped her, Livy's back bowed and her hips thrust into his hand as she whimpered into his mouth.

Breaking their kiss, Luke's forehead met hers. "I want you so bad, Livy. I want what we had all those years ago," he breathed into her.

The silence coming from Olivia could have been viewed as both good and bad. Her trembling hands covered Luke's, and if it weren't for being underneath his warm body on his couch, her weak knees would have given out. She was shaking on the inside, her heart beating so hard she wondered if he could feel it pound against his chest.

"Livy," he whispered when she didn't respond.

"I... I want you too, Luke."

"Thank God," he muttered against her mouth, grinning

as he kissed her again. Luke's hands traveled up her waist, the pads of his fingers feeling the outline of her ribcage as he rolled up her shirt and yanked it off of her. His fingertips found her soft shoulders and pulled down the straps of her bra. Luke watched as he removed the lace covering her heavy breasts, breasts that begged for his touch. Her pink nipples puckered as his fingers delicately trailed over the goose bumps that covered her flesh.

Luke stared down at Livy's breasts, his eyes growing as big as saucers and said, "They're bigger than what I remember." Luke's grin was contagious and Olivia smiled in return, her eyes soft. But Luke hesitated, unsure if he could touch her naked body the way he wanted to. Leaning down, he gently pressed kisses to the top of both breasts, his stubble grazing her supple skin.

"Yes," she sighed. Olivia's hips were moving in a rolling wave motion and it took all of him not to rip her jeans off and take her.

Luke sat back on his heels. He wanted to make love to her, but it wasn't the right time and he wouldn't dare push her. Luke knew the last few days had been emotional on Olivia and he wanted her to want him just as much, not because of all that had occurred that left her emotions running amuck. Though, judging by the look in her eyes, Olivia didn't want him to stop.

Reaching out, Luke helped Olivia to stand. Questioning him with her gaze, curious as to why he stopped, she cupped her breasts and leaned over to grab her shirt, not bothering to replace her bra.

He kissed her forehead and answered her questionable look. "Not yet, baby. Soon."

Olivia nodded, silently agreeing.

After replacing her shirt, she glanced around Luke's studio. It appeared to be a full recording studio, just more intimate and cozy. She walked over to a wall that showcased what looked to be his most prized possessions. Framed and mounted on the wall were Luke's albums, pictures of singers he was now friends with, his family, and friends from home. There was a warm, comfortable feeling to it that warmed her to the core.

Huddled near the corner on the wall was a picture of her and Luke.

Olivia's heart dropped to her stomach.

She snapped her head to Luke. Olivia was astonished he'd have anything having to do with them anymore.

"You have a picture of us in here?" Luke nodded. "Why?" She walked over to get a good look at it. It was actually a collage of pictures of them from back in the day.

"The same reason why you kept the Care Bear, and because you're the reason why I do what I do."

"What do you mean?"

"Every song, every word, every melody, it's because of you. The music never stopped for me. You're part of everything I do, Livy. You're ingrained into my skin like a tattoo. It reminds me of where I came from, where it all started. I didn't want to lose that. Some days I come here and just stare at old pictures and I'm hit with a new song. Most of them were about you, some came from being on the road, friends."

"Luke…"

"I was pissed, Livy. So hurt when you left. I couldn't fuckin' believe you threw it all out like you did and without even asking what I thought about it. I thought my had opinion mattered to you, but you said otherwise. It was shocking considering how we were. I mean, I understand why you did it now and I'm glad you did what you had to do. But at the time, I couldn't accept it."

"I thought you resented me."

"Believe me, I did," he said, speaking the truth. "For a long time, I resented you. I wanted it all with you, but you walked away, as if our relationship was an old ratted t-shirt that you had no use for anymore. And before you speak, I know that's not how you truly felt, but damn did it sure feel like it. You didn't even give me a chance, just up and left. But it's over with, Livy. I don't want to rehash the past. The past is the past. I don't want to talk about it anymore. Let's leave it there and move forward, together."

"I need time to think, Luke."

"You and your brain, always at work and thinking too damn hard. What is there to think about? Why do we have to throw away more time together?"

"So much? We have completely different lives now that don't really mesh well. It's been a long time."

Olivia was stalling. Luke could feel it, so he pushed harder. "Exactly. Let's not waste another day. We'll make it work, Care Bear...and I'll follow close by this time."

Luke brushed a strand of hair away from Olivia's face, tucking it behind her ear.

"Just give me time," she whispered.

Luke's lips curved up. "If you think about it, I've given you almost ten years. But what's a little more, right?"

thirty-seven

one week later

That night at Luke's house was an awakening.

Olivia was glad she hadn't stayed. She needed to clear her head and think about what she was going to do with her future, and she couldn't with Luke nearby. They were both learning about each other again with a different approach that fit their busy lives. So they discussed his upcoming tour for the following summer, his brothers, her family, the weather, anything really. Them as a couple was hidden in plain sight, not openly spoken about all that much even though Luke tried his damnedest. She knew where Luke stood. It was just her who was standing back.

Did she want to be with Luke? More than all the moons in the universe.

So there she was, sitting in a coffee shop with the tallest coffee she could purchase and waiting to find the courage to jump in her car and head down to Luke's. Her knee bounced and her heart was pounding as anxiety consumed her. Between the double shot she already had and her nerves, her belly was doing hurtles in record speed.

A bell chimed and she looked up, her eyes forming huge circles as her stomach dropped. It was the last person she expected to see.

Nate took her breath away. He was ruggedly handsome with a heady air of authority and sensuality surrounding him. It was almost impossible not to be drawn to him. Though, this time it was different for her. While Nate was undeniably attractive, she didn't feel the spark pulling her to him, the heat that was meant to ignite her blood.

Only one person managed to do that to her.

Olivia had a death grip on her coffee cup as Nate spotted her. He walked right up to her with a half smile like it was nothing, casually hugging her and dropping a gentle kiss to her cheek. Olivia was caught off guard for a moment, not expecting it at all.

"Hey, Liv," he whispered by her ear.

"Hi, Nate. It's good to see you. How have you been?" she asked easily.

He didn't have to say it for her to see. It was written in his eyes. Nate's eyes softened as their eyes locked. He was still hurt but was getting by.

He cleared his throat. "I'm good. Just working a lot. You look good, Liv. Beautiful as always."

She felt a blush crawl up her neck and settle in her cheeks as she smiled from Nate's compliment.

"Thank you," she said quietly. "Want to take a seat?"

Nate nodded. "And how are you doing?" he asked.

"Uh, pretty good I suppose. Same as you... Busy with work and all."

"That's good."

Talk about a stifled, awkward conversation. She needed to switch it up.

"Just so you know...I cared about you and can't help but feel awful about everything that went down between us. I know it was entirely my fault, but I never meant to cause you pain, Nate. I swear it."

He nodded in agreement. "It is your fault, Liv. We could've had it all."

She sucked in a breath at his honesty.

But," he continued, "It's over and done with. I'm moving on and I know you will too."

Olivia treaded carefully. "Have you moved on?"

His chuckle at her question. "You mean with another woman? No, not quite. And I don't plan to anytime soon, either."

She bobbed her head. "I know you'll make someone happy one day. She'll be a lucky lady."

"I wanted to make you happy."

Her throat tightened. "I'm sorry," she said as she looked down dejectedly at the table.

Nate placed a hand over hers and rubbed along her knuckles with his rough thumb. "Don't be." She looked up at him. "I'm not trying to hurt you, Olivia, just speaking the truth. It hurt like hell when I walked away. But I had to. For both of us."

"I understand. I just feel terrible about it."

"You'll get over it in time. I'm sure Luke will help with that."

She raised her eyebrows at the mention of Luke's name. Nate smiled.

"Olivia King, you can't fool me, remember? You may not have gone back yet, but you will. I left so you *can* go back to him. You go after what you want. But the difference is that not only do you chase after what you want until you get it, but you make your vision a reality whereas most give up easily. It's what I liked about you—your eyes show your strength of mind and dedication. I'm not saying Luke is your dream or chase or whatever, but somehow he falls into your plans. It's okay... Go."

Strangely, it's what she needed to hear, yet she felt so selfish hearing it.

"I just don't understand how you can be okay with that, or even utter the words."

Nate's intense, amber eyes looked deeply into hers. "I'm a grown man, Liv, not a damn child. I can accept loss when it's due and still wake up the next day. Doesn't mean it's going to be easy at first, but I'll get by."

How she ever screwed up a relationship with a man as genuine and compassionate as Nate she'd never know.

"You're a good man, Nathaniel."

Nate stood and shoved his hands into his pockets. Looking down at her, he said, "People come into our lives for a reason. Sometimes to help us guide our way for a short period of time and other times to stay. Whether they're meant to be there for a month, two months or four years, they're there. Maybe you came to let me know I can feel love again. Who knows? Only time will tell."

Olivia's lips parted in surprise as all the air decompressed from her lungs. Her chest ached from the pressure building inside as she struggled to breathe. He had given her so little of his past while they were together, and an admission like that left her with many questions.

"It's about time for me to go, Liv. You take care, okay?" She nodded.

Olivia stood and pulled Nate into a tight embrace and held on for a moment. Pulling back, it was her turn to kiss his cheek lightly.

"You too, Nate."

thirty-eight

She was finally ready.

Luke opened the door to Olivia standing in front of him in a pair of little shorts and flip flops. Her hair was swept up in a loose tie with pieces framing her sweet face. She had on the tightest tank top he'd ever seen and it made his mouth water. Her heavy breasts pushed up from the low cut neckline and a heart shaped necklace lay at the crease of her breasts, glistening in the sun. *Fuck.* His whiskey girl always looked so damn sexy to him.

"Care Bear."

And then she gave him a smile that made her beautiful face glow. And that's all it took for Luke.

He knew.

Closing the distance with two long strides, Luke didn't waste any time. He yanked Olivia to him, holding her face between his hands and looked deeply into her eyes.

"You finally ready to kiss me now? Are we gonna do this?"

She nodded her head with a tight lipped grin, her eyes glowing with happiness.

"You sure?"

She nodded again.

"And you're not going to leave me again, are you?"

The smile never left her lips as she shook her head no.

"Because if you do, you know I'm following you anywhere you go, right?"

Olivia gave Luke a big smile. "Or I can follow you."

"Well go on and kiss me then, whiskey—"

Olivia pressed her lips to his fast before he could finish the sentence. They both sighed in unison from the contact, knowing this was it. That it was finally just them. No more running, no more arguing, no more being apart. It was just them, how it always should have been from the start. They'd been apart for ten years at this point, and that was ten years too long.

Never leaving her mouth, Luke reached down to her fabulous ass that he couldn't wait to get his hands on and hoisted her up. Walking inside, he slammed the door shut with his foot. He'd love nothing more than to slam her up against the wall and fuck her six ways to Sunday, but he wouldn't. He was going to make love to her the right way, and that was in his bed where she was going to stay from now on.

Or in hers. Whichever she wanted. Luke was going to make it all about her from this day on and give her everything she wanted.

Taking two steps at a time up the stairs, Luke nearly sprinted to his room with Olivia locked around his torso, joined at the mouth the entire time. The last thing Luke wanted to do was allow her to leave the sanctuary of his arms after he finally got her back.

Luke crossed the floor of his large room to his bed while Livy's sweet ass sat in the palms of his hands. The feel of her so close had him raging for more on the inside. He didn't want to rip her clothes off and take her like a caveman, but dear God, he was so close to doing so. He was struggling to keep it reined in.

The shades in his room were still drawn from earlier in

the day, and it exuded a dark but cozy feel to it. The cool air plucked at Luke's hypersensitive skin as he laid Olivia gently down at the base of his rumpled bed.

"I'm going to try and go slow. Lord knows it won't be easy on me."

"Okay," she answered with a ragged breath.

His hands were planted near the sides of her head as he hovered above her. He cupped the side of her face and leaned down for a soft kiss, pulling at her lip with his teeth before he let go and retreated back. Ever so slowly, Luke slid his hand from the side of Livy's face. He caressed the curve of her neck to her shoulder and ran his fingers delicately over her collarbone. Olivia released a seductive sigh that made Luke's cock twinge. Her back arched and her breast grazed the underside of his hand, sending heat straight to Luke's groin.

This was going to be tough on him indeed.

Tearing his gaze away from Livy's body, Luke looked into her eyes to gauge her response.

Just as he had hoped. Olivia's heavy lids fluttered just from his touch, her cheeks flushed and lips parted. He couldn't even imagine how it was going to be once he was inside her.

Reaching for her denim shorts, his fingers slipped inside to remove them. He ran his hand up her leg and over her thigh, stopping at her hip where he tightened his grip. The pressure of his hand had Olivia's hips arching in pleasure.

"It's okay, Livy. We can stop if you're not ready."

Olivia shook her head. "I am ready. Just nervous is all."

Luke saw apprehension in her eyes. He wanted to ease it away so it would never return. Pushing her legs together and onto the bed, he laid next her and took her mouth once again, but this time in a tantalizing roughness. He was going to show her how it could be forever with him.

Their tongues linked together and Olivia felt her body melting in pleasure. She'd forgotten how seductive his kisses were and how effortlessly her body turned to liquid just from his touch. She dropped one leg and dragged it across his waist, opening herself up slowly to him. Luke took the invite and rested his weight carefully on her body. His fingers threaded her wavy locks while he got reacquainted with her mouth, this time not missing any part of it. She wound her legs around his waist, feeling his hard length against his zipper as he ground into her sex. Olivia released a heated moan, her panties already wet. The moan only fueled him even more as he ate at her mouth like he was making love to it. Luke's strong hands held her in place and with the grinding, Olivia was building, a firestorm of need lighting up her body, starting at the tips of her toes and settling in her lower belly.

Luke thrust his hips and she groaned. The sound that fled from her lips had Luke in agony. They hadn't even done much yet, and he was already dying to sink into her and stay there for hours. He wasn't sure how much longer he'd be able to hang on, but was going to try his damnedest. Reaching around, Luke swiftly yanked her panties down from one side of her hip.

Olivia widened her legs. She was soaking wet as two fingers slid down, creating a steady friction against her lips. The impending climax was a steady pressure against her sex that was building inside her.

"Luke," she moaned when his immediately found her center and thrust inside. Her hips jerked against his steady fingers as Luke produced a guttural groan from deep inside his chest.

He pulled her lip between his teeth and asked, "What? What do *you* need?"

"You. I need you. Always."

"Take your shirt off for me."

Nearly ripping her shirt in two, she threw it on the floor and Luke found her creamy soft skin. Running his tongue from her collarbone to neck leaving a trail of wetness, he grabbed her flesh with his teeth and bit down hard. The walls of Olivia's sex began to spasm around his fingers, her orgasm on the verge of release.

"Oh, no you don't," Luke said between his teeth and pulled his fingers out.

Olivia almost saw stars as Luke taunted her body. She was on the brink of an orgasm when he pulled out and looked at her. She reached for him and he pulled back. Her eyes narrowed with question as she stared at him. Olivia immediately felt the absence of him and wanted him back. She kicked out her foot and tried to grab him, but he stepped away.

"Stop playing with me, Luke."

He raised an eyebrow at her and waited.

Hopping off the bed, Olivia tracked him with a darkened gaze. An arrogant smirk formed on his face, his gleaming eyes meeting hers with a knowing look. The man knew what he was doing to her, and knew the control he had over her body.

It was the same control he had since the day they met.

Olivia followed Luke as he stepped back and pressed into the wall. He raised his arms in surrender. He had worked her up to a titillating high and then stopped, leaving her hanging and nearly begging for more.

Leaning into him, she placed her palms on the side of his chest against the wall, his leg sandwiched between hers. "What are you up to, hmmm?"

"Nothing, baby."

"Oh, really? What was that for then? To show the power you have over my body?"

"Don't know what you're talking about." He raised his thigh and pushed against her naked sex.

Yes...

Olivia pressed into his rigid body, feeling his shaft through his clothing. Reaching down, she went to grasp him in her palm, but Luke grabbed her wrist and held it behind her back. He pulled the other one down and secured both wrists tightly with one hand.

Luke hissed in a breath when Olivia bit his chest. He grabbed her hair and yanked her back, his skin pulling from the hold of her teeth.

"Tell me, Livy. You want me? Right here, right now? More than anyone else?"

"You know I do."

"Do I? Show me. Better yet, tell me what you want. It's been so long that I think you should remind me. Do you want it hard? Or do you want it soft? Or how about long hard strokes real slow? In the shower? Or on the couch? How about I just bend you over and I take you like that? I'm going to say any one of those would work, right?" His voice was rough as he spoke, like sandpaper. His piercing eyes covered every inch of her body.

Olivia whimpered as he carried her back to bed. Luke was just as affected by this sudden change as she was, and yet he was the stronger of the two as he held back. "Stop playing with me, Luke. I can't take much more."

"I want you bad, Care Bear, so bad it hurts," he whispered.

"So have me. I'm yours."

"Are you? Are you truly all mine?"

Olivia nodded her head and unzipped his jeans. "I. Am. Yours."

His cock free and she gripped his thick length with her palm. Her hand glided over the small amount of moisture he released and she used it to stroke him with a twist of her wrist. His hips surged toward her and he nearly collapsed from the sensation. He slid down her body, her knees going to the sides of her chest as the cool air shocked her wet heat. Olivia was at her breaking point and needed release so bad. She watched as Luke's eyes grew in size, licking his lips with his tongue. His hands were roughly sliding up and down the inside of her legs as he rose up on his knees.

Olivia reached for him. "Come to me."

"I plan to come," he said with a grin. "But you first."

Quickly, Luke reached into the drawer next to his bed and grabbed a condom. Rolling it on, he palmed his cock and poised it at her entrance. He inched his way in then drove inside, his head flying back in pleasure so hard veins popped from his neck. Warmth seeped through their blood, igniting the fire between them.

"I won't be able to last. Livy. It's been too long."

"Don't care. Just as long as you make love to me however you like."

Luke grinned, his face lighting up with the challenge as he slowed down and began to make long, deep strokes inside of her. He was going to give his whiskey girl everything she wanted.

"Yes..." she cried out. "Keep going."

"You mine?"

"You know it."

"No one else's? Say it. I need to hear it over and over." He continued his deep strokes, each one hitting the back of her, hitting that sweet place that was just about to take her over the edge.

Olivia grabbed his face with her hands and brought it to hers. Looking straight into Luke's eyes, she answered between pants, "I'm only yours, yours forever."

"Thank fuck," he ground out.

His strokes picked up speed, their breathing accelerated, nearly breathless as they locked eyes. She felt herself pulse around his cock as an intense orgasm ripped through her body.

"Oh god, don't stop," she begged.

"Wasn't planning on it, baby."

Luke drove in harder, and he moaned into her mouth when her hips met his. Well, if that wasn't the hottest thing she'd ever experienced. She did it again and in return Luke pushed harder into her, not only hitting that delicious spot deep inside of her, but her clit at the same time causing her sex to ache for more. Her body trembled from the sensations running underneath her skin, igniting her blood and making her pulse soar.

Weaving his fingers through Olivia's hair, he held on as she took every inch of him. They came together in a wave of delicious rapture that they didn't want to end. They both gasped when they reached the pinnacle, ecstasy gripping each other forcefully, and holding on for dear life.

Him.

Her.

Together, as they breathed each other's names in blissful harmony.

Still deep inside her, Olivia whispered against Luke's lips, "I missed you so much."

OLIVIA WANTED TO WAKE TO LUKE HOLDING HER IN HIS strong arms. She wanted to feel his body wrapped around hers more than anything tonight, holding her tight and making her feel like everything was how it should be.

"It's with you," she said, curled up against him. "I was trying to find my way in this crazy hectic world we live in, and I finally did."

"You did?"

"I did." She shrugged. "I just took a little…scenic detour," she laughed, "but I finally got there."

Luke held Olivia tightly, savoring the moment he never wanted to forget.

"And where is there?"

"Georgia. With you. Where I was supposed to be all along."

"Didn't I tell you you'd be back? That this place is in your bones, baby?" He nibbled on her lips.

Olivia breathed out a smile. While the beauty of the south was deep-rooted inside of her all along, so was Luke. He always had been.

So she said the one thing Luke had said to her years ago. "Take me or leave me."

Luke pushed her mouth with a flick of his jaw, demanding she open up. And when she did, he glided his tongue between her lips, wrapped around it and cocooned her kiss slowly and methodically with everything in him, proving how much he loved her.

But he didn't need to. She already knew.

epilogue

Luke | seven months later

Long strides take me down the back corridor, rounding corners and passing various doors. Security has boxed me in, along with my manager and entourage of people to prep me, bumping into me as I walk. I can't tell if it's cold or hot, as my mind is only on one thing as I make my way down the hallway. I still don't understand why I can't just slap on my hat and a pair of shades to take the stage, why people need to style my hair and paint my face full of crap. But I don't argue. I get to do what I want every night with my girl, and that's all that matters. If she's happy, then so am I.

My mom will be on continual treatment for the rest of her life for relapse-remitting MS. It was hard to deal with at first, especially putting a title on the stage of MS she has. Having Livy by my side helped me come to terms with it and understand that she can still live a full, healthy life. I'm a mama's boy at heart and not afraid to say it. So when I found out about her disease and different stages and treatment, I broke down.

Aside from that, life couldn't be better.

Tonight is like any other night on the road, but it's not. Goosebumps coat my skin just thinking about it, how I've fantasized about this night for many years. Only a few more feet and I reach the side of the stage. Ear phones in, shades on and the lights go down. The stadium is bound by darkness, the air thick with excitement.

The countdown begins.

10...

Adrenaline is pumping at a hefty speed. The rush of blood streaming through my veins is a high that is indescribable, but better than any drug out there. I shake my arms and legs out and do a few jumps to loosen myself up. My neck pops loudly as my joints release fluid from the cracking.

9...

The roar of the crowd as I take the stairs two at a time only grows louder. They know what's coming. They can feel it. The guitar is strapped to my back, the leather band digging into the skin of my shoulder from its weight as I fist the neck of it. The tips of my fingers slide along the steel cords, and I feel my body humming to life.

8...

The darkness surrounds me as I take twelve long strides and I hit center stage. Time is beginning to slow down as everything falls into place. I want this. I need it to move faster so it can make me fly like it always does.

7...

My chest is pumping harder than ever before. I've done this routine a million times now, but this time is different. I've never allowed her to come to a show before. It's the one place where I can drown only in my music and forget the world. Now I'll be breathing under water to the beat of her next to me and still be flying high.

6...

She begged, and I said no. Pleaded, and I still said no.

5...

The nerve endings in my fingers twitch and play the notes on my guitar without making a sound. My knee starts bobbing.

4...

Floor level can see a shadow on the stage, but no one else. I take my stance and drop my chin to my chest. They're screaming my name as I grip the lip of my hat and slide it way down low.

3...

Wait. For. It.

2...

A faint chord rings almost silently through the air letting me know we're about to play. I start a new count in my head. 3...2...

1...

The first chord ripples through the air and all hell breaks loose. The lights go up and the band plays the first note. The crowd is growing larger as the stadium lights up, the roar at its highest. I step into the one place that has always been my comfort zone.

"This one goes out to my whiskey girl..." I fling my pick across the strings and let it rip, letting Livy hear a song solely meant for her. I know she's watching from the side of the stage, I can feel her gaze on me. Turning my head, our eyes lock and I blow her a kiss. The crowd roars even louder and she blushes. The smile that glides across her face puts everything into perspective for me. Why I do what I do. And why things happen for a reason.

Damn, I love that girl. And I'm never letting her go again.

acknowledgments

My Goodness, what a journey this has been. Alyssa West, Claire Contreras, Elizabeth Lee, Roxie Madar, Pamela Sparkman, Janna Sierens, thank you all for your early early feedback and suggestions. I learned so much and without each of you, this novel might not be what it is. Thank you for being part of my first novel.

My husband. The ungodly amount of hours I spent on the computer was a bit disturbing, but you never, not once, complained. Some days I noticed it in your eyes, but you never said a word. I can't thank you enough for that alone. And when I stressed out trying to make the final changes with the kids around? You swooped in and took over. Having a supportive husband is the key to it all, and I'm one lucky chick. I love you! And to my wild and crazy boys who drive me insane everyday - I love you more than you'll ever know. I know you're probably never going to ever read this, but you two are my inspiration and make me want to be all that I can be for you guys.

Dad. Thank you for believing in me, for your stories on how you got your business started, and giving me the inspiration to keep trekking ahead. I knew you would support me in anything I did, but the way you were with me with my writing really moved me. Thank you so much!

Nadine Winningham. You're a woman of many roles. There are not enough words in the dictionary for me to express how much I appreciate you. From cheering me on, asking to read everything I wrote, your surprise promo pictures…everything you did made a difference. You're my biggest cheerleader and have supported me from the beginning through all my crazy changes and ideas. You held my hand when I panicked, and gave me motivation when I needed it the most. Thank you for remembering the scenes I forgot, sending me links, highlighting the funny typos I made and making me laughing. Most of all, your friendship means the world to me. I give you two nipples up!

To all the bloggers who took a chance on me, THANK YOU, THANK YOU, THANK YOU! When I started out, I prayed that five would help promo me. That's all I hoped for. I was blindsided by the amount of bloggers who were willing to take a chance on me. Thank you all so much!

about lucia

Lucia Franco resides in sunny South Florida with her husband, two boys, and two adorable dogs who follow her everywhere. She was a competitive athlete for over ten years – a gymnast and cheerleader – which heavily inspired the Off Balance series.

Her novel Hush, Hush was a finalist in the 2019 Stiletto Contest hosted by Contemporary Romance Writers, a chapter of Romance Writers of America. Her novels are being translated into several languages.

When Lucia isn't writing, you can find her relaxing with her toes in the sand at a nearby beach. She runs on caffeine, scorching hot sunshine and four hours of sleep.

She's written ten books and has many more planned for the years to come.

Find out more at authorluciafranco.com.

Printed in Great Britain
by Amazon